PASSION'S GOLDEN BOUNTY
RAINY KIRKLAND

ZEBRA BOOKS
KENSINGTON PUBLISHING CORP.

ZEBRA BOOKS

are published by

Kensington Publishing Corp.
475 Park Avenue South
New York, NY 10016

First printing: July 1990

Printed in the United States of America

To Andy—
for always being there
with love, support, and encouragement.
You're terrific, Dad.

To Linda and Roger Lark of Cheltenham,
England, for their hospitality; Mary Jane Nauss of
Rancocas Woods, New Jersey, for her help with
research; and last but not least to Lee Rouland,
Beverly Haaf, and Bernadette Puskar of RHAPPS for
their patience.

Chapter I

Summer 1711

The gray mist floated silently on the Caribbean waters, pausing now and then to grow in strength, then moving onward to the island drums that beckoned it home once more. Distant thunder rumbled its approval as the thick tendrils crept steadily inward, cloaking the island with fear and uncertainty. The rhythmic drums intensified and the clouds lowered. As the last remnants of silvery moonlight vanished, Samantha Chesterfield slid closer to the edge of the stone balustrade that encircled her balcony.

"'Tis the last time you'll humiliate me, Falcon," she vowed, angrily wiping her tears with the back of her hand. Bawdy laughter floated upward from the inn below, and her anger flared anew. "And you're more the fool to think a locked door will detain me."

She tucked her long hair carefully beneath a battered woolen cap. Black breeches and a dark shirt

7

completed her garb. Grateful for the dense mist, she swung her leg over the railing and reached for the nearest branch of the massive cypress tree that stood beside the inn. The muscles of her shoulder and back throbbed in protest, bringing fresh tears, but her resolve stood firm. It was not the first time she had used the old, gnarled branches to escape her father's wrath, but tonight, with stiff muscles and no moon to light her way, she progressed slowly until she reached the lowest branch. Pausing to listen to the rhythmic message within the drums, she wiped the sweat and tears from her face. Why, she wondered wearily, did Kabol always seem to send for her when Falcon was in a temper?

She slipped from her perch and edged away from the inn, careful to avoid the flickering patches of light that spilled from the lower windows. Samantha moved through the yard, blending first with one shadow, then another until the inn was no longer visible. The cool moss beneath her feet was a welcome relief from the humidity that plastered the tattered shirt to her skin and sent trickles of sweat down her back. She navigated the narrow trail that led to the island's swampy interior with a sure step, ducking beneath the thick clumps of sodden Spanish moss and soundlessly pushing the large palm fronds from her path.

As she neared her destination, the hollow beating of the island drums faded. The dense foliage opened to reveal a small clearing where the damp earth had been raked clean. In the flickering firelight, she could see the ancient skulls that guarded the circumference of the circle and the sun-bleached animal bones that lay scattered on the ground before her. Their mystical patterns had taken years to unravel, but tonight she read their secrets with ease.

She dropped to her knees, then rocked back on her heels to wait. The hunched figure on the other side of the fire remained motionless, and a smile touched Samantha's lips as she watched her silent companion. More bones than flesh, his image little resembled that of a dreaded shaman. Yet on the island, the wizened old man was respected by all. He could stop a heated argument with a glance, calm an angry mob with but a few whispered words. Even those who sailed with Falcon on the *Sea Hawk* gave Kabol wide berth while they were in dock.

Samantha hugged her knees tighter to her chest and tried to stem her impatience. Why did he not acknowledge her? Taking slow, deep breaths, she willed her mind and body to relax as she gazed into the small fire before her. The night birds ceased their chatter. Only the crackling flames dared to disturb the unnatural silence. Time ceased to exist as the colors of the fire blended, then separated only to blend once again. Mesmerized, she watched the dancing flames give way to a growing image. A face appeared. Green eyes, dark hair; the features were hazy but they belonged to a man—a man she had seen each night for months. Gooseflesh covered her arms and ran down her neck. To have the strange, shadowy image haunt her dreams was one thing, but to see it mystically appear within a living flame was another. The image flickered, growing, then fading, only to reappear. Panic soared through her veins as the image teased its way in and out of reality, never becoming completely clear. It beckoned. She felt its strength even before its hand reached out to touch her.

Cowed by her lack of control, Samantha closed her eyes tightly and pressed her forehead to her knees. Then it was gone, leaving an aching emptiness in its wake. Her body trembled despite the fire and heat of the night.

She looked up to find Kabol watching her intently, his dark eyes puzzled. Slowly, the wrinkled black man rose and moved before the fire. His hands danced lightly over the flames and a fine powder sifted through his fingers. Red, green, and blue lights instantly shot out in all directions, illuminating his shrouded figure against the darkness of the night. Abruptly he gave a tired grunt and squatted back down on the damp earth.

"He tried to come to you. Why did you turn away?"

Samantha's eyes widened with amazement. "You saw him? He truly existed? How did . . . ?"

"Nay," Kabol interrupted softly. "'Twas not my doing. You called forth the image only to deny it existence."

Samantha bit back the protest that sprang to her lips.

Tell him, her mind pleaded. *Tell him that the image heeds no master but comes and goes at will. Tell him of the haunted nights and restless sleeps. Tell him of your fear.* She clasped her hands tightly to stop their trembling, as pride defeated common sense. "Why did you send for me?"

Kabol watched her inner struggle. *Such power,*

he thought, *but so stubborn.* "You will be leaving soon."

"Aye." Samantha gave a weary sigh. "Falcon is anxious to be back on the sea. He has the patience of a child."

"A well-learned child does not mock its elders," he scolded gently.

Her spine straightened and her chin tilted indignantly. "At ten and six I am no longer the child that ran to you in tears because of her father's cruel words."

Kabol heaved a deep sigh. Although she pretended indifference to her father's rejections, to his observant eye her pain was tangible. "What has happened this time to toss you out of favor?" he prodded gently.

"When am I ever in favor?" she sighed. Her fingers rubbed the nagging ache in her shoulder. Touch alone told her it would be many days before the stiffness left.

"But this time?"

Samantha pulled off her cap, spilling silvery hair to her waist. As her fingers toyed with the cap's frayed edges, her shoulders slumped forward and Kabol thought of a wilted island flower left too long in the sun.

"Somehow the latches on the birdcages were left open," she said softly.

"Somehow?"

She shrugged. Finally the silence weighed more than her guilt. "I read the clouds wrong. I thought the winds had returned and we would be gone."

11

"So you set Falcon's prize game cock free to roam the island thinking the deed would not be discovered? It is a wonder that you are still with us, my child."

"'Tis not natural to teach birds to kill one another," she defended. "An animal should kill for food or protection, not to line the pockets of the greedy."

Kabol shifted closer to the fire and wished again that he might work his magic to bring father and daughter together. But the tapestry of time was already woven, and even with his power, he knew better than to alter the threads.

"The winds will return at midnight." His prediction seemed to hover over the fire then seep into growing mist. "Falcon's ship will sail with the morning tide."

"I shall never understand him," Samantha sighed wearily. "He possesses more than ten men could spend in a lifetime, yet he still is not sated."

"Mayhap your father worries of the day when he will no longer have your eyes to guide his ship. Mayhap he fears that without your 'sight,' he would fare no better than St. Martin."

"How can you even think that?" Samantha jerked to her feet and began to pace before the fire. "Falcon's faults are many, but his skills as a captain far surpass those of St. Martin. And whatever his circumstances, he would never resort to the buying and selling of human flesh for a profit as does that whoremonger. You do me a grave injustice even to speak my father's name in the same breath with that bastard." Her soft voice was threaded with anger.

Kabol smiled. She had grown, he thought with satisfaction. Now she questioned and argued with strength. The metamorphosis was nearly complete. Her eyes looked past the face and into the soul; her mind was strong and true. The shy, awkward child was slowly being pushed aside by the striking beauty that sat before him. An intense sense of satisfaction seeped into his aging bones. But, now the time was nigh, he felt a moment's reluctance to let her go.

Reaching deep within the folds of his cloak, he withdrew another handful of the magical dust. Again the flames danced in a frenzy of colors. "The hour is at hand," he declared firmly. "You must leave me."

"But I just . . ." The words died on her lips and she quickly resumed her position before the fire. Panic filled her slender frame. Could she do nothing right? Her outburst had displeased him. Now he was sending her away.

"You must find your other half." His words were a mere whisper above the crackling fire. "You must find the sun."

"Other half?"

Kabol watched the emotions play across her face. Blue eyes that always danced with laughter and mischief now clouded with confusion.

"You are the moon," he continued patiently. "Silver is your metal. Your hair is the color of moonlight dancing on the waters, and you carry the scent of life. You hold within you great powers, my child, but alas, you are only the moon."

Instinctively Samantha touched the tear-shaped medallion that hung around her neck. The delicate crystal encased a mystical silver liquid, and as it lay warm against her skin, each breath caused the medallion's interior to shimmer in a never-ending motion. Kabol had placed the talisman around her neck the night they met, and for eight years she had not removed it.

"You need to find the sun. Without the sun, the moon may cast no light."

"But where . . ."

Kabol silenced her with a glance. "'Tis not an easy task, my child, but you have within you the talents to see it through. You must go now, for Falcon has discovered you gone. Do not return to me until you have found the sun." With a grace that denied his years, Kabol rose, then vanished into the mist that crowded the now-dying fire.

The night air hung heavy and hot, yet Samantha huddled closer to the fading embers. Her mind spun with confusion and she clutched her knees closer to her body. *Why a riddle? Why now?* A wave of loneliness washed over her. She glanced about the shadowed clearing, but found no peace. Wearily she stood. The puzzle would have to wait, for, as always, Falcon came first.

Cursing the fog that hampered his steps, Falcon made his way down the narrow, rutted street to the Silver Serpent. The stately, whitewashed tavern stood two stories tall, but set within the steep-pitched, red-tile roof, a small set of rooms towered above the rest. He glanced up at the darkened windows and his scowl deepened. Tonight, the

14

bawdy laughter that spilled forth from the inn grated on his nerves and the usually welcome aroma of roasting goat assaulted his senses. With the fog, the inn would be more crowded than usual and that did not please him. His head ached. And those damned drums. If he ever found them, they would be instant kindling—voodoo curse or not.

Roughly he shoved the inn's swinging doors, causing them to snap back on their hinges. The startling clap pierced the merriment and a hushed silence filled the crowded common room. Oil lamps swung from the ceiling timbers casting shadowy images on the startled faces.

Falcon gave a growl of disgust and flexed his shoulders, anxious for a fight. His loose-fitting shirt could not disguise the solid, muscled flesh that lay beneath. And although short in stature, an aura of strength surrounded him. A path cleared before him as he crossed the crowded room to his empty corner table. His menacing scowl kept anyone from approaching as his eyes coldly swept the dimly lit room.

"Marie!" he barked. "Will half the night be gone before I get my meal?"

The robust maid gave him a curt nod and scurried to the hearth. Her ample bosom swayed as she sliced at the roasted goat flesh with a large knife. She ladled vegetables from a boiling kettle onto the huge tray and filled a tankard with ale. Balancing the heavy fare, she slowly made her way back to the Falcon and carefully placed the meal before him.

"Have you seen the Curse tonight?" he challenged softly.

"Nay, Captain." Her voice quivered as she busied

15

herself wiping the oaken table. "Not since you carried her through."

Falcon watched her closely, judging her words for truth. "Then she should still be there, should she not?" With careless ease, he leaned back on his chair. "Marie," he commanded, a sardonic smile touching his lips, "fetch her for me."

Marie's dark skin paled. For a heartbeat she stood frozen with fear. But as Falcon's glare hardened, her limbs found movement and she fled to do his bidding.

"Madre de Dios, let her be there," she whispered over and over.

A commotion at the door took Falcon's attention from the retreating girl.

"It is raining!" Dancer shouted. Standing just inside the entrance, he shook the fine drops of moisture from his curly hair. "The winds have returned!"

A chorus of rowdy cheers sounded, and mugs were filled all round. Dancer slowly made his way through the crowd, pausing now and again to share a word or issue an order. Reaching the back, he straddled a chair at Falcon's table. A giant of a man, his broad shoulders flexed, straining the damp fabric of his shirt as he casually rested his forearms on the back of the chair. His sharp features were softened by warm brown eyes and a rakish smile.

Scowling at his brawny quartermaster, Falcon grabbed the tankard of ale and downed half the contents with one gulp.

"You look little pleased with my news," Dancer stated. "I thought the idea of leaving would cheer

16

your sagging spirits."

"We sail on the tide." Falcon's voice was flat, giving no hint of inner feelings.

Dancer turned and called Falcon's orders to the crew, and another chorus of cheers sounded.

"I understand I missed quite a spectacle earlier," Dancer continued, turning back to Falcon. "Did you really beat her until you drew blood, or do the gossips speak falsely?"

"Have you so little to do with your time that you give heed to vicious island rumor?"

Dancer's smile grew. "What did the wench do this time?"

Falcon pictured the Curse lying in a crumpled heap on the floor of her bedchamber, her eyes bright and brimming with tears. Would that he could turn back the hands of time. He'd never leave her like that again, he vowed silently. The next time, he'd bind the cocky wench in chains.

"She's missing." Falcon's voice was hard and threaded with anger.

"Falcon, the island is too small for her to be missing," Dancer chuckled. "I'd wager she probably heard your angry bellows and decided to lay low until your temper cools."

"Her chambers are empty." Falcon stared blankly over his mug. "And she is not on the ship. She's in the swamp with that scurvy mongrel, Kabol. I know it sure as I know my own name."

Dancer's easy smile disappeared. "I thought you forbade her to go there again."

"I ordered her! But does she obey? Why I'd flog a man for less, and she knows it."

Dancer shifted uncomfortably. "How long?"

"An hour, mayhap less," Falcon shrugged.

Dancer made to rise, his intent clearly to go after her.

"It is not necessary," Falcon stated from behind his tankard. "Marie has gone to fetch her."

"On a night such as this you would send my Marie into the swamp?"

"Nay." Falcon belched, wiping his mouth with his sleeve. "The girl is no fool. She will sit on the wood's edge and wait for the Curse to return. Then they will concoct some fantastic story that I am supposed to believe."

"So you are content to do nothing but wait?" Dancer's tone clearly sounded his objections.

Falcon rocked back on his chair, and his eyes took on a glassy hue. "Aye, mayhap the fates will smile on me tonight and the wench will lose her step in the quicksand that lines the path."

For a moment, Dancer could not gather his wits. For years, Falcon had complained at having a daughter instead of a son. He had even gone so far as to dub her his Curse. But never before had his words wished her true harm.

"You've been too long with the drink, my friend." Dancer's voice was stern and he pulled his chair closer. "'Tis your daughter, Elizabeth's child, you prattle about."

Falcon slapped his tankard down on the table. "Don't speak the name of that witch in the same breath with my Elizabeth. Elizabeth was good, an angel . . ."

"They are mother and child!"

"Nay," Falcon argued. "She is a spawn of the devil. She sees into the future and plays with black magic. If it wasn't for her, I could have persuaded Elizabeth to join me all those years ago. But, nay, she wanted a proper home for the child. 'Twas that damned babe that cost me the finest thing I ever owned."

Dancer's thoughts raced back in time. He had met Elizabeth Chesterfield twice, and although it had been more than a decade ago, the memory still burned brightly. A delicate thing, she looked as if a puff of air would carry her off. But her looks had been deceiving, for no matter how difficult, whenever Falcon sent a message, Elizabeth traveled to meet him. Until . . . Dancer felt his skin grow cold with the memory of that last night. The *Sea Hawk* had slipped past the English ships and docked off the coast of Falmouth. Impatiently, Falcon had waited for Elizabeth to join him at the posting house on the edge of town. But Elizabeth had not come. At the appointed hour, an exhausted and ragged Samantha had appeared. Her frightened, whispered words still echoed through his mind. "Mother won't be coming. She's dead."

Falcon had taken one look at the tiny child who stood before him and his curses shook the rafters. He saw not his daughter, but the messenger of despair. He never asked how a child of eight had managed to travel the great distance, or of her welfare. He had simply stood and walked out.

Dancer had watched the pain eat at Falcon's reasoning until the friend from his youth became the embittered man who sat before him.

"If your true wish is for the Curse to be gone," Dancer said quietly, "then why not send her back home to your brother Edward. Let him be responsible for raising her in proper English fashion."

"Never," Falcon snarled. "I'd sooner cut off this hand before I'd give anything I possess to that bastard. We are brothers, two with mirrored faces, yet fate saw fit to pronounce him the elder." Falcon's eyes glittered with hatred. "It was ten damned minutes of life that gave that bastard the right to lay claim to everything."

"But since the Curse is such a trial, send her back to Edward. Let her wreak havoc with his life."

"I need no advice from you," Falcon spat. "The Curse is mine and I'll do with her as I damn well please. And when I find her tonight I'm—"

"Going to do what, invite me to share your table? Why, thank you, Falcon. I accept your kind offer."

Samantha settled gracefully into the remaining chair and tried to ignore the silence that had invaded the room upon her entrance. She could feel Falcon's anger, and tonight even Dancer seemed in ill humor.

"Where have you been?" Falcon growled, noting her dry shirt and cap.

Remembering her humiliation from the afternoon, Samantha's chin raised as she assumed an attitude of remote indifference. "Why, Falcon . . ." she drawled innocently. "Has it been so long since you locked me in my chambers that you have forgotten the incident? Did you not, just moments ago, give Marie permission to release me?"

As if on cue, Marie silently appeared at the table

and produced three crystal goblets and a bottle of fine brandy.

Samantha smiled sweetly and reached across the table to pull Falcon's untouched plate before her. "It was thoughtful of you to consider my hunger. Aren't you eating?" she questioned, taking a dainty mouthful.

"Don't push me any further, Curse, or the seat of your pants shall become smartly acquainted with my belt."

"As you wish," she smiled innocently. "When do we sail?"

"I'll not have you going into the swamp again. Do you hear?"

Samantha wiped her mouth with the edge of her sleeve. "Aye, in fact I'll wager half the island heard."

"Then heed my words. 'Tis not a safe place for the likes of you."

She returned her father's glare, refusing to lower her eyes in defeat. "'Tis the safest place on this island."

"Falcon speaks the truth, Curse," Dancer interrupted quietly.

Her stomach knotted, and she stiffened under Falcon's withering stare. "What a pair of hypocrites I sit with," she snapped. "If I followed your asinine orders, neither of you would be here today. Would you have had me sit and watch, dear Father, the time your belly was split open with a sword and your life flowed freely upon the deck? And you . . ." Her anger turned toward Dancer. "When you shook with fever so hard that ribs cracked, were you sorry then that I

21

ventured into the swamp? Would you have wished me no knowledge of the yellow powder that cured you?"

The stem of his glass snapped between his fingers and Falcon looked down to see his blood mingle with the wine that spilled on the table.

"*Madre de Dios*," Samantha swore softly, reaching for his hand.

Falcon flung her arm away with a savage jerk. "Do not touch me!" he bellowed, rising from the table. "This is the last time you will disobey my orders. You will not venture alone into the swamp again, or with Dancer as my witness, I'll have you tied to the capstan and flogged. Fifty lashes should go a long way to curb your wanderings." His ultimatum complete, Falcon flung his chair against the wall and stormed from the tavern.

Samantha sat as one made of stone, seeing nothing, feeling nothing. He hadn't even wanted her to touch him. Her throat tightened and her eyes stung. Masking her inner turmoil, she lifted her wineglass in a silent toast to her father's retreating shadow. Two could play his game, but try as she would, she could still feel Dancer's silent disapproval. It was not often that he sided against her, and tonight she felt his betrayal more keenly than Falcon's ire.

Resting her elbows on either side of her plate, Samantha's head dropped to rest on clenched fists. Her chest grew tight and she struggled against the tears that threatened anew. She took several deep breaths before raising her eyes to confront Dancer.

"It is not my wish to disobey him, but he should

22

not ask the impossible of me."

Dancer raised a brow, but said nothing.

Samantha pushed the food away in disgust. "Mayhaps I should have tempered my words," she conceded, shrugging her weary shoulders. "But he should understand. You should understand. Why do you fight me on this? I am completely safe when I venture into the swamp. Do you truly think that there is one on this island, save perhaps St. Martin, that would dare to harm me? I have you and Falcon standing to my left and Kabol on my right. What fool would risk the anger of all three?"

Dancer watched a familiar mutinous look settle over her delicate features. She didn't even reach Falcon's shoulder in height, yet she was the only one who openly dared to challenge him. "Falcon has made a stand in front of his crew, Curse. The next time he will not back down. If it comes to that, there will be little I can do to save you."

Samantha shrugged and emptied her wineglass. "I have survived my father's wrath for these past eight years. I have no doubt that I will survive a little longer."

"At least think on my words, Curse," Dancer said as she rose from the table. "I would stand before the very devil himself to protect you, but I grow weary when you tempt fate so often."

Samantha placed a fleeting kiss on his weathered cheek. "You speak as a doddering old man," she whispered, giving his thick gold earring a gentle tug. "But I know for a certainty that despite Marie's objections, you still bed more than half the wenches on this island."

23

Samantha dodged his threatening swing and left to seek her bed. But for Dancer, the light sound of her laughter lingered long after both she and the brandy were gone.

Samantha paced restlessly, finding no comfort in the plush surroundings of her chambers. Rich ivory silks from India covered the walls. The ornately carved teak furniture glowed warmly in the light of the single candle that reflected in the crystal panes of the French doors. A large arrangement of wildflowers in a variety of yellows and oranges provided the room's only touch of color.

Muffled laughter from the common room below filtered upward to her third-floor sanctuary, but tonight it offered no peace. Her mind replayed the angry confrontation with Falcon over and over again.

Not bothering to disrobe, she extinguished the candle and listlessly flopped back against the pillows on her bed. Tonight, no moonlight illuminated the miniature portrait she cradled lovingly in her palm. "How did you succeed, Mama?" she whispered. "How did you make him love you?" Silent tears traced a path down her pale face. "'Tis not possible for me to please him. We took half a score of ships last voyage and still he is not content. We must sail again with the tide." Clutching the portrait close to her chest, Samantha curled onto her side. "What words of wisdom did your death rob from me?" she sobbed brokenly into the pillow. "Do I ask too much? All I wish is for Papa to love me."

Chapter II

Late fall 1711

Alex Cortland impatiently paced the length of the *Windspur*'s quarterdeck as streaks of lightning raced across the blackened sky. First pirates, now a storm, he thought darkly. Was there to be no end to this travesty? Looking about the unkempt schooner, he gave a growl of disgust. The deck was bare of paint and even the sails wanted mending. No wonder the pirates hadn't boarded. They had sailed close enough to see that the mismatched crew was virtually defenseless, yet they had retreated without a confrontation.

Alex flexed his shoulders trying to work the tension from his muscles as he paced. When he got back to London, the first order of business would be to deliver a sound thrashing to James. Thinking of his younger brother, his scowl deepened. He had credited James with more sense. It was bad enough that the lad had sent an urgent message to return home without sending proper transport to see the deed completed, but to have entrusted the message with Julia Harwick was unforgivable. How would he ever manage to discourage the girl's amorous advances when James and Carolyn constantly found opportunity to throw them together? And why was she traveling with Lord and Lady Halifax?

Alex adjusted his step to the rolling motion of the deck and moved to the rail. The wind's icy fingers reached beneath his well-stitched coat, and he shivered. He had Julia clinging to his coatsleeve below deck, and a drunken captain above. He watched silently as Captain Prescott stumbled about the deck and vowed never again to sail on a ship that was not his own. Yes, James would definitely have much to answer for.

Determined to seek the comforts of his cabin, Alex turned to find First Mate Smith climbing the stairs to the quarterdeck. He was holding the collar of a very large coat with a young boy dangling inside. A dirty knit cap hid a goodly portion of the lad's face, but what was visible was covered with a thick layer of grime.

"Captain!"

"What is it now, Mr. Smith?" Captain Prescott barked, clutching his head at the sound of his own words.

"Stowaway, Captain."

Captain Prescott turned and stumbled on a coil of rope piled carelessly on the deck. "And just where did you make this discovery, Mr. Smith?" he demanded, his words slurring together.

"I's found him rootin' around in the cargo hold, sir."

"Tell me, Mr. Smith, how is it you just found this worthless piece of baggage today? Damn it, man, we've been almost three days at sea."

"I don't know where he been a hiding, Captain," Smith barked in return. "I's only knows he weren't in my cargo hold when we left Bordeaux."

"Then how did he get here, Mr. Smith?" the captain bellowed, veins bulging on his forehead.

"He ain't been here, and that's a fact!" Smith replied belligerently. "I ain't gonna be called up fer something not my fault."

Unable to watch the farce any longer, Alex stepped forward. "May I be of some assistance, Captain?" His voice held quiet authority.

"'Tis nothing to concern yourself with, sir. 'Tis just a stowaway that Smith failed to find when we left France."

"Beggin' pardon, sir," Smith interrupted. "But I ain't failed at nothin'. This little beggar weren't on this ship when we left port."

Three pair of eyes turned and settled on the lad. As Smith jerked on the boy's collar, the youth's feet were in constant danger of leaving the deck. Yet despite his precarious situation, the boy seemed amazingly calm.

"Enough," Alex said sternly. "You, lad, where have you been hiding these last days?"

The lad looked up slowly, appraising each man in turn. "What kind of friggin' ship is this what's got three captains?"

27

"Blast it all!" Captain Prescott exploded. His arm swung blindly, but the vicious uppercut found its mark. The youth's head snapped back, and the unconscious boy now dangled like a limp puppet from Smith's meaty grip.

"Mr. Smith, take the scum below and lock him up. A taste of the lash on his back tomorrow will loosen that stubborn tongue and teach him some manners. And you, sir . . ." Prescott paused, trying to control his boiling anger. "If you please, would you kindly join the other passengers below deck. That storm is going to let loose any minute."

Alex watched silently as Smith tossed the limp form over his shoulder and moved unimpeded toward the lower decks. *How curious*, he thought. *Where had the lad been hiding that would make his clothes so wet?* The unsolved puzzle intrigued him, but as large raindrops spattered on the deck, he took the captain's advice and went below to join his companions.

Several hours later, the small schooner felt the full force of the storm. Experience warned Alex to brace himself as he unfastened the passage door, but even so, he was stunned by the force of the raging wind and pounding rain that greeted him. Within the blink of an eye he was soaked to the skin. The icy wind cut like a knife through his wet clothing, and his fingers grew stiff, making it difficult to cling to the guide rope that had been hastily strung across the heaving deck. Lightning flashed, and the deafening roar of thunder followed in its wake. Another bolt of lightning streaked across the blackened sky, and Alex saw that less than half the crew was on deck to ride out the storm.

"Where is Prescott?" he demanded, slowly making his way to the small huddle of men. The ship careened violently beneath his feet and his eyes burned from the salty spray.

"Drunk in his quarters."

Alex surveyed the confusion. He had been in worse storms, but without a captain, there was no hope, and all seemed to know it.

"Bring her about," he called, struggling to make his voice heard above the angry sea. Clinging to the guide ropes as wave after wave washed over the deck, Alex slowly reached the helmsman. "Dammit, man. Set a new course. Go with the storm, don't fight it."

"But, sir, the captain said . . ."

"Damn the captain!" Pushing the man aside, Alex spun the wheel so the ship veered sharply. For a sickening moment she listed dangerously, then, giving a deep moan, she slowly righted herself.

The roar of the ocean lessened for an instant as a loud, groaning sound pierced the air. The crew watched in horror as the foremast cracked, leaving a deep split running half its length. The main casings slipped and the wind found a new toy.

"Damn," Alex swore, watching the wind tug at the line. Their situation was rapidly going from bad to worse. Giving stern orders to the helmsman, Alex moved cautiously to the foremast as the heaving deck pitched and rocked beneath him. Brushing the rain from his eyes, he saw the young stowaway braced by the mast. Struggling against the violent downpour, the boy was trying to lash a length of rope about his middle.

"What the bloody hell do you think you are doing?" Alex yelled above the storm.

"'Tis possible the casings might be refastened." The boy gestured toward the sails. "Look, Captain, when I goes over, and believe me I will, just haul me in as quick as you can. Bathing in the ocean ain't my favorite pastime."

"The hell you will. To climb that mast is sheer suicide!"

"Aye, but the alternative is a watery grave fer all." Dodging Alex's outstretched hand, the boy grabbed for the shrouds and started to scale the ratlines. Several times the youth lost his footing on the twisting ropes and dangled above the rocking deck before regaining his balance.

Bracing himself against the capstan, Alex slowly fed out the rope, careful to keep the line steady. The sea tossed the schooner relentlessly about like a toy; still the boy moved on. Several of the crew secured themselves near Alex on the deck to watch the small figure now high within the sails. Towering waves slapped angrily against the hull, washing over the deck in their fury. Alex held his breath and tried to keep his eyes fixed on the boy. Now more than sixty feet above the deck, the lad balanced on ropes as he leaned precariously over the spar.

Lightning flashed and the foremast groaned in protest as the split in its side deepened. Another towering wave washed over the deck. Alex felt the line jerk and knew without looking that the boy was gone. His muscles strained as he and several crewmen frantically pulled on the rope, unwilling to grant the sea her victim. For a heart-stopping moment he feared the line would snap. Then, as another deep wave flooded the deck, the sea spit back her treasure. Alex found the limp form of the boy crumpled at his feet.

"Is he breathing?" Smith asked, helping to untangle the lad from the knotted line.

"Aye, but just barely." Alex scooped the boy under one arm. "Keep that bloody wheel secure," he called as he slowly edged his way to the passenger cabins below.

The *Windspur*'s violent rocking was intensified below deck. Alex cautiously navigated the pitch-black passageway and entered the cabin. The faint glow from a single lantern presented his four traveling companions, their pale, strained faces filled with fear.

Lord and Lady Halifax and Francis Newly were huddled in undignified positions near the small stove. Julia, her face several shades of green, had braced herself against the wall for support.

"Are we going to die, Alex?" Lady Halifax dabbed at her tear-filled eyes with the edge of the blanket she had wrapped around her.

"I doubt we shall be that lucky, Constance." Alex moved toward the corner bunk and carefully lowered his slight burden.

The lad was breathing, but his skin was blue and pinched from cold. Reaching to remove the boy's water-soaked hat, Alex lost his balance as the ship pitched violently. He caught the bunk's railing to brace himself, but the others were not as successful. Shrieks and muffled curses filled the air as the group sprawled across the damp floor in a tangled mass of arms and legs.

"Alex!" Julia's cry was muffled as she squirmed out from beneath Constance's ample form. Not caring where she planted elbows or feet, she struggled to her knees.

Alex positioned the boy as securely as possible on the bunk, then pulled Julia to her feet. Her appearance no longer bore any resemblance to that of a high-born lady. Her new French gown was crumpled and stained. Once perfectly coiffured auburn curls now hung in a tangled mat about her shoulders.

"Calm yourself, my dear," he chided gently.

Whimpering softly, Julia pressed herself full length against him, oblivious to his rain-drenched clothing.

Alex felt her tremble, and for a moment held her close. But when he would have moved, Julia's arms tightened in a death grip about his middle. "Enough, milady." Alex firmly settled Julia onto a small stool near the stove. "'Tis not the time. Tend to the boy. Get him dried off and see if you can warm him."

Julia's dark eyes grew wide with fear. "You don't mean to leave me again?"

"I must rouse Prescott. I've no choice."

"I don't want to die!" Constance wailed as tears streamed down her face.

Alex tugged open the cabin door and Constance's hysterical cries joined with those of the screeching wind. Carefully making his way along the darkened passage, Alex opened several doors before finding Prescott's cabin. The odor of the place nearly stopped his breath. His eyes adjusted to the darkness, and he located a candle on the desk. Taking great care with its lighting, Alex surveyed the shambles before him.

Prescott was lying half in and half out of his bunk, snoring loudly. The man's head almost touched the floor with each roll of the deck, but an empty whiskey bottle was still clenched tightly in one fist.

"Dammit, man, wake up!"

Prescott responded with a deep belch that added to the stench of the room. Deciding the situation was hopeless, Alex moved closer to push the ailing captain back into his berth. The odor grew stronger, and Alex suddenly realized that the top portion of the bed was completely covered in vomit. With a snarl of disgust, he flipped the captain onto the floor. Prescott belched again but showed no other signs of life. With a final glance about the room, Alex extinguished the single candle and left the cabin in darkness.

The hour was past midnight and the *Windspur* continued to rock wildly in the angry sea, but the driving rains had ceased and the gale winds were steadily dying. Alex relinquished the wheel to the helmsman and flexed his tired shoulders. It was a miracle the schooner had withstood the storm's violent pounding, he thought as he carefully made his way across the ravaged deck.

Stepping into the cabin, Alex was rocked backward as Constance Halifax threw herself into his arms.

"Oh, Alex, I'm too young to die," she sobbed. "I know you have come to tell us that the end is near."

"Halifax, tend to your wife, man," Alex growled as he forcibly pried Constance from his chest. He smiled as Julia moved to help him. But as she stepped closer, she gave a deep groan, closed her eyes, and fainted into his arms.

Catching her, Alex swore under his breath. It was not by choice he traveled with them, nor was it his way to mock their fear, but he was beginning to lose patience. Turning with Julia in his arms, his eyes settled on the empty bunk.

"Halifax, where is the boy I brought here?" He set Julia none too gently on the vacant berth.

"Now see here, Cortland." Francis Newly, his fine powdered wig slightly askew, moved gingerly from his warm position near the stove and stood on wobbly legs. "Control your temper, man. We," he gestured to his bedraggled companions, "are not a common lot to be ordered about. What with Constance and Julia to see to, Halifax and I have been frightfully busy."

"That's right, Alex," Halifax added with new-found courage. "If you want to wander about on the deck like a common sailor in spite of your position, that's your privilege."

Alex's eyes narrowed dangerously. "What do you mean, my position?"

Halifax looked nervously from Alex to Julia and back again. "Come, man, 'tis common knowledge that you are soon to become the Duke of Coverick."

"Where is the boy?" Alex growled, the muscle in his cheek beginning to twitch.

34

"Who cares?" Newly touched a wrinkled lace-edged handkerchief to his lips. "Personally I wasn't sorry to see the little beggar go. Why, just think of all the crimes one of his sort might have been involved in. He might even have committed murder!"

"I won't stay in the same cabin with a murderer!" Constance cried hysterically.

"See what your folly has caused now, Cortland!" Halifax patted his wife's head in an effort to soothe her.

The strain of the last several hours began to take its toll, and Alex gritted his teeth in anger. "That little beggar, as you want to call him, was the only one on this blasted ship with enough nerve to climb the mast." Alex looked from one to the other, disgusted with their lack of understanding. "The storm is passing. 'Twill last a few more hours, but the worst is over." His voice was deadly quiet. "I suggest each of you find your bed and stay there till morning."

"Alex . . ." Julia's pleading cries and outstretched arms were ignored as Alex left the cabin.

"Damn," he swore as he navigated the darkened companionway. So Julia had read Jamie's note and drawn her own conclusions. That meant all of London would be speculating on his actions. Would he leave the city and return to Coverick, or would he turn his back on the Cortland Estates. Four and ten years had passed since he had seen his childhood home. He had not set foot on the family estate since the death of his grandfather. What irony, he thought sadly. William had gone to such extremes to secure the vast family fortune for his exclusive use. Now he was dying without an heir.

Alex rubbed his tired eyes. He could still see the pain and disbelief on his mother's face when the housekeeper brought the news. They were to leave the estate immediately and find residence elsewhere. His father's outrage was to no avail, for the law was clear. The elder son inherited, and William wanted it all. Suddenly, doors that had always been opened in friendship were closed. His mother's delicate nature had not tolerated the abuse, and her death came before winter's end. His father had contracted a fever and died the following spring. At ten and six, Alex found himself completely responsible for James, a lively six-year-old, and Carolyn, barely two. Rage and determination had erased any grief he might have felt, and the innocence of his youth died with his parents.

Leaving the two young ones in the care of the local church, he had carefully sold the few remaining possessions of value, then left for the sea. Five years later, he returned to England a wealthy merchant, to reclaim his brother and sister. Their home was now in the most fashionable part of London, and though all speculated on how he had made his fortune, none dared to inquire. Money once again secured his place in society, yet he remained aloof. He had no tolerance for those who judged a man's worth by the weight of his purse.

A fresh breeze swept through the companionway, and Alex breathed deeply. Now, at age thirty, he was about to become the eighth Duke of Coverick. Nay, if Jamie's letter was accurate, he already held the title.

Alex reached his cabin. First, a dry set of clothing, then he was going to find that boy and have some answers.

"Don't move, Captain." The hoarse whisper reached his ears as hard steel poked into his back. "Come in slowly and close the door."

Alex did as he was told. Turning, he found the trembling boy wrapped in a blanket. A pistol protruded from within the massive folds, and Alex recognized it as his own.

"I was wondering whose cabin I picked." The boy's teeth chattered. "But I couldn't tolerate the other accommodations, too many hysterical ladies."

Thinking of Constance Halifax, Alex started to smile and relax his stand, but the quiet click of the gun's hammer warned him to hold his ground.

Chapter III

"Easy, lad, 'tis a fine piece you now carry. It reacts to a light touch."

"All the better, Captain." The boy shivered. "And should you be wondering, I shoot better than I climb. Now, if you was to be so kind as to step this way?" The boy nudged at a straight-backed chair with his foot.

Ever mindful of the pistol and the unsteady hand that held it, Alex allowed himself to be tied. He would play the game for a few moments more, then he wanted answers. With a startling swiftness, the ropes were tightened about him.

The boy coughed violently, taking several minutes to catch his breath. With sluggish movements, he lit the wall lantern, filling the cluttered cabin with dim, dusty shadows. A narrow berth and massive sea chest claimed most of one wall, while a roughly hewn table and single chair competed with the small stove for the remaining floor space. Shifting the blanket more securely over his trembling shoulders, the boy knelt before the sea chest. Carefully placing the pistols within easy reach, he studied the ornate clasp. The lock proved no obstacle to his trembling fingers and the heavy lid creaked open.

Alex watched with a mixture of curiosity and irritation as the youth rummaged through his possessions, carelessly dumping the well-packed garments onto the floor.

"Who are you?" he demanded. "What is your name?"

A batiste nightshirt caught the boy's attention, and he pulled it from the chest.

"Are you a dandy, Captain?" he taunted, his fingers flipping against the lace edge of the sleeves.

Alex's scowl darkened. His arms strained against the bindings, but the knots held firm. *What a fool I am,* he thought with sudden insight. *Surely any lad that could climb ratlines would know his knots.* Silently cursing his own faulty judgment, Alex realized his wrists were being rubbed raw. Clearly strength was not to be the answer.

The boy stood on shaky legs. "Be patient, Captain," the husky voice whispered. "In time you will understand."

"What the . . ." Alex's curse was muffled as a damp blanket was tossed over his head. The sickening smell of wet wool invaded his nostrils. He heard muffled sounds as the youth moved about the cabin, but none gave a clue to the lad's mischief.

When the blanket was pulled away, Alex's eyes grew wide in disbelief. The water-soaked boy had vanished. Standing in his place was a bewitching sea nymph.

Clad in the thin nightshirt, the nymph silently knelt near the small stove and tried to untangle the long strands of hair that clung damply to her shoulders. The lantern silhouetted a petite form with soft, womanly curves. Her ivory skin glowed in the candlelight, and even the darkening bruise along her cheek did not detract from her beauty. Alex tried to picture the fragile creature before him clinging to the mast, but the image escaped him.

Mesmerized, he watched the heat from the small stove bring her hair to life. Never had he seen such a color. Too pale to be honey or gold, it was that soft, elusive silver color so often found on small children who spend hours in the sun.

"Who the hell are you?" he queried softly. "Where in God's name have you come from?"

"Is a name really that important, Captain?"

"If this be madness, at least put a name to it, milady." His smooth, rich voice commanded an answer.

She gazed at the flickering candle, her eyes vague and unseeing. "Samantha . . ." Her voice hesitated.

"Just Samantha? No family?" Alex watched her eyes cloud with visible pain.

"Ches—" A violent cough consumed her, and Samantha jerked back to the present. *Good Lord,* she shivered, *what was she doing?* She had almost confessed her most guarded secret to a stranger. She rubbed her burning eyes. Her arms were heavy with exhaustion. *Think,* her mind screamed. *Think.*

She rose slowly and leaned against the massive sea chest for support. Her throat was raw, and it hurt to breathe. Her strength was fading, every muscle ached for rest. To tarry longer would be madness. Trembling, she reached for the long knife that lay on the table.

"So m'lady has found her wits at last." His voice was stern. "Untie me now and put an end to this foolishness."

Samantha's spirit revived with his words. Did he think her a half-wit to meekly bow to his orders? Angrily she straightened and moved toward her captive.

"You are in a rather perilous position, Captain," she taunted. The sharp edge of the knife forced his chin upward. "You speak boldly for one on the wrong side of the blade." Angry green eyes locked with hers, and Samantha felt her strength drain. Prickly fingers of doubt traced an icy path down her spine and settled as a knot in her stomach. There was something terribly important about green eyes, but her tired mind refused to find the thought and her head ached from the effort. She fought back the fear that coiled tighter in her middle and on unsteady legs moved behind him.

The ship pitched deeply and Alex's breath stopped as he felt pressure from the knife against his back. The wet cloth of his jacket yielded easily to the sharp blade, but the sleeves proved more difficult. Alex watched in stunned silence as his jacket fell to the floor in pieces. His waistcoat and stock quickly followed. As she pulled his shirt from his breeches, the icy touch of her fingers against his bare flesh brought his speech back with a gasp.

"What are you doing?" he demanded, finding his wits at last.

She leaned forward to reach the buttons of his shirt but said nothing.

Alex watched her trembling fingers closely, trying to anticipate their actions. They were fine-boned and delicate. Fingers made to wear rings, he thought, yet hers were bare. As she moved behind him, the fresh scent of sandalwood from the nightshirt mixed with the salty fragrance of her hair to surround him. The heady mixture clouded his mind, and he had the sudden impulse to rub his cheek against the pale lock of hair that trailed across his shoulder. But as his shirt was tossed to the growing pile on the floor, the frigid air of the cabin brought him to his senses.

"Samantha, untie me. I swear, lass, you won't come to harm by this hand."

Samantha cast him a dubious glance but said nothing. Kneeling before him, she tugged at his boot. The force tumbled her backward as his foot pulled free.

"Let me help you," he argued as she struggled to her knees again. "Whatever your plight, I am not a man without means." Alex wondered even as he spoke the words why he was offering. The girl meant nothing to him, yet as he gazed into her troubled eyes, a seed was planted. It started with a tightening in his loins and a growing ache in his arms to hold her. The thought of this fragile creature alone and in danger enraged him, and his frustration grew.

Samantha tugged his other boot free, and a wave of exhaustion engulfed her. Her head dropped forward to rest against his thigh. The hard muscles tensed beneath her palm as she braced herself against his leg.

"Don't stop," she muttered weakly. "Keep moving, just don't stop." With effort, she steadied her breathing and raised her head. Panic whispered through her veins as the magnitude of her error came to light. *Green eyes,* her mind screamed. Why had there been no warning? Why hadn't she realized sooner? It was not the face of a stranger that scowled down at her, but a face that had lived in her thoughts for weeks, haunting her dreams, plaguing her mind.

Reluctantly she gazed back up at him. As in her dreams, she could feel his strength. His well-muscled chest and bronzed skin were not of one who spent idle hours. There was a ruggedness to his handsome features which exuded authority, and his bold eyes followed her every move with a curious intensity.

"Samantha . . ."

"Nay, Captain, enough chatter." She struggled to her feet, trying to ignore the icy panic that filled her. His breeches would just have to remain, she decided, finding it hard to keep her balance on the rocking floor as she stood.

She used the table for support as she moved to the small stove and wrapped a blanket around it. When the blanket was warm to the touch, she sluggishly crossed the narrow cabin till she again was standing behind him.

Alex sighed in gratitude as the warmed blanket covered him. She rubbed the top of his shoulders and arms briskly until the chill was gone from his flesh.

The effort exhausted her remaining strength, and Samantha felt tears of frustration well in her eyes. Why could she do nothing right? Why did it have to be him? Why wouldn't the damn blanket stay in place? She wiped the growing moisture from her eyes with the back of her hand and pushed the blanket back onto his broad shoulder. She needed desperately to find sleep. Her gaze settled on the berth, but her mind flashed a warning. She had come too far to let her guard down now. She turned back to the captain, realizing for the first time how easy it would be for him to overtake her.

Alex felt the gun press against his back as the ropes on his wrist were cut away. "Go easy, m'lady," he commanded softly. "I would take great offense if my death was the result of an ill-timed sneeze."

"Move to the bunk, Captain, and if you do value your life, go slowly."

Alex moved cautiously across the cabin, ever aware of the cold metal pressing into his flesh and the trembling hand that held it there.

Samantha stood at the head of the bunk. *Hurry*, her mind pleaded. *Hurry*. The finely crafted pistol was no light object, and the muscles in her arm began to scream with pain as she fought to hold the gun steady.

Alex stretched out on the bunk and placed his hand over his head as directed. He had seen the pistol tremble within her grip, but at such close range it was not worth the gamble. He would bide his time, for a moment would come, of that he was certain.

Samantha used several short lengths of rope to bind his wrists to the bunk's railing. Satisfied he was secure, she wrapped the blanket about him, then pulled up another quilt to cover him.

"I don't know if it will be enough," her voice rasped. "But I know no other way to keep you warm."

"And is that so important?" he questioned, stunned by her actions.

"You saved my life tonight," she said quietly. Wrapping herself in the second blanket, Samantha gazed longingly at the soft feather tick beneath him, then resigned herself to the floor. Placing both pistols within easy reach, she curled into an uncomfortable position before the door. If anyone came to call, she would be ready.

"M'lady, I did not drag you back from the sea to watch you freeze to death."

"Go to sleep, Captain," she whispered hoarsely.

"Samantha . . ."

"Enough. You will rest easier without a gag, will you not?" Samantha wrapped a second quilt about her and tried to find a warmer position. Her eyelids felt like lead weights and refused to do her bidding. Despite all efforts to stay awake, exhaustion finally took its toll.

The thick quilts were slowly soaked by the dampness that seeped through the creaking wood, and Samantha shifted restlessly within the sodden garments seeking warmth.

Alex tried to flex his arms, but the bonds held firm. Turning his head he watched the huddled figure with fascination. It was a dream, he decided. That could be the only explanation. A delicate female who climbed the lines better than any seaman he knew. A bewitching nymph who preferred the floor to his bed. Nothing made sense, including the overwhelming desire to protect the tiny bundle now shivering on the floor. Where had she come from, he wondered, and what delightful revenge would he extract when he was free?

The *Windspur* moved into calm waters, safe now from the raging force of the storm. But for two on the small schooner, the night held no peace.

Alex came awake instantly as a lumpy bundle joined him on the bunk. Hopelessly tangled in the damp quilts, she was trying to snuggle next to him on the narrow berth.

"Cold," she mumbled sleepily. "So cold."

With that, Alex could agree. Even through the blankets, she felt like a giant icicle pressed to his side.

"Push the quilt away and get under the covers." His voice was soft, hypnotic. His words drifted into her fogged mind, and Samantha sat up in confusion. He held his breath. It was clear that she was still more than half asleep. "Samantha," he crooned softly. "Untie my hands, then get under the covers."

She stared at him like one stricken of mind.

"Come, little one," he coaxed. "Let me warm you."

With a herculean effort Samantha rid herself of the damp quilt and clumsily slipped under the blankets.

Alex started to speak, but his words caught in his throat. For finding the heat of his body, she had draped her scantily clad figure directly over him, her thigh sliding intimately between his own.

"Samantha," he whispered against her forehead.

She wiggled against him trying to get as close as possible to this haven of warmth.

"Untie me, Samantha. Let me hold you close and

warm you." But he was too late. By her deep even breathing, he knew she was already asleep.

Alex groaned and shifted beneath her slight weight. His hand ached to caress her softness, and his loins throbbed with the need to possess her. For the first time in his life, Alex Cortland felt completely helpless.

Samantha awoke, sensing danger. A steady thumping sounded beneath her ear, and the desire to follow it back to her dreams was strong. Without moving a muscle, her eyes darted about the cabin, trying to clear the clouds from her mind. Her heart quickened. Somehow she had left her cold pallet by the door and had joined the captain in his bunk. The thin nightshirt was the only thing now separating her from the heat of his body.

For several minutes she listened to his steady breathing, and her greatest fear was confirmed. He was free. One arm pressed against her back and anchored her firmly to his chest. His other hand had pushed the nightshirt up and was resting boldly on her backside.

Cautiously, she tried to ease herself from the bunk, but his arms tightened about her and she froze with fear. Samantha raised her head and found herself mere inches from the captain's smiling face. His teeth were straight and white and his eyes twinkled with a devilish gleam. A night's growth of beard shadowed his cheeks, and thick dark hair curled insolently about his forehead. She might have enjoyed his rugged features, but her heart was pounding so fiercely it made thinking quite impossible.

"Good morning, m'lady." His voice was deep and rich, but Samantha was only aware of the hand that caressed her spine and pressed her hips more firmly against his burning desire.

"Let me go!" she snapped, angry at the blush that now heated her face. She struggled but to no avail, for as she tried to push away, he pulled her back with a grip that was gentle but unyielding.

Alex flipped her beneath him and let his weight hold her until frustration and exhaustion stilled her frantic movements. The faintest sunlight filtered in through the cabin's narrow windows, yet he could still discern her heightened color, and his smile grew with satisfaction. She had held the upper hand, now all was in reverse. Revenge would be sweet.

Shifting slightly to her side, Alex kept one leg firmly tucked over her squirming body as he slipped his arm under her head. Her fist lashed forward but was entrapped mere inches from his taunting smile. Alex drew her clenched fingers to his lips. His mustache caressed her knuckles as his teeth nibbled at each finger.

The bunk rocked hypnotically beneath her, and Samantha stared wide-eyed as he gently placed her limp hand on the pillow beside her head. Trapped beneath the hard length of him, she was completely helpless, while he still had one hand free. The tempo of her pounding heart increased twice over as she saw the flash of satisfaction deep within his emerald eyes.

Panic filled her anew as she realized what it had cost him to be her captive. He would not grant quarter easily.

"Now, little one," he said firmly, "you are going to tell me who you really are and how you came to be here."

Her energy foolishly spent, Samantha turned a mutinous face toward the wall, refusing to acknowledge his question. Never had a man touched her so boldly, and his nearness was playing havoc with her senses. Her eyelids, still heavy with fatigue, wanted nothing more than to escape into sleep. His strength was frightening and her perilous situation was becoming more desperate with each ragged breath.

Alex brushed soft tendrils of hair from her heated face. "Well, there is more than one way to unravel a puzzle," he whispered. "If the lady won't cooperate, then . . ." Slowly, he began to unbutton the front of the nightshirt.

"Stop that!" she demanded, snapping her head back. But her voice was a raspy whisper that held no strength. Samantha twisted frantically against his firm grip, but his lean fingers did not pause till they rested on the last button near her waist. She began to tremble and tears stung her eyes.

"Please, please don't," she begged. Humiliation burned deeply and she loathed herself for the pleading words that spilled forth. "Please stop." But even as she spoke, the nightshirt was slowly peeled open. Her breath refused to come and her eyes closed tightly as her body quaked with shame.

Alex looked down at the feast before him like a starving man. Slowly his hand came to rest on the

50

silver medallion. "Very beautiful, but very expensive for a stowaway." As he examined the necklace now lying in the palm of his hand, his knuckles rested against the gentle swell of her breast. The carved crystal sparkled, and the silver liquid inside moved constantly with a life of its own. Letting the warm medallion slip from his hand, he circled her breast with the tip of his finger and watched the rosy nipple spring to life. "Are you a sea nymph?" he whispered, his breath warm against her heart. "Will you disappear if I get too close?"

"You couldn't be much closer."

Alex chuckled deeply at her answer. "Are you really an innocent, milady?" His cheek brushed against the soft mound. Her skin was smooth, like a mixture of honey and cream, but he could still taste the tang of the sea as he nuzzled at her breast. *'Tis a sea witch I hold*, he thought, shifting more fully over her as his need to possess her became a consuming flame.

Alex felt her body go rigid. Looking up, confusion washed over him. Pale curls tangled about her drawn face and her eyes were pressed tightly closed. Silent tears seeped from beneath the long, dark lashes to trace a silvery path down her cheeks. There was no response here, only fear.

Letting out a breath of exasperation, Alex felt his desire cool sharply. "Easy, little one, easy." He shifted to the side and pulled her gently against his chest, tucking her head safely beneath his chin. "Calm down, Samantha. You'll come to no harm by this hand." Tenderly he held her. His fingers traced through the silky tangles of her hair, soothing and caressing. Gently his arms cradled her until her trembling eased. *She must be a witch,* he thought with frustration. She had woven a spell of magic about him and somehow had become entangled within her own web. Her breast burned a brand against his chest. His loins ached for release, yet the desire to protect her was stronger, even if it meant denying himself. *Madness,* he conceded. His lips brushed against her forehead as he continued to rock her gently, *truly madness.*

Samantha sensed the change and wondered at its source. Slowly her eyes fluttered closed as a blissful peace surrounded her. The gentle motion of his hand in her hair soothed the fright and stilled her fears. His skin was warm and firm beneath her, yet even at rest, she could feel the strength of his muscles. The curling dark hair on his chest tickled her chin and his male scent enveloped her. She breathed deeply, trying to absorb the sensations. Never in all her memories had any man sought to give her comfort. She shivered, and the captain's arms tightened, shifting her more securely against him.

Samantha raised her head and looked up at him, unable to believe what she saw and felt. Surely no dream could be so real. Warm emerald eyes gazed back at her until she felt herself drowning in their magic.

Alex watched the emotions play across her face, but despite his resolve, her trembling lips were his undoing. Slowly his mouth lowered to cover hers. At the first feather-light touch of his tongue, her lips remained motionless with uncertainty. Gently he touched again, tracing their outline, tantalizing her with feelings she didn't understand. Under his insistence, her lips parted. Alex moaned as he reached his goal and began to drink of her sweetness.

Samantha felt herself aflame. His lips moved like liquid fire across her cheek to nuzzle at her ear. A curious feeling settled in the pit of her stomach, then radiated outward. His mustache dusted lightly over her lips, brushing ever so close yet not touching, moving from eyelid to cheek, from forehead to nose, teasing again and again.

Turning her face, Samantha pressed her lips boldly against his so the magic could continue. Needing no encouragement, his tongue plunged to intimately explore her mouth, shattering the last of her resistance. Slow, ardent kisses robbed her of her will and created a longing for what she knew not.

Samantha felt flames of desire threaten to consume her as his teeth gently scraped down the cord of her neck. Her ragged breathing quickened as she felt the sleek texture of his tongue caress her neck, then move lower. Her head rocked from side to side as he tasted first one nipple then the other. The gentle tug against her breast seemed to pull at the very heart of her and she floated in exquisite ecstasy.

Their eyes met and held, saying nothing yet telling all. His hand moved to her leg and his fingertips traced intricate patterns against her silken skin. Her heart clamored crazily as his calloused palm moved steadily higher until it came to rest on the gentle swell between her legs.

A loud banging rattled against the door of the cabin and reality returned with a jolt.

"Sir, can you come on deck, sir?" The voice

boomed in the passageway. "There's trouble. I can't rouse Captain Prescott and a ship a-flying the black bones is coming fast on the port side."

"I'm coming," Alex groaned, resting his forehead against hers, their breath mingling. His blood was pounding and he ached with frustration. 'Twould be no release found in a hasty coupling, he decided. She was like a fine brandy and needed to be tasted slowly to savor the full richness. "Stay here," he commanded. "I'll deal with the matter above and be back shortly." A flicker of fear crossed her face and her bottom lip trembled at the anger in his voice.

Sensing her distress, Alex claimed her mouth for one last kiss before levering himself from the bunk. "Be easy, little love," he whispered gently as he reached into the sea chest for a new shirt. With quick, efficient movements he slipped into the garment and searched the cabin floor for his boots. "Together we shall see to all your difficulties. No one shall harm you. You have my word."

He checked the pistols, then tucked both into his waistband. At the cabin's door, he paused. Unable to leave her, Alex moved back to the bunk. "I truly think that you have bewitched me." He brushed the damp tendrils of hair from her face, then pressed his lips against her forehead. "Rest easy, love." He pulled the covers to her chin, then he was gone.

Dull, gray-black clouds streaked the sky, obscuring the sun with a hazy film. Alex squinted against the glare as he watched the approaching ship. Smith and two others he recognized joined him on the quarter-deck.

"'Tis the same one as before." Smith's voice was tinged with fear. "Why would she leave us be and then come back?" A pale-blue flag streaked with black now flew beneath the black bones on the approaching ship. "Oh, my God, 'tis the Falcon."

Alex's eyes settled on the powerful lines of the two-masted brigantine. Through the eyepiece he counted more than two score of men lining the decks, each fully armed. A single figure clad in black stood alone on the quarterdeck. The Falcon.

"Mr. Smith." Alex's voice was slow and steady. "Get every available firearm on deck. Spread the word for each man to arm himself with whatever he can find."

"Aye, sir." The tension on the *Windspur*'s deck became a tangible thing as the pirate ship moved ever closer. "Lordy, look at all them cannons." Smith took a shaky breath as he stood beside Alex. "Ye think they gonna fire all them?"

Alex shrugged. "With the Falcon, 'tis hard to say. Coming this close, I think they mean to board us."

"But we ain't got no cargo," Smith argued. "What good would it do?"

The pirate ship was almost upon them when a shrill whistle pierced the waiting silence. All eyes turned upward, but Alex was the first to see her. Clad once again as the stowaway, Samantha climbed high within the sails. Straddling the main topyard, she cautiously edged her way to the spar's outer point. Alex felt his heart jump as she stood on shaky legs, then dove neatly between the ships.

Surfacing, she caught the line tossed from the mighty brigantine and was hauled aboard. Alex watched in utter disbelief as the pirate ship changed direction and moved away.

Samantha sputtered and gasped for breath as Robbie helped her over the rail. The icy water of the sea clung to her clothing, cloaking her in frigid agony.

"You shouldn't have done that, Curse." Robbie's voice was filled with concern as he pulled the seaweed from her hat. "Falcon was madder than hell when we couldn't find you last night."

She tried to smile her thanks, but all she could do was shudder. Robbie stepped aside and Samantha found herself face-to-face with her father.

"You have pushed me too far, my dear," he said coldly. "You have made a fool of me for the last time."

"Falcon, calm yourself. I am fine." Her teeth chattered uncontrollably and her speech slurred. "'Twas no harm done. Why all this fuss?"

"Fuss!" he bellowed, causing everyone save Samantha to back away. "What if we had not discovered you gone? What if I had been unable to find the ship? They hang pirates in England! Did you forget that?"

Samantha swayed and leaned back against the rail for support. Fatigue clouded her reasoning, making her chafe with impatience. Why didn't he just go away? All she wanted was to get warm and find sleep.

"Stop shouting and leave me be," she commanded hoarsely. In her exhausted state, she didn't hear Dancer's gasp, or see the danger that glittered in Falcon's eyes.

Falcon stared at her in disbelief. There was no remorse here, no begging forgiveness. He looked about at his waiting crew, then made his decision. Slowly, he began to unbuckle his belt.

Samantha stared at his hands like a bird caught in a trap. "Now, Falcon, don't be hasty." Trembling, she let the water-soaked coat slip from her shoulders, then edged her way along the rail. "What good is all your worry if you kill me?"

Falcon pulled the wide leather belt from his breeches. "I'm not going to kill you." His voice was flat. "Though you might wish it before I'm through. Your wandering ways are going to come to an end."

"Not if I can help it." Samantha swung herself to the railing and started up the ratlines. Falcon followed.

She moved as quickly as she dared. If only the tightness in her chest would ease. Stopping briefly at the watch, she saw Falcon following at a slow, measured pace. She had nowhere to go and he knew it. She climbed higher.

Her mind darted frantically from one plan to another. Could she soothe him? Nay, the anger on his face erased that thought completely. Desperate now, she groped wildly and her hand caught a support line. Did she dare? Her eyes settled on the foremast, more than twenty feet away. Was the line secure? Would it hold her weight? Her hands reached again to the line, and she tightened her grip. The coarse rope sent splinters of pain shooting through her fingers. Blinking salty tears from her eyes, Samantha looked back to see Falcon steadily closing the distance between them.

In wild desperation, she swung her legs forward from the spar, and her heels caught the rope. Her shoulders strained and her arms trembled as she hung more than sixty feet above the deck. Panting, she tried to force as much breath as possible into her starving lungs. Slowly, ever so slowly, she began the laborious hand-over-hand motion down the support stay that connected the foremast with the mainmast.

A gust of wind caught the sails and the ship heeled slightly. Unprepared for the sudden lurch, Samantha's foot slipped. Every muscle screamed in protest as she dangled from the line. Dredging forth her last ounce of strength, she forced her leg back over the rope. Salty tears burned her eyes and the pain in her hands made clutching the line a living hell as she continued across.

A lifetime later, she felt her foot touch the topgallant. Her body trembled violently as she pulled herself over to straddle the spar on the foremast. Sweat covered her forehead. Her palms, raw and bleeding, were embedded with slivers of hemp. The golden splinters glittered in the sunlight and sent daggers of pain through her hands. Her breathing was reduced to shallow gasps and her shoulder muscles throbbed in agony. Wiping the tears from her eyes, she spotted Falcon high on the mainmast. For the moment, victory was hers and defiantly she saluted.

Falcon climbed down from the mast and stood on

the deck below her. His anger had been dulled only for a moment when he thought she was going to fall to her death. Now that she was safe, his rage increased. "Curse, get your ass off that spar and get down here before you break your fool neck."

"I shall stay here." Her voice drifted downward. "The ladies of London tell me bruises are not in fashion this season." Dancer choked on his pipe and Robbie turned quickly to the rail, his shoulders shaking.

"Damn her then." Falcon turned. "Robbie, Mc-Neal, stand guard at the foot of that mast. The minute that cocky wench comes down, bring her to me."

Samantha shivered. The clouds had vanished, but despite the bright sunlight, she was freezing. The harsh glare from the water hurt her eyes and she shifted on the narrow beam trying to find a more comfortable position. She watched the movement on the deck below, but the motion made her dizzy. Leaning her head back against the foremast and closing her eyes, she tried to still the queasy feeling that was creeping into her stomach.

Falcon was no longer on the deck, of that she was sure. But if he was waiting for her to come down so he could beat her, he could wait forever.

Chapter IV

Samantha shifted as much as she dared on the narrow beam, trying to ease the cramped muscles of her neck and back. The harsh glare from the water hurt her eyes, bringing tears that would not cease. Her clothing, dried stiff from the wind, gave little protection. Terrified of falling, she awkwardly twisted a length of rope about herself and the mast, then slipped her legs under a loose line on the spar. The simple movements were pure agony for the raw flesh of her hands and perspiration covered her forehead before she finished.

Satisfied that she wouldn't fall, Samantha leaned her head back against the hard wooden foremast and willed the queasy feeling in her stomach to vanish. Watching the horizon rise and fall did little to stem the fear that grew with each passing hour. She searched her mind for some spell or charm that would command her tortured muscles to do her bidding. But even the simple act of pushing hair from her face caused her arm muscles to scream in protest. Her battered hands, now too stiff to move, paused as the sun sparkled against the band of gold that ringed her middle finger.

Blinking through her tears, she studied the ring more closely. The image of a golden snake coiled twice around her finger, then stretched its head toward her fingertips. Two goodly sized emeralds glittered as eyes. The captain's ring with the captain's eyes, she thought as she watched the sunlight bounce from gem to gem. Had she taken it? A warm glow started in the pit of her stomach and began to radiate outward. Just the thought of him made her heart quicken. How strong his arms had been, yet how gentle his touch.

Dreamily, her eyes closed. She could picture his face smiling down at her, the curl of his dark hair, the rugged slant of his brow. The warmth of his body surrounded her. He would protect her, she reasoned with childlike innocence. With that thought, a smile touched her parched lips and she floated into darkness.

Oblivious to the pallet of colors nature washed across the night sky, Dancer paced the *Sea Hawk*'s deck and wrestled with demons from within. It was more than ten hours since the Curse had perched within the sails. No food, no drink; by the time Falcon came to his senses, the lass would be dead. The magenta sky faded to a dusty gray and his agitation grew. Denied the warmth of the sun, winds chilled with dampness crossed the deck and filled the sails.

With a determined step, Dancer crossed the deck and stood before Falcon. "You can't leave her up there. She'll die of exposure."

Falcon sat on the bottom step that led to the quarterdeck. His eyes searched the sails briefly, then turned back to the pistol he was cleaning. "She'll come down when she's ready."

"And if she can't?"

Falcon shrugged. "I did not place her there. 'Tis by her own choosing she beds within the sails."

Dancer's face grew red with anger. "I'll not stand by and watch your stubbornness take the life of that child."

Falcon rose and stretched to his full height. Rage knotted his brow as he glared at the giant before him. Abruptly, he turned and mounted the steps to the quarterdeck. "Fetch her down." He tossed the words over his shoulder with a casual indifference, but Dancer never noticed, for he was already climbing the rigging.

Dancer's breath caught in his throat as he reached her. Pain swelled in his chest, and for a heartbeat he couldn't move. "Dear God, I'm too late." Her arms hung limply at her sides and her head rolled lifelessly with each shift of the mast. "I'll kill him for this," he vowed. "I'll feed every inch of his flesh to the sharks." Taking his knife, he carefully cut the ropes that tangled about her legs.

Pulled from the gray fog that surrounded her, Samantha whimpered in protest as the blood rushed back into her stiff limbs. Her legs burned with white-hot pain and she struggled against the source.

Dancer blinked away the forbidden moisture that

had gathered on his lashes as relief washed through him. "Can you hear me, Curse?" he whispered. "Let go now . . . I'll not drop you."

"Drop me?" Her mouth moved, but only a strange moaning sound whispered forth. She floated through a cloudy mist. Where was the captain? Why didn't he come to her? "Mustn't fall," she whispered against Dancer's shoulder. "Falcon will be angry if I fall."

The *Sea Hawk*'s crew breathed a collective sigh of relief when Dancer's feet finally met the deck. "Is she dead?" Robbie moved closer. The deck lanterns had been lit, and their eerie glow now surrounded the limp form that dangled in the quartermaster's arms. "'Tain't never seen her so still before."

"Nay, she lives." Dancer cradled her tighter against his broad chest. "But she is burning with fever. Where is Falcon?"

"Gone below." MacNeal stepped forward and carefully lifted her dangling arm, gasping when her bloodied palm came to view. "Oh, the poor wee lass," he crooned. Gently, the wrinkled old seaman rested her injured hand against her chest. "Them's one fine pair, they is. She be as crazy as he."

Seated at his chart table, Falcon looked up in anger when the door to his cabin flew open. Dancer stood in the entranceway only a moment before, striding inward to lay his bundle gently on the wide berth. "Why bring her to me?" Falcon snapped, rising from his chair.

"She burns with fever." Dancer's voice was strained and tight. "She tries your temper to be sure, but death is too harsh a punishment."

64

Falcon's mouth hardened to a thin line as he struggled to remove her clothing. Her hair lay in a knotted mat on the pillow, and the bruise along her jawline was dark and ugly against her sunburned skin. "My God," he gasped as the last of her clothing parted under his knife. "When did that happen?"

Dancer looked down and found the source of Falcon's distress. He knew the Curse would not stay a child forever, but never had he imagined her to be the beauty that now lay before him. The gentle swell of her breast rose and fell with her labored breathing. Her waist was so tiny he knew he could span it with his hands. And the delicate curve of her hips . . . Dancer looked away, uneasy with the knot that was growing in the pit of his belly.

"I'll get the rainwater to bathe her hands," he muttered, needing to flee the confines of the cabin.

Falcon gazed down in wonder at the creature that was his daughter. "What am I to do?" he barked at her silent form. "I cannot tend a sick woman." Then with a gentleness that belied his harsh words, Falcon wrapped his daughter in his last clean shirt.

Fevered and witless, Samantha traveled through the passing days. Her captain was nowhere to be found. And tears came when she realized she had no proper name to call him. Her troubled mind raced backward in time in search of peace as her fever rose and her body raged in delirium.

Samantha watched her mother, clad in a vibrant red dress, glide across the room. How beautiful she was. Everyone had said so. And what a tragedy to be widowed at such a young age, they had whispered. Samantha pressed her lips together tightly. Never would she reveal their secret. Father wasn't dead, she smiled, but everyone must think him so. Another shadowy figure appeared beside her mother. Samantha shifted restlessly in the bunk. It was Falcon. She watched the young couple embrace, and anxiety filled her. The image of her father was somehow wrong. The body was too plump, the face too full. It was Uncle Edward.

Since that night so long ago when she had first crouched frozen in fear behind the chair in the library, she watched the hideous scene replay itself. She tried to scream a warning, for she knew now what was coming. Edward and her mother struggling on the floor. The grotesque sight of Edward's nakedness and the hideous things he had done. Her mother's fading cries as Edward choked the life from her body. Samantha thrashed wildly, smothered in a burning heat. Willing the dreams to go away, praying to awake and find her mama still alive. She should run . . . but as always her body wouldn't move. Call for help . . . but her voice refused to come. *Get Falcon,* her mind screamed. But what would she tell him? Violent tremors consumed her, making her teeth chatter. How could she admit that she had watched Edward rape and strangle her mother while she had done nothing to stop it? Edward rose from the crumpled body on the floor, then turned to face her. His eyes were red and wild, his features distorted. He was coming after her. Gasping for breath, Samantha turned to flee, but, as before, her feet refused to do her bidding. Ever so slowly, she crossed the library floor. Edward was closer now. She could feel the warmth of his breath on her neck. The strong odor of brandy filled the air making it impossible to breathe. The door was but an arm's length away when the heavy hand clamped down on her shoulder. The scream that had been building inside was suddenly set free and it shattered the misty darkness.

Struggling against the hands that now held her captive, Samantha screamed again and again. The hands were rougher now, causing pain, shaking her violently. She opened her eyes to see Edward's face staring down at her and her terror increased.

"Damn it, Curse. Stop screaming. You'll wake the dead with that noise." The harsh voice bellowed through the cabin as Samantha slumped back against the pillows and slipped once more into the misty darkness.

Dancer lit his pipe and joined Falcon on the quarterdeck. His eyes scanned the gathering clouds with a practiced air. "Tomorrow, mayhap late evening."

Falcon took a deep swill from his bottle before turning back to lean against the rail, his gaze on the growing whitecaps. "Aye, she'll probably hit late tomorrow, and by the looks of it she'll be a rough one." Both men stood silent, each thinking of how much they had grown to depend on the Curse and her ability to navigate their course. Her skill with figures had far surpassed anything that either had taught her, and her unnatural talent of sensing danger they had come to take for granted.

Falcon's voice broke the silence. "Tell Robbie to set a course for home."

"Aye, and will you leave her behind next time?" Dancer questioned.

Falcon sighed deeply. "Nay. The Curse has the 'sight.' Besides, if I left her on the island, she would spend all her time with that maniac, Kabol. The nightmares come too often as is without adding more voodoo witchcraft."

Dancer cleared his throat and knocked his pipe against the rail. "You wish not to hear this, but I think you should send her back to England. Edward could find her a wealthy suitor and marry her off."

"Nay." Falcon stretched. "I have need of her here."

"And the next time she jumps ship to look at ladies from London?"

"I'll probably kill her," Falcon said quietly, draining the last of his bottle.

Feet braced slightly apart and hands clasped behind her back, Samantha stood on the quarterdeck and stared at the horizon, hungry for the first sight of land after so long a time at sea. In the months since her illness, Falcon's foul moods had increased twice over. She had tolerated his fiery temper, but his icy indifference cut to the very heart of her, and life aboard the *Sea Hawk* had turned into a nightmare. No matter how simple her task, or how hard she strived, he still found fault, even when there was none to find. Despair became her constant companion, and her resolve weakened. Yet from somewhere deep within came the knowing that she would never give up. Somehow, she would find a way to make him love her.

The waves rocked hypnotically before her, and again Samantha set her mind to Kabol's riddle. Find the sun. She was the moon and she needed the sun. Wearily she rubbed her forehead, for no matter how she directed her thoughts, the sun remained high in the sky, and she saw little hope of charming it down. Her thumb twisted the golden snake that coiled around her finger. It was the only thing of late that offered comfort. Dreams of her English captain were a constant companion now, for she had only to touch the ring and his image came swiftly to mind. She raised her hand to shade her eyes from the glare of the sun and then she saw it.

Formed by a magic from days gone by, twin volcanic peaks rose majestically from the crystal waters of the Caribbean. At their base nestled a secluded island, ringed with jagged reefs and silent bays. The horns of the devil, the Spanish had whispered. And Cuernos del Diablo they had named her. Samantha smiled. It was easy to understand why so many avoided the island. It looked like the cap of the very devil himself. Yet to her, the whitewashed city of her home glistened like precious pearls in a lush bed of green. The island drums sounded their welcome as the *Sea Hawk* navigated the reefs, then floated gently in to bump against the dock. Waiting for no one, Samantha vaulted over the side and was swallowed by the growing crowd.

Wearing a clean shirt as a dressing gown, Samantha flopped back on the thick pillows of her bed and stretched lazily. Refreshed from her bath, she luxuriated in the comforts of her surroundings. Pressing her cheek to the pillow's soft covering she breathed the fresh scent of newly washed linens and sighed with satisfaction. It was two weeks since the *Sea Hawk* had docked, and each day on land had been a treasure. From the balcony a perfumed breeze stirred the airy curtains that lined the French doors, yet she could not rouse herself to venture forth. It would be cooler on the shaded balcony, but her eyes were growing heavy. *'Twas so nice to be back.* She smiled sleepily to herself. Even Marie's odd mood did not unduly detract from her pleasure. Her chambers had been aired and polished, and a bunch of gaily colored flowers rested in an earthen vase that stood beside the door. Had the added work of having them home distressed the maid? On the nightstand, crystal goblets and a decanter of deep-red wine cast rainbows of sunlight against the wall. She felt her eyes grow heavy as she watched their shimmering colors and, within moments, she slept.

Samantha woke to the sound of loud angry voices. The dusty shadows that filled the room and the rumbling of her stomach told her the hour was growing late. Hastily she jumped from the bed and bent to pull on clean breeches. They were old and the fit was much closer than she usually wore, but before she could exchange them, Dancer banged on the door and strode into the room.

"If you desire a meal tonight, best make haste. Falcon is in a foul mood."

Samantha wrapped her hair about her head and

pulled the knit cap into place. "When of late is his mood not foul?"

Dancer stood mesmerized as he watched her hair disappear. "Since when have you taken to keeping wine in your chambers?" he questioned abruptly.

Startled as much by the question as the way he voiced his concern, Samantha threw him a haughty glare. "I am eight and ten." She glanced toward the wine. "Some people have already realized that I am not a child."

"You're a brat," he said with affection. Picking up the decanter, he filled a glass and looked to her.

"Nay, let me find my boots and we shall be on our way."

Dancer leaned against a darkly carved chest and downed the wine while she scooted under the bed. His pulse quickened as he watched her wiggle out feet-first with the missing boot, and the evening breeze did little to cool the heat that fired through his veins. Suddenly the room grew too close. "I'll wait for you in the common room," he called, making a hasty retreat.

Samantha sat on the edge of her bed and pulled on the soft kid boots. Where was her captain tonight, she wondered, for this was a game she often played with her mind. Would he be . . .

"Curse!" Dancer's impatient bellow startled her from her dreams, and she quickly snuffed the candle. The click of her heels echoed on the wooden floor as she crossed the hall and started toward the common room. But as she reached the second floor, a piercing scream filled the air.

Samantha descended the stairs two at a time. The

71

scream had turned to a high-pitched wail, and she recognized Marie's voice as she drew closer. Her heart beat in triple time, then stopped all together as she rounded the corner. Dancer lay sprawled on the floor, his body twitching in convulsive spasms.

She could not breathe, or move, then she was kneeling beside him. Her eyes filled with tears, and just as quickly, she blinked them away. She rested a trembling hand on his neck. His heartbeat was rapid and his muscles twisted beneath her fingers. Bending closer, she smelled his breath, then pulled at his lips with her fingers to look at his tongue.

"'Tis poison." Recognizing the angry contortions of his muscles, she dashed to the table set with full trenchers of meat and bread, but nothing looked disturbed.

"Madre de Dios, Curse, do something," Marie cried. She had taken Samantha's place on the floor and held Dancer's head cradled in her lap.

Samantha took in the startled expressions of the crew and Marie's tear-streaked face. "McNeal, take him quickly to his chambers. Marie, bring me hot water and lots of it, and Robbie, find Falcon. Tell what has happened and beg him to make haste." No one questioned the quiet authority of her voice, and within a heartbeat everyone scrambled to do her bidding. While McNeal and the others struggled to carry Dancer's twitching body to his rooms, she raced up the two flights of stairs to her own chambers.

Her hands shook as she tried to light a candle. *Stop,* she commanded silently. *Dancer's life depends on clear thinking.* Kneeling before her sea chest, she raised the lid and tossed aside the neatly folded

72

clothing. Reaching the bottom, she carefully extracted two large woven baskets and set them on the floor before her. With poison, the wrong antidote could itself prove deadly. A tear escaped and trickled down her cheek. Which one? her mind cried as her fingers moved over the packets of herbs and powders. If only there was a clue. Pressing the heels of her hands against her burning eyes, she tried to block out all emotions and think. There had to be something. Dancer would have had to eat . . . or touch . . . or drink . . . Her eyes snapped open. There on the nightstand, sparkling in the candlelight, was a decanter of wine from which only one glass was missing.

She sprang to her feet. The bottle was heavy and cool to the touch. Her blood chilled as she poured a small draught and held it over the candlelight. Her hands trembled as she touched a finger to the liquid, then raised it to her nose.

"Damn it to hell," she cried, and the costly decanter crashed to the floor. It was poison, and from a plant she knew well. Time was now her enemy. Hastily wiping her hand against her breeches, Samantha grabbed one of the covered baskets and flew down the stairs.

Four days passed, and Dancer still struggled in agony, as if his belly contained a giant rodent that was trying to eat its way out. Falcon paced the length of the room and back again. He had searched the island from stem to stern and still he had no answers as to who would want Dancer dead. His frustration grew with each passing hour as he watched his quartermaster grow weaker and weaker. "Why aren't you doing anything?" he demanded abruptly. Dancer's skin had turned a sickly shade of gray and his face was gaunt and hollow. But looking to his daughter, Falcon saw not the deep shadows of sleeplessness or the exhausted look of her eyes.

"I have done all I can," her voice trembled. "I can do no more."

Falcon felt something akin to reason snap inside him. His best, nay only friend in the world, lay close to death and the Curse did nothing. His arm lashed out and his hand caught her full across the face, knocking her hard against the wall. "You will not leave this room until he is out of danger, do you hear me?" Falcon's face flushed red, and the veins on his temples grew visible. Picking up a vase of flowers she had placed near the bedside, he heaved it against the wall above her head. Glass and flowers splattered in all directions. "You will not step across that threshold," he snarled. "And if Dancer dies, mark the hour, for it will be the one in which you draw your last breath. Now clean this mess and be quick about it." Falcon stormed from the room oblivious to the sound of his daughter's quiet weeping.

Samantha tried to push her exhausted body from the floor but fell back when her legs refused to do her bidding. She had not slept in four days, and her eyes burned as tears ran down her cheeks. Leaning against the wall for support, she managed to rise, brushing bits of glass and broken flowers from her clothing.

Does he truly think I would do nothing if there was but something more for me to do, she thought wearily. She struggled to her knees, and with a damp rag, tried to gather the bits of broken glass. She wiped at her tears with the back of her hand and a sad smile touched her lips. For resting under the bed was Falcon's best sword. He had obviously placed it there thinking it would help cut Dancer's pain.

Trembling, she rose and set the rag aside. With a painful sigh, she eased her battered body onto the wooden chair beside the bed and raised a hand to her face. Her lip was cut, she could taste the blood. Gingerly she touched her eye and winced when the pressure brought fresh tears. A weary sigh escaped her. What good were her visions if she couldn't tell when a friend was about to drink poisoned wine? Her hands folded limply on her lap. Someone wanted to kill her, but who and why? Exhausted, she had not the energy even to be afraid. She tried searching her mind for answers, but none would come. Leaning forward, she again cooled Dancer's fevered brow with a damp cloth, but she knew in her heart that time alone would not dictate his recovery. "Come back to me soon, old friend," she whispered, "I don't know how much more of this madness I can stand."

Dancer woke the next morning like a cranky child, demanded food, then promptly fell asleep before she could fetch it. Giddy with relief and exhaustion, the sound of his strong, even breathing was music to her ears. "Marie," she called. "The worst is over! He will live!"

Marie rushed into the room and nearly knocked Samantha over in her jubilance. "'Tis a miracle," she whispered. Her hungry eyes drank in every detail of Dancer's haggard appearance. But when she turned back to Samantha, her face was cold and hard. "I will sit with him now. Why don't you leave?"

Samantha rubbed the grit from her eyes with the heel of her hand and missed Marie's hostile glare. "If he should waken, there is still broth." She pointed to a warming pan that sat on the chest.

Marie nodded. "You go now." Firmly she ushered Samantha from the room. "I shall stay with him."

Samantha slowly made her way to the third floor of the inn. Dancer would recover. Standing at the opened doors of her balcony, she breathed deeply. The fresh morning breeze stirred the fragrant hibiscus and frangipani that grew beneath her window. She watched as the marketplace came slowly to life. Village women in bright, gaudy dresses balanced huge bundles on their heads as they scurried to claim the choicest of spots. Wealthier merchants pushed open the thatched fronts of their huts. It would not be long before the square would fill with noise and confusion as many sought to buy and sell. Turning, she stumbled toward her bed. Her eyes refused to stay open. Flopping backward across the high mattress, she was asleep before her head even reached the pillow.

It was two hours past noon when she awoke, and although greatly refreshed from the nap, dark shadows still ringed her eyes. Hastily she splashed cool water on her face and donned fresh clothing.

Falcon stood near the foot of Dancer's bed as she entered the room.

"Good afternoon," she said quietly as she moved

to touch Dancer's brow. It was blessedly cool. He was still pale, but the pasty look of death no longer marred his features.

"Are you sure all is well?" Falcon demanded.

"Aye, his fever is gone, and when he woke, he asked for food."

"'Tis about time." Falcon began to pace. "Your lack of skill in this has already cost me precious days. The *Sea Hawk* will sail on the morning tide."

Samantha turned to her father with alarm. "I said he will be well, Falcon, and he will, but not to sail on the tide. 'Twill be two weeks or more before he shall be strong enough to leave the island."

"Cease, you addlebrained twit," Falcon snapped. "Do you think me completely without reason? A fool could see that the man can't even walk, let alone sail. But I am leaving on the *Sea Hawk* tomorrow. You shall stay here and see to his needs." He gestured toward Dancer's prone figure. "Robbie will remain with you until Dancer is fit."

"Falcon, please . . ." She touched his sleeve. "Do not decide in haste. Wait but a few days more. Dancer will probably be able to protest on his own behalf by evening tomorrow. And how shall you sail without a quartermaster?"

Falcon shook off her hand as if the merest touch repulsed him. "Leave off, Curse," he snarled. "I can abide this place no longer." His decision made, Falcon left the chambers.

A cold emptiness settled over her as Samantha eased herself onto the chair beside Dancer's bed. He had flinched from her touch, and suddenly she knew it was not the island that he could no longer abide, but the sight of her. His revulsion was so great that he would even leave Dancer behind to be done with her.

Surely there is something I can do, she thought frantically. *He cannot sail alone.* An icy chill raced down her spine and left her trembling. Danger and death lurked nearby. She could feel their cold, ominous presence. The premonition vanished as quickly as it had come, leaving total confusion in its wake. Who was in danger? Was there to be another attempt on her life? The words rose in her throat to call back her father, but died before she voiced them. Could she face Falcon if he learned that she had been the intended victim, or would he blame Dancer's near death on her as she already blamed herself. She blinked rapidly, trying to bring an image to mind, but none came. From the open window, the sweet songs of the island birds floated forth in a sea of afternoon sunlight. Dancer moaned and shifted on his bed. Thoughts of death and darkness fled as she turned all her attention back to the living.

Chapter V

Dancer's recovery was rapid. Still, he was up and testing his strength long before Samantha thought he should be. But short of tying him to the bedframe, she had no choice but to let him have his way. When the first light of day streaked into the eastern sky, Dancer would rise, seeking the privacy of the courtyard behind the inn. There, using his lightest sword, he would execute a deft sidestep and thrust. Over and over he practiced the intricate move before progressing on to another that was even more complex. Then, switching to a heavier blade, he repeated the routine from the beginning.

Samantha sat on the veranda and watched in fascination as the muscles of his back and arms flexed under the strain. The sun rose higher in the sky, bringing forth the stifling heat of the day, coating his skin with a film of sweat, and still he practiced. The sword and the man became one, and the grace and speed with which he moved gave little doubt as to how he had come by his name.

Once satisfied that his own skill had returned, Dancer turned his attention to her. From the first cool hours of the morning until the sun was high at noon, he made her thrust and lunge, lunge and thrust, until she could execute a thrust and riposte with lightning speed. Her reach, only half of his, would always place her at a disadvantage, but Dancer knew that agility and speed could be her allies. And until he could place a name upon the guilty, he would see her well protected. His determination became a fierce taskmaster.

Ignoring her aching muscles and dripping sweat, Samantha granted Dancer this time and gloried in how proud Falcon would be when he witnessed her new skill. She studied Dancer's moves over and over again until, to his astonishment, she nearly bested him with new combinations of her own. And so the hours passed into days, the days to weeks, and the weeks to months.

It was the last month of the year, and the hour was just past midnight when her piercing cry filled the air. Dancer flew up the stairs to her rooms, sword drawn ready for action. Without knocking, he kicked in the door and froze. The room was filled with candles, two score or more. Eerie shadows flickered against the walls. Samantha, her head in her lap, lay sobbing on the floor. Before her lay the bones. A quick search of the room found no one about, and he turned back to her trembling figure.

"What happened?" he questioned, not sure if he should touch her. "What troubles you? Are you ill?"

Her tears glistened in the candlelight as she stared at him in horror.

"He's dead." Her voice was a threadlike whisper.

Despite the heat of the night, Dancer felt a cold apprehension settle over him. "Who's dead?" he commanded, giving her shoulders a shake. "What in the devil are you talking about?"

She said nothing, but extended a shaking hand, her finger pointing to the bones. "Don't you see?" she cried with frustration. "'Tis my fault he sailed without us and now he is dead." Her violent sobs were halted as Dancer's palm connected flatly against her cheek. Her head snapped back, and although tears ran freely, sanity crept back into her eyes.

Dancer breathed a sigh of relief and eased his crushing grip. "Are you telling me that you can look at those bones and see that Falcon is dead?" Slowly she nodded and he felt her trembling begin anew. "Nay, you prattle with madness," he snapped, letting her go and rising to his feet to pace.

Samantha studied her hands clasped tightly in her lap. "You don't believe me." Her voice faltered as tears choked her words.

Dancer turned and watched her trembling figure still huddled on the floor. *'Twas madness,* he thought. He had allowed her too many hours with Kabol, or maybe she'd contracted swamp fever. He knew the stories of insect bites that could send a man out of his mind.

"I think you are mistaken," he started haltingly, not wanting to upset her more.

Samantha shook her head; long tendrils of sun-streaked hair sparkled in the candlelight. "A trap was set." Her voice was hollow and her eyes fixed on the polished bones before her. "A deliberate trap, and Falcon sailed right into it." A shudder wracked her slender frame as she continued. "He was trying to get free and they shot him. His blood flows all about the deck. He no longer breathes." With her final statement, she collapsed against her knees and wept.

Dancer sat on the edge of her bed and struggled with his thoughts. What should he do? What could he do?

It was less than a month later that Dancer found himself slowly climbing the path that led inward to the lookout's tower. The small stones beneath his boots bounced down the path behind him as he navigated the steep trail. He dreaded telling her the news. The memory of her agony that night so many weeks ago still burned bright. Had she truly known, he wondered, or was it the result of the monstrous guilt that Falcon had heaped upon her head?

He reached the point and saw her. Sitting high on a large boulder, she stared at the turquoise water that ringed the island. *You have not planted your seed wisely, old friend,* he murmured to himself. *You have left your only child in the midst of hell. How will she ever survive it?*

Dancer eased down beside her. Clad in snug black breeches and a floppy shirt, she hugged her knees against her chest as if warding off a sudden chill. "You were right," he said in a weary tone. "The Good Lady just brought the news." She said nothing but continued looking straight ahead. "The English are taking great pains to spread the tale. The Crown now has a dim view of pirating and they mean to see it ended," he continued.

"I want the name." Her voice was coldly hollow. "Do you know it, the one who was responsible for setting the trap?"

Dancer shifted uneasily. She shed no tears, but an icy hardness settled over her features, and the quiet command of her voice left him shaken.

"A Captain Cortland is credited with masterminding the plan," he said slowly. He watched in awe as a strange light glittered in her eyes.

"Will you sail with me?" she questioned. Silently he nodded his agreement. "Then Captain Cortland is about to feel the sting of the Falcon's Curse."

London, England, 1716

Colorful lanterns swayed gently in the midnight breeze, casting patchwork patterns of soft light about the massive garden. The fragrance of roses and honeysuckle blended with the lyrical notes of a single harpsichord. Heat lightning flickered silently, illuminating a solitary figure on the terrace.

Alex Cortland flexed his shoulder muscles and breathed deeply of the night air, its freshness a welcome relief from the overperfumed bodies packed tightly together in the crowded salon. Resting his hip against the stone balustrade, he listened as violins joined with the harpsichord and the music took on a distinctly Spanish flavor. Scarlatti was in fine form, he thought as the sonata progressed. On the morrow, news of Domenico's visit to London and praise for his performance would fly about the city, and Julia would bask in the glory of having hosted the handsome Italian's first recital of the season.

Alex's gaze wandered back to the crowded salon. Tonight, even the virtuosity of the master himself could not dissipate his dark mood. It was becoming more and more evident that Julia fancied seeing herself as the next Duchess of Coverick. Alex's brows drew together with the troubled thought. He had no wish to see her hurt, but then, neither was he willing to become a reluctant husband to a child who couldn't distinguish the difference between grand passion and simple social politeness. Tonight, even though he had arrived extremely late, she still tried to cast him into the role of her partner and host of the evening. Alex turned back toward the gardens that ringed the terrace and watched the fireflies dance among the shadows. If his desire to hear Scarlatti perform again had not been so strong, he would have rejected the invitation completely.

"Alex, you out here?"

Alex turned to watch his younger brother stride across the terrace. Joining him near the far corner, James leaned against the stone wall and relit his cheroot. Almost as tall, but of a much slighter build, there was no doubt as to the relationship between the two. But while James's features were soft and classical, Alex had a rakishness that lined his face with strength and determination.

"I know not whether to offer my congratulations or condolences." James's voice carried more than a hint of laughter as he watched the smoke from his cheroot spiral into the velvet night.

"You speak in riddles, little brother."

"Julia will be angry that you left so abruptly," he teased, looking back toward the crowded room.

"Domenico will understand," Alex replied pointedly.

"It is of no great importance," James continued. "What I want to know is why I had to hear of your engagement from the gossips and not from you."

"What?"

James struggled to contain his amusement at the outraged expression on his brother's face. "Surely you knew that Julia has been hinting to everyone who would listen that you intend to marry."

"The devil she has," Alex hissed through clenched teeth. "And what, pray tell, put that foolish notion into her empty head? I have done nothing to encourage such a false hope."

James leaned closer. "I have it on the best authority," he whispered in a conspiratorial tone, "that the reason for your tardiness this evening was a late visit to your jeweler's to pick up a ring."

Alex relaxed slightly, but James could still see the tension that flowed through his brother, and for a brief moment he actually felt sorry for Julia.

"Part of your story is true, Jamie," Alex replied, deciding to give his brother a taste of his own medicine. "I did go to Fenwick's this evening, and I did retrieve a ring that I had ordered." Now it was Alex's turn to laugh at his brother's startled expression. "But this is the ring I received." Alex held out his hand to show a golden snake coiled about his smallest finger.

"Ah, so you found it again." Relief filled James's voice as he admired the family ring. "I thought the piece had been lost."

"'Tis not the original," Alex said sharply, remembering all too clearly the sea nymph that had shared his bed and stolen his ring. He twisted the new ring against his finger. "Fenwick has made it too small, but for now I am content to wear the copy."

Relieved to find that his brother was not making a disastrous marriage after all, Jamie's teasing manner resumed. "And what are you going to tell Julia?" he chuckled.

"The truth. I have given no reason for her to come to such conclusions, and although I do not wish to cause her distress, the problem is of her own making. Besides, since I shall sail on the morrow, they," he gestured toward the salon, "may speculate any way they wish."

"Sail? In heaven's name why?" James stared at his brother's face intently, more startled by this revelation than by the news of the fictitious engagement. "When did you decide this? Have you spoken to Carolyn?"

"The Merrywood docked this morning," Alex replied tightly.

"And the cargo?"

"Picked clean like the others."

"Damn it!" Jamie tossed down his cheroot and ground it against the flagstone with the heel of his boot. "How is this possible, Alex? We send decoy ships and they sail straight through. Yet the minute we put out a cargo of value, it's picked over by vultures."

"Nay, not vultures, Jamie," Alex said angrily. "It was the flag of the Falcon again." Even in the darkness, Alex watched Jamie's face grow pale.

"Do you think the curse is coming true?" His voice was the merest whisper.

Alex rested his hand against his brother's shoulder. "Jamie, we have been through this before."

"But . . ."

"Nay . . ." Alex interrupted, tightening his grip. "I was there. Falcon died trying to escape, but not by my hand. I know that in his delirium he said his curse would never leave me, but men say many things when they are face-to-face with death, and I will not let the irate words of a madman dictate my actions nor will I give them more credit than they are due."

"But the ships, the cargo . . . In the past two years since the Falcon's death, we have lost more than any three merchants combined! Others sail through and our ships are hit."

"True." Alex spoke harshly. "But 'tis a man and not a ghost that plagues us, Jamie. Our opponent is very clever. Somehow he knows our course of action, no matter how secret the plans." Alex looked about the terrace, assuring their privacy. "Someone is selling information to the rogue sailing under Falcon's flag, and I mean to find out who. For this time they have traded more than they realize."

Jamie shook his head. "Now it is you who speak in riddles."

Alex took a slow breath. "The captain of *The Merrywood* carried information from France, and there are many who would pay a handsome price for the knowledge."

87

Jamie whistled softly through his teeth. "'Tis the very stuff that wars are made of. Do you have a plan?" Alex explained in hushed tones, and Jamie's face again reflected his horror. "My God, Alex, why not just take a knife and slit your throat right here and save yourself the trouble of the voyage."

"Does that mean you don't think my idea has merit?"

Jamie shuddered. He had been only six years old when their parents had died, and it was Alex who had dried his tears and offered comfort. When Alex had left them, Carolyn had cried for days. But somehow he had never felt abandoned. And despite the heartless words of others, an inner faith reassured him that Alex would not desert them. Now in his twenty-fifth year, Jamie understood and appreciated Alex's devotions all the more. "And what of the Falcon?" he challenged in fear. "Do you think he will let you sail to his island without a struggle?"

Alex's features became hard, and a cold tone edged his voice. "Falcon is dead, Jamie. True, the new captain that sails under his flag is more cunning than the first, but I will make you a promise. Before this is out, he, too, shall fall at my feet as did the one before him." He gave his brother a determined look. "I sail on the morrow."

locked with her as he carried her fingers to his lips.
The emerald eyes of the snake on his finger winked in

Chapter VI

Dancer knocked, then entered without waiting for a reply. The sheer curtains on the balcony doors billowed inward, and he crossed the room on silent feet. There in the shade of the giant cypress tree, she was seated on one chair, while her feet lay propped on another. Eyes closed, her head rested back against the wicker rim and her newly washed hair spilled downward nearly touching the ground as it dried in the afternoon breeze. Her light dressing gown did little to disguise her figure as it clung sensuously to her body.

"What news have you, Dancer?" Her voice was a soft whisper, her eyes remained closed.

He settled himself in a chair, resting his elbows against his knees. There was no way to keep the knowledge from her, he reasoned. In fact, most times she knew things before they even happened. He rubbed his hand against his jaw. "An English ship docked this morning. The captain is paying good money for information about you."

"Me?" Her eyes opened, but it was the only indication that she was even slightly interested in their conversation.

"Curse, 'tis Cortland himself." Dancer watched as she transformed before his eyes. Gone was the soft, vulnerable figure from moments before, and in her place sat a pirate queen, every nerve in her body alert. Her eyes sparkled with a dangerous light that ofttimes made even him nervous.

"Is the man mad?" She jerked from her chair. "All this time I thought I had a worthy opponent. Now I find I have been trifling with a fool, for fool he is to have sailed here." Angrily she stalked the length of the balcony and back again. Cortland here on the island. Her mind replayed the words again and again. Cortland, the man who had set the trap for Falcon, stealing her last chance to win her father's love. Cortland, the man bearing the name she had come to hate, was here on her island. Anxious tremors ran down her spine and settled as a knot in her stomach.

"Does he not realize that with but one word from me, he would not live to see the sunrise?" She stopped pacing and looked to the sea, her knuckles white as she gripped the railing. Her eyes flashed in hatred as she stared at the swaying masts of the English ship. Cortland's ship.

"Do you wish him dead?"

Despite the sweltering heat of the day, a chill settled over her. "I . . . know not." She hesitated. Her pacing began anew. Was not an eye for an eye the best revenge? She pictured a man stretched on the racks in Jake's dungeon. Strangely, the thoughts brought no

90

comfort, and as quickly as they came, she dismissed them. Killing would not bring Falcon back. Besides, with Cortland playing the fool, the task would be too easy. "What can he hope to gain by coming here?" Her arms gestured wildly. But even as she spoke, she knew the answer. It bore the royal seal and was tucked safely away.

"The color of his coin will tempt many, Curse," Dancer warned.

"Bah!" She flung herself back into her chair. "They will judge the weight of his purse and kill him for it as he sleeps. How could anyone be so dim-witted?"

"I have seen the man, Curse, and he may be many things, but dim-witted is not one of them. I know not the reason for his actions, but the man is no fool."

The afternoon breeze stirred as the trade winds shifted and the branches of the cypress swayed under the gentle caress. Samantha absently pushed several strands of hair from her face and a mischievous grin began to bloom.

"Dancer," she said softly, shifting to sit on the edge of her chair. "I think we should teach Captain Cortland a lesson. After all 'tis not good manners to arrive where one is not invited."

Dancer watched her with apprehension. That tone in her voice and the look in her eye meant trouble. "Curse, this is not a man for you to play with like the others. He will not be so easily put off. And if he finds out who you really are . . ."

She waved aside his protest with a flick of her hand. "Where is he staying?"

Dancer sighed. He was losing and he knew it.

"Here at the inn. His room is directly below yours."

"Why, Dancer . . ." she drawled, her eyes sparkling with anticipation. "How thoughtful of you to make things so easy for me."

"Nay, Curse, stay away from him. This man means trouble. 'Twas not by choice I placed him there, but at least here I can keep a close eye on you both."

She slumped in the chair, her bottom lip in a pout. "Don't be angry with me," she pleaded softly. "I only seek a little fun for my dull life."

Dancer wasn't taken in for a minute by her actions. "A little fun, you say? Curse, the last English officer you said that about barely escaped with his life and you nearly burned the inn to the ground in the process."

She shrugged. "The wind shifted."

"Curse . . ." Dancer sighed with exasperation. "You can't set a man's bed aflame just because he is unfaithful to his wife. Especially if the man and his mistress are still in it!"

Samantha grinned impishly. "Well, you have to admit he was quite a sight as he ran from the inn, naked as a plucked chicken ready for the stewpot." She smiled absently as the beginnings of a plan began to take form. Captain Cortland would rue the day he sought to best the Falcon's Curse, she mused. Her body relaxed as she again settled herself in her chair. "I feel a need to be back on the sea. What say we sail in two days?" Her mind raced forward. In two days, she could accomplish much. "Will that plan set you at ease?"

"The sooner the better," Dancer grumbled. He watched as she leaned back in her chair and closed her eyes. A growing sense of unrest settled over him. She was planning something, he could feel it. Her hatred of Cortland ran too deep to be so easily abated. The breeze grew stronger, wiping her pale, sun-streaked hair into a tangled mane of curls, but she seemed not to notice. With a weary shrug, Dancer rose. Until he had her safely away, she would bear close watching.

Samantha woke as large drops of rain began to fall. Groaning, she pried her stiff body from the chair and tried to straighten. *I must have slept for hours,* she thought, noting growing shadows. Her neck and back ached, and gooseflesh rose on her arms as the wind howled, sending a spray of rain onto the balcony. Retreating as quickly as her stiff muscles would allow, she entered her chambers and firmly closed the tall French doors behind her. First Cortland, now a storm, she grumbled, making her way across the darkened room to light the tapers that lined the desk. Her hands ran briskly up and down her arms against the chill as she slipped out of her light robe and hastily donned a dressing gown of black velvet. The neckline plunged to a deep V, hinting at the shadowy curve of her breast, but the sleeves were long and the warm fabric gave instant comfort to her chilled flesh.

Lightning flashed, illuminating the room with an eerie brightness, and from the corner of her eye she saw a movement behind her. Her hand flew to her throat as she spun about in fright. Realizing it was her own reflection did little for her jumping nerves.

Damn, but she hated storms. Lightning flashed again, and her body grew rigid as the thunder cracked loudly overhead. She peered closer into the looking glass and groaned with dismay. Her hair resembled the mane of a lion as it hung past her waist in a tangled mat of knotted curls. No wonder she had given herself such a fright. For a moment she contemplated stuffing her hair under her cap, but the image that came to mind was too ludicrous. She thought of changing to her breeches and shirt, but the gown was too warm and comfortable. Resigning herself to the chore, Samantha settled on the corner of her sea chest and began the laborious task of combing her hair.

She was nearly finished when the door to her chambers flew open and Marie rushed in. From below, she could hear the noise of loud, angry voices, and then a single shot rang out.

"There is trouble just outside," the maid gasped. "Dancer is on the ship; you had better come."

Oil lamps had been trimmed and hung about, and in their shadowy light Samantha entered the common room to find mass confusion. A single man lay facedown draped over a chair. A long knife protruded from his shoulder. He was drenched from the rain, and the water mixed with his blood as it dripped in growing puddles on the floor. A terrified manservant stood beside him armed with a sword and horse pistol.

"Robbie, what goes on here?" A hush fell over the room, and all stepped aside as Samantha moved toward the injured man. "A guest in my house so sorely abused? There must be a good explanation or

94

my temper will be greatly aroused." Her soft voice was the barest whisper, yet all strained to hear her words. Her eyes scanned the crowd, stopping when she reached a burly seaman in a red-striped jersey. A deep scar ran the length of his cheek and his cocky smile made her bristle. His was a new face on the island and she wondered on which ship he sailed.

"'Tis my fault, mistress." Charlotte, one of the younger maids stepped forward clutching her torn chemise and wiping her tears. "I didn't want to go with him." Her eyes darted to the red-striped shirt, then back to the floor. "But he carried me off anyway." Charlotte's eyes filled anew and her shoulders shook. "When I tried to get away, he," her shaky finger pointed toward the wounded man, "came to help me. He was walking me back to the inn when that one comes back with his mates. But at five to one they was too much for him. That one in the red knifed him while he struggled with the others."

Samantha's blood boiled with rage. Rape was one folly she could not abide, and it took much effort not to give in to the trembling that threatened to overtake her. Her cool gaze wandered slowly about the group until it rested again on the man Charlotte had accused.

Slowly she glided to the center of the room. "You have abused my hospitality." Her voice was hard as she stared at the stranger. "You will leave my island immediately."

With eyes locked, the man slowly shrugged forward, then gave a mocking bow. "Forgive me, lovely lady. I would never have trifled with a mere serving wench had I but known that the likes of you were about." He gave a lecherous wink toward his mates and hooked his thumbs in the wide belt that circled his thick waist. "As for leaving, I think I fancy staying awhile." The lust on his face was open and degrading, and a gasp of horror echoed in the room.

Samantha suppressed the urge to take her nails across his leering smile. Boldly she gazed him up and down appraising his worth, then threw back her head and gave a low, throaty chuckle as if she found him lacking. She turned to go but took less than half a step before she spun around again to face her prey. Her long curls flew in all directions as she turned, giving an ominous effect to her small frame.

"You, sir, are a fool." Her voice was quiet and cold as ice. "You dare to do battle with the Curse of Falcon? Do you not know that I am a witch?" Firelight danced from the emerald eyes of her snake ring as she flexed her fingers in catlike motions before her. "Aye, sir," she hissed, "a witch. You have insulted me in my own house, and now your days are sorely numbered."

The smile faded from the seaman's face as he watched her stalk around him, her fingers constantly reaching, then pulling back only to reach again. Nervously, he shifted, suddenly afraid to have his back to her.

"Even now you feel your chest growing tighter." As she spoke, her soft words forced him to meet her stare and her eyes hinted of madness. "You find your breath difficult to draw."

The burly man seemed to shrink into himself. He clutched his chest first in disbelief then in pain. Slumping, he grabbed a chair for support.

"Make her stop." His high-pitched cry spoke of fear and desperation. "Dear God, make her stop." But within the hushed circle, none moved to come to his aid.

"I believe I asked you to leave my island." Her voice was quietly cold and her eyes never left his twitching figure. "Leave me and your pain will subside. But if you ever dare to cross me or threaten what is mine again, you'll wish your life had ended on this night." The threat echoed throughout the silent room.

The sailor's mouth gaped open in a soundless cry and spit dribbled from his lips as he stumbled toward the door. Samantha turned her attention to his mates who stood wide-eyed at what they had just witnessed. And as her calm gaze moved over them, anxious grunts and shoves followed as they hastened to make their exit.

"Charlotte, fetch hot water. Marie, clear that table. We'll see to his needs here." Samantha moved toward the wounded man, but the growing silence made her pause. Turning, she found both Marie and Charlotte staring at her, eyes wide, as if she had grown another head. Robbie, the only member of her crew who had remained behind, also stood motionless.

"Enough." She clapped her hands smartly. "We've a wounded man here, and much time has already been wasted. Now make haste, less you make me angry, too."

With her threat, Charlotte and Marie jumped to do her bidding. Robbie took a deep breath, and rubbing his hand nervously against the side of his neck, ventured closer. Satisfied, Samantha turned her

97

attention back to her patient. Kneeling beside him, she grimaced, noting how dangerously close to his heart the knife was placed. Gently she raised his head to better view his face.

Her hands began to tremble as the shock of discovery hit her full force. *'Twas her captain!* Her mind raced in a thousand directions as a soft gasp of astonishment escaped her lips. For five years she had re-created this face in her dreams, remembering a night of wonderment that she had found in his arms. Hesitantly, her fingers touched the black curls at his forehead, fearful that as with her dreams, she would blink and find him gone. The wiry feel of his mustache, the thick dark brows, how could this be? For all the times she had wished for his presence, dreamed him her defender in her battles with Falcon, yearned for the safety of his arms or the warmth of his lips, she had never thought the fates would allow it to be. Her knuckles traced down his cheek. He was English, could he have sailed on Cortland's ship? His low moan broke her thoughts and her heart hammered wildly as the irony of the situation returned to taunt her. Had she found him only to watch him die?

Calm resolve pushed aside any uncertainty, and she rose with determination. "You . . ." She glanced toward the servant. "Help Robbie take your master up to my chambers. Move gently less you alter the knife's position."

Charlotte had returned with a steaming kettle, and she looked at her mistress with uncertainty. "Dancer won't be liking you taking the mate here to . . ." Her eyes glanced upward as if she couldn't voice the words.

98

"The man has been stabbed, Charlotte," Samantha said quietly. In her mind she was already gathering the herbs and potions she would need. "I can hardly be faulted for seeing to his wounds. After all, we owe him a debt for having saved you from that slimy toad."

The group moved slowly to Samantha's private chambers. Robbie glanced about with apprehension as if he expected to find remnants of skulls or dark, creepy creatures. Instead, he found a set of elegant but simply furnished rooms where Marie reluctantly turned down the spread on her mistress's bed.

Mindful that the Curse watched their every move, the men lowered their burden gently upon the soft feather ticks. Taking care not to disturb the knife that still rested in his shoulder, they began to disrobe him.

Confident they could accomplish this task, Samantha turned toward her sea chest, and kneeling before it, began to rummage inside. She shifted several wicker containers until she found the one she sought. But before she could rise, a large hand clamped firmly about her shoulder.

"I would speak with you." The voice was cold and lashing.

"You startled me," she gasped. She closed the trunk and stood with the basket clasped tightly in her hands. "Let me tend to his wound." Her eyes glanced toward the bed, her soul angry for another look at the face from her dreams. "I will join you presently."

Dancer's hand took a firm hold on her upper arm, and he none too gently ushered her from the room. "I would speak with you now." His grip tightened painfully as she accompanied him into the hallway.

Once there, he dropped her arm and stared at her, his face contorted with rage.

"What is the meaning of this?" she demanded, angry with his interference and the careless way he handled her. Her arm throbbed, and she knew her flesh would carry a deep bruise from the pressure of his fingers.

Dancer's look was incredulous. "You bring him here, and you dare to ask me what is the meaning? Whatever possessed you to do this?"

"I realize things might seem amiss." She struggled for words. Her joy was too new to share, even with Dancer. How could she ever explain the stolen hours that she and the captain had shared. Her fingers twisted the snake ring, his ring, and her courage returned. She looked up at Dancer, and the force of his anger hit her anew. "Be patient with me," she pleaded, resting her palm against his forearm. "I will explain in time."

"Be patient!" Dancer's voice dropped, his brown eyes darkened like angry thunder clouds. "How can you ask that of me?" His hand threaded impatiently through his hair. "I know not what you play at." Intense fury coupled each word. "But, dammit, Curse, your bed is no place for Alex Cortland!"

Chapter VII

Samantha drew her knees up against her chest and wrapped her arms about them. The rain had ceased, leaving only a light mist to taunt the flames of Kabol's small fire. Oblivious to the dampness that seeped into her clothing, she rocked back and forth in silence. Tears burned at the back of her eyes and her throat felt thick with emotion.

"Why did it have to be him?" Her voice was an anguished whisper. "Of all the bodies that walk this earth, why did his face have to belong to Alex Cortland?"

Kabol pulled the blanket higher about his frail shoulders. He had known this day would come. She was being forged for greatness, and if she didn't shatter, each pass through the fire would leave her stronger. But tonight, even as he watched her pain and his heart ached to share secrets that would ease her torment, his voice remained silent.

Samantha shivered. Her hand twisted the golden snake that wound about her finger. Once, just to

101

touch it brought peace and contentment. Now it painfully coiled about her heart. Its chilling force seeped into the very marrow of her bones and she doubted she would ever feel warmth again. *Toss his ring and your foolish dreams into the fire and be done with it,* her mind argued. But her hand stayed tightly clenched. Frustration turned to anger and she glared at Kabol.

"Just what good is my sight?" she demanded. "I have known Cortland's face for years. Why did it not come to me when Falcon died?"

"Mayhap your heart did not wish to acknowledge what the mind already knew."

"Bah!" Her arms gestured wildly. "Tell me now how I go about avenging my father's death. Do I plunge a knife into the heart of the man who saved me from a watery grave? Do I torture the soul who prevented Charlotte from being raped?"

"Sit." Kabol gestured beside him.

Wearily, Samantha dropped to the ground. Her fists still clenched tightly as they rubbed absently against the coarse fabric of her breeches. The fog grew thicker, crowding closer to the small fire. Daylight would soon be upon them. She watched as Kabol reached into the folds of his shroud to withdraw a worn leather pouch. His fingers danced over the flames and the fire suddenly grew brighter. Satisfied, he tipped the bag, spilling forth a diamond twice the size of a walnut.

"'Tis called the Midnight Star," he said quietly. "It has great power."

Samantha gazed in awe at the fortune he held in the palm of his hand. The legend of the stone was one she knew well. A sultan had first used the diamond to secure the freedom of his only son; a king had bartered it for the love of his bride; and once an entire army had been enticed by the fortune it would bring. The multifaceted stone caught the light and magnified its brightness until it seemed Kabol held a living flame. Her eyes searched the old man's face for answers. Never had she imagined such a treasure on her island. His look hushed her questions.

"The stone also carries a warning." His voice was the barest whisper. "To possess it brings great wealth and power, but to desire it causes only destruction." He uncurled her fingers and placed the diamond into her palm. "'Tis a gift, 'tis yours, you must take it."

Samantha stared down at the gem in disbelief. Its history had caused both passion and bloodshed, and she had no use for either. And unlike her father, she possessed no desire for wealth. "I cannot accept such a fine gift."

Kabol rested his weathered palm against the side of her cheek. "You must. I know not how, but this stone will save your life."

Samantha smiled, pleased that she could so easily see through his words. The diamond was priceless to be sure, but it carried no magic. And when she thought of all on the island who could benefit from its fortune, her mind was set.

"Your path is not to be easy, Curse." He took her hand in his. "And many of your trials will be caused by your own willfulness. But you must remember always that you are the moon. When she tries to stand alone, the moon can shed no light. Accept the warmth of the sun and your life will shine brightly."

She pretended to slip the stone back into the battered pouch. "I must leave you now," she said slowly, looking about for a likely place to set the gem. "I promised Dancer we would be off by sunrise." As she spoke, her hand dropped innocently to her side and, making a grand show of tucking the pouch safely into the folds at the front of her shirt, her other hand carefully placed the stone into a small cooking bowl that sat beside her. He would be sure to find it on the morrow, but by then she would be gone. "'Twill not be a long voyage," she continued, forcing a cheerful tone. "But my crew is restless, and I need to find them new sport." Rising, she placed a fleeting kiss on Kabol's wrinkled forehead. "Think of me till we meet again." Then she ducked quickly into the thick, predawn mist.

Kabol watched her retreating form until she was completely consumed by the shadows. His heart ached with her torment, yet deep within his soul he knew the worst trials were still to come.

"Give her strength," he whispered to the coming dawn. "Open her eyes so that she may recognize the sun as it shines before her." With a weary sigh, he reached into the clay cooking bowl and retrieved the diamond. "And please," he beseeched the shadows, "give me patience." Leaning heavily on his staff, he climbed slowly to his feet, his mind already searching for a solution to the problem she had placed before him.

Samantha entered her chambers on silent feet. The dawn was fast approaching and she had much to do before her ship sailed. Already Dancer would be at the docks, barking orders and seeing to their provisions. Quietly she approached the bed where Alex Cortland still slept.

Dark hair clung damply to his forehead, and even in sleep his features were striking. Her hand lifted to touch his brow, but just as quickly she pulled it back. Had she finally gotten her wish to have Falcon's killer destroyed? Cortland was completely at her mercy. But instead of revenge, her thoughts were filled with the memories of a night spent in the narrow confines of a ship's berth. A night when strong arms had held her close to offer comfort and still her fears.

Carefully she pulled the sheet higher about him. The white cloth that bound his shoulder was a striking contrast to the bronzed skin that covered his chest. Was it possible that he was even more handsome than she remembered? Knowing she ached for something that could never be, her frustration grew. Eyes, she thought as she gazed down at him. What she remembered most was the shocking green color of his eyes. Deep emerald eyes that could see into a soul and steal a heart. Cortland's eyes that now wanted revenge and probably wished to see her hang.

The hands of the clock refused to slow, and reluctantly she turned to more pressing matters. Her clothing was already on board; she now needed to choose the herbs and powders she wished to take along. With a practiced hand, she selected from the baskets that were scattered on the floor.

A deep moan filled the room, and Samantha was instantly on her feet beside the bed. This time her hand didn't hesitate as she touched his brow. It was hot, but not overly so. Taking a damp rag, she bathed his face with cool water.

"You, sir, are a fool," she chided gently. "You dare to come to my island with little thought to the consequences. No wonder it was so easy to steal your ships. You are as dim-witted as the rest. How you ever lured Falcon into your snare is beyond me."

"Carolyn, good Lord, woman, be careful." Samantha jumped at the sound of his words. His eyes remained closed, but his voice was clear. "Don't cry, love. All will soon be well."

"Carolyn, Carolyn you call." Angrily she tossed the cloth back into the dish, heedless of the water that sloshed over the edges. "Well, where is your precious Carolyn now that you need her?" she questioned angrily. "Was it Carolyn who tended to your wound or sees to your comfort? Nay, she is probably home in England spending what little money you have left."

Never in her dreams had Samantha considered her captain married. A large knot settled in her throat, and again her eyes stung with unshed tears. She fled to the balcony doors and threw them wide, breathing deeply of the fresh morning air, trying to regain her composure.

"Samantha . . . come to bed." It was the slightest whisper, but she heard every word. Slowly, as if in a trance, she turned back to the bed. Did he know her? Did he remember as she did? *But this is Cortland,* her mind screamed. *The man who wishes to see you hang.*

"Samantha, don't be scared . . . You're cold. Come, let me warm you."

106

A violent trembling started somewhere about her knees and quickly traveled upward. Did he dream of her as she did of him? And would the dream turn instantly to a nightmare when he realized who she was? Cautiously she returned to stand beside the bed. His eyes remained closed.

"Ah, Captain Cortland," she sighed quietly, reaching once more for the damp cloth. "Once, a very, very long time ago, you pulled me from the arms of the sea. That night you gave me my life. And for that we are now even." Her hand pressed the cool cloth to his fevered brow. "Marie shall see to your comfort, for I am off. I'm finished with childish dreams that can never be. I'm a woman now, and my days for foolish play are finished." Carefully she leaned over his sleeping form, touching her lips lightly to his. "And when we meet again, Captain Cortland, as I'm sure we shall, you will still owe me a debt for the death of my father." Leaving the cloth to cool his forehead, Samantha turned, and with a determined step, gathered her basket of herbs and went to join her ship.

It had been two months since the ship left port. The sea was calm, the sky a vast expanse of clear blue that stretched as far as the eye could see. In silent mockery, the sun smiled down on the solitary ship. Merciless rays beat upon the deck until the pitch seams began to sizzle and the brass fittings were too hot to touch. Hands calloused from years at sea grew raw as day after day they rowed. But the elusive wind could not be found. The sea remained smooth as glass, trapping the *Sea Witch* in the doldrums.

Dancer pulled an empty wine keg to the starboard side and sat with his sword resting across his lap. Sweat ran freely down his face and dripped from his bare arms and chest. Trouble was brewing, he could feel it in his bones as he watched Samantha pace. The crew blamed her for losing the wind, and her relentless motion was making them crazy. His gaze dropped back to his sword and his hand tightened on the hilt. With long smooth strokes he caressed the blade's edge with the whetstone. Over and over, his muscles flexed and stretched as he struggled to find a plan. Talk of mutiny had reached his ears, and even he could not protect her if their words turned to action. He had to get her away from the crew, but how? Short of setting her adrift in the long boat, nothing came to mind.

Dancer rose and stared up at the windless sails, then slowly made his way to the Curse on the quarterdeck. He gasped as she turned toward him. Her cheeks blazed with fever and her eyes were circled with dark shadows, giving her thin face a haunted expression. Dancer took a steadying breath. He had to do something and now.

"Curse, there is trouble." He struggled to keep the urgency from his voice, for hers was the counsel he always sought when trouble was at hand. "We must go below," he continued quietly.

Samantha stood motionless. She heard Dancer's words, but her mind was too tired to put them together. She made no protest when he gently grasped her arm and led her from the deck to her cabin.

Dancer steered her toward her bunk and tried to ignore the blazing heat that filled the small chamber. *There had to be another way*, his mind argued. Angrily he gave her shoulders a rough shake.

"Damn it, Curse, snap out of it." His harsh tone and the sudden jerk of her body brought a glimmer of recognition back into her eyes.

"I've failed." Her voice was a scratchy whisper. "I've lost the wind and I don't know why."

Dancer squatted beside the bunk and stared at her intently, as if he might find the answers to his questions in her eyes. "Will you try the bones?" His gaze shifted to the small pouch of animal bones that rested on the chart table.

Samantha shuddered. "I have."

He watched the color drain from her face, and despite the suffocating heat, a chill ran over his flesh from the hollow sound of her words.

"They showed death." She drew her knees to her chest and wrapped her arms about them. Silently she began to rock on the narrow berth.

Dancer jerked back at her prediction and then rose to his full height as fear flowed through him. "Whose death?" he demanded, picturing the group that had gathered at the mizzenmast. She said nothing but continued her silent rocking. Dancer felt his patience snap. Roughly he grabbed her arms, drawing her to her feet. "Whose death?"

Her tortured eyes looked into the future, then back to his eyes. "Mine," she said quietly.

Denial knotted his muscles, stealing his air, making breathing almost impossible. "Nay!" He shook her shoulders in protest until her face grimaced with pain and he realized he was the cause. "Nay," he challenged again. "I'll not let anything happen to you." Carefully, he eased her back onto the bunk and turned to the shelf where she kept her herbs.

Samantha searched her mind for a plan, some way that would keep her ship from harm. She ignored Dancer's movements within the cabin. He never believed the bones anyway, she thought wearily. When he returned to her and pushed a mug of wine into her hand, she drank without protest.

"I have to go back on deck," she said finally as fatigue pressed down upon her. "'Tis too hot in here, my mind will not work." But as she tried to rise, she felt her legs crumble beneath her. She cried in fright, but Dancer caught her limp form and eased her back into the bunk. The room was growing dim with an alarming speed and Dancer's features shifted across his face, making her stomach lurch in protest.

"Be easy, Curse." His voice floated somewhere above her. "'Tis only one of your own sleeping potions in the wine. I need to keep you from the men for a while and this seems to be the only way. Trust me to see to your safety."

She tried to rise, but Dancer's hand pressed gently against her shoulder, forcing her to lie flat. She tried to speak but no sounds came forth. Panic surfaced. She had to warn him. Danger was near, she could feel its presence coming closer with each beat of her heart. But her muscles refused to do her bidding as her eyes struggled to remain open. Slowly the black void that circled edged closer until she slipped completely within its icy grasp and knew no more.

110

Chapter VIII

Samantha wandered through a maze of darkness. Her cramped muscles jerked in spasms as the clamor of confusion into her dreams. Swords crashed and outraged cries of agony pierced her mind. Thunderous sounds of death rang about her. Then abruptly, all grew silent.

She drew a shallow breath and winced. Reluctantly she forced her eyes open. Darkness. Her head dropped forward and crashed into a wall. Her mind throbbed with confusion as she tried to piece her awareness into some type of order. With her back braced against the wall, her hands reached forward and encountered rough wood. The familiar touch tugged at her memory. The cargo hold? Her head wobbled and her eyelids fluttered with fatigue. Why was she in the cargo hold? Awkwardly she reached outward again letting her fingers drag over the wooden surface in search of the catch. Only she and Dancer knew of this hollow tucked neatly between the walls. It was her hiding place whenever they took

111

a ship. But now, something was wrong. She had no memory of sighting a ship, and she couldn't find the damned catch. Gingerly leaning against the back wall and using the forward wall for support, Samantha struggled to her feet. Maneuvering in the small space was difficult and she lost her breath quickly. There was only a creak of warning before the board behind her shifted and sent her tumbling backward onto the floor. Stunned, she lay sprawled, looking upward at the beams overhead. Thoughts returned in sluggish disarray. Dancer . . . the wine . . . A rat scurried near as she struggled to her feet. Dancer had drugged the wine and hidden her in the belly of the ship, but why? Her legs quivered like jelly as she started around an empty crate. Bile rose in her throat, a bitter reminder that after two months she had still taken no ship. The floor beneath her feet swayed, and she awkwardly fell against a crate. Breathing deeply of the stale damp air, Samantha tried once more to make her legs support her. Then it hit . . . danger. Her awareness sharpened. Gone were the familiar sounds of her ship; only silence prevailed.

With eyes now accustomed to the dark, she crept cautiously toward the upper levels of the ship. A sharp breeze stung her face as she peered out from the companionway. Her heart leaped into her throat. Surely this was part of her nightmare, for beyond the deck of her ship lay another. Grappling hooks now held the *Sea Witch* securely to the rail of an English war vessel.

The decks of the *Sea Witch* were heavily stained with blood, yet none of her crew were about. Silently,

Samantha made her way back toward her cabin.

Chairs had been overturned and chests emptied of their contents. Herbs that she had painstakingly gathered were crushed and scattered about the floor. Angrily she fought against the urge to reach down and salvage her possessions, for she knew that to tidy anything would give proof to her existence. With quiet determination, she carefully doffed her white shirt and exchanged it for one of the black ones that littered the floor. Her eyes searched until she spied her cap and mask half-hidden beneath the rubble near the chart table. These, too, she retrieved, careful to move as little as possible. With each measured step about the cabin, her anger grew.

The sun had long since dipped below the horizon as she made her way from the cabin. Keeping well to the shadows, Samantha eyed the two English soldiers that now guarded her empty decks as they lounged near the capstan. Cautiously she edged closer to the English vessel and peered over the railing. Stunned by the sight that greeted her, Samantha used all her strength to suppress a wail of anguish. Dead bodies were piled high about the English deck and only a handful of her crew appeared to be still alive. Frantically her eyes searched through the carnage. *Dear God, where was Dancer?* Her fingers tightened on the rail and her heart thumped wildly. Then she spied him. He was tied to the pinrail at the base of the mainmast. His head hung loosely between his outstretched arms. He stirred slightly and relief soared through her. For the moment at least, he lived. But if the war ship transported him to London, they would hang him first and ask questions later.

Cold determination filled her. The English would pay for the destruction of her crew. Her hand reached down to touch the rim of her boot and she vowed they'd never find what they truly sought. A deadly calm possessed her as she moved quietly back to her cabin, a daring plan forming in her mind.

"Blimy, 'tis raw tonight." The seaman rubbed his hands briskly against his arms and shifted from one foot to the other. "One day yer so hot ya think yer sailing with the devil himself, then with a blink, 'tis cold enough to shrivel yer nuts off."

"Aye," his companion grunted. Anxiously, he peered into the darkness. "Ya think taking the Falcon's ship what's brought the cold?"

The seaman shrugged and cast a wary eye over his shoulder. "Ya'd think the captain would let a body celebrate, not make him guard an empty ship. Besides, what chance do we have to stop a ghost? I hears he can float right through a solid wall." Again his eyes traveled nervously over the deserted deck. "Here." He pulled a flask and cup from beneath his cape. "What we needs is a little nip to take the chill off."

"Nay, mate." The first backed away, setting the filled cup on the rail. "If the captain was to find out . . ." He shuddered. "I've no wish to feel the lash on me back."

"Aye, ye'd rather freeze and go dancing with Falcon's ghost then. Well, not me. If Falcon's ghost is gonna walk these decks tonight likes they says, then at least I'm gonna be warm." Hastily he grabbed for the cup and downed half the contents before it was roughly snatched from his hand and emptied by his partner.

"Do ye really think we'll see em?"

"Who?"

"Falcon's ghost!"

The answer never came as both men slumped over to the deck. A catlike creature sprang over the railing behind and tucked a small green vial into the sash at her waist. The men were heavy, but she positioned them atop kegs and lashed them to the railing. To the casual glance, all would be well. The men were clearly visible and still on post.

Blending into the shadows, she stole onto the English deck. A weighted pin, hastily swung, took care of the guard near the helm. Steadily she pulled him into the shadows and lashed him securely out of sight. The guards drinking near the quarterdeck never saw the slender arm emerge from the darkness to administer to their cups, and within moments each fell into a deep slumber. These, like the first, she propped back into position and tied to the step posts.

Dancer watched in fascination as she moved about the deck. But his heart stopped when she slipped into the companionway that would lead to the bowels of the ship. Every moment seemed an eternity as he waited the alarm to be sounded. Twice his heart froze as a senior officer ventured on deck, glanced about, then, satisfied all was well, returned below.

The Curse was mad if she thought to take on this English ship, he thought wearily. The guns on one side alone would be adequate to blow the *Sea Witch* from the water. Her mumbo jumbo might work on the island, but it wasn't going to work here. Why hadn't she released him? Dancer tried to breathe deeply. Dear God, this was not the time for one of her schemes. Anxiously, he strained against his bonds. He had to get her off this ship. She didn't realize what they would do when they found a woman in their midst. Rage soared through him, filling his battered limbs with determination. He'd die before he'd see her spread beneath some English bastard. The skin on his wrist began to rip away in his frenzy.

The sergeant moved onto deck and noted Dancer's struggles. With great satisfaction, the small man sauntered over and stood before the bound giant.

"Well, laddie," he sneered, "not so high and mighty are we now?" His hand touched the split skin over his eye and he winced. "And I think I owe you a debt." He cast a quick glance about, then his thick club crashed into Dancer's ribs with a sickening thud.

Dancer groaned as the pain exploded in his chest and radiated outward. With herculean effort he raised his head, gasped for breath, then deposited a healthy amount of spit on his captor's fine red coat.

"Temper, temper, laddie," the sergeant growled. His club poked roughly at the bruised skin near Dancer's eye, then smashed against his nose. Dancer's head fell forward and blood coursed down his face. Grabbing a handful of hair, the sergeant jerked his face upright to better survey the damage. "You need to be more careful, laddie," he sneered with delight. "We don't wants you to go and hurt yourself now. Just think of all them fine folks that would be disappointed if they was deprived of seeing ya hang."

His crackled laugh grated on the silence of the night.

"Penwick, you and Bookman get below now. Captain will be up shortly and you know how he feels about drinking on deck." There was no response, and the sergeant's attention now turned toward the motionless pair on the step.

"Slimy bastard," Dancer cursed. "Care to untie me, Sergeant, and we'll see who's to hang on Sunday?" The man's club swung again, and Dancer slumped unconscious within his bonds.

The sergeant turned back toward the step. He could see them sitting in the shadows, their bottle clearly in sight, yet they did not answer. If the captain came up and found them so it would be his ass as well as theirs in deep waters. "Penwick, Bookman . . ." His voice hissed with a hint of fear. "Answer me." Nervously the sergeant edged closer to the silent men. He fought down his inner panic. All afternoon, stories of Falcon's ghost had floated about the ship, each telling more gruesome than the last. These thoughts vividly filled his mind as he stared at the silent Penwick. The sergeant felt sweat begin to trickle under his collar as he moved timidly forward.

"Penwick . . ." The whisper was almost a plea. His trembling hand reached out to the silent man's shoulder. Unbalanced, the body toppled over. Penwick's jaw hung slack and his open, unseeing eyes stared up from the deck.

"Dear God," the sergeant gasped. "'Tis the ghost to be sure." A soft shuffle sounded behind him and he felt the icy hand of death even as his pee ran warm down his leg. "Capt—"

The cry never left his throat as a pin connected

117

with his head in a meaty clunk.

With agonizing care, Samantha dragged his body into the shadows, then repositioned the man on the steps. With a toss the wine bottle sailed over the rail. Now, all was ready. Quickly she moved to her crew scattered about the deck, thanking God they were only tied and not yet shackled.

Dancer watched through swollen eyes, and his ire built as she purposefully moved to him last. "I thought mayhap you were going to leave me here." The cut on his lip made speech difficult.

Samantha winced at his battered face and rested her cool palm against his swollen cheek. "'Twould be no more than you deserve for that trick with the wine. Now listen closely," she whispered to the small group. "Each of you is to take the powder keg and the wick from a cannon on the starboard side. They have more below to be sure, but the act will buy us more time. When you push off, Robbie, keep to the starboard side and move straight away."

Dancer rubbed his aching shoulders and straightened to his full height. "'Tis good, Curse, but we'll still be in range when she swings about."

Samantha smiled. "Aye, but I've cut the till line almost through; with a sharp turn of the wheel, the line will snap all together. So they sit, unable to turn, while we sail away." The men nodded their heads and she continued. "I'll see to the wheel and try to keep the ship steady while you lift the hooks. We don't need any visitors on deck just yet."

Dancer stood mesmerized as her form once more blended into the shadows. Never would he have thought of such a plan. Robbie's sharp tug forced

118

him from his trance and quickly they made their way to the *Sea Witch*'s deck.

At Dancer's signal, the *Sea Witch*'s sails were hoisted as the grappling hooks were removed, freeing her from the English vessel. With fluid grace the *Sea Witch* silently began to slip away and the space between the two ships widened.

Samantha secured the wheel of the English ship, then started toward the rail. She'd have to go quickly or the distance would be too wide. Already the *Sea Witch*'s sails were full as she began to gather speed.

"What the bloody hell is going on out here?"

Samantha spun about, scooping a pin from the rail as she turned. A giant shadow filled the steps of the quarterdeck, effectively blocking her retreat. Frantically, her eyes searched for a means of escape. The distance between the two ships grew steadily by the heartbeat. She was trapped. The giant man rushed toward her, released the wheel, and spun it sharply. The deck quivered as the line snapped. The wind caught the sails and the ship careened dangerously to one side. Her feet left the deck and, despite a cry of warning, a thousand lights exploded before her eyes and a searing pain shot through her head.

Samantha woke to a sea of pain. Eyes closed tightly, she bit down hard on her lip to keep from crying out. Tears seeped between her thick lashes and silent tremors shook her body. Something cool and wet was pressed on her forehead and over her eyes. For once her quick mind didn't bother to ponder the source but only grab for the slight relief it brought.

"Please . . ." her voice pleaded in anguish when the cloth was removed. Her eyes were too heavy to open and tears threatened anew. Then the treasured coolness was back. Time and again the process was repeated. As the cloth warmed against her fevered skin, another was set in its place. The pain receded, and slowly her breathing became more even. How strange, she thought. Whenever she was hurt, she had always been left to her own devices. Who then cared so much about her comfort? Her mind could find no answers and reluctantly she forced her eyes to open. The hazy figure of a man now sat on the bunk beside her.

"Lie very still, little one. You are safe, just be very very quiet."

The voice was familiar, and her body relaxed at his command. Blinking, she gathered strength to fight the haze and slowly the image grew clearer. A gasp echoed her lips as she stared into the fierce green eyes above her. The face was that of Satan himself.

"Cortland."

"At your service, m'lady."

Samantha tried to rise, but intolerable pain seared through her head. "My ship . . ."

"Be still," he scolded. His hands effortlessly pinned her shoulders to the bunk. "You received quite a blow to the head when the boom broke loose. All this thrashing about is only causing you more distress."

Samantha's eyes darted about the cabin, and Alex's smile deepened. "You're in my bed again," he taunted. Lifting her hand, he uncurled her tense fist and again studied the snake ring she wore. His eyes

120

locked with hers as he carried her fingers to his lips. The emerald eyes of the snake on his finger winked at her.

His voice was soft, his breath warm upon her skin, and his mustache tickled. "'Twas you on the island?" he questioned. "I've a hazy memory of a sea nymph floating about my bedside." Her eyes cast a fleeting glance to his shoulder, and he had his answer. Alex shifted to sit more comfortably on the bunk. Bracing one arm on the far side of her, he kept her fingers neatly trapped within his. "According to Judd, you are a witch that saved my life." His hand carried hers to his shoulder to touch the now-healed wound.

"It pains you?"

"Nay." He smiled gently. "I had excellent care. And now it seems, 'tis mine to return the favor."

Samantha tried to blink back the wave of fatigue that washed over her. "My ship?"

Alex's smile vanished. "The *Sea Witch* is gone. Spirited away by Falcon's ghost. But then you wouldn't know anything about that, would you?"

Samantha stared mutinously straight ahead.

"Aye, I have lost the *Sea Witch*, but then I have gained a more valuable cargo, would you not agree, m'lady?"

Fear now coupled with the pain that filled her. Dancer had been right, Cortland was no fool, but how much did he know? She flexed her toes, relieved to realize she still wore her boots. She had to get away. Lying before this man made her too vulnerable. His thigh rested against her hip, and where they touched, her skin burned. Consumed by panic, she tried again to rise.

"Be still, you witless child." Alex's scowl deepened as his hands held her flat against the bunk. He could see the lines of strain about her mouth pulling tighter, and his frustration grew. He had thought her dead at first, hearing the crack of the beam against her skull. And when he had pulled off her cap and mask, his heart had stopped, for lying at his feet was the sea nymph that still haunted his mind. Thank God he had gotten her to his cabin before the watch had aroused. But now what to do with her? If it were true she had masterminded the *Sea Witch*'s escape, there was no telling what other mischief she might be about. His thumb traced a pattern on the soft skin of her wrist and he felt her pulse quicken.

"What are you going to do with me?" Samantha closed her eyes, unable to meet his harsh scowl. Her heart jumped each time his hands touched, and despite the thundering pain in her head, a fierce longing filled her. Her captain, the man from her dreams, she could breathe of his scent and not call on memory. She could feel his strength and, strangely, it brought comfort.

The cloth on her forehead was removed. She felt the brush of his mustache as his lips traveled over her fevered skin. A slow ache started deep in her soul and grew steadily brighter. His lips teased at the corners of her mouth, coming close only to shift to her cheek, her jaw.

Samantha opened her weighted lids and stared deeply into the green eyes that for years had haunted her. But this time it was not a dream. And when the lips taunted again, she raised a hand to lay against his cheek. Closing her eyes on a sigh, she smiled as his mouth settled firmly over hers. His tongue traced against her lips, and when he pressed more closely against her soft frame, she found a sweetness that she had only imagined in her dreams.

Alex fought against the urge to throw caution to the wind, bolt the cabin door, and join her in the narrow bunk. He had desired women before, but never with the consuming passion that now burned his flesh. Still, if his plan worked, he would get her to London without the crew ever knowing, and then time would be on his side. His lips traveled the velvet smoothness of her neck, and her sigh caressed him. He would take her slowly, feasting on her flesh until she was a quivering mass of need. Then and only then would he sate his own desire within her honeyed flesh.

Samantha's arms wound about his neck, and when her fingers threaded through his hair, Alex tossed the last of his common sense aside and slipped onto the bunk beside her. Shifting her more securely beneath him, his lips again traveled the side of her neck, causing her to moan and arch more firmly against him.

"My crew thinks that Falcon's ghost is responsible for the disappearance of the *Sea Witch*." Each word was punctuated with a featherlike kiss across her forehead. He shifted his hips more fully against her. "I've never bedded with a ghost before."

The sound of her father's name washed over Samantha like an icy bath. This was Cortland, her father's killer, who rubbed his body boldly against hers.

"Get off me, you English bastard." Her words hissed against his lips and she struggled to turn her head aside.

Startled, Alex drew back. "What the . . ."

Samantha's fist smashed into his cheekbone. "Get your slimy hands off of me. I'm not some whore for you to use at your leisure." The contempt in her voice caused Alex to draw back even farther as fire and hatred shot from the bunk beneath him.

Samantha tried to swing again, but Alex was out of reach. Relieved of his weight against her, she jerked into a sitting position and froze in agony. Her hands grabbed her head as lightning-white pain exploded behind her eyes, stealing her breath, making her stomach lurch.

Alex watched her frozen form and knew well the cause. Her soft pain-filled cry ripped at him, and his anger fled as quickly as it had come. His voice was soft and low as he supported her shoulders and gently lowered her once more onto the pillow.

Samantha tried to concentrate, using every trick Kabol had ever taught her to block the blinding light that threatened to consume her. She felt the treasured coolness again on her forehead and fleetingly wondered why Cortland would want to comfort her. A damp cloth patted gently against her parched lips. Her breathing eased slightly as the pain dulled.

"Water . . . please." The words were an effort, but were rewarded when a spoon touched her lips. The liquid dribbled down her chin. A frustrated curse sounded, then Cortland's hand was slipping under the pillow that she rested upon. Ever so gently he raised her until she could sip against the spoon. Her eyes opened, and she stared at him with confusion. Again the spoon touched her lips, but this time the liquid was bitter and hard to swallow. She recognized the sleeping potion instantly, but her resistance was no match for his determination.

"'Tis better on the inside, my lady," Alex scolded, and again the spoon met her lips. "'Twill help ease the pain."

Satisfied, he eased the pillow back to the bunk. Samantha blinked wearily. The pain had stolen her strength. She was defenseless, and they both knew it. His hand at her neck could easily have snapped it in two, yet his fingers smoothed the damp, tangled hairs from her face.

Alex stared at the sparkling eyes· before him. The softness of her skin still amazed him, and he let his thumb lightly trace the curve of her jaw. Who would believe this innocent-looking bit of fluff was the most talked-about pirate in London? She returned his gaze with equal intensity and, strangely, that pleased him.

"Little Samantha." He replaced the cloth against her forehead. "Whatever is London going to think of you?"

"I can't go to London," she gasped. Memories from her childhood jumped forward and demanded to be noticed. She had stood with Edward near the front of the mob. He had gone to such lengths to procure her a good view. The crowd throbbed with excitement. She felt the sensations swirl about her. Then she saw the gallows, and excitement turned to horror. The infamous privateer, William Kidd, was brought forth and the chanting of the crowds grew in

125

volume until she thought she would scream from the sound of it. She tried to run, to escape the brutality, but her uncle kept her hand in a tight grip. The crowd, drunk on the spectacle of it all, surged forward. Samantha looked up. She could smell Kidd's fear. Sweat poured from his face as the hangman and his assistant affixed wide metal bands around the pirate's body. For an instant, their eyes met, his filled with frenzied fear that pleaded for salvation, hers filled with horror steeped in helplessness. Samantha tried to look away. But even with her eyes pressed tightly together, she could not block out the terror that lay before her. The hangman pulled the lever. The crowd gasped, then booed, for the rope had broken. Kidd was hauled back up to the scaffold. Finding no pleasure in hanging an unconscious man, the henchman had tossed a bucket of icy water over Kidd's crumpled form. The pirate coughed and sputtered, and the chanting of the crowd began anew. Satisfied Kidd was again conscious, the hangman dragged the stunned pirate to his feet. The roar of the crowd was deafening. Samantha had struggled to cover her ears, but Edward, braced behind her, held her hands firmly at her sides. She closed her eyes, but she could still see the picture too clearly. She heard the thud of the platform snap open, and the crowd cheered anew. Her eyes opened to the horror before her. Despite death, Kidd's eyes were locked open with terror. His body twitched and quivered, then swayed gently in the noon breeze.

Samantha shuddered. "I'll not go to London and be hanged." Her eyes sparkled defiantly.

Alex silently agreed. She was a treasure he would

not be content to share.

As the numb feeling began, Samantha silently cursed herself for a fool. She had lain like a besotted ninny while Cortland had spooned laudanum down her throat.

"Get away . . . I must get away." She didn't realize the words were mumbled aloud.

Alex halted her restless movement less she do herself more harm. "Relax, Samantha," he crooned gently. "'Tis the easiest way. Now you won't feel the pain."

"Nay," she cried in a whisper. Did he think to drug her would lessen the brutalities she would suffer in prison, or just make her easier to control? Would it lessen the humiliation she would face, or simply make her incapable of resistance.

"Nay," she cried again. She struggled to keep her eyes open and the numbness from her mind.

"Rest, Samantha." His hands were gentle but firm. "Don't fight the drug . . . or me. I've told you before and I'll tell you again, I will be master here before this is finished."

Her response died on her lips as they were covered by his. The warm taste of his mouth was the last thing she remembered.

Samantha snuggled deeper under the covers and tried to recapture her dream, but the gnawing pangs of hunger would not give her ease. Reluctantly, she pushed herself upward and stretched like a cat unwinding from its nap. Abruptly she paused. The pain was gone. Cautious fingers moved to the back of

127

her head. It was still tender to the touch, but the mind-wretching agony did not reappear. In a moment of joy, she swung her legs from the bunk and froze.

Sitting less than two feet away was Alex Cortland. He leaned back in his chair, his stocking feet stretched lazily before him. His shirt, open to the waist, revealed dark curling hair on his chest. He did not smile. And his eyes watched her every move like a hawk about to devour a mouse for lunch.

"I see you have decided to rejoin the living."

Samantha shrugged and tore her gaze from his. Steadying herself on the edge of the bunk, she tried to stand.

Alex was on his feet instantly, not to push her back as she expected, but to lend a steady hand as her knees quivered. Her feet tangled in the long nightshirt she wore, and as she tried to gain her balance, the reality of their situation hit her with a force that made her dizzy.

"Where are my clothes?" She tried to keep the desperation from her voice as she glanced about his cabin.

Alex chuckled, relieved she felt well enough to be demanding. For days he had cared for her, tortured both by her pain and then by her beauty. "Since 'twas your choice the last time, I thought m'lady would be pleased."

"I want my clothes back now." Her voice gained strength as she glared at him.

"Easy, my sweet," he cautioned. "You don't want to displease me when you have so much to lose. Besides . . ." he taunted, delighted with the high color in her cheeks. "You are quite a fetching sight in my shirt. And I quite enjoyed putting you there."

Samantha felt her anger begin to surface. Who did he think he was talking to? If he thought her some feeble-minded wench who would lose her heart to his handsome face, he was in for a rude surprise.

"But if it distresses, my lady," he continued, watching the fire blaze in her eyes, "I shall remove it most willingly." His long brown fingers deftly moved to the front buttons.

"Nay . . ." Samantha knocked his hand aside, but when she looked up, he was grinning. "Nay." Her voice was soft but firm. She lifted her wrist up to admire the lace edging. "I think I find this quite to my liking."

"A wise choice, my lady."

Samantha tried to step away from the bunk. She could feel his presence too strongly. His power both frightened and enticed her. But as she moved, her feet tangled again in the cursed nightshirt. Instantly she was caught against his hard chest.

Alex closed his eyes in silent pleasure. Her hair, soft as silk and the color of moonlight, spilled over his arm. He could feel the rapid beating of her heart. His hand caressed her back, then strayed lower, pressing her still closer to the manly hardness of his body.

Samantha's resistance melted. Rock-hard thighs pressed against hers while the hair on his chest tickled her cheek. The male scent of him engulfed her, and the warmth of his body lit a strange spark deep in her soul. Of their own volition, her arms encircled his waist to maintain this glorious closeness. She trembled as his breath brushed her ear, then her throat. Her neck had no strength and her head fell back against his arm to give his lips new freedom.

Alex felt her pulse leap as his hand settled possessively on her breast. Annoyed with the thin fabric that kept him from total possession, he brushed her nipple with his thumb. As it reached pebble hardness, the desire to taste it grew stronger, but her soft moan of pleasure drew his attention back to her mouth. Here was a treasure worth taking. His lips settled firmly over hers. Leisurely he let his tongue taste the intimate sweetness of her.

Samantha was grateful for the solid security of his arms. He was taking the very breath from her body, stealing her senses and claiming them for his own. A curious ache of emptiness was pulling deep within her, and unknowingly she pressed closer to his growing hardness.

The sharp knock on the door caught both off guard, bringing them swiftly back to reality.

Alex watched in frustration as color filled her cheeks and awareness replaced the drugged look his kisses had created.

"Who goes?" The anger in his voice startled her, and she struggled to move away. "Be still," he hissed in irritation.

"Beggin' your pardon, Captain," a timid voice called from beyond the door. "Land's End is in sight. You said I should call."

Alex ignored Samantha's struggles to move away and rubbed his chin atop her head. "All right, Judd. I shall return shortly." He listened to the retreating footsteps, then sighed wearily. "Why, wench, do I always find myself interrupted with you? Now let us make haste and seek our pleasure while we may.''

"Nay, Captain, I'll not bed with you," Samantha tried to squirm from his embrace.

Alex frowned. "There are names for women like you, madam, and none of them complimentary. To lead a man on and then dance away seems to be a game with you. So hear this my lady. 'Tis going to change and now." Her resistance against his strength was no match, and as her struggles became more frantic, Alex only became more determined.

Samantha found herself unceremoniously dumped on the bunk, not quite knowing how she got there. Alex doffed his shirt before letting his body weight settle over her, thus pinning her to the bed. Samantha squirmed and managed to get her arms between them, but pushing against his chest was like trying to move a brick wall.

Alex chuckled at her unsuccessful attempts and watched her strength fade. Swooping down, he placed a hard, swift kiss on her lips, then propped himself on his elbows so she could better breathe. She was exhausted, yet angry fire still burned in her eyes and, strangely, it pleased him.

"Please, Captain . . ." Her voice hesitated with the plea. "Let me up. I need my clothes."

"Nay, m'lady, for too long it has been a game with your rules. Now I think I have found a suitable way for you to pay for my losses." His purpose was only too clear as he pressed boldly against her thigh.

"Nay." Turning her head from side to side, she tried to avoid his mouth.

"Give me one good reason, love, not to take you

here and now." His voice was husky as he nibbled against her throat.

"I'm hungry."

Alex's eyes opened wide with surprise. Whatever he had expected, it certainly was not that. "Are my kisses not food for your soul?"

"'Tis not my soul that is hungry, Captain, but my stomach." As if on cue, her stomach emitted a low rumble.

Alex laughed aloud. No lady would ever admit to hunger. He thought of Julia, she would have fainted before voicing such a request. Alex gazed down at the beauty beneath him and mentally ticked off the time. Even if he allowed this delay, there would still be opportunity to sample her wares.

"Ah, witch." He kissed her forehead, then reluctantly levered himself from the bunk. "I feel I am already caught within your spell. If 'tis food my lady wants, then 'tis food she shall have." Alex moved to the door of the cabin, then nodded toward a folded screen in the corner. "I shall give you a few moments to see to your needs, but be warned, my lady, no tricks or you shall feel the full force of my temper for the first time."

Samantha breathed a sigh of relief as he closed the door behind him.

Chapter IX

Samantha gazed at the now-empty dishes that Judd cleared from the table. She had been starving, yet she had no idea what had just passed between her lips, for each mouthful had brought her closer to the hell that awaited. Again and again her mind played over her choices and found them wanting. Resentment burned for having to grant Cortland even the smallest victory.

"Enough." Alex's voice broke through her thoughts, his patience at an end. "Now, m'lady, after you." He stepped from the table and waited for her to do the same.

Stiffly she moved toward the bunk, then perched on the edge. "A moment, Captain, please!"

Alex paused and waited for her new ploy. Didn't she know how he burned for her? What sweet torture it had been tending her these past days yet never easing his needs within her soft flesh? His scowl deepened as her words rushed forth.

"Tell me, are you a gentleman, sir?"

133

Alex laughed. "If you mean to set me from my goal, nymph, then rest assured that with your beauty, I find it easy to cast my gentleman's ways aside."

"But what of your word, Captain?"

Alex stared at her silently, then sat facing the bunk and began to remove his shirt. "When I give my word, m'lady, 'tis my bond, and as such, not broken."

"Then what say you to a bargain?"

Again his laughter rang out. "I fear, love, that I already have all I seek. The captain of the *Sea Witch* and a nymph for my bed."

Samantha watched in awe as he rose and pulled his shirt free from his breeches. The men on her ship had often worked without their shirts; what then caused this fascination with Cortland? His muscles flexed as he discarded the garment and began to unfasten his buckle. With nerves threatening to shatter, she took a deep breath and plunged forward.

"Really, Captain?" She strove to keep her voice calm as he approached. His tight-fitting breeches gave strong proof to his intentions. "I seem to remember a great desire on your part to obtain a certain document."

Alex halted midstride. "What do you know of it?"

"Mayhap nothing, then again mayhap quite a lot. Why not sit, Captain." Graciously she nodded to the chair he had just vacated. "It seems we have something to discuss after all."

"Nay, love, I'll not bargain with you. You stall for time."

"My, my, Captain, when a fine gentleman like yourself puts his personal pleasures before the safety

134

of his country? What is this world coming to?"

Her azure eyes grew wide, and Alex wondered how she managed to appear so innocent. She had the looks of an angel and the soul of a witch. "Cease your prattle, wench. If you know of the document, then tell me."

"Three sheets, fixed with the king's seal . . . You tell me, Captain. If both were laid on a table before you, my life for Newgate or the document you covet, which would you choose?"

"If, madam, and I repeat *if* there were indeed a choice, then we would discuss it. But since there isn't . . ."

"Oh but there is," her soft voice taunted. "If 'twas my desire to do so, I could have the document delivered to your hands as we docked. Now, Captain, what of choices?"

Alex eased back into his chair. It was a trick. Every word rang false. Her description fit any number of official papers. Still, if she had even the smallest bit of information . . .

"So we bargain, Captain?" Her confidence began to seep back. "You may turn me over to the authorities and London will have her hanging, or I produce the document, and in return you set me free."

A sardonic smile touched Alex's lips. "I think you bargain with an empty hand, love. I shall have you for my bed, and if you truly know of the document, then there are ways of making you talk."

Samantha felt her blood run cold as he rose. Alex paused as he watched her withdraw his dagger from beneath the covers on the bunk. His face showed

135

surprise, then anger.

"Do you mean to stop me with that toothpick?" he challenged, towering before her.

"Nay, Captain, I am not a fool like some in this room." Her face was cold and determined as the dagger pointed toward her own heart. "Now," she continued in a deathly quiet voice, "if you wish my life, then 'tis yours by right of my capture. But if you wish the papers that could destroy England, then I will have my freedom by your words and by your oath as a gentleman."

Alex stared in amazement. What manner of woman was this? She must be mad. Angrily he took a step toward the bunk.

"You wish my life then?" Large eyes searched his. "You don't believe me," she stated sadly. The dagger moved, and a red stain instantly appeared on the white nightshirt. "'Tis easy to end a life, Captain, so very easy."

Alex heard her hiss of pain as the blade pierced her skin. "'Tis madness, madam." Yet he retreated, lest she press the blade deeper. Already the stain was too large for his liking. "I'll not bargain with a pirate."

"And I, sir, will not go to prison."

"Enough." His eyes locked with hers, and Alex suddenly feared she would see the deed through. "You are going to bleed to death. I can't believe someone of your few years should be so willing to end her life."

"Nay." Tears now stung her eyes and she struggled to keep his image in focus. "If to die by the hangman or in Newgate, then this be my choice. But *if* I am to die, that, Captain, is your choice."

136

"I think you bluff, madam . . ."

Her hand shifted before he could add to his words, and to his horror the blade moved deeper into her flesh. Alex stifled a curse. He had no way out. The twit would sit there and kill herself if he didn't do something.

"I yield, madam," he snapped grudgingly. "Now put that damned thing down."

Weakly she shook her head. "A bargain first, Captain, an oath by your own words from your own lips."

Alex growled impatiently. Her face was totally devoid of color and her eyes struggled to remain open. Yet he now had no doubt of her determination. And if he didn't take action soon, there would be no choice to make.

"Madam . . ." He clicked his bare heels together and bowed formally. "I, Alex Cortland, agree that upon receiving the papers I desire, will do all in my power to keep you from Newgate Prison and from the hangman. I will see you gently cared for and always kept safe from those who would harm you. To this, madam, I give you my word."

With great effort, Samantha nodded her head. "The documents are in the lining of my boot."

"Damn the papers!" Alex couldn't be still **another** moment. Two angry strides brought him to the bunk and the dagger was struck to the floor. None too gently he pushed the nightshirt open and sought to stop the flow of blood with his handkerchief."

"'Tis not as bad as it appears," she said, but her voice trembled and lacked conviction.

Quickly, Alex cleaned and bound the wound.

"You're a fool, madam," he said through clenched teeth as he worked. "How you have survived this long when you gamble with such high stakes is a wonder to me."

"I'll not go to prison." Her voice was barely a whisper, but the determination rang through.

"Ah, love, 'tis ture." His voice gentled as he replaced the blood-soaked shirt with a clean one. "Newgate will never see the likes of you, on that you have my word."

Samantha stared deep into the green eyes that floated before her and knew she would be safe.

Gently, Alex tucked the covers around her shoulders. *How innocent she appears,* he thought as he studied her sleeping form, and how deceptive. For a fleeting moment he admired her strength and courage, but her willfulness was going to cease. As his mistress, she was going to have to learn obedience, and quickly. He had dealt with her gently but with no results. "By heavens, madam," he whispered softly as his thumb caressed the curve of her jaw. "If it takes a heavy hand to steer you, then rest assured, love, you shall feel it." A quick kiss sealed his vow, and reluctantly Alex left the bunk for more pressing matters.

Alex tried to quicken his step as he moved unsteadily along the dock. It had taken the better part of three days and two sleepless nights, but he had succeeded. In the taverns, the story was always the same. The pirate ship had been easily taken, only to be reclaimed that same night by Falcon's ghost. The crew, never aware of Samantha or her presence on deck, had found the failure easier to tolerate with such a famous spirit to cast into their stories. But on the second day, when news of the delivered documents leaked out, the laughter and the ribbing ceased.

"True enough," the crew muttered. "The captain be the devil himself when in a temper." Silently, though, the thoughts of their captain sealing a pact with Falcon's ghost on their very deck caused many a hand to tremble as the tale grew with each telling. Within hours, all on the wharf knew the story, and Alex's presence caused a hushed reverence wherever he went.

Alex rubbed the grit from his eyes and prayed his luck would hold for another hour. The crew would have departed for their leave. Only Judd would be left aboard to guard his prize. He stumbled and cursed at the coil of rope at his feet. *Get her off the ship without being seen.* The thought ran through his mind over and over again. He would send Judd to fetch a carriage and then they could be away. The sooner he had her off the ship and away from the wharf, the better he'd feel.

As Judd left to do his bidding, Alex paused at the door to his cabin. Even tired as he was, his anticipation was keen. Samantha curled dreamy-eyed on his bed, or stretched beneath him. God, how the image stirred. The ache in his loins grew stronger as he unlocked the cabin door.

But the sea nymph had vanished and Alex was greeted by an angry Samantha who paced the length of his cabin.

"Where the devil have you been?" she demanded.

Alex stood mesmerized by the movement of her rounded hip in the tight breeches she now wore.

"Answer me, damn you!"

"Ah, I beg pardon, m'lady." Alex bowed unsteadily before her, raising a bloodshot eye to meet icyblue ones. "I have been seeing to our bargain, of course. The papers have been safely delivered."

Samantha snorted with irritation and snatched her mangled boot from the table. "Look at this," she railed. "'Tis ruined." She dangled the leather strips before him. "Did you have to cut it to bits? Could you have not retrieved your precious document without destroying my boot?"

Alex stood silent, transfixed by the sight before him. When she had lain curled on his bunk, he found it hard to believe that she even sailed with the *Sea Witch*. Now, her icy tone had him ready to apologize for a simple boot. He watched in fascination as she stuffed papers into the toe of one of his and pulled it over her shapely calf. She had located her cap with the rest of her clothing and as she tucked her hair out of sight, the transformation was complete.

Samantha gave him a cold stare, then moved toward the door, her gate slightly uneven in the mismatched boots. But as she reached for the knob, his hand wrapped around her middle and she was pulled back against his solid frame.

"And just where do you think you are going?" He snatched the cap from her head and sailed it across the room. His voice was husky as his breath hit her ear.

140

"We made a bargain, Captain, and I am leaving." Alex ignored the stiffness of her body and the icy tones of her words. For three days and nights her image had haunted him to distraction and now she was in his arms.

"Nay, little one." His lips traveled the length of her neck making her stomach quiver.

"You gave your word as a gentleman." She struggled, but his arms only tightened about her.

"I promised to keep you from prison, m'lady, and I shall. I vowed to see you gently cared for and I will."

Samantha felt the manly warmth of him surround her as the hardness of his body pressed boldly against her backside. Fear coupled with the sudden realization that Cortland had never intended to let her go. His arms tightened, and Samantha fought against the panic that threatened to buckle her knees.

"Captain . . ." Her voice was breathy with anticipation, and she relaxed her body to rub back against his. "You move too quickly," she chided gently. "Have you not learned to slow down and savor the moment?" She brushed a promising kiss against his cheek, then twisted deftly from his arms. Giving Alex her most bewitching smile, she maneuvered to put the table between them. "After all, Captain," she cooed, "There is no need to rush."

"Captain? Captain?" A timid voice echoed in the companionway just outside of the cabin.

Alex's eyes never left hers as he answered. "What is it, Judd?"

"The carriage is ready at the end of the lane, sir."

Alex glanced at the ornate clock that sat above his

141

chard table. "Judd, take the driver and share a pint or two. Come back to the lane at midnight precisely. Do not come to the ship, but wait for me there." After a moment of silence, Judd's response, then his footsteps, echoed in the empty hallway. Alex locked the cabin door, then glanced pointedly to the clock.

"How wise you are, m'lady. 'Tis not the night to rush. Two hours should take the edge off this ache I have carried for the last three days."

Samantha forced her smile as Alex slipped his jacket onto the chair. A single lantern burned high on the wall behind him, and in the flickering light his shoulders appeared wider, his muscles stronger, the task before her harder. "You should sit and relax, Captain." Her voice was soft and coaxing. "Let me fetch you some wine to make the night even sweeter."

Alex shoved the key deep into his pocket, then turned toward the bunk. Samantha tried to keep her hands steady as she prepared the wine. She had found the small bottle of laudanum when searching for her clothing, and now she prayed that the few drops left would be sufficient. She turned quickly and approached the bunk where Alex stretched against the pillows. He had removed all but his breeches, and there was no doubt as to the state of his arousal. Samantha knelt beside the bunk as she handed him the goblet.

Alex took a healthy drink, then, grabbing her wrist, pulled her closer so that she, too, sat on the bunk. "You are so beautiful." His free hand caressed the hair that cascaded over her shoulder. "Who

142

would have thought such a rare diamond would exist."

Samantha jerked and turned to face him. "What do you speak of?" Her mind raced to the *Midnight Star* that Kabol had shown her and she wondered if Cortland, too, knew of the stone.

Alex drained the last of his wine and leaned over to set both his goblet and hers aside. "You remind me of a diamond, love." He sat forward now, and his nimble fingers tugged at the wrapped tails of her shirt. "You sparkle with a thousand lights, and although some would shy from your brilliance, I am attracted to that fire I find deep within."

Samantha sat mesmerized by the hypnotic quality of his words. How did he know that the ache in her belly intensified each time his fingers traced down her arm. Or that the warmth of his breath against her skin both chilled and burned her. Then her shirt was free and his palm against her bare stomach fanned the flame into a blaze that threatened to consume her. Why did he not sleep? His lips followed his fingers and her shirt was eased from her shoulders and pushed aside. She tried to steel herself against the growing desire to lose herself in his embrace. Her eyes fixed on the flickering lantern and she prayed for sleep to overtake him. Alex's fingers danced over her breast and Samantha felt a jolt of longing shoot to her toes. She should not be lying with him, yet she had no desire to move.

Be patient, reason argued, *the drug must take effect soon. Give him no reason to suspect foul play. Enjoy,* her senses countered, *sample the secrets of the*

143

universe. His mouth found hers. A frenzy of feelings washed over her. Was this the source of the radiant smile Marie always wore after a night with Dancer? The heat of his body grew, and Samantha suddenly realized they both were naked. She stiffened. What sorcery had he performed? Had she consumed the drug? Fear of the unknown cooled her, but she could no more turn away than a moth from a flame. His lips fastened against hers and threatened to steal the very breath from her body. She tried to shift against him, but escape was clearly impossible.

Impatiently, Alex kissed the lips that had tempted him even in his dreams. Her skin, softer than he had remembered, caressed his body as he covered hers. The desire that burned within threatened to consume. His kisses grew more frantic, but still 'twas not enough. Her silken thighs rubbed against his hips and his resolve came undone. With a strong thrust, he penetrated her warm flesh to find his release.

Samantha curled into a tight, trembling ball that threatened to fall out of the bunk. She bit hard on her lip and vowed not to cry. Alex stared at the beams on the shadowed ceiling and tried to clear his senses. A virgin, she had been a virgin. Dear God, he took more care with the seasoned women that he visited. And tonight he had been her first. How could she have lived as a pirate's mistress for all these years and still be an innocent? Why had she not said something? Why had he not realized?

Samantha tried to still her uneven breathing, for if

she gave in to the tears that threatened, she feared they would never cease. What had she done wrong? Why did she feel so helplessly empty? Marie always carried a glow that lasted for days. She felt Alex behind her on the bunk and her body stiffened. For the first time in her life she felt shame, and the taste was bitter.

Alex propped himself on one elbow and gazed down at her trembling form. He didn't need to see her blood on the sheets to know that he had hurt her, and the thought plagued him. His mind replayed the act again and again until he recognized her hesitant attempts for what they truly were. Yet still, he had only to touch her and his flesh burned. Never had a woman caused the flames to stir so quickly or so hot. Even now, knowing what he had done, he wanted her. But this time he would see her tremble with passion before he took his ease. He lifted his hand to caress her shoulder, and a deep weariness washed over him. Alex blinked, then rested his head behind hers on the pillow. His arm snaked around to pull her securely back against him, and he felt her tremble.

"Hush, love, hush." His voice was soft, almost a whisper. "Let me rest but for a moment, then I shall show you the true joy of passion."

Samantha tried to be still when his arm tightened about her. And despite her fear, the sound of his voice was soothing to her senses. But she knew that repeating the act itself would be more than she could bear. She wanted to hide, to find a dark hole she could crawl into to conceal her shame. Dear God, what had she been thinking of? She had let Cortland, the man who had killed her father, make love to her. Her trembling began anew, and she jerked herself from his grasp on the bunk. Alex, deep in sleep, made no protest. He only clutched at the pillow in her absence.

Samantha stared in horror at the bloodstained sheet. How could she have ever thought that she would find peace with her father's killer? What sorcery did Cortland use to make her body burn with lust instead of hatred?

Unsure of how long the laudanum would detain him, she struggled to dress quickly. She had to get away, for another such encounter with Cortland would surely destroy her. Giving his slumbering form one last glance, Samantha pulled the snake ring from her finger and placed it on the pillow beside his head.

"Now, there is nothing to bind us together," she stated quietly. Then, turning, she fled the cabin.

The night was still. Water lapped gently against the hull of the English ship as she silently made her way to the main deck. All was deserted, but she took no chances and kept well to the shadows. The moon flirted with the stormclouds overhead as a thick mist floated about the water. Samantha tested her legs on the cobbled street and waited for the rocking motion to ease. Cautiously, she made her way to the end of the lane. There she could see a covered carriage. The driver was not about, and the horse nodded, sleepy in his tethers. The cobblestones felt strange beneath her feet and the stench of the city overwhelmed her. There was no doubt in her mind what many of the

146

dark corners she moved through were used for. A lamppost glowed on the deserted street, and she resisted the urge to seek comfort beneath its light. This was London, and her memories were not pleasant. Carefully, she continued onward, blending into the shadows. The fog horn moaned again in the lonely night and the answering mist grew denser.

Chapter X

Samantha paid the driver and paused, gasping for breath. She would never become accustomed to the stench of London's back streets. On the island, the air always carried the heady scent of fragrant blossoms. Here, garbage and human waste made her stomach turn.

"Want me ta walk with ya, miss? Ol Bertha will tear me limb from limb if you was ta get lost." His words snapped her back from thoughts of home, and a sad smile touched her face.

"Thank you, Jim," she replied softly. "But 'tis best if I make my own way." She started to step away, then turned back. "You will wait for me, won't you?" She tried to conceal her trepidation as she searched the ruddy face that stared back at her.

"You be about your business with an easy mind, miss. Ol Jim will be right here when ya gets back." He gave his black mare an affectionate pat on the rump. "Can ya see me facing Bertie if I was ta come back without ya?" The horrible grimace he made brought forth a chuckle, and Samantha relaxed with his teasing. "Now that's what I likes ta hear, miss. Laughter sweeter than sunshine. You be gone now and Jims will be here awaiting."

With fresh resolve, Samantha smiled and slowly made her way into the crowded city street. The sun warmed the coarse brown material of her gown. The thick veil that covered her head and face made her hot, and sweat trickled into the high collar of her dress. The numerous petticoats were cumbersome, and silently she longed for the unrestricted freedom of her breeches. But her costume served her well, for no one gave the small lady in the plain brown dress any notice as she quietly made her way into the bank.

As the clerk ushered her into a small, private room, she wondered if Falcon's claims were true, or if this was just another of his farfetched tales; how much did this banker, Radford Linstrom, know of her identity? Lifting the heavy veil from her face, she surveyed the tiny office. A large desk in need of repair filled most of the room, and shelves lined with books went from floor to ceiling. Packing cartons cluttered the corners, and several smaller boxes had been stacked upon the desk. Her foot tapped impatiently on the dusty floor. Somehow this wasn't quite what she had imagined when she thought of a rich banker's office, but then the city, too, had been worse than she had remembered. Her fingers traced the dust from the desk's surface, and she grimaced. She gazed longingly at the sealed windows and wished for a breath of fresh air. Then it happened.

A chilling jolt ran up her spine, and despite the heat in the cluttered room, she shivered. Her senses sharpened as the knob twisted slowly, then the door burst open. Her eyes widened in amazement as a tall, lanky man bustled into the room. His arms dangled at his side as he nervously shifted from one foot to the other. Why, she wondered, would such a strange, bungling creature cause such a strong sense of danger? She eyed him critically, but the man seemed more intent on getting in his own way than in hampering hers.

"Please accept my sincere apology, Lady Chester-field." He gestured helplessly. "Our clerk is new and has much to learn." All but tripping over his feet, he retrieved a goblet and decanter from the shelf, then made a grand show of pouring her wine.

Forcing a smile, she accepted the goblet, but set it on the table before her.

"Forgive me, sir," her voice was soft, "but are you Sir Radford?"

The man's eyes widened in surprise. "But no, madam, please forgive me." He executed an awk-ward bow. "I am Philip Sedgewinn, Sir Radford's personal assistant."

Samantha hid a smile as Sedgewinn's chest puffed with his own importance. His coat was too small for his reed-thin body and he constantly tugged at the worn cuffs to make them meet his angular wrists.

"Then will you tell Sir Radford I am here, sir? I am about matters that need his attention."

"That will be quite impossible madam." Sedge-winn looked down his beaklike nose with a superior air. "Sir Radford is on holiday and shall not return for several weeks. I am handling all banking matters in his absence." With a smug look, he pushed aside several boxes, then settled himself at the desk before her, heedless of the dirt that covered the surface on which he rested his elbows. "How may I assist you, Lady Chesterfield?"

Unused to being addressed as such, Samantha straightened in her chair and forced memories of her mother from her mind. The sense of danger was back—and stronger, making her shoulders stiffen.

She glanced again about the cramped office. Falcon had always been most precise in his instructions. If she ever found herself in London, she was to deal with Linstrom and only Linstrom. But now she was here, and Radford Linstrom was on holiday. Her options were few. For the moment, Bertie and Old Jim believed her story of being a runaway. But the old, dilapidated tavern that she had thought would give her refuge had turned out to be one of the most popular near the wharf. It would be impossible to stay there much longer without rousing suspicion. Reluctantly, Samantha turned back to Sedgewinn.

"Tell me, sir, are you familiar with my account in this bank?"

Sedgewinn, who had been leaning back in his chair, straightened like a puppet whose strings had been given a swift tug. "Surely you do me an injustice, Lady Chesterfield." He put on a wounded face. "'Tis common knowledge that you hold the two largest accounts that the bank handles."

"I beg your pardon, sir," she replied gently, trying to sooth his ruffled feathers while assessing this new information. "Then, since you know of my accounts and Sir Radford is not available, you must assist me in making a slight withdrawal."

Sedgewinn shifted uncomfortably in his chair. "Certainly, m'lady, whatever is your pleasure. I am only here to serve. How much do you wish?"

Samantha paused, knowing that to ask the exact amount of the account might rouse suspicion. "I think I should like a quarter of my money at this time," she stated in an offhand manner. Sedgewinn's eyes snapped from the clock on the far shelf back to hers.

"One quarter of the account?" His face held disbelief. "M'lady, I don't know if the bank can ready that much cash with such short notice." He rose and collected an assortment of documents from various shelves, then sat again at the desk. "Usually one contacts us a few days in advance with a request of this nature."

Samantha kept her face void of expression. Judging from Sedgewinn's reactions, the account was even bigger than she had thought. "Please don't distress yourself, sir." She smiled sweetly, leaning toward the flustered clerk. "If you can advance me but fifty pounds now, I shall be most content to return in a few days to collect the remainder."

"As you wish, Lady Chesterfield." Awkwardly, he shuffled the scattered papers over the desk, then he began to cipher with amazing speed, glancing at the clock all the while.

Samantha's uneasiness grew. Sedgewinn's words and actions did not go together. Glancing at his papers, she realized he was working a random pattern of numbers. Did he think she could not read figures? The clock struck, and Sedgewinn nearly jumped from his chair. Clumsily, he adjusted the stock at his neck.

"Ah, I pray you will excuse me for a moment, Lady Chesterfield. I shall return with your money shortly."

As he closed the door behind him, Samantha turned back to the papers he had scattered on the desk and sorted through them. Not a one mentioned her account. The tension that had been lurking at the base of her neck shot out in all directions. Danger was near; she had to leave. Rising quickly from her chair, she cursed her cumbersome petticoats as she made her way around the desk to the small window. Voices sounded in the outer hallway and her fingers struggled to undo the catch. But the window faced the back alleyway behind the bank and had not been opened in years. The catch refused to budge. Reaching for a heavy candlestick to break the glass, Samantha spun about as the door behind her swung open.

"Dear God in heaven . . ." she gasped. Her heart pounded furiously within her chest and her knees threatened to buckle. "Edward."

"My, my . . ." Edward Chesterfield stepped into the tiny office. "If it isn't little Samantha, and all grown up. Isn't she a beauty, Sedgewinn?"

Sedgewinn nervously bobbed up and down. "I did do as you asked, sir. The minute I heard her name, I sent for you straightaway." Sedgewinn eyed his massive companion expectantly. "I will get my reward now, won't I, sir?"

Samantha's eyes held those of her uncle, and in that split second, she knew that he, too, was remembering that night of so long ago. When last they had faced each other he had been leaning over the dead body of her mother.

Samantha straightened. "Hello, Edward."

Edward ignored her and turned to the clerk hovering over his shoulder. "Did she sign the draft yet? Do you have the money?"

Sedgewinn's eyes grew round. "You said nothing of money, sir. Your instructions were only to send for you immediately if someone came to inquire about the account. She is the one you've been searching for, isn't she?"

Edward turned back toward his niece and a portentous smile traced his lips. "Aye, she's the one. Now write a draft, Sedgewinn, so the twit can sign it and we can be on our way."

"I'll not leave with you, Edward." Icy contempt filled Samantha's voice.

"Of course you shall, my dear," Edward mocked pleasantly. "You have no choice."

"Over my dead body."

Edward grunted impatiently as he eased his massive form onto a chair. "As you wish." The brass candlestick sailed through the room and connected with Edward's head with a heavy thud. Stunned, Edward slumped forward as Sedgewinn rushed to his aid.

Samantha turned toward the window, scooped up a heavy volume, smashed the glass, but got no farther. A large hand clamped cruelly on her arm and spun her sharply about.

Edward glared at her in hatred. Blood trickled from the wound high on his temple and his grip on her arm threatened to snap her bones. "That was a very foolish thing for you to do, Elizabeth," Edward's voice rumbled with anger.

"But, sir," Sedgewinn interrupted. "I thought you said that was Lady Samantha. The account's in her name only."

Edward's eyes never left his niece as he snapped his orders. "Get me that money now."

"I'll never sign, Edward," Samantha taunted, trying to ignore the growing numbness in her arm.

"Sir Edward," Sedgewinn whined. "I can't get the money."

Edward shoved his niece onto a chair and turned his fury toward the bank clerk. "What do you mean?"

"No one can draw from that account without Sir Radford's signature." Sedgewinn edged nervously toward the door. Despite Chesterfield's portly figure, he knew that beneath the rolls of flesh there lay a dangerous man. He had heard of his foul temper and did not want it to turn in his direction. Chesterfield could do what he wished with the girl, that was not his affair. But he needed to stay on his good side until he received his money. Sedgewinn cleared his throat uncertainly. "I will get my reward sir, won't I? I mean you did promise . . . At least I was of the understanding . . ."

Edward belched loudly and tugged at his waistcoat. The buttons strained at the abuse, and the stains from his lunch were obvious. The pounding in his temple increased. *My own private treasure*, he thought silently. He'd go back to the club with his pockets filled and this time they'd all sit up and take notice. How sweet it would be to have them grovel before him for favors. He stared down at his niece.

Even garbed in that hideous dress, she was more beautiful than he remembered. The tightening in his loins joined the throbbing in his head.

"Get Linstrom to sign the damn papers then," Edward snapped.

Sedgewinn continued to twist his hands together in distress. "But, sir, Sir Radford is on holiday for another three weeks."

"Then sign the damn papers yourself," Edward bellowed in rage.

"But, sir . . ." Sedgewinn's voice took on a pleading tone. "The board of directors would know that he hadn't signed the draft and I would lose my position. The only choice you have is to make an appointment for when Sir Radford returns."

Samantha lunged from her chair in a feeble attempt to reach the door, but Edward easily caught her skirts and hauled her back.

"Why do you insist on running away?" Grabbing her shoulders, he shook her like a rag doll, his face growing red with anger. "If you hadn't run from me before, I wouldn't have had to live all these years with creditors snapping at my heels. You're too selfish, Samantha," Edward hissed. "And it's going to stop. Sedgewinn . . ." Edward turned to the clerk. "Fetch my carriage and have it brought to the back entrance. My niece is feeling poorly and I don't wish to subject her to curious eyes."

Grateful for an excuse to leave the room, Sedgewinn hastily made his exit. Edward smiled as he spied a length of packing twine. But when he reached for Samantha's wrist, he felt her teeth sink into his hand. "Damn you," he swore. His other hand lashed out and caught her full across the face.

Stunned by Edward's blow, Samantha found herself no match for her uncle as he tied her arms tightly behind her. She gagged as he stuffed his handkerchief in her mouth, then pulled the thick veil over her face. Unwilling to grant him victory, her foot landed sharply against his shin. Edward grunted in pain and his grip on her arm tightened.

"Don't make me hurt you, Elizabeth," he warned darkly. "I don't ever want to have to hurt you again." Then he led her through the rear entrance of the bank and into the waiting carriage.

Sir Radford Linstrom paced the length of his office several times before finally taking his place. The rich mahogany finish of his desk had been well polished, and the crystal goblets that sat on the far corner sparkled in the morning light, casting rainbows of brilliance about the room. But he was not content. He had been gone just over a fortnight and had returned to find his schedule in shambles. He stared down at the deep stack of correspondence Sedgewinn had arranged for him and groaned when he noted the first of his many appointments. Edward Chesterfield.

With an irritated sigh, he pushed his spectacles into place on his thin nose and started to read. Maybe he could send Chesterfield a note to cancel the appointment. He removed his glasses. Taking a snowy handkerchief from his pocket, he began to polish the lenses. No, canceling would only provoke the man, and although it was unlikely, mayhap this time his claim would prove to be true.

The timid knock sounded a second time, and the door to his office inched open. "Sir Radford?" Sedgewinn wedged his lanky frame into the narrow opening.

"Dammit, man! I gave specific instructions that I was not to be disturbed."

Despite Sedgewinn's feeble protests, the door swung wide. "Then you must rant at me, sir," the intruder's eyes twinkled, "for when your clerk said that you were not receiving, I would not take no for an answer."

Linstrom rose from his chair. A broad smile covered his face for the first time that morning. "Alex, my boy, how good to see you."

"The Duke of Coverick," Sedgewinn announced to the ceiling.

Linstrom clasped Alex's hand in a firm grip of friendship, and glared at his clerk. "Be gone with you, and this time, see to it that I am not disturbed."

"Don't be cross with him, Sir Radford." Alex settled himself into one of the overstuffed chairs positioned before the desk. "I did give him a rather bad time in your outer office." Alex's hand rubbed absently over the costly leather armrest. "My patience is rather short these days."

Linstrom settled himself and gave a halfhearted smile in sympathy. "Then don't make the mistake that I did and take a holiday." He shook his head sadly. "Alice insisted that we go to Bath, said it would calm my nerves." He reached for the decanter on his desk and poured a small draught for each. "The trip itself was pleasant enough, but I have re-

159

turned to even bigger problems than when I left." He gestured helplessly to the stack of papers that covered his desk.

Alex stood. "Then I shan't keep you."

"Nonsense, my boy." Linstrom waved him back to his seat and offered the wine. "I fear you are to be the only bright moment in my day. Pray tell me that this is just a social call and that you have come to share your latest adventure with a feeble old man." He leaned forward and winked conspiratorially. "I hear that you actually met with Falcon's ghost."

Alex's smile faded. "Nay, that was not the case. But as you well know, 'tis often easier to believe a fantasy than the hard cold truth."

"But why the long face? You are a hero, my boy. All of London sings your praises."

Alex's scowl deepened. "That may be so, but the matter was not settled to my satisfaction."

"Will you sail again?"

Alex stared out the window before turning back to his host. "Nay, I think not. I have resigned my commission. I was thinking of retiring to Coverick."

Linstrom's smile faded. "Resigned your commission? Alex, my boy, do you have any idea what you are undertaking? Your uncle ran the estate to the ground before he died. It will take a fortune to make the necessary repairs. Have you even seen it recently?"

"Nay, I've not been back since the death of my grandfather. The day that dear Uncle William drove my family from their home." Alex was silent for several moments with his painful memories, then he straightened in his chair. "But with William's death, the estate is once again mine. It has come to my ears that life in the country is hard. I think the time is at hand to return home. Mayhap with the estate open and working again, all of us shall live a little easier."

Linstrom felt a strong sense of pride for the young man that sat before him. With his striking good looks and impeccably tailored clothing, Alex Cortland could turn the heads of any fashion circle. But no dandy was this. Alex would always be a man of principle.

"And what of your ships? Do you plan to make Truro your base port?"

"Nay . . ." Alex hesitated slightly. "I've sold most of my ships. I still have a missing piece of baggage to find, but when that is done, I will be finished with the sea." He thought back to the morning when he awoke in his cabin and found that Samantha had vanished, and again he cursed himself for a fool. His frustration had increased when his search for her had proven futile. He had hired ten men to search, but in three weeks not a trace of her could be found.

"It won't be easy, my boy, and as your banker, I must warn you that in my estimation it will take more than your current account to make the estate the showpiece it once was."

"'Tis not a showpiece I desire, Sir Radford, but a home. My memories as a child are happy, and Coverick Manor was my home."

"Ah, then you'll soon be acquiring a wife? Alice would like nothing better than to have you to introduce at her soirees."

Alex smiled, but held up his hand in protest. "Nay,

Sir Radford, do not push me to the altar yet. There is much I would do first."

"Bah! Always the wary bachelor fearful of the trap. You are a duke, my boy. 'Tis only fitting that you have a dynasty of sons to run your estate."

Alex's laughter rang deep and clear. "I'll leave the chore of populating London to James. I believe my brother already has a good start in that direction."

Linstrom smiled warmly. "'Tis hard to believe James has grown to manhood. I remember him as a little tyke at the parties your grandfather held. Why, Carolyn was just a babe at the time." Linstrom sighed, deep in thought. "What grand affairs they were. Why, Alice and I and half of London would travel clear to Cornwall to attend."

"Were those the same people who wouldn't even receive my mother when William cast my parents from the estate?"

Alex's quiet words pulled the banker from his pleasant memories. "Ah, my boy, society is like a woman . . . an extremely fickle creature. As to your uncle, William reaped his own reward. In the end he died a broken and bitter old man."

Angry voices sounded in the hallway, and Alex looked from the door to Sir Radford. "Are you expecting trouble?"

Linstrom rubbed his temples wearily. "That fool, Sedgewinn, granted Edward Chesterfield an appointment." Nervously Linstrom downed the remainder of his wine.

"If you don't wish to see the man, tell your clerk to cancel the appointment."

Linstrom rose and began to pace behind the desk.

162

"If only it was that easy lad. Chesterfield is a loud-mouthed buffoon. Still, he does have some claim on my time."

"You allow him to keep his accounts here?" Alex asked in surprise, for he, too, had heard of Chesterfield and his ways. It was common knowledge at the gaming tables that Chesterfield was always in debt, and Alex couldn't think of one who would willingly seek out the man's company.

Linstrom sat again. "Chesterfield banks with Pasco," he said quietly as he began to collect the papers on his desk. "But his family does have an account here, so I imagine that he is here to try to dupe me again."

Alex raised a brow in question. "How so?"

Linstrom leaned back in his chair. "Before Edward, the Chesterfield family was very well-to-do and much respected. There were two boys, Edward and Francis, twins, I believe. I came to know the family when my godchild became involved with Francis. Then to complicate matters, it seemed that Edward was also enamored of Elizabeth, and a terrible row ensued." Linstrom smiled sadly as the memories surged forth. "But my Elizabeth was a headstrong little thing, pretty as an angel but stubborn as they come. It mattered not that Francis was the younger, and as such would receive none of the titles of monies, for she was determined and much in love. Despite the family protest, the two wed.

"When their child was born, Elizabeth bloomed with a radiance like to take your breath away. But children cost money, and as you well know, love won't put bread on the table. I offered to help, but

Francis would have none of it and took to the sea to find his fortune. Poor Elizabeth was distraught. And when the news came of his death, for a fortnight Alice and I thought we might lose her, too." Linstrom heaved a deep sigh as he stared into the past. "But you know, my boy, I often wondered if the rumors of Francis's death were really true. Elizabeth's mourning suddenly passed, and although she never returned to the carefree girl she once was, ofttimes she carried that glow that only Francis could bring to her eyes. Even Alice noticed it."

Alex smiled and politely refrained from suggesting that perhaps a lover and not memories of a dead husband had caused that certain glow. "But what does Chesterfield have to do with the story? Other than the fact that his brother died at sea?"

Linstrom pushed his glasses back onto his nose. "Before he left, Francis set up a fund for Elizabeth and the child. His instructions were most unusual, but I promised that I would see them not altered. Every year a sizeable amount was deposited in the account. The same messenger was never used, and even though Francis was dead, the money continued to come. I questioned Elizabeth, but she claimed to have no knowledge of the money's origin. She insisted that it was something that Francis must have arranged for the child and refused to touch it. She lived meagerly on the small stipend she received when her grandmother passed over."

"And now Chesterfield is trying to attach himself to the account?"

"Aye." Linstrom's eyes grew sad. "Almost twelve

years ago, there was a terrible tragedy. Thieves broke into Elizabeth's house in the middle of the night. She was killed and the child was abducted."

"Why have I not heard of this?" Alex questioned.

Linstrom tried to smile, but the sparkle was now completely gone from his face. "You were deep in family troubles of your own, my boy. In fact, I do believe you had already left for parts unknown to seek your own fortune."

"And the child?"

"I waited for weeks to be contacted for ransom, but the only one who ever inquired was Edward. Somehow he had learned about the account and decided he was the only rightful heir." Linstrom shook his head wearily. "When I explained that the money was in the child's name, the man flew into a rage. Now he bothers me every few years, claiming to have found his niece. He drags in some misbegotten wench and tries to pass her off to get the money."

"Then why do you bother to see him?" Alex questioned. "Why not send the fool on his way and not waste your time?"

Linstrom removed his glasses and tossed them on the desk. "I realize that after all these years my hopes are foolish, but I guess that in spite of the man's obnoxious ways, each time he appears, I hope that this time he will truly have Samantha."

Alex felt every muscle in his body snap to attention at the mention of the name. *Dare he hope?* He tried to piece together the scattered information. Could the child have been sold into slavery to the pirates?

"And how will you know if Edward is successful?"

he questioned carefully. "Surely after all these years you'll not recognize her. When last you saw her, she was a child. Now she'd be a woman grown."

Linstrom smiled. "As a babe, she had her mother's face but her father's sparkling blue eyes. In my heart I feel I will know her. That is why no matter how unpleasant, I . . ."

he questioned carefully. "But he after all these years
would not recognize her. When last you saw her, she

Chapter XI

Linstrom's words halted as the door to his office crashed open. Edward Chesterfield's massive frame filled the doorway, bringing both men to their feet.

"You can't go in there," Sedgewinn whined from the hallway. "Sir Radford is in conference with the duke."

"I don't give a damn," Edward billowed. "We have an appointment and I'll not be put off any longer."

Alex started to move forward, but Linstrom placed a hand on his arm and fixed Edward with his sternest scowl. "I beg your pardon, Sir Edward, but your appointment does not start for another quarter hour and I am not available to see you at this time. If it is inconvenient for you to wait, why don't you reschedule the appointment. I'm sure Sedgewinn will be most happy to oblige you."

Heedless of Alex's presence, Edward moved farther into the room. "Convenient? I'll tell you, sir, what would be convenient. Bankers should be available when they are needed. They shouldn't be gallivanting about the countryside on some frivolous holiday." Edward placed his hands on the desk and leaned toward the shocked banker. "If you had been here three weeks ago, sir, when I needed you, then I would not be here now to interrupt this ah . . . important meeting."

Alex glanced at Edward Chesterfield with complete disgust. The man hadn't even bothered to wipe the egg stains from the front of his shirt. But Alex's full attention centered on the small, veiled figure that moved unsteadily behind Chesterfield.

"Enough of your stalling," Edward bellowed, pounding his meaty fist on the desk. "In all this time you've been wasting, you could have signed the draft for my niece and been done with it!" Edward reached back and jerked his companion forward. "Tell the man you want your money."

Linstrom turned his attention to the girl. Cloaked in a nondescript gown, she was covered from head to shoulder by a thick gray veil.

"Well, come here, child, let me have a look at you." The girl hesitated, but Edward impatiently shoved her closer. Linstrom turned to Edward. "Stop scaring the child, man. Violence does your cause no good."

"Then be done with it." Edward reached down roughly and flipped the veil back.

Alex's hand tightened on the arm of his chair as Samantha's face was revealed. A strong sense of satisfaction surged through him, yet he suppressed the desire to stand and reach for her. He leaned back in his chair, biding his time for the moment that was sure to come. He watched as ever so slowly her eyes moved about the room, but when her gaze passed over him without the slightest recognition, he felt his muscles tighten. Her face was too pale. Her eyes held no sparkle. And she didn't know him. Alex shifted to view her better. She rested heavily against an armless chair, almost as if she had no strength to stand. He looked from Edward to Samantha's vacant gaze, and a feeling of dread began to take hold. Had she spent the last three weeks in Chesterfield's charge? God in heaven, what had the brute done to her?

Linstrom moved to view her closer. His face held total disbelief as he scrutinized the girl before him. "My God, Samantha," he gasped. "You're the very image of your mother."

"Now, if you're satisfied," Edward gloated, pushing himself between the two, "we would like the money from my niece's account."

Linstrom totally ignored Edward. Tears filled his eyes as he took her trembling hands. "Child, where have you been all these years? Half of London searched for you for weeks after your . . . after that terrible night. Were you abducted? Dear God, child, tell me you were safe." But Samantha remained silent.

"Enough of this trivia! It matters not, sir, where she's been, but that she's here now and wants her money." Edward pulled her from Linstrom's grasp and shoved her none too gently onto the chair. "Now see to it."

Sir Radford drew himself erect and gave Edward a cold stare. "Very well, sir." He moved back behind his desk and cast a fleeting glance in Alex's direction. But Alex had eyes only for the girl. "Sir Edward . . ." He gestured to a chair. "I'm afraid there is a slight

169

problem here." Alex watched the banker unlock a small drawer where he knew a pistol was kept. Edward's face took on an ominous look, but with the drawer now partially opened, Linstrom continued calmly. "It seems, sir, that when your brother set up the account, he was unsure of his daughter's ability to handle money. As a result, no cash monies may go to your niece directly. She will be extended a line of credit in any establishment in London, and when the bill is presented, it will be paid directly and in full by the bank."

"That's absurd!" Edward choked on his words. "As her only living male relative, the money should go to me . . . to see to her welfare, that is . . ."

"Please, Chesterfield, let me continue. Also you know, that after his marriage, your brother was not received by his family." The banker looked over the rim of his glasses at Edward. "That I believe was your doing. So to ensure that no member of his family would benefit from his gains, your brother left the bank as the sole executor over Samantha's money. So in short, Chesterfield, your niece may purchase a gown, nay a hundred gowns if she wishes and the bank will honor her credit. But should a debt for one glass of your port be brought forth, it will be dismissed without payment."

Samantha struggled to make sense of the banker's words. For three weeks Edward had kept her locked in the cellar. The single candle he had left had burned out after only the first day, leaving her in constant darkness. Food and water had been scarce, but Edward's abuse had been plentiful. The bright light in the office pained her eyes and her head throbbed. She had little energy to stand, let alone flee. But the realization that after all this time Edward could still not touch the money struck a chord of irony that would not be silenced, and her soft laughter bubbled forth.

"Shut up, slut. You knew this, didn't you?" Edward unleashed his anger at the world, and his thick backhand slammed against Samantha's face. The vicious blow sent her crashing into the wall, where she crumpled into a heap. Her veil tumbled to her feet revealing matted hair that spilled over her shoulders.

"Sir, have you no decency?" Linstrom was already moving to the girl's aid.

Edward would have risen to strike her again but for the viselike grip that clamped on his arm. Turning his anger to the fool who would dare touch him, he was stunned by the icy green eyes that held his own.

"I think not, Chesterfield." Edward did not miss the quiet threat behind the words. The Duke of Coverick had a temper that was legendary. Sweat began to cover his temple at the thought of that temper unleashed in his direction.

"Your Grace, ah . . . forgive me." Edward glared at Linstrom as he helped Samantha into a chair and tried to fan her with a volume from his desk. "Being responsible for the likes of my niece becomes very trying at times."

Alex watched her head roll limply against the back of the chair and suppressed the desire to plant his fist into Edward's face. Chesterfield would look to his life if he ever touched her again. But aside from the clenched fist at his side, he gave no outward sign of

171

his anger.

"Sir Edward, I do understand your plight. Sit and have a glass of port with me." Alex poured two glasses and handed one to Edward. The mere thought of Samantha under the same roof with the man was making his skin crawl. "I believe I might have the solution to your problem."

"And what would that be?" Edward queried suspiciously as he hastily downed the wine.

"What say you, sir, if I offered you a check from my own accounts to equal that which belongs to your niece?" Alex paused. If his hunch was right, Edward had no knowledge of Samantha's past life, for if he did, the man would be fool enough to try to turn her in, claiming her a pirate and demanding reward money. He watched the sweat trickle down Edward's face, and knew in that moment he would do whatever was required to get Samantha away.

"My check, Sir Edward, for the hand of your niece in marriage."

Edward coughed, and the port added another stain to the front of his shirt. "Done, sir, and you won't regret the decision for a minute! Did you hear, Sir Radford, the duke wants to wed Samantha. You're a witness." Edward grew almost frantic with the thought of all the money again within his reach. He would let no time pass lest Cortland change his mind, but what price to name? Sedgewinn had not told him how much was currently in the account.

"You do realize, sir, you're getting quite a bargain with my niece. Actually, I think that a payment of say five thousand pounds would compensate me for the loss."

172

Alex sat forward, and Edward withdrew, regretting his hasty words.

"I shall give you a check for ten thousand pounds this afternoon after the ceremony. Then you and I will never speak of money again, is that understood?"

"Yes, Your Grace, of course, Your Grace." Edward stuttered in delightful confusion. Ten thousand pounds, twice what he had asked for! Cortland must be going soft in the head to want a bag of bones like Samantha. Why, the best whore in London could be had for a few shillings.

"Alex . . . ?" Linstrom questioned hesitantly. "Do you know what you are doing, my boy? I would like nothing better than to see you wed to Elizabeth's child, but marriage is not something that one enters into lightly."

Samantha fought against the swirling darkness as Linstrom's worried face came into view. Her head rolled limply against the chair and her eyelids fluttered, then froze. She had escaped from one nightmare only to awake in another. For less than three feet away sat Alex Cortland. Her senses reeled in confusion. She had never seen Cortland in fine clothing before. The striking whiteness of his shirt and stock deepened the bronzed glow of his skin. His fawn-colored jacket accentuated the broad shoulders and well-muscled frame that lurked beneath. Memories of their last encounter brought a rosy hue to stain her cheeks and, as if reading her mind, Alex's rakish face broadened with a deep, knowing smile.

Alex watched her pain-filled eyes grow wide with disbelief. How frail she looked, but he remembered, too, the witch that lurked beneath the surface of that fragile exterior. A witch that had taken more cargo than he could afford to lose.

Samantha struggled to form her words. She could not let this madness continue any longer. "It matters not who agrees with who, Sir Radford, for I do not agree with anyone and I shall not marry." She struggled to give Alex a scathing glance. Their eyes locked, and she felt the silent challenge he sent forth.

"Yes, Sir Edward," Alex smiled. "I do believe that marriage to your niece will suit me nicely."

Samantha could not contain her outrage. "I'll rot in hell before I'll marry you, Cortland," she hissed.

"Then that's where you'll go until you decide otherwise." Edward's booming voice rattled the windows.

Samantha recognized the clouded look in Edward's eyes and struggled to rise from the chair to place it between herself and the bulky giant. But her flight was halted when she backed into a hard chest and two arms reached to encircle her.

"Enough, Chesterfield." Alex's voice was deadly quiet, halting Edward midstride. "I'm buying your niece for marriage and I have no use for a bruised package." Samantha struggled to move away, but Alex merely tightened his grip. "You arrange to bring Samantha here at four hours past noon. I shall see to the legal arrangements and license. When the ceremony is complete, Sir Radford will present you with my check. Now if you gentlemen will indulge me but for a moment."

Alex shifted and Samantha's eyes flew wide. Her feet left the floor and she was spun about, then deftly placed in a corner with Alex's solid frame blocking her view of the room. Her heart pounded wildly as she stared at the buttons on his waistcoat. The masculine scent of fresh soap filled her senses, making her all the more aware of her own unkempt state.

Alex raised her stubborn chin with his finger. Gently his knuckle traced the dull redness of Edward's blow. He read the odd mixture of determination and defiance in her eyes and knew that no matter what the stakes, she would thumb her nose at the very devil himself. But the sight of Edward's mark on her cheek made his blood run cold. Without warning, he pulled her firmly to his chest and placed a hard kiss against her lips.

"Stay out of trouble, love," he whispered against her mouth as his breath mingled with hers. "Even you should be able to manage that for a few hours."

Samantha fumed inwardly at his audacity and this public fondling. Did he think her fool enough to do his bidding? She gave him a humble smile.

But Alex only chuckled as he read her silent challenge. Then, surprising them both, he reached down and gently brushed his lips against hers. "I meant it when I said behave. I'll not have my property so sorely abused." His lips traced down her bruised cheek, and Samantha fought against the sensations he created. Her breath caught in her throat as the strength drained from her limbs. Why did she constantly forget how dangerous this man could be?

Alex turned and placed her gently in his vacant chair before addressing Edward.

"If you value your life, Chesterfield, you'll have

her here when the clock strikes four." Alex looked from uncle to niece. "See that she's cleaned up a bit and dressed for the occasion. That should be a detail that even you could manage." Alex looked pointedly at Chesterfield. "And keep in mind that I won't be interested in damaged property." With his last order, Alex gave Linstrom a quick nod and left the room.

Samantha stared after his retreating form. His words had cut deeper than any of Edward's blows. Did he really think she chose to be dirty? Didn't he know how she ached to scrub the grime from her flesh or to see her hair free from its knots and tangles. Tears threatened. Damn him! If Cortland thought she would sit meekly by, he was in for a rude awakening.

Taking a deep breath, she tried to gather her strength when she spied the opened drawer containing Sir Radford's pistol. "Sir Radford . . ." Her voice sounded weak even to her own ears as she rose unsteadily from her chair. "Might you open the window for a breath of fresh air?" She touched her temple. "I feel a bit faint."

The banker immediately turned to do her bidding, but Edward had followed Samantha's gaze and had spied the gun also. Despite his huge girth, he rounded the desk and slammed the drawer shut, narrowly missing her fingers in the process.

"Feeling a bit faint, are we now," he sneered, taking her by the arm and jerking her forward. "Then let me get you home, my precious. We have much to do in the next few hours." Edward spun her about and pulled her arm high against her back leaving her no choice but to walk with him or have the arm broken in the process.

"Do not hurt her, Sir Edward," Linstrom called worriedly after the retreating pair. "The duke will be most distressed . . ."

Edward pushed her down the narrow hallway. "I don't understand, Elizabeth." His words slurred against her ear. "Someone always wants to take you away from me."

A dreadful premonition filled her, and Samantha struggled to keep her wits. "Think of all the money, Edward. In just a few hours you will get ten thousand pounds."

Edward paused in the doorway while Sedgewinn scurried to fetch a carriage. "Francis thinks that he has tricked me again, Elizabeth." His breath was warm against her, yet a cold chill raced down her spine. "But I shall be the victor this time. I shall have you and the money, too." Edward's sharp laughter rang out, causing several passersby to turn and stare as he none too gently shoved her into the waiting carriage.

Samantha struggled to open her eyes. Total darkness again surrounded her, renewing the desperation she had fought for the last three weeks. Pushing against the damp floor, she tried to sit. A strange, pricking sensation was her only warning before excruciating pain covered her shoulders and back. Caught unawares, her cry broke the silence, sending her furry companions to scurry back into their corners. Her breath heaved in her chest and even the slightest movement sent hundreds of needlelike pains shooting through her. Her body collapsed, her cheek pressing against the cold, damp floor. Her tears ran freely.

Thrice since their visit to the bank, Edward had ventured down into the cellar to join her. Each visit had become more painfully terrifying than the last. Her strength was spent, and as her body trembled from the tears, the agony in her back intensified. She blinked against the darkness. How many hours had passed since? Was it even the same day? She struggled to overcome the pain. Somehow she had to get away. But how, when she hadn't the strength to stand?

"Curse." It was the merest whisper, but she stilled instantly. "What have you done to yourself, child?"

Samantha's heart quickened, but she resisted the urge to sit. She blinked against the blackness.

"Kabol?" Her voice was husky with pain. "Where are you?" she gasped. "I can't see you."

"Use your mind, child," he chided gently. "You may see me if you truly wish."

"I can't," she cried against the floor. "'Tis too dark." Her muffled sobs echoed faintly in the empty room.

"Then maybe you have learned at last."

"You sent me to this?" Her voice filled with disbelief.

"Nay, child, the path you are on is of your own choosing. I would have preferred something warmer. Have you found the sun?"

Samantha closed her eyes in frustration. "You

would ply me with riddles at a time like this?"

"How can you afford not to listen at a time like this?"

Properly rebuked, Samantha attempted to relax her tightened muscles. Her breathing slowed. With effort she did not know existed, she pushed the pain from her mind and he was there.

"I'm sorry," she whispered, closing her eyes and letting his image become clearer. "I have failed again."

Kabol shook his head. "There are times, my Curse, when I feel you could hold the universe in your hand. Then you become willful and all my teaching is for naught."

"You sent me to find the sun," she whispered. "Yet all I have found is darkness."

"Aye, a difficult lesson, and much of your own making. But do not chastise yourself too harshly, child, for often from the greatest trials come the greatest treasures. Look and you will see."

"See what?" She forced herself into a sitting position, and as the pain sliced through her, Kabol's image began to quiver and fade. "Don't leave me here," she cried desperately. "Don't leave me in this darkness."

The image grew stronger as she struggled to regain control.

"'Tis dark here because you are only the moon," he continued quietly. "If you run from the sun, then you in turn seek the darkness."

Her hand reached to touch her crystal necklace. "But I don't know what to do." Her voice trembled.

179

"I'm too weak to escape alone."

"This is true." Kabol's head nodded slowly. "Alone, without the warmth and life giving touch of the sun, a human will surely die. And this will happen if you insist on being apart from that which gives you life."

"I have looked," she offered weakly.

"Curse, even a child knows that to look at the sun with one's eyes brings great pain."

"Then how . . ."

"Use your heart, Samantha." His voice was impatient. "Look with your heart. For if you don't, it will be your own stubbornness that kills you." His image began to fade, and Samantha felt the pain return a thousandfold. *I am going mad,* she thought just before the darkness claimed her.

Samantha soared high above the trees, the fresh air a welcome treasure against her face. The darkness was gone and clouds wrapped her in a cloak of warmth. Peering over the cloud's edge, she watched the mortals scurry like ants on the ground beneath her. She could see Cortland and her uncle. Pain threatened anew with the sound of their angry words so she looked quickly away. Straining her eyes against the brightness, she watched in fascination as hundreds of candles burned before her. The flames danced hypnotically, and out of their motion two golden snakes appeared. Their bodies glowed and shimmered in the flickering light as they moved before her. Slowly they rose from the velvet pillow on which they danced to coil themselves about her fingers. Samantha lifted her hand to better view the apparition, but pain sliced through the cloudy haze that surrounded her. The sound of her cry jolted her into awareness as her hands reached out to hit something solid.

"Easy, love," a voice crooned softly. "You're safe now, just rest easy."

Samantha blinked in confusion. She knew that voice. Her eyes focused to find Alex Cortland directly before her, her hands resting lightly against his chest.

"Samantha, look at me."

She looked about to discover she was no longer in the cellar. Candles burned, and the light brought pain to her eyes. She could see several people nearby, but her mind refused to function.

"Samantha, look at me." Her eyes raised to his quiet command. The strength of his voice flowed through her, and her eyes filled with tears of gratitude. His finger brushed gently against her trembling lips. "Will you trust me, love?"

Samantha nodded with a jerky movement, but his silence demanded more. Her tongue felt thick in her mouth as she struggled to form the words. "I will . . ."

Alex silenced the remainder of her words by brushing his lips against hers. She felt his power. Relief was almost tangible as she clutched his hand tightly. It was her lifeline and she refused to let it go. He would help her to escape from Edward. For the first time in weeks she felt a flicker of hope on the horizon. Voices droned on making little sense. Her back was on fire again and it hurt when they made her move, but still she clung to his hand. Her eyes grew heavy as the exhaustion of the past few weeks flowed over her.

She was floating again. But it was not the slime of the cellar that claimed her; this time her cheek rested against something warm and soft. She whimpered as the pressure on her back increased.

"Sleep, love. I'll keep the watch." The voice was gentle but firm, and Samantha obeyed, sinking into an exhausted slumber.

The carriage rocked as it wielded its way down the narrow London streets. Alex held his slight burden high against his chest and tried to still the rage that consumed him. She had been drugged. He'd wondered at first what reasoning—nay, what threats Edward had used to make her so docile. But when she allowed him to hold her close without murmur or protest, he had realized something was amiss. He saw the vagueness of her eyes, the confusion that etched her brow. His arms tightened about her and she moaned softly in her sleep. His need to get her away from London had barely won out over beating Edward senseless. And now that they were safely on their way to Coverick, the need to do Edward bodily harm burned like acid in his stomach. Gently Alex leaned forward, lowered her onto the plush velvet seat, and wondered if she would remember any of the ceremony when she woke. He placed her limp hands on her stomach and smiled at the sight of his family rings coiled about her fingers. Now she belonged to him. Tenderly he tucked the carriage blanket securely about her, his hand pausing to smooth a tangled lock of hair behind her ear. Her face still carried the shadow of Edward's blow from that morning and Alex felt his stomach tighten. He signaled the driver and instantly the carriage slowed. Mayhap if he rode outside for a space the air would clear some of his anger. Alex watched the sleeping form of his wife as the carriage drew to a halt. He would get her to Coverick, and then he would see to dear Uncle Edward.

several boxes, then settled himself at the desk before
her, his chest at the drawer that covered the surface and

Se...umably as...uncomfortably...on...
Cortland...asked as...as our ple...to say...

Chapter XII

Samantha clutched the window strap and tried to brace herself as the carriage bumped and swayed on its journey. The drugs Edward had forced upon her had worn away leaving her mouth full of cotton wool, her head aching, and her back ablaze with pain. Wearily, she rested her head against the thick leather strap as she tried to piece together the missing hours. She had no memory of donning the fine gown she now wore, but beneath it she could still feel the filth from the cellar. And the thought of Edward dressing her, touching her, made her stomach turn. Fighting back the bile that rose in her throat, she tried to search her mind for answers, but the images stayed as hazy shadows.

She remembered candles, hundreds of flickering lights . . . and Cortland smiling down at her. Had they wed? Was she now his wife as well as his prisoner? Her head grew dizzy from the thought. Her only certainty was the rings she now wore. Two golden snakes, one on each hand, coiled about her fingers.

The slowing of the carriage brought hope that the nightmare was at last coming to an end. With fumbling efforts, Samantha tried to untangle her wrist from the strap. The door swung wide and Alex deftly climbed inside, then relaxed on the opposite seat. Even before the door was latched, the carriage was moving again.

"Are we not there yet?" Her voice was laced with impatience.

"Nay, love." Alex chuckled at the futility of her efforts to keep from touching him. "Had I but known m'lady would be so anxious for her marriage bed, I would have made different arrangements." Even in the carriage's shadowy interior, he could see the color that stained her cheeks. Alex smiled, then reached over to light the small lantern so he could better view his new acquisition. She had cost him a fortune, but now she was his.

"How much longer?" Samantha gritted her teeth as a vicious bump rocked the carriage. *Cocky swain,* she cursed silently, noting the costly fabric of his coat and the fine cut of his breeches.

"'Twill be hours yet, love," he replied easily, thinking anger the source of her obvious discomfort. "Why not sit back and enjoy the journey with your new husband?"

"I am most comfortable this way," she hissed angrily. "Surely you do not mean to dictate as to how I may sit?"

Alex removed his coat and settled himself more comfortably as he unbuttoned his waistcoat. Her moods were as changing as the quicksilver in the necklace she wore. His eyes followed the silver chain about her neck until it dropped from sight behind the sprig of lace that covered her bosom, and his imagination had no difficulty in calling forth a memory that brought a smile to play about his mouth.

Samantha fidgeted on the edge of her seat. It had been agony before, but the added strain of his eyes undressing her made the ride pure torture. She thought of their last night together on his ship and her stomach churned in protest. Sweat gathered on her brow and her defenses began to crumble.

"Stop staring at me!" The harsh sound of her words was startling even to her, as her voice broke the silence.

Alex smiled. The drugs had definitely worn off and he wondered how long it would take for her true colors to show through. "My, my," he drawled slowly. "It does seem that I have married a shrew." Again his eyes raked slowly over her. "But not to worry. A few nights without her supper will cure that waspish tongue and see her eating out of my hand."

Samantha's life on the sea had granted her knowledge in many areas, and the string of phrases she lay on his head tinged the air with its bite.

Alex's smile faded and a coldness invaded his features. "So the witch is no longer hiding behind a cloak of demure gentility. So be it. But let there be no mistake, madam, you have taken from me, and on more than one occasion. You owe me a debt that I intend to see paid. You are my wife and there will be no mistake as to who your new master is."

Alex leaned forward and easily untangled her fingers from the strap. Pulling her onto his lap, he ignored her gasping protest, crushing her to his chest, and covered her lips with his own. Feeling her body go limp, he raised his head in confusion. Samantha lay in a dead faint across his lap. Thinking it some plot or trick, Alex shook her gently, but her head only rolled back limply over his arm. In the flickering light he watched her closely. He was concerned, but not alarmed. His experience had taught that women often had the vapors whenever it was convenient to their cause. She would soon learn that she'd not be rid of him that easily.

Alex tucked her head into the crook of his arm and settled her more firmly on his lap. "There are certain times, m'lady, when I shall dictate my will and you shall obey." He spoke softly to the limp form he held. "I am master of all I possess, and say you yea or nay on the matter, the fact is that I possess you." She moaned slightly and Alex pushed the stray hairs from her face, noting with displeasure that her facepaint now covered his glove. "This shall be your first lesson, love." He pulled off his glove and searched for his handkerchief. "No wife of a Cortland ever needed facepaint to ensure her beauty and you are no exception. You'll not wear this again." Gently he wiped the cloth over her skin.

Alex's hand began to tremble as the paint rubbed away. Deep circles ringed each eye and her left cheek was several shades of blue. A surging rage swept through him as he pictured Edward striking her in Linstrom's office. Damn, he'd been a fool to leave her with that madman for even those few more hours. His face hardened to an unreadable mask as he studied her. Even bruised, her beauty tugged at something deep within him. Gently Alex touched her swollen cheek, but his stomach knotted with fear. She was burning with fever, and with the blush of her anger gone, her skin was whiter than parchment.

Alex shifted her again to lie on the seat before him and roughly banged his staff against the carriage roof. The light from the sun was all but gone, and Coverick was still two days away. With a final glance to her unconscious form, Alex made his decision and left the carriage.

Samantha awoke to find herself again alone. The carriage moved at a breathtaking pace and she struggled to push herself into a more tolerable sitting position. The lantern burned dimly and its uneven sway from the rough roads turned the carriage into a well-decorated torture chamber.

"You must be gone from here," her mind cried in rhythm to the creaking wheels. "You must be gone." She pushed aside the window curtains, letting the cool night breeze bathe her warm face and dust the clouds from her mind. It seemed impossible to think. Only two things seemed real; the need to escape from Cortland, and the consuming pain in her back.

The carriage slowed and Alex was at the door the instant it drew to a halt. Relieved to find her conscious, he frowned as he pried her frozen fingers from the strap. "Sitting before an open window with a fever, my lady, is a very foolish thing to do. I have paid too much money for you to become a widower before the match is even consummated. Now can you walk, or shall I carry you?"

"Play your games with someone else, Cortland," she snapped in irritation. "I'll gladly step aside while you find some complying kitchen wench to cool your rutting needs. Now, unless you wish me to spend the night in the carriage, please move from the door." Seeing his frown deepen, she smiled sweetly. "That is what you wish, is it not, my lord?" Alex stepped back but was there to steady her as she stumbled. She tried to move away, but his sharp grip on her elbow halted all motion.

"Tread carefully, Samantha," he warned quietly. "In private I tolerate and am often amused by your foolishness, but this is my sister's home and I'll not have her upset by your rudeness. One wrong word and you'll find my wrath heavy on your shoulders. Do I make myself plain?"

Despite shoulders that were already aching, Samantha turned with her own retort, but her words never came forth as she viewed the hard coldness of his features. Her bravado fled and her strength faltered. She nodded slowly to his icy stare.

"Good, then let us go in, dear wife." Gripping her arm, they moved toward the tall entrance way.

Samantha's eyes grew wide as they entered a lavish hallway. Heavy tapestries hung from the walls, and bowls of autumn flowers adorned the tables. A massive chandelier sparkled in the candlelight and the beauty of it all left her breathless.

"Alex, oh Alex, 'tis so good to see you!"

Samantha turned to watch a tall, slender woman with dark flowing curls catch up her skirt then fly down the ornate staircase. Her soft pink gown had a wide scooping neckline that revealed the ivory whiteness of her skin. Samantha stiffened with anger. He had done this to her on purpose. Brought

190

her to meet his family without giving a thought to her feelings. She shuddered thinking of the filth that lay beneath her gown. Looking down, she realized that she had let her own skirt drag when they had left the carriage and now the hem of her gown was stained and as dirty as she felt. Even the travel cloak that Edward had thrown over her shoulders was threadbare and worn. She watched Alex with his impeccably tailored clothes greet his sister. He would pay for humiliating her this way. She would see to it.

"Terrance will be so sorry he missed you. He's off for a fortnight of gaming at the lodge. When did you leave London? Does James know of your plans? He never mentioned your visit to me. You will stay until Terrance returns, won't you? Oh, Alex, the children will be so pleased. Are you hungry? Would you like a meal?"

Alex caught his sister in a warm hug to stop her endless chatter. "Carolyn, hush," he chuckled. "You never change. Now you will ask one question at a time and then," he paused, laying his finger to her impatient lips, "you will wait until I have answered it."

Carolyn smiled and nipped playfully at his still-extended finger. "In the house barely a minute and already you scold. Really, Alex, 'tis you who never changes." Reaching up, she placed an affectionate kiss on his cheek. Alex returned the gesture, then turned toward Samantha. His eyes grew cold with silent warning as he took her arm and stiffly drew her to his side.

"Carolyn, I'd like you to meet Samantha. Samantha, this is my sister, Carolyn Treadwick."

191

Carolyn looked at the mismatched pair in confusion. The young woman was pretty enough, but with those clothes and her dirt smudged face she certainly wasn't her brother's mistress. And she looked too proud to be a newly acquired servant.

"Samantha and I were married this afternoon," Alex replied to the unasked question.

Carolyn's eyes grew wide with shock. "I don't believe you." She looked at the dark circles beneath Samantha's eyes and the battered clothing she wore. "Alex, what are you thinking of? I thought you were to be engaged to Julia. You know she comes from one of London's finest families."

"Carolyn, your snobbishness is showing and it does not become you."

There was nothing subtle in Alex's rebuke, and as Carolyn's cheeks grew rosy, Samantha almost felt sorry for her. Their eyes met, and Carolyn suddenly realized how insensitive her words had been. "That was foolish and crude of me," she said quietly. "I hope you can forgive me and accept my welcome to the family."

Samantha felt the genuine sincerity and managed a smile. "I've never had a sister before." Her voice was strained with fatigue. "I look forward to the experience with great anticipation."

"Carolyn . . ." Alex's voice drew the attention of both. "We were on our way to Coverick, but Samantha is exhausted. I didn't think you would mind if we stayed the night and then continued the journey tomorrow when she is rested."

Carolyn's smile returned to light her face with pleasure. "Of course you must stay, and for as long as

192

you desire. Alex, you go to the dining room. Jenkins will see to your dinner." Dismissing her brother with a wave of her hand, she turned her full attention to her new sister. Firmly she took Samantha's arm and led her across the hallway. "Don't fret now. You'll feel better after a hot bath. I'll have a tray sent up and we'll have you tucked in a soft bed before the hour has passed. Although knowing my brother," Carolyn chuckled, "I doubt you'll get much sleep tonight."

Samantha stumbled and Carolyn quickly caught her arm to lend a hand. Panic covered Samantha's face, and Carolyn instantly regretted her choice of words. "Samantha?" Carolyn's voice was filled with concern.

"'Tis nothing, I am but fatigued from the journey." Samantha's gaze rose to the top of the winding staircase and she wondered how she would ever manage.

"I think my brother is an insensitive brute to have carted you all the way from London without so much as a thought to your welfare. Can you make it or shall I call him? The least he could do is to carry you gallantly up the stairs." Carolyn turned, but Samantha gripped her arm in panic.

"Please . . . please don't call him."

Carolyn saw the threatening tears. It was obvious that Samantha was terrified of her brother, but why? "Very well then, you know what is best." Slowly the two made their way to the top of the staircase and Carolyn led Samantha down a long hallway. Opening one of the doors, she directed Samantha into a spacious room where a fire already burned brightly.

"This is Alex's room whenever he comes to visit," she explained. "The minute my servants see his carriage approach, they race to make all ready for him. The way they scurry to do his bidding, you would think that this was his house, not mine."

Samantha listened and noted that although her words complained, Carolyn seemed very pleased with the situation.

"The boys shall fetch water for your bath shortly." Even as she spoke, there was a gentle tap on the door. Two servants placed a large brass tub before the fire and moved the screens into position to trap the heat.

Carolyn poured some water into a china basin near the bed and handed Samantha a small cloth. "It will take them several trips to fill the tub," she explained.

To Samantha the chance to wash the grime from her face and hands was a gift to be cherished, and with great care she wet the cloth and pressed it to her face again and again. Yet now that her face was clean, the desire for a bath was even stronger.

Carolyn turned back from fluffing the pillows on the bed and gasped in horror. "My God, I thought it was just dirt . . . Your face . . . what happened?"

Samantha raised trembling fingers to her sore cheek and winced. "I ah . . . fell, Carolyn, nothing more."

"That is not from a fall." Carolyn touched Samantha's chin and turned her face toward the firelight. "Someone hit you, and I want to know who."

Samantha smiled at Carolyn's indignation. Now she could see the strong resemblance between Alex and his sister. But thoughts of Alex drove the smile from her face. "It will do no good to speak of it,

Carolyn. Please let the matter rest. I fell."

Carolyn huffed and nodded, then busied herself about the room. But her jerky movements clearly showed she did not believe one word of the story.

Samantha was grateful for her silence. When the tub was filled and steaming and the servants had withdrawn, she reached back to unhook her gown. Her muscles screamed, her stomach flipped, and sweat ran freely from her face. Swaying, she grabbed the back of a chair to steady herself.

"Here, let me help you. 'Tis so awkward with back hooks . . ." Carolyn gasped in horror. "Oh, my God." The few hooks that had pulled open revealed Samantha's back and shoulders bruised and raw from Edward's abuse. Where the blood had dried, the fabric was now stuck fast. There would be no way to remove the gown without ripping the wounds anew. "You've been beaten . . ." Carolyn's voice filled with horror.

Samantha fought back her tears. "Just help me, Carolyn, please." But through watery eyes, she saw Carolyn backing toward the door, her hand clamped to her mouth in total revulsion.

"I can't." Carolyn shook her head in despair. "The sight of blood . . . I'll get Alex. He'll know what to do."

"Nay!" Her agonized cry stilled Carolyn mid-stride. "Please, no, don't let him see me now. I couldn't bear it. I can do it myself and everything will be all right." With great effort, Samantha reached behind and gave the gown a hearty tug. Pain increased a hundredfold, and despite her resolve, she cried out as blackness swirled about her. Something warm and sticky ran down her back and her heart pounded like a drum in her ears.

Carolyn could watch no more, and with a strangled cry she reached for the door just as Alex opened it to step inside.

Alex saw Carolyn's distress as she crumpled onto a chair and sobbed in incoherent phrases. Angrily he turned toward his wife.

"What did you say to upset her like this?"

The cold fury of his words left her numb, but as he approached, Samantha cringed back with a fear she could no longer control.

"I warned you, Samantha. Now you shall pay for this little escapade." The flat, emotionless voice was her undoing. Whatever he intended, she knew she could endure no more.

"Please . . ." she begged, "don't hurt me." Her voice was the barest whisper, then she crumpled at his feet.

Bending to reach her, Alex froze. "Sweet God in heaven," he swore silently. The gaping gown revealed long streaks of broken skin and badly bruised flesh. Where she had pulled the gown away, the wounds were open and bloody. Lifting her gently, Alex placed her on his bed.

"Alex?" Remembering his sister's aversion to the sight of blood, he was surprised to see her standing at the foot of the bed. "Who beat her? Why is she so afraid of you? You didn't . . . you didn't hurt her, did you?" Carolyn's eyes were full of horror as she stared at her brother.

Alex turned Carolyn toward the door as the memory of Samantha's faint in the carriage raked his conscience. "I've hurt her, yes, but I did not do this. My God, she didn't even tell me."

"Alex, how could you ride with her all the way from London and not know? You were hours in that carriage."

Alex did not need his sister's words to remind him. He thought of how she struggled to sit erect, and yet he had never even asked of her time with Edward. "Carolyn, the important thing now is to help her. Will you fetch ointment and bandages for me without a word to the servants?"

"I could call for the physician."

"Nay." His anger surged forth. "I'll not have some butcher look at her back and then bleed her more. 'Tis my responsibility. I will see to it."

Carolyn recognized her brother's determination and knew better than to argue. "I shall only be a moment."

Alex turned to the small figure on the bed. She was still unconscious as he leaned over and pushed the tangled hair from her face. *Just don't wake up,* he pleaded silently. He removed his jacket and waistcoat and tossed them negligently over a chair. Sitting on the bed beside her, he slowly rolled up the white sleeves of his shirt.

"I shall never forgive you, m'lady," he stated quietly, "for not telling me of this. Your silence has caused you hours of pain on a needless journey. You must take better care of my property in the future, madam, or you will vex me sorely."

Carolyn paused in the doorway. Her brother sat on the bedside and raw pain etched his features. In that instant, all her doubts brushed aside. Alex loved his wife. She watched her brother for a moment longer and wondered if he even realized it yet. Taking a deep breath, she entered the room and closed the door firmly behind her.

"I could do it, Alex," she said, trying to ignore the churning in her stomach.

Alex took the tray and set it on the nightstand. "You will help me more by keeping the servants from the room." Gently he steered her back toward the door. "Make up some absurd story about newlyweds and wedding trips." He tried to smile but failed.

Carolyn looked from the bed to her brother, and a new horror sprang to her mind. "Alex?" She couldn't voice the words, but her brother knew the question.

"I don't know, Carolyn. There is no telling what indignities have been done to her." Alex turned to his wife. "Now I must cause her more pain to see to the wounds. Already she burns with fever."

Carolyn placed a comforting hand on her brother's arm. "Have heart, Alex. You have her safe now, that is all that matters. And even in pain, she will know the difference between your hands and those who beat her."

Alex wondered if Carolyn would still believe her statement if she knew the whole story. "If you know any prayers, little one, now is the time to put them into practice."

Reaching up, Carolyn placed a fleeting kiss on her brother's cheek. "Call if you need me and God be with you both tonight." Needing no further encouragement, Carolyn fled and shut the door firmly behind her.

Samantha's faint whimper brought Alex quickly

to her side. Her eyes fluttered open as he sat beside her.

"Well, little love, you've really done it this time." His voice was soft as he stroked her hair from her face and neck with a cool cloth.

Samantha's senses fought within. This was Cortland. The man who had killed her father. The man who had destroyed her crew. Her hatred ran deep but his touch was surprisingly gentle, and he had saved her from Edward. Desperation made her ache for whatever comfort he would give. She wanted to protest as she heard the material of her skirt and petticoats rip, then he was gently pulling the fabric from beneath her.

"Alex . . ."

"Don't try to speak, love." Alex paused and took a steadying breath. "Samantha, I must clean your back or it will fester. Some of the gown is stuck so I will try to soak it off. I'm going to hurt you, but I know no other way."

Samantha closed her eyes in defeat. "You wanted me to pay for taking your ships," she whispered into the pillows. "This should bring you much pleasure."

The knuckles of his fist went white, and the muscle in his cheek ticked with anger. "Do not mistake me for the madman that is your uncle, my dear. Never have I willingly hurt a woman."

Samantha remembered their last night together and shuddered. "Then how is it that you succeeded where he failed?"

Not knowing how to answer, he began his task.

Three-quarters of an hour later, Alex stood and

straightened his back. His shirt was soaked and he badly needed a drink. In a trancelike state, he moved to the sidebar, poured a liberal draught, then downed it quickly. A second followed the first. With hands again steady, he moved back to the bed and sat down. Her muscles stiffened as the bed gave with his weight. Her tears had run freely during the ordeal, but never had she moved or uttered a sound.

"'Tis over, love, 'tis over." He wiped the sweat and tears from her face with a soft cloth.

"Alex?" The pain in her voice was evident as she struggled to maintain control.

"Be still, love, shut your eyes and try to sleep."

"Alex . . . please . . ."

Confused, he watched her struggle to remain conscious. Something troubled her more than the pain. Bending close, he touched his lips to her cheek.

"Tell me, love, for God's sake don't be so stubborn and let me help you." Her body shuddered and he felt her pain cut through him.

"Please . . . I'm so dirty . . . I can't stand it . . ."

Alex wanted to laugh with relief, but her distress was too real. Carefully he poured fresh water into the basin, then proceeded to wash every inch of her body until it glowed pink and fresh again. Washing her hair had proved more difficult, and he shifted her to lie on a dry spot on the bed. He offered laudanum and brandy, but she refused both, and after what she had endured, Alex had not the heart to force her further. Taking a comb, he sat on the bed and gently worked the tangles from her hair. Her hand inched its way across the mattress to touch his thigh and his motion stilled.

He reached down and their fingers meshed.

"Thank you," she whispered hoarsely.

Alex watched as she heaved a great sigh, then slipped into sleep. Their hands still locked, he looked down at the fingers intertwined with his and wondered why he was so reluctant to let them go.

Chapter XIII

Samantha sat propped against the pillows of their bed with the sheet pulled high over her bosom. For days Alex had allowed no one to enter their chambers and she had wanted to shout for joy when he had finally proclaimed their self-imposed exile at an end. But now that several young maids tittered about the room, she found her patience strained again. It had never occurred to her that in their ignorance of her illness, they would draw their own conclusions, and her cheeks grew red each time one of the girls cast a fleeting look in her direction. Their smothered giggles and knowing smiles added to her discomfort as they moved about their chores.

Alex entered from the dressing room wearing only his breeches and stockings. He carried a fresh white shirt in his hand and seemed oblivious to the hushed silence of the girls.

Samantha frowned in irritation as they stared at the wide expanse of her husband's chest and the swirls of dark hair that traced downward. His muscles rippled as he pulled the shirt on over his head, and when he went to tuck it into his tight breeches, she watched their eyes grow round with awe.

Alex smiled and opened the door wide to dictate their exit. They bumped, shuffled, and giggled behind their hands as they scurried to do his bidding. He shut the door shaking his head in amusement.

"Was it necessary to display yourself so?" Samantha snapped.

Alex only smiled. Joining her on the side of the bed, he reached for the breakfast tray and set it over her lap. "Are you hungry?" He picked up a slice of toast and spread it liberally with strawberry preserves. Samantha watched as the toast moved to his mouth where his white teeth took a hearty bite. She snapped her concentration back from the movement of his lips and tried to rekindle her annoyance.

"Doesn't it bother you, knowing what they must be thinking?"

Alex's smile deepened and his eyes twinkled. "Nay, love, I would expect nothing less."

His smug look sent her anger soaring but she held her tongue. She had made her plan, but until she could put it into action, she had vowed to play the part. She would do nothing to arouse his suspicions. She leaned back further into the pillows. The blazing pain in her back had finally gone and only a vague stiffness lingered as a reminder. Still, it would be at least another week before she would be strong enough to successfully venture out on her own. She would not be so foolish as to gamble away her chance for freedom by leaving before she could see it through. Taking a deep breath to strengthen her resolve, she reached for a slice of toast and smiled meekly at her husband.

Alex watched her with fascination and wondered if he knew another woman with her determination and defiance. Her forced smiles and compliant ways fooled him not one bit. His gaze fixed on her lips as she chewed her toast, and he remembered too well the taste of her. His stomach pulled into the knot that was becoming his constant companion. Deciding to prolong his torture, Alex passed her a bowl of cut fruit.

"When you've finished, I'll see to your back."

Her appetite gone, Samantha pushed the bowl aside. "'Tis fine. I'm sure there is no need for you to trouble yourself."

Alex rolled to his feet in a graceful move, taking the tray with him. "'Tis no trouble, sweet." He set the tray aside, and picking up a jar of salve, returned to the bed. "Roll over, love."

Samantha pulled the sheet tighter about her and glared. "I said I feel fine."

Looking not the least disturbed, Alex sat again on the bedside. "Forgive me if I do not take your word, m'lady. But I've learned recently that ofttimes where your health is concerned, you are not the best judge of what to do."

"And just what would you have me do, pray tell?"

Alex uncapped the jar of salve. "You should have told me what that monster had done to you. We would have gone directly to my townhouse and you would have not had to endure those endless hours in that blasted carriage."

Samantha's eyes grew dark with frustration. She hated him when he was right. "I concede on that point, Your Grace, and I do appreciate all that you have done for me, but from this time on I shall see the matter through myself."

Alex shook his head, and before she could realize his intentions, he pulled the sheet to her waist and flipped her over onto her stomach. The sheet rode low on her hips and Samantha struggled to reach back and grab it.

Alex's hand pressed firmly on the small of her back. "The time for maidenly blushes is long over, love." He tugged the sheet upward to her waist. "You seem to forget that there is not one inch of your skin that I have not seen or touched."

Her struggles stopped abruptly. Samantha stilled with her memories. Alex had heeded her plea and had washed the filth from her body. Her humiliation that he would see her thus had almost overridden the pain, and at that moment in time she felt more vulnerable than in all the days she had spent with Edward. Why, she wondered, did Cortland always do what she least expected.

"'Tis healing nicely." His voice was hard. She knew he hated her for the money and ships she had cost him, yet his hands were always gentle. "Does this still feel tender?" He touched a spot high on her shoulder.

"Nay." Her voice was muffled by the pillows.

"And here?" She shook her head. Alex shifted on the bed, and the sheet over her hips slipped lower. But Samantha found she no longer cared as his hands worked their magic. The heel of his hand rubbed down her spine and up again, and her last ounce of resistance vanished. She shivered when the tips of his fingers brushed the sides of her breast, but she had not the will to bid him cease. He kneaded the stiffness from the back of her neck and sent her soaring. She wondered how he knew when to caress, and when her muscles ached for a firmer touch. Despite her resolve to stay awake, she felt her eyelids grow heavy and her muscles grow limp.

Alex frowned as he watched the scars on her back and wondered again how she had ever endured the carriage ride. He thought of the time Julia had swooned when she had but pricked her finger on the thorn of a rose. His frown softened as he watched her relax into the pillows. He would have to take great care not to underestimate her determination when she made her bid for freedom. His hands glided up her spine and down her sides until he felt the last of her resistance melt away. What manner of woman was she? Knowing she was asleep, his touch softened and he enjoyed the satiny texture of her skin finding the smooth flesh on her inner arm a striking contrast to the callus that covered her palms. She was indeed a study in contradictions. But now, he smiled with satisfaction, she was his.

Pangs of hunger woke Samantha from a sound sleep as dusty shadows of evening began to fill the room. *Damn*, she swore silently. *Another day lost*. Determined to be out of bed, she started to rise, but found herself caught fast. Turning, she saw Alex. Clad only in breeches, he had joined her on the bed.

207

Now, in his sleep, he rested on much of her hair.

Propping herself on her elbow, Samantha gazed down at his sleeping form. For days now they had shared a bed, but he had made no move to press for the intimacies that she knew a husband could demand of his wife. Dare she hope that he no longer desired her in that way? She watched the steady rise and fall of his chest. Perhaps after seeing her body coated with the filth from Edward's cellar, she repulsed him. Or mayhap, like herself, he had found no pleasure in the intimacies they had shared that night on his ship. The warmth of his body beckoned as she shivered in the chilled room.

"You'll not trick me into liking you, Cortland," she whispered. "Just because you have a handsome face and a winning smile, don't flatter yourself into thinking that I'll not try to get away. For as God is my witness, as soon as the time is right, I shall leave you."

Alex stirred and stretched in the large bed. As his hand stretched out and found emptiness, he snapped fully awake. A quick search of the room confirmed his suspicions. She was gone.

"Damned twit," he swore softly. "She's too weak to run away. She'll kill herself this time." With quick, efficient movements, he pulled on his shirt and slipped into his shoes. Grabbing his waistcoat, he did up the buttons as he moved purposefully from the room.

Carolyn met him halfway down the hall, with tears of laughter sparkling in her eyes.

"Oh, Alex, wherever did you find her?" She caught her breath before she could continue. "What a treasure she is. Come, I was about to call for you. Dinner will be served shortly." Taking her brother's arm, Carolyn led Alex toward the family's salon. As they approached the doorway, the delightful laughter of children spilled forth. Alex tightened his fingers on Carolyn's arm.

Samantha, wearing a borrowed dressing robe of soft black velvet, sat before the fire gingerly holding the baby. Jonathan sat at her knee and little Jenny, three years his junior, sat on the other side. Absorbed in the story she was telling, Samantha missed the eyes that studied her. And as her tale drew to a close, the children again dissolved into fits of laughter.

"Tell us another, Aunt Samantha," Jonathan pleaded.

"That is all for tonight, children." Carolyn bustled into the room. "'Tis time for bed, and your aunt and uncle need their supper."

At the mention of her husband, Samantha looked up to find Alex leaning casually against the doorframe.

"Uncle Alex!" Jenny squealed in delight as she untangled her legs and scrambled toward her uncle.

Samantha steeled herself for Alex's rejection of the girl. But when he laughingly caught his niece and raised her to his shoulders, Samantha's eyes grew wide with amazement. He carried a true affection for the child. And the same could certainly be said of Jenny.

"I love you so much," she stated loudly, and to emphasize her feelings, her chubby arms gave Alex's neck a fierce squeeze. Alex responded by nuzzling her cheek until she squealed with delight.

Looking past his niece, Alex found Samantha, and the warm glow of pleasure that covered her face was almost his undoing. Catching her eye, he smiled, but she quickly looked away and began to fuss with the baby's blanket as a rosy hue touched her cheeks. Alex set Jenny down with a firm good-night kiss.

Jonathan presented his six-year-old form, and put his hand out politely. "Good night, Uncle Alex." Samantha hid a smile as Jonathan tried to imitate Alex's stern tone. Quite properly the two shook hands. Then to Jonathan's delight, he, too, surveyed the world from his uncle's level. "Uncle Alex," the boys said solemnly, resting his arm on his uncle's shoulder. "Aunt Samantha is the best present you have ever brought us. Jenny and I are most pleased. You are going to let us keep her, aren't you?"

Alex turned to see Samantha's face blush with surprise and pleasure at the boy's compliment.

"Never fear, Jon," he said quietly, giving his nephew a kiss on the cheek. "She pleases me, too, and I shall definitely keep her." Setting the boy down, Alex gave him a playful swat and Carolyn bustled the two from the room.

Samantha could not look up as Alex moved closer. From her place on the floor, his size seemed more intimidating than usual. Again she adjusted the blanket as the baby cooed and gurgled at her.

"You have certainly made a conquest," he said, choosing the chair nearest her. Looking down at his wife, Alex found himself mesmerized by her radiance. Her hair had been washed and pulled back simply, allowing the loose curls to tumble over her shoulders. The light of the fire gave her skin a creamy

210

glow. But from his chair behind her, Alex found the true meaning of torture. The low neckline of the borrowed gown gave his eyes easy access to the rise and fall of her breast. As she clutched the baby closer, he marveled at the picture she presented. Seeing her thus, it was hard to imagine that one as soft and gentle as she could command a ship of cutthroats.

"I've never held one before," she said suddenly. Samantha turned slightly, and Alex felt her lean against his leg. "A baby," she continued. "I've never held a baby before. He's so tiny." She smiled in wonder as the babe's flailing arms bumped her finger and his hand clutched fast.

"Well now, two down and one to go." Startled by the sound of Carolyn's voice, Samantha turned to find her sister-in-law standing directly before them.

Carolyn smiled. "You know, Samantha," she said slowly, "you look absolutely perfect sitting there. You should have several of your own. But then," Carolyn teased, "I'm very sure you and Alex have, ah . . . discussed the matter already. So let me pop this little one in the arms of Mrs. Burke and we shall eat. I don't know about you two, but I am famished."

Without the protection of the babe, Samantha felt suddenly very vulnerable with Alex sitting so close. She started to rise, but Alex leaned forward and pulled her onto his lap. Teasingly he tugged a lock of her hair.

"Tell me a story, Aunt Samantha." His eyes twinkled with mischief, and Samantha could not suppress a smile at his efforts. He was a devil when he chose to be persuasive.

"You would not like my stories," she responded

lightly. "For although the pirates often make terribly funny mistakes, they are never, ever caught."

Alex cocked a brow and his grip about her waist tightened slightly. "Never?"

"Never." Her look might have quelled a lesser man. "My stories always have happy endings."

Alex made no move to stop her as she slipped from his lap to stand before the fire. "They are lovely children," she said quietly, trying to steer the conversation to safer grounds. "They're quick and alert. You must be very proud of them."

"I shall be more pleased when my own come along." Alex's smile became more purposeful as he gazed into the blue eyes before him. "But then, with us for parents, I'm sure we'll have more hellions than babies."

Samantha's face colored at the intimacy of his words and her eyes grew round with surprise. "You plan for me to bear your children?"

"'Twould seem a fitting payment for all you have taken from me. Besides," he mocked gently, "you are my wife, m'lady. To whom else would I assign the task?"

Samantha felt a thrill surge through her. A baby of her own . . . just like the one she held. She stared wistfully into the fire. It would be soft and cuddly . . . with dark hair and sparkling eyes . . . But as she turned to Alex, the reality of his words found their mark. Her stomach tightened with fear. He still wanted her for his bed. Their eyes locked, and painfully the thoughts of babies died. She would lose her sanity if he tried to have her again.

The flames of the fire danced high, yet despite the

heat, she wrapped her arms about her, suddenly afraid of the night ahead. Her thumbs traced the golden snakes that encircled her fingers. She had dreamed of being married, and now she was. But her husband held no love in his heart, only revenge. The melancholy of it all settled about her shoulders with the comfort of a threadbare cloak.

Samantha was relieved when Carolyn excused them from the table, leaving the men to their port and cigars. Despite having slept for most of the day, her eyes were heavy and it took much effort just to move into the salon.

"Carolyn, please don't think me rude, but I must beg my leave. I seem to be more tired than I realized."

Carolyn smiled as she reached for her needlework. "You go ahead and have a good night's sleep."

"My idea exactly." The deep voice startled the women as Alex entered the room.

"Alex, I wish you wouldn't sneak up on people like that." Carolyn fanned herself in irritation. "You could startle a person to death."

"My apologies, madam." He gave a deep bow. "I only came to see to my wife's comforts." Alex presented his arm in a most courtly fashion. "M'lady, if I may assist you."

Samantha bade Carolyn good night and let Alex escort her into the hallway. She paused only a moment at the foot of the long staircase, but Alex felt her hesitation. Suddenly she was scooped into his arms.

"Put me down," she squealed, yet her arms looped behind his neck. "I'm too heavy, put me down."

"Hush, madam," he chided gently. His breath was

warm against her face, and Samantha became aware of the masculine scent of him. His arms encased her firmly and she allowed herself to relax. She only meant to rest her head on his shoulder for a moment, but once there, she had no strength or desire to raise it.

When Alex entered their room to lay her gently on the bed, Samantha was already asleep.

Samantha trembled as she walked slowly down the darkened hallway to the pinpoint of light that glowed at its end. Blinking, she found herself crouched behind the chair in the library. Her heart pounded within her chest, for now she truly understood the obscenity of her uncle's brutal actions toward her mother. Edward turned and glared in her direction and her heart froze. She looked down into her mothers lifeless eyes and hatred pounded through her veins. Edward's lips twisted into a snarl.

"You'll not leave me again, Elizabeth."

Samantha started to back away, but her foot caught something slippery and she landed hard on the damp floor. Stunned, she looked about with confusion. She was back in the cellar. Moldy slime clung to her legs and oozed through her fingers as she tried to scoot backward. Edward stood before her, his grotesque figure illuminated by a single candle. She watched in horror as his hands reached to his stock and he began to remove his clothing.

Alex awoke to feel Samantha's restless motions on the bed. Lighting a taper, he turned and found her entangled in the covers. Her head rocked from side to side and her smothered whimpers tore at his heart. He reached for her as she cried out his name, giving them both a start.

Alex cuddled her close and crooned nonsense into her ear to stop her violent trembling. "'Tis a dream, nothing more," he soothed. "You are safe."

But it was several moments before Samantha could give heed to his words and accept his comfort. She shivered, and Alex pulled her closer to the warmth of his body.

"Mayhap, it would help to tell me, love." Her trembling increased and Alex tightened his arms. "You seem to have forgotten, little one, that you are no longer alone. Now what devils pray upon your dreams to rob us both of sleep?"

Samantha hated for her weakness to be so visible. Reluctantly she tried to push herself from Alex's chest, but he would have none of it and his grip became unyielding. "'Tis nothing." But her voice held no conviction and to her complete mortification she began to cry.

Alex felt her hot tears on his chest and searched his mind for a way to comfort her. "Tell me, love," he coaxed gently.

Samantha felt the security of Alex's arms about her, and for the first time dared to bring forth the truth. "Edward killed my mother." Hearing her words aloud brought fresh tears to her eyes and, once started, she could not seem to stop them.

Alex wondered if she meant in her dream, or if her dream meant something more. He eased them both into a sitting position and leaned back on the pillows, keeping her firmly against him. Tugging

215

the blankets more securely about her shoulders, he urged her to go on. "Linstrom said that thieves broke into the house the night your mother died."

Samantha shook her head. "There were no thieves. Only Edward."

Alex tipped her chin up to better view her face. "You were but a child," he said gently. "Mayhap the horror of what you have just endured has mixed with memories of years past. Surely someone would have realized and Edward would have been accused if what you say is true."

Samantha jerked away from the haven of warmth that he offered. "I might have been a child," she sniffed, "but I watched." Her tears began anew and she huddled deeper within her misery. "I called not for help, I just stood there and watched as he raped her." Dragging the heels of her hands over her face, she tried to erase the evidence of her weakness. "Edward strangled her with the very pearls she was wearing." Her voice was weary, yet full of conviction. Without the warmth from Alex's body to stem the chill, Samantha shivered and pulled the blanket closer.

Silently, Alex rose from the bed and moved to stoke the fire. He added several logs and, within minutes, flames shot high, adding their brightness to the shadowy room. He was going to kill Chesterfield. He knew not how, or when, but he was going to see the man pay and pay dearly. He turned back toward Samantha and his heart turned over with sympathy. But a nagging fear had taken hold, and try as he might, he could not push it aside.

"Samantha . . ." His voice struggled for control, then he continued. "Did Edward rape you?"

216

Samantha watched the naked form of her husband as he moved before the fire. But the slight pleasure was snatched away with his words. The time with Edward was too recent to be ignored or forgotten, and she tugged at the hem of the sheet to wipe her tears. If she closed her eyes, she could still see the grotesque outline of his form as he stood over her . . . feel the weight of body as he rubbed himself against her . . . and smell the terrible stench of his sweat as he cried in frustration. Then came the pain. His riding crop sliced through the flesh of her back again and again.

"Samantha?" Alex's words pulled her from her thoughts, but she noted that he made no move to return to her. *So that was it,* she thought wearily, *the reason they had shared a bed but nothing more.* He thought she had lain with Edward. The very thought made her stomach churn and she wanted to throw back her head and laugh with the irony of it all. He didn't seem to care that she had stood by in silence and watched her mother die; he only cared that Edward might have used her.

Wearily, her head dropped forward and she turned it from side to side. "He tried to have me . . . several times." Her voice was filled with remembered pain as she lifted her eyes to his. "But he never succeeded."

Alex held her gaze as relief rushed through him, but he found no pleasure. He thought of the careless ease in which he had taken her. He had been so consumed with seeking his own pleasure that he had given not a thought to hers. And she had been a virgin. Never in his life had he shown a woman less consideration. He watched her shivering on the bed

217

and wondered if indeed she viewed him much better than her uncle. No wonder she shied away when he tried to hold her close. As a child she had witnessed her mother's rape, then he had all but raped her himself. Alex steeled his longings for her. She had suffered too much of late and it was time that he began to remedy the situation. She was his wife, but he would court her gently and the next time he made love to her she would burn with a passion that would exceed his own. Taking a deep breath, Alex returned to the bed.

She gave a token resistance when he reached for her, but when she realized that all he sought was his sleep, she relaxed against him. Settled firmly in the crook of his arm, Samantha tried to sort her feelings. But Alex's fingers trailed through her hair and the soft caress stilled her thinking.

"I shall deal with Edward in due course," he said suddenly, jerking her from her sleep. "Think on him no more."

"What will you do?" Alex felt her breath warm against his skin and cursed his own good intentions.

"'Tis not your concern." His voice grew cold as he tried to stem his desire for her. "But rest assured that Edward will never bother you again."

Satisfied that for the moment at least, Alex had no plans to demand his marital rights, Samantha let her body relax against his. Her eyes grew heavy, refusing to stay open. And secure in his arms, thoughts of Uncle Edward faded from her mind.

Chapter XIV

Delighting in the warmth of the autumn sun, Samantha sat on the balcony outside their room. Earlier that morning, she had discovered the Treadwicks' library, and now several volumes sat on the small table beside her. Reluctant to leave her story, she looked up as the doors behind her edged open.

"Your Grace, your trunks have finally arrived."

Samantha turned to find one of Carolyn's young maids timidly standing in the doorway. "My trunks?" she questioned.

The girl nodded. "His Grace has been most anxious as to their arrival. He sent his manservant Judd to inquire after them several days ago. Seems there was some confusion and the trunks were delivered to Coverick." The girl pulled a cloth from her apron pocket and carefully wiped the volumes that lay on the table. Samantha noted the way her fingers traced slowly over the tooled leather covers.

"What is your name?"

Hastily the maid set the book back on the table and

took a step backward. Her hands clasped before her and her eyes dropped to the floor. "Megan, Your Grace," her voice croaked in a whisper.

"Can you read, Megan?" Samantha watched the girl's eyes grow wide with surprise. She might have asked if the girl could climb a rigging and gotten the same response.

"Oh no, Your Grace."

"Would you like to learn?"

"Oh no, Your Grace," Megan gasped. "'Twould be most unseemly." She began to twist the cloth in her hands. "People would think I was trying to put on airs and then none of my friends would want to keep company with me. I just couldn't do that."

"Do what?" A deep voice questioned.

Megan cheeks turned a vivid red as Alex stepped onto the balcony. She bobbed in respect and her head dropped forward.

Samantha rose and touched Alex's arm, casting a fleeting glance in Megan's direction. "'Tis nothing." She smiled. "Just some conversation about womanly topics."

Alex cocked a brow. "And here I thought you would be busily sorting through the new gowns that you ordered." He smiled and directed her back into their rooms. "Those," he gestured toward the two smaller trunks, "contain your old gowns and need not be unpacked until we get to Coverick. But I did think that curiosity would demand you to check the other."

Samantha stared hard at her husband. She had no gowns old or new and she wondered at his actions. She watched as Megan unlatched the largest trunk.

Stunned by the beauty before her, Megan reached for the first gown. "Oooh, Your Grace, 'tis beautiful," she sighed, holding a satin gown of midnight blue. Crystal jets covered much of the neckline and sparkled like diamonds in the light.

Samantha watched the stack grow larger. Rich brocades, soft woolens, and brilliant satins of every hue covered the bed. "These must have cost a small fortune. Surely, one does not need so many." Reaching for a gown of rich burgundy velvet, she did not notice the sparkle leave her husband's eye.

"You find fault with the purchase, madam?" His voice was tight.

Samantha shook her head and gently set the gown back onto the bed. "Nay, m'lord. If you wish to spend your money in such a fashion, who am I to complain?"

Alex's mouth pulled into a thin line. He had expected her to be thrilled with the gift. After all, Julia always was. She would toss him a kiss and race to the mirror to admire her new acquisition. She'd preen and flirt, hinting for more. Of late he had begun to think that Julia's voracious appetite for life's finer things would never be sated. Now he had a wife who was reluctant to accept a handful of gowns. He watched as Samantha ran her finger down the burgundy velvet and pictured the soft fabric against her skin. He had placed the order with the clothier just hours before they had wed. And the sum to have them ready quickly had cost him dearly. He minded not the money but the lack of interest that Samantha displayed.

"We shall start with that one," Alex stated

abruptly. "I think the color will do well on you."

Samantha wondered at his game. She could hear the tension in his voice and although his words were pleasant, his eyes were cold. Why should he be angry, she thought irritably. She had not asked him to spend such a fortune on her clothing. "What do you mean, start with this one?" Warily she looked from the gown in her hand to her husband.

Alex leaned against the bedpost, crossing his arms over his chest. "Naturally, I shall wish to view you in each."

Samantha stiffened. "If you insist, sir." She gave him a mocking bow. "Pray take your leave, and I shall join you shortly."

A dangerous smile touched Alex's lips. "'Tis no need for all that travel to and from, m'lady," he mocked softly. He removed his coat and settled into a wing-backed chair. "I am quite content to stay right here for your convenience."

Their eyes locked in stubbornness and Samantha vowed not to be the first to look away. "Am I to have no privacy, sir?"

Alex hit his head with the palm of his hand. "Ah, 'tis privacy you wish." His eyes sparkled wickedly as he turned to the befuddled maid. "You must leave us now. My wife wishes us to be alone." The husky chuckle in his voice brought a rosy hue to Megan's cheeks as she scurried to the door, closing it firmly behind her.

Samantha's look could have chilled the sun, but Alex merely smiled and loosened the buttons of his waistcoat.

"Best begin now, love," he challenged softly. "I

mean to see you in each of those before the evening meal."

Samantha scowled and held her ground as Alex tossed a fluff of material in her direction.

"Here, love, start with this."

The shift was of the softest fabric she had ever felt, and tiny blue flowers embroidered its edges. Her fingers trailed over the delicate ribbons and bows, but as she slipped her hand inside to better view the quality of the work, her eyes grew wide in amazement.

"You can see right through this," she gasped.

Alex's smile broadened. "That is the general idea. Lovely, is it not?"

Samantha stiffened and returned his gaze. It would be a dry day in the ocean before she would parade before him like a strumpet selling her wares. "I won't wear that," she said firmly, laying the shift carefully on the bed. "I'm not a whore and I'll not dress like one."

Alex jerked as if she had slapped him. Angered that she thought he would insult her, he rose to his feet. He did not give gifts lightly and never had one been tossed back in his lap so neatly. The feeling did not suit him and his anger grew.

"If these clothes are not good enough for you, madam, then you shall wear nothing." In the blink of an eye he crossed the room and the dressing gown was torn from her body. Samantha tried to bend and gather the fabric to cover her nakedness, but Alex caught her shoulders and blocked her way. Warm color stained her cheeks as his sharp eyes raked over her.

223

"Since you seem reluctant, love . . ." His voice was tight with frustration. "I shall assist you." The new shift was dropped over her head and Alex deftly moved her arms through the proper slots. "I assure you, madam, this is not the first time I've helped a lady to dress." His implications were only too clear, and Samantha felt herself rooted to the spot as he nimbly fastened the ribbons. Finished, Alex stood back to survey his creation.

His mouth went dry and his heart pounded. The filmy veil covered her body yet was more alluring than bare flesh. Long, silken legs rose to the enticing curve of her hip, and the blush of her nipples against the sheer cloth begged for his kiss. His gaze moved to her face, and Alex felt his passion drain away.

Her skin had turned an ashen gray and her eyes held a glassy stare. She began to sway and, catching her shoulders, he felt the icy chill of her body.

"Samantha?" He gave her a gentle shake.

Samantha blinked several times and her eyes grew wild and frightened. In panic, she reached out to clutch desperately at his shirt. The carriage was moving faster now. She could feel the wind as it stung her face and clawed at her hair. Cries of terror filled her ears and still the horses ran faster. She tightened her grip on the reins and pulled back with all her might. The vision was gone as quickly as it had come, leaving her as always, light-headed and shaky. Her stomach churned and she gasped for breath.

"Samantha?" Alex's concern was her undoing. Turning, she wrenched from his grip and tried to flee. She had taken but two steps when his arms closed around her. "What are you doing?" he demanded, unwilling to show how shaken he was.

Samantha looked blindly about the room but found no corner of safety. When Alex turned her about to face him, the shelter of his arms beckoned her home. With a muffled cry, she pressed her body against his and tried to stop the trembling.

Alarmed at the icy coldness of her skin, Alex scooped her into his arms and moved to sit before the fire, tugging a quilt from the bed as he went.

"What happened, love," he questioned gently, wiping damp hair from her cheeks.

Samantha stared into the fire and wondered how long his arms would give comfort if he knew. She drew a deep breath. "I see things." Her voice was faint as she struggled for control.

"You have the sight?"

She nodded and waited for him to move away, but his arms tightened. "Then you have been blessed with a gift."

She wanted to laugh at his choice of words. "Many would call it a curse." She looked about with embarrassment and tried to rise from his lap. She was weary to her bones and desperately needed to sleep. But Alex would not release her and she had not the strength to fight him.

"When did this start?"

A strange calmness settled over her as she rested her head against his shoulder. "When I was a child," her words were no more than a whisper, "I thought everyone dreamed of things that would happen. My mother understood, but she died."

"Can you talk to me about it?"

She sighed and snuggled closer to his warmth. Alex obliged by pulling the quilt more securely about her. "Usually I can control it." Her voice grew strong and, encouraged, she went on. "But sometimes when I'm very angry or frightened, it appears when I'm not prepared. 'Tis always harder then." Her eyes began to grow heavy.

"But most times you can control it?" he questioned, already wondering if he had been the victim of her gift.

"Mmm," she murmured. "Kabol taught me to use the bones. 'Twas the only reason Falcon let me stay."

Alex held her close, relieved to feel the warmth easing back into her body. Had her gift been the key to Falcon's extraordinary success as a pirate? "But this time . . ." he pressed further. "What did you see?"

She rubbed her cheek against the softness of his shirt. "A carriage. I was driving a carriage and I couldn't make it stop." Her eyes closed, and the picture was there as she knew it would be. But now there were no cries of terror, no sense of danger.

"And these . . . visions, they always come to pass?"

Wearily she nodded against his chest.

Alex felt his muscles begin to relax. "Then I see no problem, love." Unable to resist, he kissed the top of her head. "I shall simply not allow you to drive my carriage."

Samantha gave a tired smile. He made it sound so

simple. Her eyes stayed closed and her breathing evened.

Alex continued to hold her long after he knew she slept. Her words played over and over in his mind. Was it possible? Could she really see into the days ahead? He shifted her more securely in his arms. There was more here than she was telling and, like it or not, he was going to have his answers.

Samantha reclined against the bank and watched the swans float majestically with the stream's light current. Nearby Jonathan and little Jenny frolicked with several ducks that had boldly ventured from the water in search of a handout. She watched the clouds drift lazily across the sky and silently shouted for joy. When Carolyn had first suggested the outing, she had accepted the idea with due course. But when she realized that Alex and Terrance would not be accompanying them, her excitement had increased tenfold. She glanced about the deserted mill and the crop of trees nearby as her fingers peeled the skin from an orange. It was indeed an excellent spot for a picnic.

Peter, their elderly driver, lay sleeping soundly against a rock near the horses. The sun reflected off his balding head and Samantha knew that he would prove no obstacle when the time was at hand. Fleetingly she regretted the choice she had to make. Carolyn had been nothing but kind and now she would surely receive the brunt of Alex's anger when he discovered her gone. Just that morning he had suggested that they would soon be leaving for Coverick. Samantha glanced again about the secluded glen and knew she would be a fool to not seize the opportunity fate had handed her so neatly. Reaching into the basket, she withdrew the fruit knife and carefully slipped it into the pocket of her gown.

Chapter XV

"They have not returned yet?"

Terrance strained to see farther down the torchlit drive. "Nay, and Carolyn specifically told Mrs. Burke that they would return for tea. That was hours ago."

"Fetch my horse." Alex's voice was sharp and Judd hurried to his task. Alex looked back at Terrance. "Why ever did you let them go off alone in the first place?"

"I was never consulted about the matter," he huffed. "And 'tis very unlike my Carolyn to venture out on her own. I do believe this outing must have been Samantha's idea."

Alex had already come to the same conclusion, and the muscle in his jaw began to twitch. He had assumed her safe when he had left that morning to purchase the horses. Angrily, Alex watched his brother-in-law pace. If only Terrance had mentioned that he, too, planned to be away. Alex's fist drew tighter. Samantha must have thought him a fool to have presented her with such a unique opportunity.

"Where do you think they have gone?"

Terrance shook his head. "I have no idea. I just can't believe Carolyn would go off and not tell me."

Alex tried to hold his temper in check. "She couldn't very well tell you if you weren't here." Both men turned as Judd rounded the corner with two saddled horses. Alex deftly mounted the high-spirited gray.

"At least give me an idea in which direction they might have gone. Does Carolyn have a favored spot on the estate that she likes to escape to?"

Terrance drew himself erect with indignation. "My Carolyn has never felt the need to escape. She is very content with her life here at Treadwick."

Alex clenched his jaw in frustration and wondered for the hundredth time what his sister saw in the pompous fool she had married. "Very well then." His words were curt. "You wait here and Judd and I shall search."

"Alex, wait," Terrance called, anxiously rubbing his hands against the coarse fabric of his trousers. "There is more that you should know."

Alex reined in his horse.

"I spoke to the magistrate today." Terrance turned and looked into the growing shadows. "There was another killing yesterday. Down by the old mill."

Alex stilled. "What do you mean, 'another killing'?"

Terrance shifted uncomfortably. "There have been three deaths already this month. Yesterday's makes the forth. The magistrate has no idea who the culprit might be, and all the villagers have been alerted." In the dancing light of the torches, Terrance's cheeks turned scarlet and his voice dropped to a whisper. "All four of the victims were young women, and the last two were violated before they were killed."

"Carolyn knew of this and still she went on an outing?" Alex's tone was incredulous as he held the gray steady.

Terrance began to pace. "Carolyn has no knowledge of the killings. I did not want to cause her worry."

Alex uttered a foul word and looked to the heavens for guidance. If he found them safe, he was going to come back and cheerfully strangle Terrance, brother-in-law or not.

They heard the sound before the shape of the carriage emerged from the darkening shadows. Entering the drive at a breathtaking speed, it careened out of control as it approached the manor house.

Alex felt his heart stop as he realized it was Samantha who held the reins. Her words from the day before echoed in his head. "I was driving a carriage and I couldn't stop it." A icy chill ran down his spine as he kicked his mount into action. Had she seen more and not told him? A million thoughts, each more horrible than the last raced through his mind as he reached the carriage and struggled to still the prancing team. The horses, lathered with sweat, snorted and blew as they reluctantly allowed Alex to guide the carriage to a halt.

Alex dismounted quickly as Samantha stumbled down from the driver's seat. Grabbing her shoulders, he turned her to face him. Even through the leather of his gloves he could feel the icy coldness of her flesh.

The sleeve of her gown was missing, she was covered with blood, and he could see the bluish tint of a bruise already forming on her cheek.

"What happened?" His eyes raced over her, searching for the wound. "Where are you hurt?"

Samantha shook her head. Her hair streaked out in all directions and her eyes were wide and haunted.

"Peter is in the back." Her voice trembled in horror. "The blood is his. I fear he is dead." Her stomach churned as she tried to stand on her own.

Terrance tugged the carriage door open and Jenny tumbled neatly into her father's arms. Her startled expression lasted only an instant before she erupted into an hysterical wail. Helplessly, Terrance turned to Alex.

Samantha raised her trembling hand to Alex's arm. "I'll fetch Mrs. Burke." Gathering the remnants of her strength, she stepped from his support and fled into the house.

Frustrated that the answers to his questions would have to wait, Alex reached for his sobbing niece. Terrance turned quickly to help Carolyn as she stumbled from the carriage. Bloodstains covered much of her gown. Her eyes were red and swollen with tears, but her skin was pale as death.

"Dear God, Carolyn." Terrance's voice trembled. "What ever has happened?"

Carolyn took one look at her husband's face and dissolved into tears again. Only young Jonathan seemed to have retained his wits, and he jumped lightly from the carriage to the step.

"You should have seen it, Uncle Alex," Jon exclaimed, glowing with excitement. "Aunt

Samantha threw the knife and got him square." Jonathan imitated the throw of the knife, and a swishing sound left his lips.

Momentarily stunned, Alex watched as Judd pulled Peter's body from the floor of the carriage.

"He's dead," Carolyn sobbed. "His blood is all over me. Oh, I wish I had never thought of the blasted outing to begin with. When I think of what almost happened." Again she buried her head on her husband's shoulder and sobbed. Jenny followed her mother's lead and her cries increased.

"He is dead, Your Grace." Judd straightened and looked to Alex. "But 'tis a gun that did him in, not a knife."

"'Twas fantastic, Father." Jonathan tugged on the edge of his father's dinner jacket. "You should have seen her. First this thug shoots Peter, then they dumped all our food onto the grass, even Mrs. White's cake. We didn't know what to do, but when one of them grabs Jenny, Aunt Samantha pulls a knife from her skirts, and swish she lets him have it."

Carolyn raised her tear-streaked face from her husband's shoulder. "Terrance, he was going to . . ." Carolyn could not control her shaking breath.

Jon impatiently waited for his mother to finish, and when it seemed she could not, he anxiously resumed his tale. "Then the big one gets really angry, Uncle Alex. He grabbed Aunt Samantha and slapped her till she fell down. Mother was crying, so I poked him with my stick, hard." Jon's chest puffed with pride. "He was gonna hit me, but Aunt Samantha rolled over and grabbed the dead man's gun. Pow, she got him neat as you please right in the head."

Alex turned to Carolyn. "Where did this happen," he demanded.

Carolyn swayed, but Alex pressed further. "Carolyn . . ." His voice was stern. "You must tell me where. Did anyone other than yourselves witness this?"

Her eyes were dazed as she fought for control. "We went to the pond near the old mill. The children like to watch the swans."

"And what of the bodies?"

Carolyn shuddered and pressed closer to her husband. "Samantha insisted that we bring Peter back with us. Dear God," she cried. "What will happen now?" She turned to Terrance. "Will the magistrate call? I couldn't bear having to tell this all again."

Alex swore soundly, silently agreeing with his sister. What he didn't need was an investigation that would involve Samantha and her past. Questions would surface about her abduction on the night of her mother's death, and until he had all the answers himself, Alex knew he was not willing to take a chance. Besides, there was no way under heaven he would ever be able to explain to the magistrate how a lady of genteel background had managed to throw a knife. His decision made, he turned to Terrance.

"You see to things here," he stated quietly. "Judd and I shall ride to the mill and take care of things on that end." His meaning was not lost, and Terrance gratefully nodded in agreement.

"Alex, there is a boarded-up well on the far side of the wood . . ." Terrance began. "It might be possible . . ."

Alex silenced him with a look and nodded toward Carolyn. "It will be taken care of." Again he mounted his steed, then paused. "See to Samantha for me until I return."

Three hours later, Terrance mopped his brow as he nervously paced in his study. Again and again his fingers threaded through his thinning hair. Alex had been gone for hours now. Surely the deed should not have taken so long. He downed his brandy and poured another. The click of the study door made him whirl about.

Alex entered, brushing the dust from his coat.

"Did you find them?" Terrance questioned, pouring Alex three fingers of brandy.

Alex nodded. "Right by the pond, as Jonathan said." He moved to warm himself before the fire. "The old well was an excellent idea." He toasted Terrance. "With the boards securely in place, none shall be the wiser. Did you speak with the servants?"

Terrance mopped his brow again and flopped back into a high-backed chair. "Aye. They're all completely devoted to Carolyn and shall say nothing. 'Tis the unfettered exuberance of my son that has me worried."

Alex sighed and finished his brandy. "I'll speak with the lad in the morning. Mayhap that will help. Are the ladies composed now?"

"Jenny fell asleep the moment her head hit the pillow; and even Jonathan dropped right off. But Carolyn is still distressed. I had to force her to take laudanum to calm herself."

Alex frowned, thinking Terrance's choice a bit severe. "And Samantha?"

Terrance stuttered with embarrassment. "I knocked at your door, but she would not bid me enter." As Alex's scowl darkened, Terrance rushed on. "I meant to go back, Alex, but there has been no time."

Alex rose, and with a withering glance to Terrance, grabbed the brandy bottle and left the room.

He felt his anger surge as he entered their chambers. No candles burned. The fire was dying and the balcony doors stood wide open. As his eyes grew accustomed to the dark, he saw her, a silver shadow that floated in and out of the moonlight that streamed into the room. Clad only in a light chemise, she silently paced the room. Like a trapped animal, oblivious to his presence, her restless motions never ceased. Fighting the urge to go to her, Alex closed the tall French doors and moved straight to the fire. A damp chill had filled the room and, as he stirred the coals back to life, he silently cursed Terrance for his ineptitude.

The flames in the hearth sprang to life, bathing the room in golden shadows. As their warmth began to grow, Alex turned to his wife. Even from a distance he could see the bruises on her arms and shoulders. Jonathan's story danced through his mind, and the terrified look in her eyes when she stumbled from the carriage was etched against his heart. Snatching a blanket from the bed, he shook it open to warm by the fire.

His touch on her shoulder stopped her pacing, but she stared straight ahead like one stricken of mind. Her flesh felt like ice as he wrapped her against the cold. Settling into a chair before the fire, he cradled her in his arms and offered her brandy. When she made no move to drink, Alex tilted her head and let some of the amber liquid trickle down her throat.

Samantha gasped as the fiery spirits burned through her haze. Her eyes watered and her breath caught in her throat. Alex took advantage of her confusion, and another mouthful was downed before she struggled to push the glass away. The fire in her stomach began to grow and, as the numbing cold faded, the pain returned.

"Did they hurt you, m'lady?" he questioned softly, hating the trembling that shook her body.

Samantha said nothing, then turned her tortured eyes to his. "I killed them."

Alex pulled her back to rest against his chest. "Would that I could have killed them myself for the evil thoughts they harbored."

Samantha shivered. "I've spent so much time learning to heal, and tonight I threw it all away."

Alex looked at her with confusion, and her eyes dropped with shame. "In all my years, I have never taken a life."

Alex hugged her tighter. Her shoulders were too slight to bear such a burden. "You had no choice," he said, quietly trying to let her know he understood. "But Carolyn and Jenny are safe tonight thanks to your cunning and skills. Do not berate yourself for sending some bloody scum to his death."

Samantha jerked to her feet and whirled to face him. Her eyes blazed with a fury that knew no bounds. "And is that how you justified the killing of my father, Cortland?"

Alex felt the impact of her beauty like a shot

through his gut. Her hair tumbled freely down her back, and the creamy smoothness of her skin bathed in the firelight begged for his touch. But her words drew his brows together in confusion.

"I know not of your father, little one, much less of his death."

Samantha planted herself directly before him as her frustration and anger found its target. "And I suppose you stake no claim to the plot that killed the Falcon?"

Alex's smile faded. "Aye, I planned the venture. But 'twas not my sword that took his life. Was your father one of the Falcon's crew?"

Samantha threw back her head with ragged laughter. Slowly her eyes lowered to Alex. "You play the fool well, my lord." Her words were cold. "Wl do you think I have plagued you all these years? Have you never wondered why others sailed with clear passage while ships under your flag were hit?"

Alex watched in fascination as she moved before the fire. The face of an angel in the body of a witch. Then he knew. The answers he had searched for were as clear as the eyes that held his own, eyes that had turned to him in the moments before death and sought to curse him.

"Falcon was your father."

Samantha's eyes locked with his. "Aye, and you're the man who killed him."

Alex was silent, but his gaze never left her. "Your father chose a treacherous path to travel. Surely you realized the dangers." His brow lifted. "Or did you think that the laws that govern piracy were for everyone but him?"

"He had no choice." Her voice rose with frustration. "Those damned laws you're so proud of forced him."

Alex felt his own frustration grow. "What childish gibberish. Every man has a choice of what path he is to walk."

"Hah!" Her eyes flashed with fire and indignation. "Do you think Megan would choose to be a ladies' maid if she had the opportunity to be the lady? Do you think my father chose the life of a pirate because he wanted to? He was forced from his home." Her fist clenched in anger as she paced before him. "Those fine English laws of yours took everything he thought was his and gave it to Edward as the eldest brother. What choice had he then?"

Alex rose to tower above her. "The same choice that I had. Falcon was weak of character, and you're too blinded by your loyalty to see it. The day my grandfather died, my uncle, the eldest brother, threw my family from the only home I had ever known. My father took us to live in a gaming lodge on the edge of the property." Alex turned to stare at the fire as memories intruded. "He and my mother died that same year." Alex cocked a brow and his eyes narrowed. "Should I have turned pirate, m'lady?"

Samantha stood mesmerized. Bathed in the angry red glow of the fire, Alex appeared more intimidating than any man she had ever known. But her chin moved upward and brazenly she returned his stare. "You might have made a good one."

"And would you have found me any different? Does it take the lack of value in another to give worth to Falcon?"

Samantha felt her foundations begin to crack. He was right and she hated him. "You chose the easy way."

"Because I take responsibility for my actions and refuse to cast the blame on others? Because I choose to live within the law? Because I choose to make my own way and not survive on the sweat and tears of others?"

Samantha cringed, hating his strength and her father's weakness. "Mayhap all your decisions are not as noble as you would let on," she challenged, grasping blindly for hope.

"And mayhap the biggest mistake I made was taking you from the bosom of the family you hold so dear. Was I wrong in thinking you chose not to stay with your uncle? Did you plan to meet those two thugs by the mill? They were like those you sailed with, weren't they? Common crooks no different from your father?"

Alex regretted the words even as they left his lips, and his anger doubled that she held the power to push him to such lengths. She tied him in knots with her twisted reasoning. Never had he explained his actions. He lived to suit himself and no one else. But now as he watched the blood drain from her face and the horror of the day cloud her eyes, there was no taste of victory. There was only fatigue and the bitter feeling he had struck a blow on one with no defense. Alex watched her begin to tremble as she struggled to hold her tears at bay. She could flay him with a glance and her words often drew blood, yet as she stood trembling before him, the sense of satisfaction was strangely missing.

A solitary tear rolled slowly down her cheek, and Alex felt the weight of her distress settle firmly on his shoulders. Moving with a grace that always caught her unawares, Samantha gasped as he scooped her high into his arms and moved toward the bed. Panic filled her as she realized their destination.

"Nay!"

Alex winced at her panicked cry, disgusted with himself for adding to her terror. "Be still, little one." His voice was gentle as he cradled her close. "Enough has passed for one day. I would seek my rest."

Samantha tried to resist, but the warmth of his body seeped into hers, and she began to wonder what power Alex had to steal her anger. Her head dropped to the pillow as he lowered her onto the bed.

Alex would have drawn away, but the panic in her eyes refused to release him, and reluctantly he eased onto the bed beside her.

Samantha closed her eyes against the memories that threatened, and as her head rested on his chest, the steady rhythm of his breathing soothed the harsh edges of her day and cloaked her in security.

Alex pulled the blankets high about them. Her trembling eased, and her hair, a tangled disarray of curls, caressed his hand as he held her close.

"You took the life of my father." Her words were the barest whisper against his neck. "But you saved my own. Mayhap the deeds are now even."

Alex waited at length, but her breathing evened and he knew she slept. Her words echoed in the silent room. The deeds even? He thought of the frustration he had felt each time one of his ships had returned empty, but that was nothing compared to the confusion she had tossed so neatly into his life. He should beat her and toss her to the dogs, yet he only had to look at her and his body ached.

In sleep she willingly curled against him, and Alex wondered yet again what spell she had cast on him. For surely had he been in his right head, he would not willingly condemn himself to yet another sleepless night.

Chapter XVI

The predawn sky had been dark when Alex chose to make their good-byes. Carolyn, too distraught from the day before, did not leave her bed. But Terrance, although still in his dressing gown, had risen to bid them farewell and safe journey. As he ushered them to the door, Samantha could not help but wonder if his anxiousness to see them gone was really just to escape the chill of the morning air, or something more.

On the second day, the carriage entered Cornwall and the road turned toward the sea. Samantha drew back the shade and let the damp wind tug at her hair and brush against her face. Nearly four months had passed since Alex had plucked her from the decks of her ship. She watched the untamed landscape unfold before her and thought of Dancer's bruised and battered face on that last terrible night. Her mind ached to know the fate of her crew, but each time she had tried to call forth their image, her head had filled with pain, forcing her to cease. Did he worry? She thought of the care he had taken with her training. Did he think her dead? Or did he wonder as she did, still these many months later?

The villages had thinned considerably as they moved along the coastline. And despite the inner yearning to be back on her ship, Samantha felt strangely drawn to the desolate beauty of the countryside that surrounded her. The carriage jolted from side to side, and suddenly she knew they had crossed the estate boundaries and were in Coverick. Perching on the edge of the seat, she peered out the carriage window. The cottages that sprinkled the hillside were run-down and in vast need of repair. The carriage made several sweeping turns, then angled upward before drawing to a halt.

Alex dismounted and stood before the grand entranceway to his family home. His chest tightened and his muscles tensed. The east gardens, once celebrated for their beauty, were now obliterated by weeds and bramble. Shattered glass crunched beneath his feet as he took a brass key from his pocket, and the old oaken door creaked its welcome.

The musty odor of stale air greeted his entry and Alex knocked several thick cobwebs from his path. Weaving his way through the maze of litter that covered the floor, he struck a flint to light a wall lantern. In its glow the destruction was even worse. Furniture lay overturned and no semblance of order remained.

Filled with self-condemnation, Alex tried to contain his rage. It was inexcusable that he had taken such little care with the home of his ancestors. Now he had a wife, patiently waiting for him in the carriage. Why had he ever thought to bring her here? Angrily he kicked a broken chair from his path, then looked about and laughed in despair. For like a youth green with love, he had wanted to flaunt the grand Cortland estate to prove his worth. The realization did not weigh lightly and his self-contempt grew. He had humiliated Samantha by labeling her father weak of character, but as he gazed about, he considered himself no better.

Not content to wait for Alex to come for her, Samantha opened the carriage door and gazed in wonder at the massive gray structure that was to become her home. *'Tis a palace,* she thought as her eyes surveyed the gabled roof with its high-rising pinnacles. Towers majestically flanked each corner, and the great mullioned windows sparkled in the sunlight like a glowing fire. Noting the intricate side gardens and making a silent promise to explore their treasures as soon as she dared, Samantha followed Alex through the doorway.

Her eyes widened in horror at the chaos that lay before her. Window casing were torn and tattered. Alex's footsteps showed clearly in the dirt on the marbled floor and several chickens roosted on the staircase. Massive tapestries lined the walls, but the dust was so thick, it was impossible to name the design they carried.

"Alex?"

Alex turned to find Samantha in the doorway behind him. Unable to bear her contempt, he turned his back to her and silently made his way down a shadowy corridor.

Momentarily confused, Samantha watched his

retreat, then reality washed over her with the pleasantness of an icy wave in winter. She was the cause of this. In all the years she had plundered his ships and helped herself to his fortune, never once had she given thought to the consequences. She had cast his home in ruins, yet he had still rescued her from Edward and at the price of his own freedom. He should hate her as she did him. But his hands were always gentle when he touched her. Carefully she stepped around a broken chair. *Well, no more,* she thought with a weary sigh. *I'm done with revenge and the havoc it sows.*

"I owe you a debt, Cortland, for saving my life." She rescued a porcelain vase from the rubbish pile and placed it safely to the side. "I shall see this place to rights again before I take my leave." Her mind set, and eager to begin her task, Samantha went in search of Alex.

Standing in his grandfather's study, Alex fought his emotions. With unleashed anger, he swept clean the desk and righted a chair to sit behind it. He wanted to laugh out loud with the irony of it all. Coverick was now his, but his stables in London were in better condition. Tangled in guilt and memories, he didn't hear her enter the study. His muscles tightened and his black mood darkened as he felt her hand rest on his shoulder. Bracing himself for the verbal onslaught he knew would come, Alex turned to face her and her perfume filled his head.

"Alex, your happy memories of this house are forever yours, and what has gone before is over and done with. Don't let the bitter seeds of resentment keep you from your goal. We have too much to do."

246

Alex took a deep breath. Whatever he had expected, it was certainly not her understanding. He tried to picture Julia standing quietly beside him, and the image paled. She never would even have set foot into the squalor, let alone seen promise amid the destruction.

Samantha felt his pain and ached to offer hope. As she gently leaned against his side and silently pleaded for his forgiveness, her quiet strength reached out and touched him like a tangible force.

Alex let his arm slide around her waist and breathed deeply of her scent. "'Tis not fit to live in," he said finally.

"The main foundation seems sound."

A sad smile touched his lips. "Aye, the structure is sound enough, but I won't have my wife living in worse than a pigsty."

Samantha cocked a brow, then surprised them both by plopping down on his lap. His arms circled her as she leaned fully against his chest. "'Twas a long journey, m'lord, and I fear since you are sitting on the only chair in the room, I shall have to sit on you."

Alex chuckled and felt his mood lighten. "Best beware, madam, or you will never find more than one chair in any room of our house." His hand rubbed along her spine and she sighed in pleasure. Then, abruptly, she pulled herself from his lap and turned to survey the room.

"I want to move the desk." Her words were brisk as she paced the length of the room. "Move it over here near the window."

Alex stared at her in disbelief as she began to tear

the tattered shades from their moorings. "What?"

Samantha squatted down to better examine the sea dog table, then rose, surprised to find Alex still seated. With her hand resting on the head of the intricately carved winged chimeras, she raised a brow to her husband. "The desk wants to be over by the window. Or do you plan to follow this fellow's example and 'make hast slowly'?" Her foot tapped impatiently at the table's tortoise base until Alex rose to do her bidding. Satisfied, her attention turned elsewhere.

Alex shed his coat and pushed the desk to its familiar spot beneath the eastern window. Was it only a lucky guess that had her choose the location? Or had her sight given a clue to what the room had once looked like? Not ready to probe further, Alex remained silent and did as she requested. For nearly an hour she had furniture shifted first one way and then another.

At last Alex mopped the sweat from his brow and leaned back against the desk to better survey the room. The transformation was amazing. For although many of the pieces ended where his grandmother had once placed them, enough were different to give the room an original touch. Samantha had found a broom and, as he had shoved the massive pieces from one place to another, she had been busily sweeping away the clutter. And now, even though everything still needed a thorough scrubbing, the room no longer looked as hopeless as his first impression.

"See." She smiled in satisfaction. "With a little effort it will look even better than you remember.

Now if I could just decide . . ."

"Nay." Alex chuckled and turned her to face him before she decided to move the bookcase yet again. He could almost hear her mind making lists and ticking off chores to be attended to. Gently he pulled her to stand between his outstretched legs as he leaned against the desk. Tenderly his fingers brushed the dust from her cheek, then lingered to trace the shadows beneath her eyes.

"'Tis going to take a great deal of work to make this a livable place."

Samantha rested her head against his chest. She had cost him dearly, but she would see this debt settled. His breath stirred her hair. Looking up, she found herself again a prisoner of the green eyes she knew so well. Her knees grew weak and she felt her insides begin to melt from his gaze.

"I see no reason not to make this our home, m'lord." She watched the cool reserve leave his face, a surprising softness touched the hard planes. She could not resist when he increased the pressure on her arms to draw her still closer. Nor did she object when moments later his mouth settled firmly over hers. The male scent of him touched her weary mind, and her senses reeled. Her palms rested lightly on his shoulders, and again she marveled at the strength that lay beneath her hands.

A stirring in the doorway drew them reluctantly apart. Samantha turned to see Judd shifting from one foot to the other with a wide smile on his lips. "Beggin' your pardon, Your Grace, but I finally located the Browns. They returned with me and are waiting in the foyer."

"Tell them I'll be along in a moment, Judd," Alex sighed with frustration. She rested so easily against him. He glanced about the room and desperately wished he had silken sheets on which to lay her, and only the finest wines to offer. Instead, his wife, the Duchess of Coverick, had been forced to take up a broom like a common maid the first hour in her new home. His arms tightened, pressing her still closer, and as his lips brushed against the softness of her cheek, Alex silently vowed to erase all the wrongs she had suffered. He would work every hour of the day to make Coverick a home she would be proud of.

Samantha felt the heat begin to grow and wiggled her arms. "Who are the Browns?" she questioned.

Reluctantly, Alex let her step away. "Brown was the majordomo at Coverick when my grandfather was alive. He and his wife lived here before I was born. When I think of William . . ."

Samantha stepped forward and laid her finger to his lips. "From this moment on, I will hear no more of what was. I only wish to know what is going to be."

Alex scowled slightly. He had never let a woman dictate to him, and his wife would be no exception. But noting the lines of fatigue that etched her flawless beauty, and still warmed from her kiss, he felt himself soften. "Come, love, they will be delighted to make your acquaintance."

Introductions made, Samantha watched tears of gratitude fill the old couple's eyes as Alex spoke. She felt her husband's anger as Brown retold the story of how William had cast out all the servants, most of whom had spent their entire lives serving at Coverick. Unable to stay any longer as they spoke of days gone by, she silently slipped away to continue her explorations.

Entering a bedroom, Samantha leaned wearily against the doorjamb. Her explorations were far from over, but her energy was rapidly fading. At least this room and the rest on the second floor seemed in a better state of repair than those on the lower levels of the house. Here much of the furniture had been covered and, with care, she removed the casings along with most of the dust. She threw the windows wide to let the cool night air drive out the musty dampness. The panoramic view was breathtaking. In the distance, she could see the ocean. As she watched, the vivid colors of the evening sky grew deeper as the sun bid its farewell. On the shore, a light flickered. Seconds later, it was answered by another. Puzzled, Samantha continued to watch, but all remained quiet. Bathed in a shadowy hue, the rolling expanse of untamed land that lay before her seemed calm and settled for the night.

With a shrug, Samantha turned back to the task at hand. The wood box was full, and in no time she had a blazing fire glowing in the hearth. She smiled and wondered if Alex would ever notice that one of his flints was missing. The warmth of the fire touched the room with new light, and despite the work that lay before her, she felt strangely content.

A large tester bed faced the glowing fire, and she fought back the urge to climb on. Quickly she stripped the coverlets from the bed and pushed them into a corner. Samantha wiped the dust from the walnut caryatides that supported the richly carved tester roof of the bedstead. The fluted posts were tapered to a melon shape that held an intricate carving of the Temptation in the Garden. She wiped the dust from Adam and Eve as she watched the serpent slither toward them. She thought of Alex, and despite the warmth of the fire, she was chilled, though earlier, his kiss had left her mind spinning and her knees weak. She wrapped her arms about her and, with her eyes closed, she could feel the pleasure when he held her close. But when she envisioned them naked in the Garden of Eden, the form became that of Edward as he grunted over her.

Samantha jerked herself from the bed with a strangled cry. Trembling, she moved before the fire. The thoughts of Alex commanding her to participate in that dreadful act again made her stomach churn, and sweat dotted her forehead. With a tired sigh, she turned back to her task. Her search finally unveiled a chest that had been packed with fresh linens. Rose petals had been tucked between the layers, and as she drew forth the linen, the light perfume scented the air.

Laying the bed was not easy, and her arms became clumsy with fatigue. Finally she stepped back and surveyed her handiwork with satisfaction. It was not neat, but for tonight it would do. She perched on the corner of the bed to rest the growing ache in her back and glanced about. Tomorrow she would see the room scrubbed from top to bottom, and the dingy curtains at the window would be the first to go. Meaning to rest her eyes for only a moment, she stretched out along the foot of the bed.

An hour later, Alex found her there, still deep in sleep.

Samantha awoke the next morning to find herself alone in the large bed. Curled on her side, her hand reached out to touch the pillow where Alex's head had rested. The fabric was cool beneath her questing fingers and she knew she must rise. But for the moment she was completely content just to close her eyes and lie curled under the covers. Her stomach, however, suddenly had other ideas and she found herself flying from the bed in search of the chamber pot. Falling to her knees before the porcelain bowl, her stomach turned over again and again as if trying to rid itself of some unseen demon. But since she had missed dinner the night before, the effort proved futile, and left her exhausted and trembling when the spasms finally ceased. On legs that quivered uncontrollably, she straightened as much as she dared and inched her way back to the bed.

Climbing back onto the bed, Samantha stretched out on her stomach and sighed with relief. The nausea was gone as quickly as it had come and the doubts that had plagued her mind for the past weeks were finally put to rest. Taking great care, she slowly rolled onto her side and her hand reached down. Hesitantly, her fingers traced the contours of her stomach, searching for signs of change.

A baby, her mind thought with wonder. She carried Alex's baby. Silently she luxuriated in the knowledge until she felt she might burst with pleasure. She wrapped her arms about her and, closing her eyes, remembered the joy of holding Carolyn's little one. Now she would have a baby of her own to love and cherish. It would have hair the color of midnight and sparkling green eyes. Not as tentatively this time, her hand again touched her stomach. Alex had certainly planted his seed well to have trapped her so neatly. A smile touched her lips as she thought of his easy way with Jonathan and Jenny. She remembered the tender look on his face that evening when he had spoken of children. Her eyes closed in pleasure. He would be so pleased. But when to tell him? *Tell him?* Her eyes snapped open. In her mind, Alex stood before her, and in that moment she knew he would never cease the chase if she escaped with his child. Her hand rested possessively on the life she carried within, and each beat of her heart strengthened the knowledge that if she fled, she would never be able to leave the baby behind.

Samantha jerked upright on the bed, glancing anxiously about the room. Her gown rested on a chair near the bed. Dare she try to escape before he realized she carried his seed? Her hand clenched tightly in her lap. But what then of her promise? She had vowed to stay until Coverick was put to rights again. She looked up at the decorative plasterwork on the ceiling then down to the ornate woodwork along the floor. There was so much to see to. Her shoulders slumped forward. And what of the estate? Cottages ready to collapse with the first strong wind of winter? And she had to see the children better cared for. How would they survive the winter if she left?

Weary from the weight of the world that rested

upon her shoulders, Samantha flopped back against the pillows. Her eyes closed in frustration. What should she do . . . what could she do . . .

Alex found her as she lay, sprawled across the covers with the pillow tucked beneath her cheek. Silently he approached the bed, then hesitated at its side. How fragile she appeared in sleep, he thought, admiring the gentle slope of her hip and the curve of her shoulder. Carefully, he moved closer. She looked so innocent. Why, he wondered, had he never noticed how delicate her features were? Oh, he knew she was a beauty, it had taken him only one look on a storm-filled night to realize that. But now, as he watched her sleep, he wondered why he had never noticed how frail she was. Her hand curled near her cheek on the pillow and he wondered how fingers so slender had ever managed to wield a sword. He tried to recapture the image of her dressed in black breeches and commanding a ship, but the only picture that came to mind was Samantha sitting before a fire, with a babe cuddled close to her breast. Alex watched the steady rhythm of her breathing and wondered yet again how even in sleep she pulled him nearer. Quietly, he left the room.

A short while later, garbed in a white, bobbed cap and flowing apron that completely covered her gown, Samantha stood with Mrs. Brown and surveyed the cookroom with disgust.

"I don't believe this," Mrs. Brown gasped, holding

a perfumed handkerchief to her nose. "I know the old master was daft, but however did the livestock get in?"

Samantha stood silent as she surveyed the filth that filled the room. On the floor, bags of grain and flour lay split and rotting. Her hand reached for a broom and her fingers tightened. Children on the estate were in want while the rats in her husband's home dined like kings. *Well, no more,* she vowed. Brandishing the broom before her, Samantha waded into the chaos. Pausing to open the windows that lined the south wall, Samantha gasped for breath as the fresh air washed into the room. Tightening her grip on the broom, she started to sweep the trash from the table.

"Your Grace . . ." Mrs. Brown stepped forward, then hastily retreated as a mouse scurried near her skirts. "You can not do that."

Samantha looked in confusion from the filthy room to the distraught housekeeper.

"You are a duchess," Mrs. Brown stammered as she watched a blank look cover her young mistress's face. "'Twould be most . . . unseemly."

Realization hit Samantha, and exasperation followed on its wake. "Mrs. Brown . . ." she began patiently. "'Twould be more unseemly for the Duchess of Coverick to have a kitchen unfit for swine." Samantha watched the old lady pale at her words. *Damn,* she swore silently. How she hated the rules that governed the English. Second sons were left with naught a half penny to their names, and it was scandalous for a duchess to see to the tidiness of her own home.

Samantha leaned against her broom. "Mrs.

Brown . . ." Her voice was soft and soothing. "Why don't you get Judd and have him take you to the village." The idea took hold and began to bloom. "You know the running of the houses better than I, so I'll leave the numbers to you. Engage as many as you wish."

Mrs. Brown's face reflected her horror. "Your Grace, the townsfolk are mostly out-of-work miners. They have no skills, no training."

Samantha brushed aside the protest. "Then you shall teach them. If they can scrub and push a broom, or if they be handy with hammer and nail, bring them back. I have the greatest confidence in your ability, Mrs. Brown. With your help, we shall have Cortland Manor shipshape in no time."

For a moment Mrs. Brown stood silent. Shipshape? Where on earth had the young mistress ever heard such a term? And how would she ever begin to train common village girls to serve in such a grand house as Cortland Manor? "As you wish, Your Grace," she replied slowly. "And perhaps, if it pleases you, while I am in the village, I will stop at the inn and purchase some cooked meat and vegetables for the noon meal."

Samantha's smile deepened. "I am sure Ale—His Grace . . ." she hesitated over the stiff title, "would be most appreciative." With a deep, perfect curtsy, Mrs. Brown turned and fled. Samantha clasped her hands in satisfaction and returned to the kitchen.

Her broom again found the tabletop and, humming a tune often used to hoist the sails, she began to clean its surface. She had made considerable headway when a large hand placed a lustful swat firmly on her

257

backside. A shriek escaped her lips as she turned, scrubbrush in hand, on her assailant.

"Alex . . ." Her words halted abruptly for it was not her husband who stood before her. Curly wheat-colored hair tumbled across the youthful forehead of an extremely handsome face, a face that looked more than vaguely familiar. James.

"So 'tis true." Casually the young dandy perched on a corner of the table. The twinkle of his eye spoke of pure mischief and his smile deepened. "I heard Alex had come to the estate. Tell me, did he bring the new duchess with him?"

Samantha smiled in amusement and wondered how soon the dampness from the oaken table would seep through his well-cut breeches. And as his smile grew bolder, she realized that Carolyn's stories of her brother's rakishness were not exaggerations. He carried less muscle than Alex and his features were softer in the classical sense. But when he suddenly jumped with a start from the table and looked from the damp wood to the scrubbrush still in her hand, his green eyes sparkled with laughter.

"Ah, you little minx," he scolded softly as he brushed at the damp fabric on his seat. "You did that on purpose and now you owe me a favor."

Samantha stifled her laughter at his outraged expression and noted that the sparkle never left his eyes.

Selecting a dry spot to lean against, James again surveyed the dainty scullery maid. "Alex always did know how to pick them," he sighed. "Tell me, buttercup, are you among the crowds already besotted with the duke, or are you free for a little tumble?"

Samantha's laughter rang out. She knew she should be offended, but his boyish charm and the openness of his leer delighted her.

Taking her laughter for a yes, James swooped down upon her and quickly swung her high in his arms. Around and around the cookroom he danced, humming an off-key tune. "Let me take you away from all this," he crooned joyfully. "You are too beautiful to be scrubbing floors, or tables," he added, giving her a crooked smile and raising a brow in the manner of his brother. Samantha could not stem her laughter and clung tighter to his neck lest he drop her.

Rounding the table, James came to a sudden halt. Samantha's bobbed cap slipped forward to cover her eyes, but when she pushed the cap back into place, she realized she was face-to-face with her scowling husband.

"Well, aren't you going to welcome me home, Alex?" James smiled fondly at his brother but made no move to release his treasure.

"But of course." Alex moved slowly into the kitchen. "I didn't expect you so soon. And then," he looked pointedly toward Samantha, "to find you so involved . . . you must forgive me for my lack of manners. Will you stay?"

James smiled warmly. "I was hoping you'd ask. But tell me, dear brother, I hear you are married, and if it is true, I shall be quite vexed with you for not inviting me to the ceremony. When can I meet this marvel, this elusive beauty that has so entranced you that you must sneak away in the dead of the night to marry without a word to your siblings. What paragon of woman is it that has at last captured the elusive Duke of Coverick?"

Alex said nothing, but looked from Samantha to his brother and then back again.

"Oh, no," James groaned. Carefully, as if holding priceless china, he set Samantha on her feet and firmly nudged her toward his brother. "I knew 'twas too good to be true."

Alex smiled for the first time as he pulled Samantha to his side and locked his arm firmly about her. "Allow me to introduce to you my madcap brother, my dear. Samantha, this is James. James, this is Samantha, the new Duchess of Coverick."

James surveyed her closely. It was easy to see why Alex had chosen her, for even clad as a serving wench, she was bewitching. But his mood dampened as he realized there would be no hidden kisses with this little beauty. Throwing caution to the wind, and giving his brother a wink, James pulled Samantha into his arms and placed a not so brotherly kiss on her lips. "Congratulations are surely in order," he quickly pushed Samantha back toward her husband, "so you can't begrudge me a kiss for the bride." Then, giving them a courtly bow, James quickly turned and made his way from the kitchen, whistling a jaunty tune as he went.

"My brother is a jackass." Alex scowled as he brushed a smudge of dirt from her cheek and wondered why her eyes had to be so blue. "London's population has probably tripled as the result of his antics.'' He pulled the white cap from her hair and let his fingers trace the silky softness of the curls that tumbled to her shoulders.

Samantha's eyes grew wide with disbelief and laughter at Alex's words. Without warning, he pulled her close and his lips settled firmly over hers. She clutched at the front of his shirt. James's kiss had been tolerated, but this one was making her senses spin in confusion. Her fingers tightened, and Alex took the kiss deeper, stunning them both with its intensity.

Samantha felt her world tilt. The touch of his lips sent her nerves soaring. Reality vanished and only the warmth of his body pressed close to hers kept her tied to earth.

Carefully, regretfully, Alex raised his head and stepped away. Her touch left him more shaken than he dared to admit. "Did you think I would leave you with another man's kiss on your lips, m'lady?" He took comfort that her eyes mirrored the dazed confusion he felt.

Samantha listened to his words, and somewhere in the back of her mind, she knew she should refute them. But with the taste of him still on her lips, she lacked the will to move. And felt Alex rest his chin atop her head, and for one blessed moment the world stood still. Warm, protected, she gloried in the comfort she found in his arms.

"You belong to me now, and 'tis something you'd do well to remember."

Samantha stiffened with his words. Was that how he sought to bind her to him? Did he really think that with a few smoldering kisses he could steal her desire for freedom? Had he already placed her with the hordes of besotted fools that James spoke of? Samantha leaned back to view the green eyes that haunted her. The intensity of his gaze shocked her, but her resolve strengthened. She would start immediately, and separate bedchambers would be the perfect place. Two could play at this game, she thought recklessly, giving her husband a saucy smile. And when it was done, she would be the victor.

Alex felt his pulse quicken with her smile but reluctantly stepped aside. They were home now and time would be his ally. When he took her again, it would be with candlelight and scented sheets, not on a coarse wooden table where mice scurried underneath.

"Come . . ." Alex took her hand. "Judd has returned with Mrs. Brown, and between them they have collected a feast. And," he smiled, "believe it or not, the main dining room is now fit to sit in."

Samantha gave her husband a bewitching smile. "Is there more than one chair?"

Alex's laughter returned, and for a moment he looked back at the wooden table with new thoughts. "You'll just have to come and see, love."

Chapter XVII

The days passed, and Alex watched his home come
to life. Samantha had embraced the task as a mother
would her child. She had insisted he hire Blacky
Teach as their foreman, and the man was proving to
be a wonder. The dirt and filth had been scrubbed
away and floors were now polished until they
glistened in the sunlight.

But now it was not his home that brought him
worry. He was losing her. Each day his feelings for
Samantha grew stronger, yet each day she slipped
farther away. Oftimes, when she thought no one was
about, her eyes filled with a sadness that haunted
him. For deep in his heart he knew the one thing that
would truly make her happy was the only thing he
was unwilling to give. Her freedom.

Alex cut another rose and carefully removed the
thorns. He was not a man to stay idle and wait for
things to happen. If he wanted her to love him, then
by God, he would make it work. But how did one go

about courting one's wife?

Samantha gazed about her bedchambers with mixed feelings. French lace hung at the windows and stirred with the autumn breeze, and the fire glowed warmly in the hearth, but tonight, memories of another time and place refused to be pushed aside. Closing her eyes, she could see their faces: Marie, Dancer, Kabol. Did they still think of her? Or had time erased her memory? Her fingers toyed with her necklace. If she could just let Dancer know she was safe, then maybe she would find contentment. Her hand touched her stomach searching for signs of the child she carried and tears threatened.

Coverick seemed less her home now than when they had first arrived a fortnight ago. She was not to clean and she was not to scrub, for she was the lady of the house. Mrs. Brown had patiently suggested that the mistress might turn her hours to needlework. Surely she had some exquisite piece of fine stitchery tucked away in one of her many trunks. And wouldn't now be the perfect time to see it completed?

Samantha sighed with frustration. Her last piece of 'fine needlework' had been on a man's flesh. She pulled the woolen blanket more securely about her as she continued to watch the fire. The restoration was progressing well, but as the house improved, the local gentry were starting to call. And with each visit, her feelings of inadequacy grew. Who would have thought there was a wrong way to pour tea?

A sad smile touched her lips as she gazed at the roses Alex had placed on her nightstand. Would she ever understand him? He was a duke, yet when the thatcher's assistant fell and broke his arm, it was Alex who climbed to the top of the widow's roof to lend a hand until another with skill could be found.

Her hand reached up to touch her lips where the taste of his kiss still lingered, and she cursed herself for insisting on separate bedchambers. She missed the warmth of his body, and waking to find his arm wrapped around her. But how did one ask a husband to share a bed and not claim his marital rights? She glanced again about her chambers. By day she could fill her hours until exhaustion overtook her, but no matter how tired she was when she found her bed, the lonely nights were becoming more than she could bear. The clock struck three and Samantha couldn't help but wonder if Alex slept, or if he, too, was impatient for the coming dawn.

Alex was drawn from his study by the sound of voices in the hall. Opening the door, he was astonished to see his distraught sister with his niece and nephew in tow. "My God, Carolyn, why didn't you send word that you were coming? Where is Terrance?" Alex scooped up the exhausted Jenny who flopped like a rag doll against his shoulder.

The reason for Carolyn's look of anguish was answered as Julia Harwick rounded the corner.

"I couldn't keep her from coming, Alex. I tried, truly I did."

"So you decided to tag along with your brats." Julia moved past the stunned group and into the study. "Good Lord, Alex, how on earth do you stand them. That one . . ." she gestured to the now-sleeping Jenny, "cried the entire trip. While he . . ." she pointed an accusing finger toward Jonathan, "talked incessantly. God, what a nightmare that was."

"I would warn you to take care with your tongue, Julia," Alex said quietly. "You speak ill of my family while you are under my roof. That is not a wise path to follow."

Julia gazed about the room appraising its worth, then, giving Alex one of her most flirtatious smiles, walked her fingers up the buttons of his waistcoat. "Don't be cross with me, darling." Her lashes fluttered. "We've had the most disastrous journey. But as much as I hate to travel, I just couldn't stay in London for one more day without you. There were the most ridiculous rumors flying about. What else could I do?" Her bottom lip pulled into a suggestive pout.

Carolyn flopped onto the settee and pulled her gloves from her hands. "Julia would not believe me when I told her you were married." Carolyn's voice was filled with fatigue and irritation as she carefully untied her travel bonnet. Alex removed Julia's hand from his chest and stepped away. "And just what did you hope to gain by arriving unannounced at a bachelor's residence?"

A young maid tapped on the door, then entered the study carrying a tray of tea, brandy, and cakes. Setting them before Carolyn, she took one glance at the dark look on the master's face and fled as quickly as she had come.

Julia smiled brightly, confident now of her prize.

"Why, darling, my reputation is in shatters. You will have to wed me now to make an honest woman of me."

Alex's laughter rang out, rousing his niece from her resting place on his shoulder. "Julia, I doubt that marriage to me or to any other poor bloke would ever make you the honest woman. But since Carolyn spoke the truth and I am no longer the gay bachelor, your reputation, m'lady, is still as it was."

A dark blush crept over Julia's features. "You have trifled with me for the last time, Alex." Her foot stomped against the worn Persian carpet. "I don't believe you. I don't believe you're married. This is all some sort of vicious plot against me, and I don't think it's one bit funny."

"What you think no longer matters to me, Julia." With Jenny still on his shoulder, Alex poured three glasses of brandy. Graciously, he handed a glass of the amber liquid to his sister, then to his irate guest. "You have had a long and needless journey. I will be honored to see to your comfort tonight, then in the morning, you can be on your way. Carolyn . . ." Alex turned toward his sister. "You and the children are 'of course' welcome to stay as long as you desire."

Carolyn smiled in gratitude as she sipped the fiery liquid. The length of the journey and coping on her own with two young children was beginning to take its toll.

"Why did Terrance not accompany you?" Alex questioned gently.

Carolyn's fingers traced an agitated pattern on her glass.

"Father doesn't know that we came," Jonathan

267

chimed in, taking a cake from the tray.

Alex raised a brow to his sister. "He is in London for a fortnight on business," Carolyn defended. "So I had to make the decision on my own."

"And made a mess of it I'd say," Julia snipped. "So if I am to believe this farce, just where is this paragon? Doesn't she realize 'tis rude not to greet one's guests?"

Alex felt his temper rise and wondered why he had tolerated Julia for so long. She was pretty, to be sure, but the long hours she spent on pleasure were beginning to take their toll, and the shrew beneath the paint was beginning to show through.

Jenny, snuggling closer to his cheek, heaved a sigh and Alex felt his tension melt. Her chubby arms wrapped around his neck and her soft breath touched his skin. He wondered, not for the first time, if it would feel the same when the child was his own.

"Carolyn, can't you manage those two brats any better than this," Julia snapped, giving Jonathan's hand a smack as he reached for a second cake. "Your brother is a duke now, not a nanny for those two monsters of yours."

Alex stiffened. "Julia, I shall give you two choices." His voice was deathly quiet. "Either you are civil and mind your tongue while you are under my roof, or you will find yourself spending the night in the barn with the other animals."

Julia had the grace to pale and Carolyn turned to her brother with a look of disbelief. She had heard rumor of his temper, but never had she witnessed it firsthand.

"Uncle Alex . . ." Jonathan squirmed, eager to be

away from the lady who pinched him whenever his mother wasn't looking. "May I speak with you?" Alex nodded, and with Jenny still in his arms, knelt so his nephew could whisper in his ear. Alex smiled and nodded toward the lad. Rising, he moved to Carolyn and gently placed the sleeping Jenny on the settee beside her.

"I shall send Mrs. Brown to help you with her in a moment. But right now, Jonathan and I have a pressing matter to see to." Alex dropped a kiss on his sister's cheek and, giving her a wink, quickly departed with his nephew.

Julia glared at the door. "That child is a brat." Turning, she generously poured herself another brandy.

Samantha paused in the doorway with James and viewed the unhappy group. Something was definitely amiss, and she cursed the sight that so often vanished when she needed it most.

"Carolyn, forgive me for not being here to greet you." Samantha moved to take Carolyn's outstretched hand. "I've been ah . . . working in the garden."

"So we can see." Julia looked pointedly toward the mud that streaked the hem of Samantha's peach gown.

James cleared his voice. "Samantha, I'd like you to meet an old school chum of Carolyn's. May I present Lady Julia Harwick."

Samantha turned with a ready smile and came face-to-face with pure, undisguised hatred.

"Old school chum!" Julia's laugh, a mixture of anger and disbelief, chilled the blood. "Darling . . . ," she cooed, brushing her gloved fingers over James's lapel. "Surely a man of your experience can do better than that. The child will never fall for such an old and trite story."

"Lady Julia . . ." Samantha hesitated, trying to place all the pieces into the puzzle. "We welcome you to Coverick. I hope your journey was a pleasant one?"

Julia seethed with anger as she viewed the young woman before her. Her gown was stained, her hair needed combing, and Alex had made her his duchess. Jealousy inflamed her. For years she had dreamed of becoming Alex's bride and the mistress of Coverick. Her eyes darkened. Never would she grant an easy victory to the little thief who had stolen it from her. "Really, darling." Julia looked to James, pointedly ignoring her hostess. "How in the world did a man with your brother's superb instincts ever choose so beneath himself?"

"Julia, please . . ." Carolyn gasped.

Ignoring Carolyn, Julia turned back to Samantha. "I simply mean that Alex was always so particular of what I wore, when I wore things, that is, that I am astonished he would let his duchess entertain in a gown that is so . . ." Her words trailed off as she casually leaned over to pluck a bit of dried leaf that had stuck in Samantha's windblown curls. Lifting the bit of leaf, Julia studied it for a moment, then, with a face that mirrored hopeless disbelief, she let the leaf flutter from her fingers.

Samantha looked down at the grass stains and streaks of dirt that covered her skirt. In her eagerness to see Carolyn and the children, it had never occurred to her to change her gown for a new one. But as she viewed Carolyn's friend, in stunning green velvet, with her auburn curls perfectly coiffed, she wished she had tarried if only for a moment to wipe the dust from her face.

"All this must come as quite a strain to you, my dear," Julia droned on. "You obviously are not at all ready to accept the position that Alex wishes to offer to you."

Samantha felt the burning start in her cheeks even as her shoulders drew erect. She might not know the proper rules that governed the English gentry, but surely they did not include enduring insults in one's own home. And Alex was greatly mistaken if he thought her willing to stand docile while this cat sharpened her claws.

"Samantha . . ." Alex's voice spun her about. "I wondered where you had disappeared to. Have you met our guest?"

"Uncle James!" Jonathan interrupted, darting past Alex to reach his uncle's outstretched arms. James caught the boy and spun him about until his giggles filled the room.

Julia folded her arms and rolled her eyes. "How utterly charming," she muttered, drawing a dark look from Samantha.

"Aunt Samantha!" Giving his uncle a quick kiss on the cheek, Jonathan scrambled down to stand formally before his aunt. "I am most pleased to see you again," he stated in his most grown-up voice as he bowed very stiffly before her.

Samantha dipped into a gracious curtsy. "And I am most delighted to see you again, too, Master Jonathan."

Julia heaved a deep sigh. "Alex, darling, your little bride is just too precious for words. Where ever did you find someone so . . . untouched by society?"

Samantha missed the dark scowl that Alex sent in Julia's direction. "Samantha . . ." His voice was tight. "Mrs. Brown is preparing rooms in the east wing. Would you show Carolyn the way?"

"Bless you." Carolyn rose, cutting off Samantha's words. "If I don't rest before dinner, I fear I will fall asleep in my soup."

"That's great," Jonathan said with an open mouthed yawn. "Can we go now, Aunt Samantha?"

Samantha turned toward Alex, an acid reply already on her lips, when the reality of the situation suddenly dawned clear. Julia was more than Carolyn's chum, or a friend of the family. She was Alex's mistress. Her mind soared back to a storm-filled sea and a ship with ladies from England. My God, he had been with her then. All the years that he had haunted her dreams he had found his satisfaction in the bed of the witch that stood before her. Samantha felt her throat grow tight. What a naive fool she was.

Carefully, she gathered Jenny from the settee and with Jonathan and Carolyn in tow, left Alex and Julia in the study. They had taken less than three steps down the hallway when the lilting sound of Julia's laughter rang out.

Samantha turned, but Carolyn touched her arm. "Be calm," she whispered softly. "You have nothing to fear from Julia."

"She is his mistress."

Carolyn shook her head. "Nay, only in Julia's mind. Oh, I'll not be so naive to believe that Alex never bedded her," Carolyn continued quickly. "But for years I've watched Julia manipulate and scheme to become my brother's wife. He's had opportunity a plenty, yet he chose you."

Samantha cast an uncertain glance toward the study. "Mayhap he now regrets his choice."

"Stop worrying." Carolyn chuckled, taking Samantha's arm and leading her down the hallway. "Have you told Alex about the babe?"

Samantha stopped dead, but Carolyn only smiled. "I know the look," she whispered softly. "After three of my own . . ." Her voice trailed off.

Samantha shook her head. "Please say nothing, I beg of you."

"Be at ease." Carolyn reached for her daughter. "Your secret is safe with me. I know you are waiting for that special time. Only take my advice and do not tarry too long." She smiled again at Samantha's uncertain frown. "My brother has a reputation for being quite the connoisseur of the female form. And I'll wager 'twill not be much longer before he discovers for himself that which you believe to be hidden."

Samantha curled on her chaise before the fire and tried to ease the pounding behind her eyes. Dinner had been a complete disaster. Despite James and Carolyn's valiant efforts to ease the way, Julia snapped at them and flirted outrageously with Alex

273

the entire time.

Samantha pulled her knees up beneath her dressing gown and locked her arms about them. Why had Mrs. Brown decided that tonight was the time to set the table with enough silver for a king's feast? Her head dropped to her knees. She had tried to quietly follow Carolyn's lead as to which spoon to use when, but the situation had become completely hopeless. Julia noticed every mistake and delighted in drawing it to Alex's attention. Alex had completed the meal in stormy silence, and Samantha felt her composure slip another notch. It wasn't her fault she had never been to a grand dinner. Angrily she wiped at the tears that threatened and rose to pace before the fire. Why a person couldn't use one blasted fork to eat a single meal was beyond her. Frustration gnawed at her confidence. She knew not of fancy ways and agreed little with those she did know.

What a fuss, she thought with irritation. Her contact with women had been brief, at best, during her days with her father. And although the pirate whores did often fight over a chosen lover, it was openly with teeth and nails and a roll in the dirt. If Julia had physically tried to best her, she would have understood. But the verbal claw marks she had made were deep and, to Samantha's dismay, still stung.

Wearily she dropped down onto the chaise, and again pulled her knees up before her. Why did she care anyway? It was not as if she was in love with Alex . . . but why then did her chest grow tight when she thought of him lying with Julia?

*   *   *

Alex paced within his bedchambers and tried to ease the growing frustration that plagued him. Despite his earlier warning, Julia had flirted constantly during dinner. Alex rubbed the tension from his neck with a weary hand. Samantha's trust in him was growing, but it was still as fragile as the young plants she so lovingly tended. Tonight, Julia had scattered seeds of doubt with every word she uttered. He reached for an iron and stoked the fire. The image of Samantha silent and regal at the head of his table brought a smile of pride to his lips. For despite Julia's often crude remarks, she had maintained a dignity that only showed Julia in the poorest of lights.

Alex replaced the poker and rose to pace again. What must she be thinking? Had she believed Julia's innuendo? Reason urged him to open the door that connected their chambers and speak with her. But pride held him rigid. There was no need to explain, his vanity argued. He had done nothing wrong. In fact, he had not taken a woman since the night they had been together on his ship. With an angry motion he removed his jacket and pulled his stock free. More than three months without a woman, he mused. His fingers moved on the buttons of his waistcoat, and that, too, was removed. Mayhap he would go to her and apologize for Julia's scandalous behavior. He loosened the buttons of his shirt and pulled it from his breeches.

The click of the door spun Alex about. Julia floated into the room amid pale-pink silk. The transparency of her gown once would have sent his desires racing. Now she only looked cheap and vulgar.

"What in God's name are you doing here, woman?" he hissed. "My wife is in the next room."

"Don't be cross, darling," Julia purred, advancing so the charms of her body became more evident. "I've decided I shall no longer be angry with you." Her eyes lowered seductively and her lashes fluttered. "Can you really say you have forgotten the hours that we spent in pleasure? Am I really so easy to cast aside?" Julia pressed her body against his, and her arms locked about his neck.

As her body rubbed against him, Alex realized that the only thought that filled him was disgust. Roughly he pried her fingers from his neck and stepped away. "Julia . . ." he snapped. "Since the first night you connived your way into my bed, you were aware that I didn't love you. I have never loved you. We had an arrangement that for a time was convenient to both of us. I have never led you to believe that it was or could ever be anything more than that. Now get out of this room"

Julia paled, but moved to the bed and turned to smile over her shoulder. Her hands rose to the silken ties at the front of her robe and it slipped to the floor in a puddle about her feet. Her gown was the thinnest whisper of fabric, leaving nothing to the imagination, as she climbed into his bed.

A determined tap at her door pulled Samantha from her thoughts. Young Hanna opened the door, closing it quickly behind her.

"Beggin' pardon, mistress . . . Your Grace," she stammered. "Mrs. Brown would have me head if she knew I was here. But I don't know whats to do."

Samantha watched the girl twist her hands and

276

shift from foot to foot. "Tell me what is wrong, Hanna."

"'Tis little John," she sniffed as the tears started. "He's doing so poorly. Me ma sent word that she don't think he'll live the night."

Samantha gripped Hanna's shoulders. "Did the tea not sit well with him? I thought he was growing stronger."

Hanna wiped her tears with the back of her sleeve and gave a hearty sniff. "The tea was wonderful. It put the color back in the little mite's face and even eased the devil on his chest. But that's the joke of it all. He used to sit indoors all the while with me ma, and now all he wants to do is be outdoors with them other hellions. Yesterday, he slipped from the rocks and fell into the bay. The other boys got him out right quick, but the wind carries a chill and he's been burning with fever since they brought him home. When I got the message this evening," Hanna lifted a tearful face, "I didn't know whats to do. It be late and all, but could . . . would . . ."

Samantha laid her hand on Hanna's shoulder. "You did right in coming to me." Her voice was calm and soothing. "You must go down to the stable and have Peter ready a carriage. I will be with you as soon as I dress."

Samantha pulled Hanna from her seat by the fire and steered her toward the door. "Time is valuable. I'll be with you shortly." As the door closed behind the distraught girl, Samantha sprang into action. She selected a gown of warm brown wool and cursed the rain that beat against the panes of her windows. Gathering her basket and shawl, she glanced about the room. She should tell Alex. Her body tensed, and if he had not yet returned to his room, then she'd just leave a note. Giving herself a shake, she set the basket on the bed and moved to the door that separated their chambers.

Alex fought to control his anger "Get out of my bed, Julia, and do it now." His words were cold, but Julia ignored their warning.

"Nay." Her lip pulled into a pout as she let the covers slip to her waist. "You wanted me once. I can't believe that simple fool you married could please you as I can. Does she know how to make your blood run hot? Are her breasts as firm?" Julia lifted a hand and let her finger trace lazy circles about her nipple. "Is her skin as soft?" she taunted. "Nay, Alex, I'll not leave your bed. I'll not let you throw away all we shared together. If you wish her to bear your children, 'tis fine with me. Let her figure be ruined, not mine. But I will not let you go."

Alex listened to her words and wondered why he had ever wanted to bed her in the first place. And strangely, he wondered why the only moments of true passion he could remember were when he had gifted her with a necklace or bauble she had pleaded for.

Alex moved to the bed. "Get out, Julia." His words were soft and menacing. He was dangerously close to striking her, and never in his life had he willing hurt a woman.

Julia shook her head and let the covers drop lower. A deep smile touched her lips, and Alex realized she was no longer looking at him but at some point beyond. Scowling, he turned to find the source of her pleasure. His heart stopped as he viewed Samantha, frozen in the doorway.

"You didn't tell me you wanted us both tonight, darling," Julia purred. "Tell her to wait and you can go to her when we've finished. Unless . . . Oh, Alex, how dreadfully wicked. Do you want her to join us?"

Alex watched as Samantha's eyes filled with anger, then betrayal. He felt the pain stab deep within and wondered if he would ever survive the haunted look that covered her face.

"Alex, love, come," Julia whined softly.

Samantha grew paler still. Then, gathering her wits, she turned and fled, locking the door behind her. Alex heard the click of the key as the bolt slid into place.

"Alex, love, come. Let her be. She isn't half the woman I am."

Alex turned and stalked back to the bed, whipping down the covers. "Get out of this room, woman." Julia's head snapped back in fear. He had never used that tone with her before, and a cold chill ran down her spine. Alex pulled his shirt closed and moved to the outer doorway. "If you value your life," he stated quietly, "you'll not cross my sights until you are in that carriage tomorrow." With a deadly sound, the door clicked shut behind him.

Finding the entrance to her chambers also locked, Alex gained access by the balcony door. A quick search found the room empty and his pulse quickened. Where would she have gone? Feverishly, he began his search through the mansion. He called upon all her favored haunts, but still he found no trace. Angered at her ability to slip away, he returned to her chambers to pace before the fire. He could rouse the servants to search. But what would he say? He had lost his wife because she had found an old lover in his bed? Lightning flashed and Alex moved to the window. The rain splashed against the glass, and seeds of dread began to take root and grow. Had she been angry enough to flee the manor? Would she have tried to run off into the night with naught but the clothing on her back? With a determined stride and fear in his heart, Alex made his way to the stables.

An hour later, Alex returned to her room and brushed the rain from his hair. He held his hands before the fire to warm them. She had gone to Hanna's again to help the boy, and thank God, Peter had had the good sense to travel with them. Alex removed his wet coat and sat on her chaise before the fire. She wouldn't welcome his presence at the moment, and knowing there was naught he could do to help her, he would wait. She had to return sometime, and no matter how late it was, he was going to be here. Alex lifted his legs onto the chaise and let his head drop back. He'd wait all night if he had to.

But when Alex awoke to find the first streaks of light pushing the darkness from the sky, Samantha's chambers were still empty.

Chapter XVIII

Samantha watched Alex leave her chambers before she returned to seek dry clothing. She was weary to the bone, but pride demanded she not sequester herself away. This was her home, and if Alex thought to make a fool out of her, he had better think again.

Clad in a gown of soft sky blue, Samantha entered the dining room and moved directly to Carolyn. "Forgive my lateness." She took Carolyn's hand. "I saw the carriage outside and Brown tells me you are leaving. Surely you do not have to go so soon. We have had no time together at all."

Carolyn noted the lines of fatigue that ringed Samantha's eyes and felt guilt that she had supplied the cause. "I fear we must," she said quietly. "With luck, we shall be home before Terrance arrives. Somehow I feel he will take the news of our travels much better if I am already there to reassure him that all is as it should be."

Samantha smiled sadly and wondered if things in *her* life would ever be as they should be. But a quick glance down the table set her most immediate fear to rest. At least for the moment, she was spared Julia's presence. Her resolve stiffened. *Julia be damned, she would not be defeated.*

Alex rose and pulled back her chair. "M'lady?" She allowed him to seat her, but remained silent toward him.

"Will you come again?" she questioned, conscious of Alex's nearness as he continued to stand behind her.

"Nay." Carolyn shook her head. "I think not until the spring. But that doesn't mean that you and Alex cannot come to visit any time you choose. Terrance and I would love to have you for houseguests."

Samantha held her tea with both hands to take the chill from her fingers, and wondered if Terrance would share Carolyn's enthusiasm after hearing of this latest adventure. "Alex . . ." Her voice was tight, but her eyes stayed fixed on her teacup. "Peter tells me that the storm last night played havoc with many of the local roads. It might be wise of you to accompany the carriage until you are sure all is safe."

Alex said nothing until his silence drew her eyes to his. "And will you be safe until I return?"

Unable to hold his stare, Samantha turned away. "I can find no reason to think not, m'lord."

James chose that moment to join the solemn group. He accepted Carolyn's silent plea, but despite his efforts, the conversation remained choppy at best, and all were relieved when the meal was over. As they rose to leave, Samantha realized that no one had commented or inquired after their missing guest.

Julia appeared as Carolyn and the children were

making their good-byes. Avoiding Alex's eyes, she gave Samantha a smug, satisfied nod, then, with a haughty turn of her shoulders, brushed past the group to enter the carriage. Mrs. Brown helped Carolyn settle the children, and Alex stepped near Samantha while he waited for Peter to bring his horse. The wind stirred, and he watched her shiver. He should send her back into the manor, yet he was reluctant to release her from his sight. He longed to reach out and touch her for reassurance, but he dare not until he could see the deed through to the end. She was building a wall, and even now he could feel its presence.

"What of the boy?" he questioned, trying to find a safe topic she would warm to.

Samantha drew her shawl more tightly about her. Her eyes were flat and haunted. "He died."

Stunned, Alex watched as she turned and fled into the house. He'd seen her tears, and her pain was such that it touched him as well. He had taken but two steps after her when Peter appeared.

"Your Grace?" Peter struggled to still the prancing steed.

Alex looked toward the doorway with frustration, then turned back. "Keep a close watch on the horses today," he instructed as Peter handed him the reins to mount. "If your mistress wishes to go about, be sure you take her yourself. James . . ." Alex called. James stepped closer to his brother's horse. "The child who Samantha attended last night died. See if you can do something to cheer her."

"I will ride with the carriage, if you wish. Then you could stay . . ."

Alex hated to admit how sorely tempted he was by his brother's words. The less he saw of Julia the better, but Carolyn had gone to great efforts on his behalf. The least he could do was see her and the children safely on their way. "I'll go," he snapped, annoyed with his own sense of frustration. "Just see to Samantha." Alex waited not for his brother's reply but gave the carriagemaster the signal and, with a lurch, the carriage was on its way.

Hours later, Alex returned to Coverick. His clothes were soaked and his temper foul. The rains had resumed before the carriage had even cleared his land, and the gray, stormy weather had continued for the better part of the day. Peter had been right about the roads, for in several places the carriage had had rough crossing. He had traveled with them farther than he had planned, but he needed to know they would be safe for the remainder of the journey. Leaving them to the comforts of a posting house, he then turned and made his way home. He was weary from a full day in the saddle, and more than once he had contemplated joining Carolyn in the carriage to escape the pouring rain. But each time the thought surfaced, he knew he could not. His hands itched to do Julia some bodily harm. So he had stayed in the cold and rain until his mood rivaled the stormclouds that filled the sky.

Alex pulled on a dry shirt and stood by the fire to warm himself. "Do you know the whereabouts of your mistress," he questioned as Judd gathered his wet clothing.

"Aye, Your Grace. She and Master James have spent the better part of the afternoon in the ballroom. I believe they are still there."

Alex frowned as he tied his cravat. The ballroom? He knew that the floors had been scrubbed and polished, but to his knowledge the room was still empty of furniture. Pulling on his coat, he left to find his wife.

A footman rose hastily from a high-back brocade chair that had been placed at the entrance to the hall. "Ah, Your Grace, . . ." he stammered, looking at the space past Alex's shoulder. "Her Grace asked that I stay here and see that she and Master James were not disturbed."

Alex paused only for a moment to look at the nervous footman, then silently continued down the hall. Nearing the ballroom, he heard Samantha's laughter ring out and sent a silent thanks to his brother for lifting her spirits. But as he stepped closer, the sound of clashing swords made his heart stop. He rounded the corner only to stop short at the sight before him.

In the middle of the empty ballroom, James was patiently instructing Samantha as to the proper handling of a sword. Relieved to find his wife in no distress, Alex advanced on the unsuspecting pair. James was the first to notice his brother.

"Alex, come and join us," he called as he carefully handed the sword back to Samantha. "We didn't expect you to be gone so long and Samantha has been worried."

Alex turned toward Samantha only to receive a decidedly icy glare.

"Were the roads bad?" James continued.

"Aye. Near washed away in some places. But I left them in good hands at the posting lodge in Tavistock. The proprietor promised to ride the rest of the way back with them as he had a need to travel to London."

James nodded, thankful that Alex had possessed the common sense not to mention Julia's name. "You must wonder what we are about," he said easily. "While you have toiled in the rain, I have had the pleasure of teaching your wife how to play chess."

Alex frowned, noting the solitary table drawn close before the hearth. "And you are having a duel to determine the winner?"

James laughed, and Samantha managed to suppress a smile. "Nay, we played for a token. I won the first game, so Samantha had to recite a piece of poetry."

Samantha glanced at Alex, but as their eyes met, she could not look away. Her shoulders stiffened. If he thought to make a fool of her in her own home, he was sadly mistaken. She quirked a brow and brazenly returned his stare.

"I also won the second game," James announced, suddenly aware of the heat that radiated from the two before him.

"And what did you demand for your token?" Alex's eyes never left his wife.

"I asked for a song."

"A song?" Alex turned to James to find his brother several shades of red. Samantha continued to say nothing, but a slow mocking smile touched her lips.

"'Twas quite . . . educational," James continued,

wondering if he would remember all the words to the lusty ballad or if he dare beg her to sing it again.

"I'm sure it was." Alex's voice held the barest trace of sarcasm. "And now?" Alex glanced pointedly back to the swords.

"Well, I must be a very good teacher, Alex, for on the third game, she trounced me solid. She had me in checkmate before I even saw it coming."

Alex thought back to the nights he had spent in Samantha's room on the island. On a table in the corner had stood an elegantly carved chess set. He turned to his wife, the question clearly in his eyes, only to see the answer plainly in hers.

"So my wife wishes to be instructed in the fine art of fencing?"

"'Twas her request." James shifted, growing more uncomfortable by the minute.

"Then you have done me a service, little brother," Alex replied easily, shrugging out of his coat. "But I feel I must return the favor." He tossed his coat in his brother's direction. "I think it will please me much to help you in this matter."

Samantha's eyes grew round, and then a smile of satisfaction bloomed on her face as she realized his intent.

"I would be honored to receive, ah . . . instructions from you, m'lord." Her voice was soft and taunting as she dipped into a deep, flawless curtsy before her husband.

"So be it." Alex lifted James's sword and tested its weight in his hand. "And what stakes shall we play for, m'lady?"

Samantha raised a brow. "I thought this was the

reward for a game already won."

"If it was won fairly, then that would be the case. But I think I would see us begin again. What say you to the original price? A favor to be granted to the winner."

Samantha watched an arrogant expression cover Alex's face, and there was no doubt in her mind what he would require of her as his favor.

Alex watched her pale slightly, then her eyes narrowed with determination. "As you wish, m'lord. A favor to be granted without reserve."

So she thinks to leave me if she wins, he thought darkly. *Well, the day will never come.* Alex gave her a courtly bow and raised his sword. "En garde."

Samantha had taken less than a step when she bid them cease. "Wait," she commanded. "The advantage is too much in your favor." She ignored Alex's scowl. "Here, I am hampered overmuch."

James watched transfixed as she tossed the sword to his brother with a move cleaner than he could execute himself. She turned and fumbled at her waist, and suddenly a puddle of white petticoats formed at her feet. James felt his mouth grow dry as she gathered the billowing white lace and tossed them in his direction. "Hold these," she instructed, taking no notice that she was giving him her most intimate apparel.

Alex said nothing as he held both swords. He watched as she gathered her flowing skirts to drape them high over her left arm. Her slender legs encased in sheer white stockings, were now visible to well past her knees.

"Ready," she said, nodding.

Caught by the sight of her legs and the tantalizing way her lacy garters peeked from beneath her skirt, Alex had to blink hard to clear his mind. She was magnificent as she stood before him. Arrogance stiffened her shoulders and determination set her form. He swallowed hard to take the dryness from his throat and tossed back her sword.

James gasped at the move and marveled at the easy way that she caught it. She tested the weight in her hand, then the metal cut through the air with a swish that left him gaping.

Samantha raised her sword and gave a mocking salute to Alex. "En garde, m'lord," she challenged softly.

James scurried to remove the yards of white petticoats from their paths and watched with astonishment as the pair moved back and forth to the clang of metal upon metal. He knew his brother's style and ability far surpassed his own, yet Samantha was meeting him move for move. He attacked; she parleyed. She attacked; he defended. James clutched the petticoats to his chest and watched in disbelief as the pair danced about the highly polished floor.

Samantha felt the power flow through her and reveled in the release. He was good, she realized, perhaps even better than Dancer. And the knowing that she held her own spurred her confidence and she pressed harder.

Alex found himself distracted time and again by the sight of her legs as she gracefully moved before him. She was skilled, more than he had ever imagined, but his reach was greater and he couldn't bring himself to duel at full pace. It seemed she sensed this and, giving her skirt another tug higher, she lunged and artfully removed one of the buttons on his coat.

Alex paused and looked down to the missing button. The fabric had not even been nicked, such was her skill. His playfulness ended, and again the pair met in the middle with a salute.

"I shall be the victor, m'lady," he taunted.

Her laughter rang out. "In a pig's eye." She lunged, but Alex sidestepped and returned to flick a bit of lace from her collar.

James felt his blood drain from his body, and his knees grew weak. He had seen the golden button sail from his brother's coat, and then the wisp of lace. It was no longer a playful game to while away a rainy afternoon that he was witness to, and he realized that he didn't wish to know the winner. Still trying to hold the billowy petticoats, he advanced upon the dueling pair. He had almost reached them when his foot caught in the dangling fabric, sending him face-first to slide across the floor.

Samantha never saw what hit her as she backed from Alex to trip over James's prone form. In his hasty effort to sit, he sent petticoats sailing in all directions. Fearing she had been injured in the fall, Alex threw down his sword and quickly knelt beside her trying to find her under the mound of fabric that James had unknowingly tossed in her direction.

He feared her injured, or at least full of rage, but when the last of the white lace was pulled from her hair, Samantha's laughter filled the room. "Is your skill so lacking, m'lord, that you must enlist members of your family to give assist?"

James struggled to his knees and tried to keep his eyes from taking a closer look at the curve of her calf. "Have I hurt you? Are you injured?"

Samantha allowed the pair to assist her to her feet. "I am fine," she chuckled, rubbing her sore backside. "But I do believe that your tactics gave your brother an unfair advantage."

"The match is a draw," Alex stated, reluctantly releasing her hand. "There is no winner, thus no favor will be granted."

James sighed in relief and turned to the chess table much in need of a brandy.

"I could have had you, you know," she said quietly, making Alex turn back as she folded the petticoats before her.

"Only if I had wished it, m'lady."

"Your Grace?"

Reluctantly, Alex turned from his wife. "Yes, Judd?"

"We have visitors, Your Grace. Sir Richard Cavandish from London and the local magistrate."

Alex straightened. Richard sat on the king's Privy Council. What was he doing in Cornwall?

Samantha rose from the floor and gathered her petticoats. "Just give me a moment, then I'll join you."

"Nay!" Samantha and James both flinched from the harshness in his tone. "Nay," Alex repeated softly. "I will see Richard privately in my study. When I know what he is about, then we shall see."

"As you wish m'lord."

Alex wasn't fooled by her words as she turned to go. Her frosty tone and hostile glare let him know only too well; there would be hell to pay later.

Annoyed with herself for allowing Alex to sequester her in her chambers, Samantha paced anxiously.
Why didn't he want her there? With eyes pressed tight
she tried to imagine Alex with Sir Richard in the
study. *Damn*, she swore as her mind remained empty.
She couldn't even remember what the study looked
like. Wearily she rubbed her temples. If only she
knew of what they spoke. Had she been found out? A
dozen plots came to mind, each more ludicrous than
the last. Could Edward have put together all the
pieces? Her flesh chilled with the thought of her
uncle, and despite the blazing fire, she chafed her
arms to warm them.

She crossed the floor and paused only as her hand
reached for the doorknob. *Don't be foolhardy*, her
mind challenged. She turned and leaned her back
against the door. Why did he not want her there?
Knowing she would find no peace until she knew
what Alex was about, Samantha reached behind her
and set the lock in the door. With the key securely in
her pocket, she moved to the carved panel wall to the
left of the hearth. Her fingers found the cluster of
grapes and pressed lightly against the third one in. As
before, the panel creaked open.

Samantha peered down into the darkened passageway. The air was close and damp. Carefully she lit a
taper, then, giving her room one last look she stepped
into the tunnel and pulled the panel closed behind
her. Shielding the candle with her hand, she
progressed slowly at first. Ten steps down and then

she reached the landing. A single wooden chair stood propped in the corner, and Samantha lit the wall candle behind it and wondered again if Alex was aware of the maze of tunnels that ringed his home. In her determination to see her chambers shine, she had worked on the wooden panels herself with polish whenever Mrs. Brown was not about. The first time the door had creaked open, her heart had almost stopped from the shock of it. But each day she explored further, and within her mind a map had begun to take shape.

The tunnel before her stretched dark and foreboding. With a hand on the damp wall to steady her, Samantha began to count the steps as she moved forward. She had learned the hard way that every seventh step was uneven in set, either too high or too low, causing the unsuspecting traveler to pitch forward into the darkness.

Reaching her goal, Samantha knelt before the wall and placed her fingers on the wooden peg before extinguishing the candle with a silent breath. The peg slipped free, and with her eye to the hole, she had limited vision of the study. Their voices, however, carried clear.

A man, slightly older than Alex, reclined in a chair before the fire and toasted him with the brandy glass he held. "The king will be most pleased, my friend, most pleased."

"And I can't begin to thank you, Your Grace." Samantha shifted to better observe the other man. Clad in uniform, he was surely the magistrate Judd had spoken of.

Alex moved in and out of her vision. "'Twas not a

planned move, Captain. I simply am taking advantage of the situation you have provided me with."

The captain shook his head. "But to give her up? I can't believe you would be so willing."

"London is still singing your praises, Alex, for dueling with Falcon's ghost," Sir Richard continued pleasantly. "You are a hero whether or not you want to be one."

"And you'll really give her to me?" the magistrate inquired eagerly.

Alex shrugged. "As you can see, Captain, I returned to find much to occupy my time." He gestured to the room and moved out of sight. "And although I find the decision more than regrettable, I feel I no longer have a choice."

Samantha felt a tickling sensation against her shoulder and looked down. The light from the small knothole showed a healthy black spider moving steadily over her shoulder. Without thinking, her hand jerked out to brush it away and knocked into the wall. Her heart flew to her throat as the conversation in the room before her grew silent. Holding her breath, she slowly drew again to her knees to peer out. The men gazed steadily in her direction.

"Rats," Alex stated with irritation, moving so his back blocked her view. "We still have much to see to. So I am grateful you understand my plight. However much I would like to see her remain at Coverick, I simply do not have the time to teach her all that would be required."

"Well, I thank my stars that I took the chance to call, Your Grace. This will bring quite a boost to my reputation. Do you think she will find the move an easy one?"

Alex stepped out of sight again. "She is high-spirited to be sure, and stubborn as they come. But with your knowledge, Captain, I feel sure you will find success. My only request is that you remove her as soon as possible. I've grown quite accustomed to her presence and I would hate to regret my decision any more than I do at this moment."

"Done, Your Grace." The captain stood. "I thank you in advance for your gracious hospitality and shall leave you now to make the necessary arrangements. I have several good men staying at the Coverick Inn and I see no reason as to why we can't be away with her at morning's first light."

Samantha flopped back on her legs. Her heart beat so loudly, she felt surely they must hear. Her hands squeezed into fists. He meant to give her to the magistrate in the morning. Their voices droned on, but she heard no more. A violent trembling started in her legs and slowly consumed her. They would take her to Newgate and there she would hang. Her stomach lurched and her hand clamped to her mouth. Without replacing the wooden peg, Samantha turned and tried to make her way back down the darkened corridor.

She wanted to scream her frustration, the sound of it already echoing in her head. The pain of it sliced through her again as her mind replayed Alex's words over and over. "I have not the time to teach her. I would be grateful if you'd relieve me from the burden of her care."

Forgetting to count the steps, Samantha tripped

several times as she slowly made her way back. Stopping when she reached the landing before her chambers, she broke down and sobbed. Her stomach lurched again as she thought of Newgate. The pirates had often outdone themselves when sharing their tales of horror. Few who went in ever came out. Bile rose in her throat. What a fool she had been to trust him. Angry tears ran down her cheeks and her body stiffened. *Dear God, the baby.* She wrapped her arms about her stomach. Would he still send her away if he knew she carried his child? Her head dropped forward. If he knew, he would keep her until the babe arrived and then send her away. Her hands tightened against the babe and, despite her will, her sobs increased.

Long moments passed, and with her tears finally spent, Samantha sat up and wiped her eyes on the skirt of her gown. She had carried Alex's seed for only three months, but nothing was going to separate her from her child. She took a deep, sustaining breath. She would leave, immediately. Slowly she rose on legs that quivered. Her hands trembled as she reached for the clothing that she had placed on the wooden chair. She had pilfered the breeches and shirt from James's wardrobe just three days before. Confident he would never miss them, she had taken thread in hand. The breeches now fit her well, but she had had no time for the shirt. Never had she imagined needing them so soon. Samantha shed her skirts and pulled on the snug breeches. A calm determination filled her as she stood in the borrowed clothing. Her fingers no longer trembled as she undid the many buttons on her bodice and removed it to don the oversize black shirt. For the first time in weeks she felt as herself again.

Samantha leaned back against the wall. Her delicate slippers were not a good choice, but her riding boots would be adequate. Stepping to the hidden panel, she reached for the lever and pulled. Samantha stepped into the room to find Alex sitting directly before her.

"Well, well," he said slowly. "It seems I have caught a pirate."

Chapter XIX

Samantha slammed the panel closed and turned on Alex in her fury. "You bastard," she hissed. Her fingers closed on a brass candlestick and sent it sailing.

Alex ducked and rolled out of his chair as a crystal goblet sailed past his head.

"You two-faced, arrogant bastard." Her voice, hard and menacing, carried a venom that chilled the blood. "What a farce you play at. All that brotherly devotion and concern that Carolyn be safely on her way. Tell me, m'lord," she sneered. "Did you stay to see your mistress safely abed before you struggled home? Is she waiting for you now?"

Heedless of the objects that sailed in his direction, Alex closed the space between them in less than three strides. "What madness has possessed you, woman?" Grabbing her arms, he tried to pull her close, but Samantha would have none of it. She twisted and squirmed from his grip.

"Unhand me, you slimy toad," she gasped as

Alex grabbed her about the waist and plunged both of them onto the bed. "Get off me."

Alex let the weight of his body hold her, yet still it was no simple feat to pin her arms above her head. She was freezing. Her hands were like ice within his own and he could feel the chill of her body beneath his. "How long were you in that blasted tunnel?" he demanded, angry that she would take so little care with herself. "You're frozen through."

"And will you wait until my bed is cold before you place your mistress in it? Or does Julia arrive even as I leave?"

Alex dropped his forehead to hers and tried to fathom her twisted words. He could feel her anger. It poured forth, stunning him with its intensity, confusing him as to its source.

"You accuse me of being unfaithful?"

Samantha turned her head and refused to look at him.

Alex, cold and tired from a hellish day, felt his frustrations rising. "You say that you have no desire to share my bed, yet you rave as a madwoman because Julia wishes to do so. I would know why."

"Take your hands from me," she gasped, his weight making her breathing difficult.

Alex shook his head. "Your words claim that you care not for my kisses, but your heart beats too fast, m'lady. I think 'tis you who play me false." He lowered his lips to hers, but she jerked her head aside. Undaunted, Alex feasted on the column of her neck and paused to nip at her ear.

Samantha shuddered. She could wish his head on a platter, yet the feel of his lips against her skin made her senses turn traitor. Her anger drained, but its loss left her empty and broken. To complete her mortification, she felt tears well in her eyes. "Please stop."

Alex raised his head and watched her lip tremble. "I sent Julia away," he said patiently. "She'll trouble us no more."

Samantha shook her head and tried to blink back her tears. "Just stop." She struggled to swallow back the knot in her throat. "I heard," her voice trembled. "You know I was in the passageway. Do you think me a complete fool?"

Alex frowned. "I heard the knock and suspected. But why are you so distressed?"

Samantha's head snapped back. "Did you really think I would thank you for signing my death warrant?"

Alex felt her trembling increase, and her hands grew colder still within his own. "What are you talking about?"

Samantha could no longer see his face for the tears that filled her eyes. "How can you do this?" Her voice broke. "I know you have cause to hate me, but, my God, if you wish me dead, just take a knife and be done with it. Don't sentence me to Newgate."

Alex released his grip on her wrists and gently wiped her tears with his thumb. "Why do you suddenly think I wish you harm?" His voice was soft and coaxing. "Just what do you think you heard?"

Samantha pulled herself from beneath him to sit on the bed. Her hands clenched in her lap and her head slumped forward. "You told the magistrate he could take me in the morning." Her voice was flat, lifeless.

Alex rolled to his feet and began to pace. "You actually believe me capable of sending you to the hangman? My God, woman, you certainly have a poor enough opinion of me."

Samantha's head throbbed with confusion. Why did he act the victim? "I heard . . ."

Grabbing her arm, Alex pulled her to her feet and gave her a rough shake. "You heard me give my best new mare to the man, nothing more."

Samantha rubbed her hands across her eyes. "I don't understand."

"'Tis little wonder," Alex snapped, looking pointedly at her breeches. "You were already jumping to conclusions and seeking an excuse to flee." He could still see the tracks of tears in the firelight, but he hadn't realized her distrust would cut him so deeply.

"But if they know I'm here . . ."

"They know no such thing." Alex continued to pace. "Richard Cavandish is a member of the king's Privy Council. He came to seek my help."

Samantha slumped onto the end of the chaise, her legs suddenly too weak to support her. "I still don't understand."

Alex tried to stem his frustration. "Someone is stealing state secrets and sending them to France. Cavandish has traced the path to Cornwall."

"But you said . . ."

Alex knelt before her. She was paler than parchment and her eyes were clouded with fear. With his forefinger he gently raised her chin so their eyes met. "The magistrate came only to requisition a horse."

"Then you're not sending me away?"

Alex rose and began to pace again, angered that she couldn't see what lay before her eyes. "Don't you realize yet that as long as there is breath in this body, I will keep you from harm?"

Stunned, Samantha tried to sort through his words and her hands began to tremble anew. The truth burned through her fear, but the relief that came was a pain unto itself for the harsh thoughts she had harbored against him.

Alex stared into the fire and wondered yet again how she had managed to turn the tide. What mountain did he need to climb to win her trust? His shoulders stiffened with anger. And why should it matter so much if he didn't? Taking a deep breath, he searched the flames for answers.

Samantha watched him pace the room, then pause before the fire. Even with his back to her, she could feel the hurt her mistrust had caused him. No one in her life had ever placed her first, and she had thanked him by thinking the worst. Her hand touched her stomach and suddenly she knew she had the words that might ease the way between them.

On legs that were no longer unsteady, Samantha rose and stood beside him. Gently she touched his sleeve.

"M'lord?" she whispered as he turned toward her. "Again I have played the part of a fool."

Alex almost smiled. She got no argument from him on that point. His hand reached for hers and their fingers intertwined. She was so damn fragile, he thought wearily, how could she ever have thought he would send her away?

Samantha studied the hand that held hers so

gently. There was strength there, enough to see a man dead if he wished it. But when he touched her, there was only gentleness. She opened their clasped hands to take his between each of hers. "Forgive me, m'lord, for harsh words spoken in haste."

Alex watched her bent head and heard the emotions clogging her voice. He touched her chin with his free hand, ready to see her tears. But when eyes lifted to his, they were strong and clear. Slowly she raised his hand to her lips and placed a kiss within its palm. The simple gesture hit him with the force of a blow to the stomach, making his heart pound faster.

Their eyes locked. The intensity of his gaze gave her strength and became her courage. She stepped closer. "You have risked much for my sake, m'lord." She moved their joined hands to cover her secret. "Know then, that even as you care for me, you care for your child as well."

Alex stared at her in wonder. "You carry our child?"

Emotions again clogged her throat. "Aye."

His arms moved about her, cradling her against his body, sharing his warmth. She could feel the beat of his heart against her cheek and thrilled to know it was as unsteady as her own. Never in her life had she felt such peace, or so protected. For each, time stood still, allowing every emotion to be touched and savored, then stored away in the making of memories.

They had dined alone in her room, but Samantha

had no memory of what had passed her lips. After the meal, he had left briefly, returning to find her dressed in a gown of the finest blue lace. But despite their joint pleasure, Alex noted the wary look that had seeped back into her eyes.

He moved to her quickly and caught her high in his arms, delighting in the way her arms looped about his neck. The door to her chambers was secured, the fire blazed warmly in the hearth, and he held in his arms both his wife and his child. For Alex the pleasure was almost overwhelming. But as he held her close, he knew one last obstacle remained in the path of their happiness. Gently he lowered her to the bed.

Samantha gloried in the strength of him as she clung to his neck. But her joy fled when he moved to set her down. He would not hurt her, of that she had no doubt. And somewhere in her mind she knew that if he pressed, tonight she would submit. Somehow she would find the strength to endure it to bring him pleasure.

Alex tugged his boots off and removed his shirt, reading the emotions that flashed across her face like lines in an opened boot. Tonight she would not fight him if he chose to take her; that, too, would be her gift. Knowing the price she was willing to pay touched him deeply and strengthened his resolve. Without removing his breeches, Alex slipped into bed beside her and gathered her close under the covers.

"You are beautiful," he whispered against her forehead, his hand sliding down to lightly touch her stomach.

Samantha smiled and, placing her hand against his, pressed it more firmly to their child. "I am not fragile, m'lord."

Alex's breath touched her cheek a heartbeat before his lips. "You do yourself an injustice, madam," he scolded, pulling her closer. "You pretend, and swagger about in breeches, but underneath you are delicate and soft." His lips brushed across her cheek. "You are more fragile than the petals of a newly opened rose, and more priceless to me than all I own."

Samantha felt her world begin to spin with his words. Never in her life had she felt cherished. "Then I take it you are pleased with my news of a child?"

"Not just any child, madam, but our child."

Samantha heard his words, but something was amiss. "Then what is wrong?" she whispered, turning to face him.

Alex leaned down until their foreheads touched. "I am plagued by the knowledge that the child you carry was not conceived in candlelight and tenderness."

Her fingers traced the lines of worry that marred his brow. "And is that really so important, m'lord."

Alex captured her fingers and kissed their tips one by one. "To me it is. In my careless haste to have you, I have given you cause to fear one of life's greatest pleasures."

Samantha forced herself to remain calm. "And if I bid you to prove different?"

He felt her brief tremor before she managed to bank it, and his heart turned over. He ached to take her and lose himself in her honeyed softness, but tonight, even as she gave, he would give back. Tonight would be perfect for her regardless of his own desires, he would see to it.

He kissed her again and then pulled the covers more securely about them. "There will be a lifetime to seek pleasures of the flesh," he whispered as a plan sprang to mind. "Tonight I would simply lie abed with my wife as an old married couple seeking to share their warmth."

Samantha fought back the tears that threatened and again her hand found his as it rested again on the baby. "Our son shall grow strong and find much pride in the man that he calls Father."

Alex smiled and shook his head slowly as their eyes met. "If you would honor a request, m'lady," he whispered as their breath mingled. "I would rather fancy a daughter. She would have her mother's clear blue eyes and hair the color of moonlight. She'll be a hellion to be sure, but then . . . He kissed her gently. "The secret will be to let her run about in breeches from time to time."

Samantha felt her last defense crumble. No flickering candlelight or sugared promises could ever have touched her as deeply as his simple words, spoken from the heart. In that moment, as she gazed into the green eyes that had held her captive for so many years, Samantha knew she loved. Instinctively her arm reached up to circle his neck. And for the first time, she slowly pulled his lips to hers and touched the sun.

Chapter XX

The air was crisp, the day clear and bright. Alex slowed his step to match Samantha's as they wandered down the street of shops in Truro. He smiled, thinking of his plan. He had thrust upon James the task of setting the stage, trusting his brother to make things right. And as the sun beat warm upon his back, satisfaction made his step light as they wandered from shop to shop.

Caught up in the perfect day he had planned for her, Alex allowed her to set the pace. But as the sunlight dimmed and each turned his feet toward home, he knew that there was not one man in all of Truro who didn't envy him his bride. He was content, he realized as he held the reins to the carriage. For the first time in his life he felt truly complete.

Sleepily, Samantha snuggled nearer, closed her eyes, and let the motion of the carriage rock her toward her dreams. It had been the most wonderful day of her life, she decided, resting her cheek against

Alex's arm. They had stood with the children and watched a puppet show, and eaten the most delicious meat pasties. Now as her eyes stubbornly refused to stay open, all she wished for was her bed.

Alex felt her shift in weight and knew she slept. All the better, he thought as he turned the carriage in the opposite direction of home.

Samantha awoke, slowly realizing the carriage no longer moved. Expecting to see the bright lanterns that lined the drive to Coverick, she was confused. Tall trees surrounded her, their shadows dark and menacing against the blue-black sky. The horse whinnied softly and shuffled. Off to the left, a single cottage stood sheltered among the trees.

"Alex?"

Alex quickened his step at the sound of her voice. "I'm sorry, love." He reached her, taking her hands. "I thought you asleep, and I but wished to see to your comfort before I woke you."

"Where is this place?" she questioned, trying again to see the position of the moon within the trees.

Alex scooped her up in his arms and walked steadily toward the cottage, setting her down just inside the door. "Warm yourself by the fire while I see to the horses." He gave her a gentle nudge inside. "I'll be only a moment."

Hesitantly, Samantha stepped forward. Candles burned, and by their shadowy light she surveyed the tidy room. A table set for two was positioned near the fire. And on the hearth a great black kettle issued forth an aroma that set her mouth to water. How strange, she thought, carefully lifting the lid to find a thick stew. Gently she replaced the lid and turned to face the room. Closing her eyes, she waited. Vague, dusty images of sadness from long ago teased her mind, but faded almost before they came. Her thoughts reeled with confusion as she opened her eyes. This place had stood empty for longer than the manor house that was now her home. Her finger traced a line along the table and came away clean. How was it possible? She twisted the snakes that ringed her fingers as she explored farther. Foodstuffs were fresh and carefully stored away. A decanter of wine sparkled in the firelight, casting its rainbow of colors against the wall. A second room opened off the first, and here, too, a fire burned. A massive tester bed, covered with fresh linens invitingly turned back, filled most of the room. Stepping closer, she gently touched the lacy gown that rested near the foot of the bed and recognized it as her own.

The click of the door told her Alex had returned, and she slowly stepped back into the main room to join him. His back was toward her as he stoked the fire higher, then carefully swung the kettle away from the flames. As the aroma of the stew again filled the air, Samantha's stomach sent out a noisy call of protest.

"Are you hungry, m'lady?" Alex laughed as he straightened from the fire.

Samantha watched him in the firelight. "Aye, m'lord. But for the moment, my curiosity almost rivals my appetite. Where is this place? And how is it that furniture that I saw polished just two days ago has found its way here?"

Alex removed his cape and then took hers from her arms, and hung both on pegs by the door. "This is a hunting cottage near the south border of our property." His eyes took in the stage his brother had set for them. When he had last been here, save for the frame of his parents' bed, the cottage had stood empty. Now the furniture gleamed and the walls sported a fresh coat of wash. James had indeed done well. Alex turned back to Samantha. "I wished to have time alone with you."

"And we could not have done that at home?"

Alex smiled at the easy way she referred to Coverick as home. Now she even sounded like a wife. "At the manor," he replied, taking the crystal decanter and pouring them both a glass of wine, "there is always that which must be attended to. It will be a time, I fear, before either of us can complain of boredom. Here . . ." he gestured about them, handing her the glass, "there is nothing that needs our attention."

Samantha sipped her wine, enjoying the bite of the fine vintage. "And did you cast a spell to make all this appear, m'lord?"

Alex smiled. "You will certainly agree that magic does have its uses."

Samantha lowered her eyes seductively. "And am I going to be seduced by a wizard, m'lord?"

Alex grinned and tried to calm the frantic beat of his heart. "Perhaps." He turned back to the table and, taking one of the china plates, began to fill it with stew. "But I did think that I would feed you first."

Samantha's light chuckle sent his blood racing and Alex found his hands suddenly unsteady.

"'Tis a most wise decision, m'lord." Her fingers traced down his arm and deftly captured the plate before his hand went limp. "I would be sorely grieved if you had planned to starve me." Giving him a slow wicked grin over her shoulder, Samantha moved to the table and took her place.

Alex felt the throbbing need deep in his belly and knew it was not for food that he hungered. But as her skirts swayed he began to wonder who was seducing whom. Deciding that in truth it didn't matter in the least, he filled his plate and, retrieving a basket of warmed bread, he joined her at the table.

They ate in silence, their eyes rarely leaving the other. Alex downed the last of his wine and wondered how long she would manage to hold her fear at bay. He had made her a promise, and until she desired him as much as he did her, he would not take her. A smile tugged at his lips, for tonight he had planned many ways to show her pleasure.

Samantha found herself floating in his gaze. The meal over, Alex pulled her onto his lap as they sat before the fire in comfortable silence. The flames danced as a log hissed and snapped, but Samantha was only aware of the wide chest that she rested against. She could hear his heart, and as her fingers reached up to touch his cheek, she felt his pulse quicken. Alex tugged his stock loose and tossed it aside, then his fingers made quick work of the buttons on his shirt. It was both heaven and hell to feel the cool touch of her hands against his flesh. Slowly, he pulled the pins from her hair, stirring the elusive scent that seemed so much a part of her.

Samantha pressed her cheek against the bare flesh of his chest, the muscles hard and warm. Never had she imagined such pleasure from such a simple act.

Alex rose and, dipping slightly, caught her under the knees to cradle her high against him. Her hair tumbled over his arm in careless disarray. Their eyes met and held as he walked slowly, into the bedroom.

His arm lowered, and Samantha felt her legs slide down his body until she came to stand unsteadily before him. Folding her into his embrace, his lips brushed lazily against her neck as he worked the back hooks of her gown.

Of their own accord, her arms moved up to encircle his neck, and as her gown loosened, his lips sought new purchase tracing the milky softness of her shoulder. "You smell so good," his warm breath fanned her cheek, "like lavender and sunshine."

Samantha felt her knees grow weak as Alex slipped layer after layer of clothing from her. But when his fingers tugged on the tiny blue bow of her chemise, her sanity returned. Desperately she caught his hands within her own and tried to stop the violent pounding of her heart.

"Hush," he whispered, gathering her close. "The night is early." Easily he lifted her onto the high bed. Samantha watched the muscles of his back with fascination as he pulled off his boots and stockings. But when he stood and reached for the buttons on his breeches, the last of her bravado fled and her eyes quickly turned away.

She struggled to quell her trepidation when the mattress dipped with his weight. He was her husband, it was his right to have her, but despite her resolve, her lips trembled with anxiety, not passion, as he grasped her shoulders and gently turned her toward him.

Alex had seen the brief moment when naked fear had filled her eyes. His fingers gently raised her chin and his lips touched hers. Not hot and demanding as was his wont, but soft as the feather-light touch of a butterfly as it moves from flower to flower. His mustache brushed against her lips, her cheeks, her eyes, then back to tantalizingly taste her lips again. His fingers threaded through the silky softness of her hair to cradle her face. His tongue traced a path across her sealed lips even as his thumb tugged gently against her chin. "Open to me, love." His warm breath caressed her skin. "I need . . ." But his words never finished as her lips parted and she melted against him. Her moan was captured by his mouth. Alex pressed deeper, drinking of her sweetness, striving to satisfy a thirst that would not be quenched. His tongue caressed hers and Samantha felt a strange languor seep into her body. She felt only gratitude when he lowered her to rest against the softness of the pillows. Drugged by his kisses, her limbs grew pliant beneath his wandering hands. His fingers skimmed across her collarbone to the back of her ear, sending shivers of gooseflesh down her arms. And when his hands trailed lower, his knuckles brushing against the soft swell of her breast, a shaft of ecstasy shot through her.

Alex tugged at the thin blue ribbon that secured her chemise, and slowly the tiny bow pulled free. Their eyes met. Using just one finger, he loosened the hooks until the fabric parted before him. Gently he flipped back one side, then the other. "You are so beautiful." His voice, husky with desire, was as intoxicating as his lips.

Samantha smiled doubtfully at the green eyes that held hers. She could climb a ratline and wield a sword, but never in her wildest imagination had she pictured herself as beautiful. Her hand reached up to trace the line of his mustache. "I think the light deceives you, m'lord.

"You are the most beautiful thing that has ever come into my life," he whispered softly. "When our years are many and my eyes grow dim, I shall still find pleasure in the sight of you." He lowered his lips to hers, and found them warm and waiting. Her arms rose to encircle his neck. Hard muscles flattened soft.

Alex shifted to gain access to the feast that lay before him. His fingers traced the silver chain from her throat to the medallion that shimmered between her breasts. His knuckles brushed across the hardened tip of her nipple. The thought of his child seeking nourishment there sent his passion raging. His lips lowered and tasted of the forbidden fruit, touching it hesitantly at first with his tongue, then drawing the bud gently into his mouth.

Samantha gasped. The tug of his lips ignited a spark deep within and created a yearning akin to pain. Her fingers threaded through his hair, loving the wiry texture as she pulled him closer still.

His mouth trailed wet kisses from the tip of one breast to the other as his hand traced down her leg. Catching the hem of her chemise, he drew it upward, as his fingers danced enticingly over her flesh. But when his hand moved to her inner thigh and tried to reach the feminine warmth of her, Samantha stiffened and jerked upright, pulling herself from his touch. Mortified by her childish

316

response, her head dropped to her knees and her breath came in uneven gasps. She forced a swallow past the growing lump in her throat. Her chemise was tangled about her waist, leaving her hip and legs bare to his gaze, but pride demanded she not embarrass herself further by pushing it lower.

Alex collapsed back against the pillow and struggled to even his breathing. One arm flopped across his face while the other absently rubbed against the tense muscles of her back. "It is not going to work," he said quietly. He felt her stiffen with his words.

"I'm sorry . . ."

His hand slid up to her shoulders and tugged, but she only curled tighter. "Nay, 'tis not you, little one." His hand drifted to rub along her lower back. "I pushed too fast. My wish was to seduce you, now I find 'tis not the case."

Samantha felt her blood run cold with fear. Had she repulsed him so completely? Had she finally found love only to have it snatched from her waiting fingers? Her heart pounded in her ears, but she needed the words. Gathering her courage, she turned to look at him. Long and lean, his naked body was magnificent as it glowed in the firelight.

"You no longer want me?"

Alex sat up beside her and captured her chin before she could turn away. "I find that I don't want some pliant creature who bends to my will." His hand raked through his hair as he sought to find the words. "I want a partner. One who meets me in all ways." Tenderly, he pushed tangled strands of hair from her heated face. "I want someone who will give back, even as I give." His lips touched hers, then withdrew. "'Tis not my wish to seduce you. I find I want more, much, much more."

Samantha felt her tears dry, and hope flared anew. Her eyes dropped to her clenched hands. He had captured her heart just as surely as he had captured her body. She took a deep breath and tried to calm the erratic beating of her heart. Her hands trembled only slightly as she reached down and, grasping the hem of her chemise pulled it over her head then tossed it carelessly to the floor. Hesitantly, her eyes raised to his.

"Then teach me what to do."

Alex released his breath as a slow, easy smile softened his rakish features. He captured her hand and uncurled her fingers. His lips pressed a kiss to her palm, and a jolt of pleasure shot straight to her heart. Then he drew her hand to his chest. "I am flesh and blood, little one." He moved her knuckles through the hair on his chest. "Not some monster who wishes to harm you." Her touch made his heart quicken, and he struggled to keep his voice even. "Know that what brings you pleasure," his lips dipped to hers, "does the same for me." His kiss deepened, then he drew back.

Slowly she smiled. Her fingers traced round his ears, then moved to encircle his neck. But instead of pulling him close, Samantha raised her own lips until they pressed firmly against his, warm, wet, willing, and rapture was kindled anew.

As his hands touched her breast, hers slipped from his neck to do the same. Alex groaned against her lips at the pleasure her caresses evoked, but when she pushed him back against the pillows and her lips timidly traced down his neck to taste his nipple, his arms tightened about her with an intensity that stunned them both. Their lips touched and flamed and danced about them. Samantha drew back and reveled in this newfound power she had over his body. Her nails raked lightly down his ribs and, fascinated, she watched his body tremble with passion.

Alex shuddered beneath her questing hands. "You are a witch, m'lady." He pulled her down to nibble on her lower lip. "What madness do you weave?"

Samantha's low, throaty chuckle was almost his undoing. "I shall cast a spell, m'lord," she threatened, her breast sensuously brushing back and forth against his chest. "I shall bind you to me for all times."

Alex tipped her chin up so their eyes met. "You did that the first time you looked at me."

Samantha felt her heart turn over. And when his lips again found hers, she answered with a longing that sprang from the very depths of her being. Alex shifted, and she gloried in the weight of him as he settled over her. His leg slipped between the softness of hers and she felt the hardened proof of his desire. Hesitantly, her hand moved lower until she brushed against him with the back of her fingers. Startled, her hand pulled back. So hard, so hot, so incredibly soft. Curious, her fingers again traced the length of him. Alex shuddered, then placed his hand about hers and taught her the motion that would bring him pleasure. And when his hand fell away, hers stayed to continue the exquisite torture. She felt his breath catch and, encouraged, her caresses grew bolder.

Alex soared in ecstasy, for the fumbling uncertainty of her innocence touched him deeper than the practiced skills of a favored courtesan. Following her lead, he let his hand trail down her silken belly to the warmth of her that held his child.

"Your skin is so soft," he whispered, dropping kisses along her neck, then down toward her breast. Again his lips closed over her, and the gentle pull and tug of his mouth coupled with the rhythmic motion of his hands between her thighs.

Samantha's breath caught in her throat as his fingers caressed closer, then slipped inside. Her head reeled as he worked his magic. A slow, sweet yearning for more seeped through her until her hips rose to meet his hand in a motion that was older than time. She moaned in protest when his fingers left her, but then she felt him shift more completely over her. He waited, until her eyes raised to his. Needing to know she ached for release as much as he, Alex poised above her but moved not a muscle.

Samantha smiled at the fierceness of his gaze. He would not take her, such was his honor. She could refuse him no longer, such was her need. Her hands traced up the corded muscles of his arms to his wide shoulders. The air about them steamed with passion as gently but surely her hands glided down his ribs to guide him home.

She braced herself for the pain, but instead felt only the hard warmth of him as he slid deep within her. The ecstasy of it flooded her senses, and just when she was sure she could stand no more, he began to move. She shuddered and arched beneath him. Passion washed over her, drugging, delirious, and wonderful. Samantha clung to Alex like a lifeline as his strokes deepened and pushed her higher, then higher still. Her breath came in short gasps as her body rose to meet his. Her pulse quickened, and as her heart pounded, an exquisite ecstasy raced through her until the very joy of it pierced her soul with a force that drew a startled cry from her lips.

Alex felt her shudder, then, placing himself deep within, joined her in sweet oblivion.

The room grew still as he held her close, her body still shivering from the passion they had shared. "Now you are truly mine," he whispered against her forehead.

Despite the sated lassitude that filled her, Samantha raised herself up on one elbow to gaze down at him. "I was yours from before we met," she said slowly, realizing the truth of her words even as she spoke them. "You came to me in a dream." She blinked in confusion, and wondered why it had taken her so long to see what had been right before her eyes. "You are the sun." She gazed at him in wonder. "My other half. The answer to the riddle."

Intrigued, Alex wanted more. "And of what riddle do you speak."

Amazed that it should now be so clear, her eyes glowed with satisfaction. "Kabol, my shaman, once told me that I was the moon." She touched the medallion that lay warm against her heart. "The last time I saw him, he bid me go and find the sun. Without the sun, he said, I would never be complete." Her eyes filled with love and promise as she looked down at him. "You are the sun."

Alex found himself floating in the clear azure eyes before him. He knew not of riddles, but he did know that she was his and his she was going to stay. His passion stirred again as he watched her. Slowly his lips raised to meet hers. "Your teacher was a very, very wise man."

The fire in the hearth grew dim from want of attention, then faded completely. But nestled under thick quilts and wrapped in love, if either noticed, neither cared.

Chapter XXI

It was almost noon when hunger finally forced the pair to leave their warm nest. After feasting on fruit and cheese, they wandered hand in hand down narrow paths until they arrived at the sea. The day, like the one before it, was clear and bright. Samantha's laughter mingled with the cry of the gulls as she danced before Alex, playing tag with the waves. She collected shells, and presented them to him one by one. Alex carefully examined each as if it were a priceless work of art. In her company, he found a peace he had feared lost to him forever, while Samantha discovered a joy she never knew existed.

Resting on a pile of flat rocks warmed by the sun, Samantha broke apart their last pastry. Alex ate from her fingers, and when the flaky confection was gone, he sucked the last traces from her fingertips, rekindling a flame that had yet to be extinguished. Shifting, he pulled her to sit astride his lap. She accepted the bawdy pose with ease and leaned more fully against him.

Alex gave a quick glance about the deserted coastline, then slowly tugged her skirts from beneath her until only his breeches separated them. His raw sensuality thrilled her as she felt him press boldly against her softness. Never had she felt so alive. Every nerve in her body sang with delicious anticipation as her lips parted, welcoming the seductive invasion of his tongue.

Her eyes widened with surprise, then slid closed with pleasure as his hands moved down to the buttons that pressed so intimately against her stomach. His fingers were cold against the warmth of her skin, and she sucked in her breath as they completed their task, then paused to linger, seeking then finding that moist place that already ached for his return. He shifted her on his lap, and she moaned with ecstasy as he entered, then sent her sailing, to fly higher than the gulls that still soared above them.

The following day, the sun had not yet reached its peak when the sound of a horse and rider invaded their solitude. An urgent pounding at the door brought an angry scowl to Alex's face as he pushed Samantha into the back chamber.

"Wait here until I see who has the nerve to call at this ungodly hour."

Resisting the urge to remind him it was well past daybreak, Samantha quietly retreated and began a frantic search for her scattered clothing.

"Alex? Come, man, open the door." James, fist raised to pound again, stepped back when the cottage door swung open. But the look of anger that covered his brother's face made him retreat even farther.

"I thought I made my plans perfectly clear." Alex blocked the doorway and made no effort to invite his brother in.

James took a deep breath and prayed he had made the right decision. "Sir Richard is back at the manor," he said quickly, hoping to divert Alex's anger from himself. "He arrived at daybreak demanding to speak with you."

Alex felt his entire body grow tense. "And you were not able to convince the man that I was away on business?"

Samantha, now dressed, touched Alex's arm as it braced across the doorway. "Darling, let James come inside." She ignored his angry scowl as it turned in her direction and smiled patiently. "Do not shoot the messenger, m'lord."

Alex stepped aside to let James enter, but his look stayed far from pleasant. The two sat at the table while Samantha turned to the hearth to warm the water for tea.

As his brother's scowl grew more impatient, James's words rushed forth. "Alex, I could not put the man off. He demanded to know where you were and seemed intent on finding you no matter what."

Alex's brows drew together in a frown. "I feared this would happen. But I had hopes it would not be so soon."

Samantha poured the tea, added a shot of brandy to each, and joined them at the table. "But why has he returned?" Her fingers clenched her mug tightly as she strove to keep her voice calm.

James accepted the hot brew gratefully. "He would tell me nothing. But I'll tell you this . . ." James turned to Alex. "The man is obsessed with finding you."

"Then it would seem best for all involved that I should help him." His decision made, Alex turned back to James. "I would be grateful if you would harness the carriage for me. When that is done, return with haste to Coverick and tell Richard that I will arrive shortly." Alex rose, pulling Samantha's stiff body to his side. "Leave us now, for there is much to see to."

James nodded. "I'm on my way."

Samantha waited until the door closed after James. "Why has Cavandish come back?"

Alex sighed and turned to his wife. "Richard is working on instructions from the king himself. The situation with France is growing more tense." Green eyes locked with blue. "He wants my help."

Samantha felt his tension. "And . . . ?"

"I have no choice," Alex said quietly. "I must leave."

Samantha shivered as an icy premonition settled over her. "There is danger." Her voice shook with fear.

Alex pulled her close, his hand resting low on her stomach. "If the choice were mine, I would never leave you. My greatest wish is to watch you grow with our child." His breath was warm against her forehead as he held her close. "But there is no help for it, love. Richard is like a dog with a bone. Once an

326

idea takes hold, he'll not let go. If I refuse, he'll speculate on the reason why. And at present, we can little afford to have someone probing into your past." He felt her tremble and held her tighter. "Trust me, love." His teeth nibbled against her cheek, then raked down her neck. "I shall join Richard as he has requested, but in doing so, I shall keep the man well away from Coverick. You will be safe there, on that you have my word."

Samantha gazed up at him and saw the raw hunger in his eyes. He would keep her safe, this fierce warrior who was her husband. And as anxiety was pushed aside, a deep aching took its place. "I want you." Her voice was clear and steady even as her fingers tugged clumsily on the buttons of his shirt. "I want you now."

Alex felt the thin threads of his control snap. Never had so few words inflamed him so completely. Their lips met and fused together in a blaze of passion that threatened to consume them. Clothing was ripped and tossed aside as they struggled to touch each other. Alex swung her into his arms, but barely made it to the bed before desire made his knees grow weak. With an abandonment she had never known, Samantha rubbed her hands through the thick mat of hair on his chest to grasp the broad shoulders that would protect her always. Her hands encircled his neck to pull him closer still. Seasoned by the parting that would come too soon, Samantha felt a hunger that could not be denied. She could no longer think, she needed only to feel. His hands slid possessively over her, then, cupping her bare buttocks, lifted her to receive the strong thrust of his manhood.

Samantha was lost, cast adrift in a sea of passion so sweet she ached from the joy of it. His hips ground against hers, and she felt herself slipping into an abyss of sensuality from which she hoped to never be rescued. Then he moved and her world shattered into ecstasy.

Sleepy from pleasure, she sighed with regret as Alex shifted his weight from her. She watched as he sat on the edge of the bed and reached for his breeches. "I wish we didn't have to leave." Her hand reached out, then collapsed against his back.

Alex felt his passion rise anew. Never had he experienced such pleasure. And never had he lost control so completely. Reluctantly he placed a fleeting kiss against her bruised lips. "Was I too rough with you?" His voice was tight with desire, but as his eyes trailed down her body, he saw the red brush burns from his unshaved chin. "Did I hurt you?"

Samantha shook her head against the pillow. "Nay, m'lord, you could never hurt me." Her hand traced up his back, marveling at his strength. He made her body quiver with passion, but as he reached for his boots, she realized he also made her feel cherished. "Do you really think that you will be able to keep Cavandish from Coverick if you join him? What if he has information about me?"

Carefully Alex took her hand. "I shall keep you safe till my dying day," he declared solemnly.

Samantha felt tears sting her eyes, but refused to release them. "Then it will be in my interest to see that you live a very, very, long time, m'lord." Their lips met, not hot with passion, but in a soft kiss of promise, filled with the hopes that their newfound allegiance would stand the strain of time.

Autumn faded into winter, and Christmas had come and gone. Determined to make the best of their time apart, Samantha had turned her full attention to the running of her home. Plaster was scraped and recrafted, and woodworkers painstakingly stripped old finish and carefully applied new. Silver was polished, then polished again. The crystal chandeliers were scrubbed until they glistened, and the tapestries that lined the walls were cleaned and restored. The baby now moved within her, yet still she was not content.

The cliffs above Coverick Cove became her private haunt as she impatiently awaited the day that Alex would return. Walking along the rocky path, she could watch the rhythmic motion of the waves and feel the power she always derived from the sea. Pulling her shawl more tightly about her, Samantha turned her face into the misty spray. The sun readied itself to slip below the horizon, and as gulls soared overhead, the last of the day's sunlight turned a fiery red to streak across the sky. It would be dark soon, but still she stayed watching the waves pound their fury on the rocks below.

What caught her attention she would never know, and she cursed the growing mist that clouded her view. Something was there. Afraid to blink lest she miss it again, she stared straight ahead until she saw them. About two hundred yards from shore she watched the shape of three longboats appear. She leaned forward on a huge boulder and squinted against the fog that rolled in behind the last of the boats.

Fascinated, she watched the boats pull ashore in the inlet beneath her. Smugglers. Her eyes narrowed as she hastily glanced about the edge of the cliff, but the rocky ledge revealed nothing. Save for the gulls that swarmed about, she was alone. Her brow wrinkled with confusion. Had they posted no watch? Carefully she made her way to the ledge to better view their activity. They carried only one torch, but it provided enough light for her to recognize Blacky and several others whom she knew by name.

The longboats were quickly unloaded and their cargo transferred to four mules that stood tethered and waiting. Suddenly, from the corner of her eye, Samantha saw a light flicker, then grow brighter. Carefully she straightened and moved around the boulder to get a better view. She watched the light grow steadily closer until the truth hit.

Dear God, she thought, it was the coast patrol. Her head snapped back to where the men were still loading cargo. The way the inlet curved, the patrol would be upon them before they knew what was happening. Why hadn't the fools posted a lookout? Her heart pounded and the babe began to kick within her. She watched the patrol move steadily down the beach. Her hands clenched into fists of frustration even as she turned to make her way down the steep path to the inlet.

She was almost upon them when the loose stones beneath her feet alerted them to her presence. Silently she prayed they wouldn't shoot her before they realized who she was. Blacky looked up and was the first to recognize her. Cursing, he quickly climbed the path to grasp her arm and help her down.

"Love of God, woman, what in hell's name are you doing here?" he challenged.

Completely winded from her frantic descent, Samantha pointed a shaky finger toward the bend. "The patrol is coming." She pressed a hand against the stabbing pain in her side. "I was up above, and I saw their torches. Why didn't you place a watch?"

Nat Wilkens grabbed Blacky's arm and pointed behind them. "Look!" The light from the coast patrol was just rounding the corner. "Run for your lives!"

"Nay!" Samantha's voice lashed out with such authority that each man froze. "If you run, they'll shoot you. Get those boats back into the water now; the rest of you stand and be calm and follow my lead. Nat, fire your gun into the air. The rest of you yell as if you were chasing someone off. Now!"

Not knowing why, Nat Wilkens fired both pistols into the air. Instantly the wild shouts of the men echoed in the secluded inlet. The longboats caught the tide and steadily moved farther into the sea. And as the shouts of the men began to fade, Samantha's piercing scream filled the night.

Blacky took her arm. He was going to get her out of there if it was the last thing he did. "Come." His voice sounded his fear.

Samantha pulled from his grasp. "Shut up and do as I say." Blacky Teach, six feet four and well over two hundred pounds, fell silent from the lash of her

331

words. His hand dropped from her arm, and as a doomed man, he watched the patrol close in for the kill.

Samantha staggered a step forward and reached back to clutch Blacky's arm. "Oh, Sergeant . . ." Her voice was breathless and full of fear as the patrol reached the nervous group. "Thank God you heard our cries for help. I was so scared."

Blacky's eyes grew wide as tears began to trace down her face and her lips trembled. Desperately he searched his pockets for a handkerchief. Finding nothing, he turned toward the sergeant with hand extended.

Momentarily thrown off track, Sergeant Ferguson lowered his gun and searched several pockets before finding the required piece of linen. "It looks like our information was right," he stated quietly, but his eyes stayed fixed on the striking beauty before him.

Samantha reached forward and placed a shaky hand on his arm. "I thought I was doomed." Her tears threatened to increase. "I was so scared of what they were going to do to me."

Sergeant Ferguson motioned for the torches to be brought closer. "My God" came the whisper. "'Tis the duchess."

Blacky felt her fingers dig into his arm to pull him forward. "Of course it's the duchess," he said sharply. "Can't you see how upset she is?"

Samantha turned her tear-stained face back toward the sergeant. "I'm just so grateful for all of your help," she sniffed.

The sergeant frowned in confusion. "But we, I . . ."

Samantha raised her hand from his arm to rest against his chest. "I was walking above . . ." She looked up toward the cliffs overhead. "When those men," she shuddered visibly, "they tried to take me." Her body shook with her sobs.

Sergeant Ferguson stiffened with anger, and not at all sure what to do, placed a comforting hand on her shoulder. "You are safe now, Your Grace. Arrest them," he barked over his shoulder.

"Oh, nay," Samantha gasped. "These are not the culprits, Sergeant." She leaned more fully against him. "These are the men of Coverick. That's Blacky Teach, Nat Wilkens, Bart Soloms . . ." Her voice faded, then she took a shuddering breath to continue. "When the duke realized that business was going to take him from home, he arranged for several of the men to patrol the inlets each night so we would be safe." She glanced back at the nervous group, willing each to accept her story. "Thank God they were here tonight." Her tears started anew. "Why, if Blacky," she pointed to the dark-haired giant, "hadn't seen what was happening and sounded the alarm . . . why I can't bear to think . . ." Her head dropped to rest against the sergeant's chest.

Sergeant Ferguson tore his eyes from the duchess to stare at Blacky. "And you say that you saw a group of men trying to kidnap the duchess?" Too stunned to speak, Blacky nodded. "And you fired the shots that we heard?"

"I have no gun . . ." Blacky started. "But I signaled to Nat Wilkens." Hesitantly, Nat stepped forward.

"I fired the shots, Sergeant."

Samantha pulled back from the sergeant's chest

and turned back to the group. So far they had done well, but too much was at stake to take chances now.

"Thank you so much." Her voice trembled as her hand pressed against her heart. "I shall be forever grateful, and I know His Grace will wish to speak with each of you personally when he returns. But now . . ." She turned back to the sergeant. "I'm terribly sorry, but I suddenly feel so queer . . ." Her words faded as she crumpled to the ground.

The sergeant swung her limp form easily into his arms. Something was amiss here, of that he was sure. But as he stood watching the men before him, he realized that none had made a move to escape. And why should they, he thought. Innocent men had nothing to be frightened of. And what other reason would explain the duchess being on the beach at this hour? His mind set, he turned to his men.

"Confiscate those boxes." His voice was sharp. "Then secure the area. We've got to get the duchess home before she takes ill. And you . . ." He turned to Blacky and the others, "Be off with you now, and from now on leave the patrols to those who know what they are about."

Nat Wilkens turned to the others. He was still not sure of exactly what had happened, but he knew they were being set free. He gestured to the group and quickly, lest the decision be changed, they blended into the growing fog and darkness. Only Blacky stayed behind.

The manor was aglow with lights as the patrol approached. James, alerted by the footman, was already racing down the steps to meet them.

"My God, what happened? Did she fall?" James

gathered Samantha from the sergeant's arms, then led them into the salon. Mrs. Brown and Hanna followed on the sergeant's heels. "Sergeant, I demand to know what happened!" James's soft features hardened as he gently lowered Samantha onto the sofa nearest the fire. Mrs. Brown spoke softly as she began to loosen the stays on the duchess's gown while Hanna fanned her mistress with the dustrag.

Sergeant Ferguson's eyes grew wide as he glanced about the room. He had heard that the duke was restoring the manor, but never had he expected to see such splendor. The chandelier alone would cost more money than he could hope to make in a lifetime.

"Sergeant!" James snapped.

"Her Grace was nearly abducted by smugglers down by the inlet tonight," Blacky replied easily, warming to the story that cast him as the hero. "I was near the cliffs myself when I heard her cry for help."

James's mouth fell open, he turned toward the sergeant.

"That seems to be the size of it, sir. We came upon them just as the longboats pulled into the sea."

James paled with the sergeant's words and slumped onto a chair. "Blacky . . ." his voice was choked with emotion, "however can we repay you?"

Samantha's soft moan turned eyes back to her as she struggled to sit up. "Perhaps he could come to the manor tomorrow and we could discuss it then?" Her voice was breathless, and she tried to stand with Hanna supporting her. "But now . . ." she held out a trembling hand. "James, would you be a dear and help me to my room. I desperately need to find my bed."

James was at her side in an instant and scooped her back into his arms. "Sergeant, thank you for your help with this matter. And Blacky, we'll discuss this more completely tomorrow. Now if you will excuse me, Brown will see you out." Both men watched with envy as James carried the duchess from the room.

Clad in a soft gown of deep-blue velvet, Samantha sipped her tea as Blacky was ushered into Alex's study. He had been unsuccessful in his attempts to tame his ebony hair and it stuck out wildly in all directions. Despite his massive stature, his approach was hesitant as he took the chair opposite her.

"Tea?" She smiled, nodding toward the silver service that rested on the table between them. Blacky shook his head. "Then tell me," she continued softly, "just who was the ass responsible for that pitiful situation last night?"

Blacky jerked upright with her words. "We made a mistake."

"A mistake?" Her voice filled with sarcasm.

"I let someone else plan it."

"And will you plan the next one yourself?"

Blacky stared for several moments without speaking. "The need is great." His eyes turned to hers and demanded understanding. "Those fat pigs that set the taxes and constantly raise the tariffs care little what it cost the common folk. I say take what you can and the devil with the rest."

Samantha picked up her tea. "'Tis my habit to walk at night on the upper cliffs." Her voice was soft, almost as if she was talking to herself. "And I've often thought it strange that the coast patrol never checks the same inlet twice in a row." She looked up at Blacky. "Don't you find that odd? 'Tis little wonder that they are having no success. Why, if someone as simple as I can notice their pattern, one can only wonder . . ."

Blacky felt his heart begin to pound. If her words proved true, then he had the answer he'd been looking for. But as he leaned forward to question her further, his mouth grew dry as she looked up at him. Her eyes were bluer than the Cornish sky, and though she was heavy with child, a fierce desire to possess her filled him. He rubbed his calloused palms against the rough texture of his breeches. The duke was a fool to leave such a treasure.

"But still . . ." The sound of her voice surrounded him, seeping into his blood. "They must save face."

Blacky pulled himself from his thoughts. "Who must save face?"

"The patrol," she continued patiently. "If they become the laughingstock, they only try all the harder. A good plan would include regular feeding of their pride."

Blacky's forehead wrinkled as he followed her scheme. "They would be most pleased if they were to happen upon a take every once in a while," he said slowly. "They would look like heros, stamping out the riffraff. But if those times were planned . . ."

Samantha's face lit up with surprise. "What a brilliant idea. You mean you could actually follow their movements and arrange such events to happen?"

Less than an hour later, Blacky left the duke's study with a spring to his step and a smile on his lips.

Wrapped in a shawl and seated before the fire, Samantha shifted yet again to accommodate the babe she carried. Almost a week had passed since her flight down the cliff, and since that night the babe now moved constantly. No position was comfortable, and sleep was all but impossible. Staring into the fire, she wondered yet again why the poets thought being in love was glorious. Never had she ached the way she longed for Alex. He had managed to send only two messages during the long weeks of his absence and she had read them over and over until the paper crumbled from the handling. He loved her, of that she was sure, but now rumors were starting to surface. The duke had been seen on several occasions with Lady Harwick. The whispered stories carried many variations, but the theme was always the same. While she sat in Cornwall and grew larger with his child, Alex was spending his time with Julia in London.

The babe gave a violent kick, and Samantha pulled from her thoughts. "Be still, little one," she whispered, rubbing the ache in her side and trying to keep her doubts at bay. "Your father will be home soon, then everything will be explained."

Straightening in her chair, Samantha glanced down at the wrinkled note Blacky had delivered. The handwriting was unfamiliar, but somehow she couldn't dismiss it. She touched her necklace but, of late, no images surfaced. Whenever she tried to see into the future, only thoughts of Alex came to mind. Over and over her hands smoothed the folds as she read and reread the strange message. Finally, submitting more to curiosity than common sense, she requested Brown to instruct Blacky to ready her carriage.

Chapter XXII

It was just past noon when the small coach drew to a stop before the Wayward Traveler Inn. Samantha checked to be sure that her heavy veil was securely in place, then unlatched the carriage door. She accepted Blacky's hand as she took in her surroundings. It was a small two-story building of gray stone with a thatched roof. But located as it was, far from the main roads, she wondered how it succeeded in business. One would have to know of its existence in order to find it.

"Good afternoon, madam. If you'll just follow me, I'll take you right in." Before she could reply, Samantha found her arm clasped in a firm grip and she was quickly led inside. Turning to look over her shoulder, she watched Blacky hang back with the carriage. She noted the sweat that dotted the innkeeper's brow and realized that something or someone had made him very nervous.

The common room was empty, save for a barmaid cleaning glasses, and Samantha was led down a dimly lit hallway. Pausing before the last door, the owner turned the knob, gave her a gentle shove inside, then latched the door firmly behind her. Samantha leaned back against the locked door and wondered why she felt more curiosity than fear. Her hand reached up to clutch her necklace as she cautiously stepped farther into the shadowy room.

"I knew I would find you." A deep voice broke the silence as a large form unfolded itself from the bed.

Samantha felt her heart beat hard against her ribs and knew surely he could hear it. On legs that trembled like unset jelly, she took a step forward, then reached for the hem of her veil to lift it back over her head. "Dancer?" Saying his name, she pushed the cape from her shoulders. But as she stepped forward, he stepped back.

"My God, Curse!" He collapsed against the bed like a puppet with cut strings. "You are with child!" Instantly he jerked to his feet, knife drawn and at the ready. "Did Cortland do this? I'll kill the bastard with my own hands."

Samantha smiled. "Then you would deprive the babe of a father and me of a husband." Her eyes filled with tears of joy. "I feared I'd never see you again." Hesitantly she took another step forward, then she was locked in his arms.

"I thought I would die when we sailed without you." His voice against her ear was uneven with emotion. "Over and over I saw the beam break loose to strike you down."

Reluctantly she stepped from Dancer's embrace and, reaching up, touched the scar that lined his cheek. Time had etched deeper the lines on his brow.

But she knew with a wink those warm brown eyes and rakish features could still claim the heart of any he chose.

"'Tis so good to see you, old friend." Her voice trembled. "Come, you must tell me all the news. Did you travel well back to the island? How is Marie? Have you seen Kabol? And . . ." She paused for breath. "What are you doing here?"

Dancer chuckled softly and pulled a chair, motioning her to sit. "You haven't changed a bit." As Samantha glanced pointedly down at her stomach, a smile touched his lips. Taking another chair for himself, he joined her at the table. "We made it back to the island but just barely. The *Sea Witch* sails no more." For a moment, each was locked in their memories of the past. Then Dancer's eyes grew hard. "As to Marie . . ." He looked off into the shadows. "I thought it strange when she cared not that you had been taken. And with time I realized she was even pleased with the turn of fate."

Samantha gasped. "What? I don't believe you."

Dancer reached to take her hand. "Marie was the one who placed the poison in your room that night. It seems that she thought you and I were getting too . . ."

"But that's ridiculous." Samantha jerked to her feet. "You've been my best friend for as long as I can remember. How could she have gotten things so twisted?"

Dancer shrugged. "Mayhap because I would never stay with just her. The sea is my true lady, and she knew that, but I don't think she ever completely understood."

Samantha sank back into her chair. "So she tried to poison me and, instead, almost killed you." Her voice was tinged with fear. "What did you do when you found out?"

Again Dancer looked away. "You've been dear to my heart since the day I first laid eyes on you, brat. You've been the child I'll never have." He turned back to watch her face. "How could I excuse one who wished to harm you?" When she would have interrupted, his finger touched her lips. "Leave it that Marie no longer calls the island her home."

Samantha blinked back her tears. "Now what?"

An ironic smile touched his lips. "I came to rescue you."

Not knowing whether to laugh or cry, Samantha wiped at her eyes. "So you sent me a note?"

Dancer shrugged. "You know planning's not what I do best. I figured if you could get this far on your own without being caught, I could get you the rest of the way."

Samantha smiled and shook her head slowly. He would never change.

"But . . ." Dancer looked at her costly gown of fine wool and the radiance that glowed about her. "It appears that you don't need rescuing after all."

Reaching across the table, she took his hand. "I never thought I would say this . . ." She paused, and Dancer watched her eyes grow soft. "But I love Alex Cortland. He's the father of my child, and at his side is where I have chosen to spend my life."

Dancer's other hand locked over hers. Had he planned it himself, he couldn't have been more pleased. Cortland was just the man to keep her safe and out of trouble. He glanced back to her protruding stomach and a grin covered his face. "Being a duchess becomes you," he said proudly. "And it seems I have brought you a fitting wedding present."

She watched him reach into a sack beside the bed and withdraw a battered pouch. But when he tipped the contents into her palm, her breath all but left her body.

"The Midnight Star."

"Aye, Kabol threatened to see my flesh slivered into pieces and fed to the sharks unless I gave my word to get this to you."

"But I can't take that . . ." The legend of the stone made her shudder.

Dancer slipped the stone back into its pouch and then tucked it into the pocket of her cape. "'Tis a gift," he said quietly. "And you must keep it with you always. Kabol was most insistent on the point. He fears your life is in danger without it, so 'tis not worth taking the chance. Besides, you really have no choice." His eyes twinkled with humor for the first time. "Unless you want to see me fed to the sharks."

Samantha shook her head as a smile touched her lips. "And what will you do now?"

Dancer rubbed a hand against his bearded cheek. "I've signed on with a Captain Thorngold out of Falmouth. In fact, now that I know you are safe, I must be on my way."

Samantha leaned forward to touch his arm. "I have money . . ." she hesitated. "Would you like a ship of your own? Be your own captain?"

Dancer rose and shook his head. "I've no use for being captain," he said firmly. "You know how I hate making decisions. No, quartermaster is fine with me." His eyes began to sparkle again. "But I do want something from you." He smiled as a puzzled look crossed her face. "I like the cut of the man you call Blacky and I've persuaded him to join us when we sail. You'll not be giving him a hard time should he choose to tell you now, will you, Curse?"

Samantha smiled and rose from her chair. "Nay, in fact I thought he'd make a good mate the first time I met him. He has a way of getting the most out of those he works with." Dancer reached for her cape and slipped it over her shoulders. "But I am losing a damn fine foreman." She pouted.

Dancer laughed. "Just consider the diamond fair payment." Arm and arm they walked to the door. "I'll come again if I can," he said quietly, giving her cheek a kiss before he tugged her veil into place. "I have a strong desire to see just what kind of monster you and Cortland finally produce."

Reaching up, her hand rested against his cheek for what she feared would be the last time. "Just see that it's sooner rather than later," she commanded softly.

"You stupid fool, this is not the inn. Those are stables!" Julia Harwick angrily stepped from her carriage. "Have you not a brain in your head? Now stop this dillydallying and take me to the inn."

The young carriage driver shifted nervously from foot to foot. "We dare not go any farther, mistress," he stammered, rubbing his hands together briskly against the cold.

Furious, Julia stomped around the carriage to

inspect the damaged wheel. Three spokes were deeply cracked and a fourth completely broken. "It doesn't look too bad to me," she challenged. "I want to press on."

The youth looked helplessly about him. "'Tis liable to break completely if we venture farther." His voice trembled and not from the cold. "Could you not just walk around to the inn?" He gestured to the other side of the stables. "Truly, 'tis not far."

Snatching the horsewhip from the side of the carriage, Julia flung it in his direction. "You stupid fool. The next time a wheel breaks, stop in front of the blasted inn, not by the stables." Her screams were muffled by the growing wind. Julia turned and kicked the offending carriage wheel. Pain shot through her foot, adding to her frustration and anger. "You are hopeless," she cried. "Completely hopeless. But if you wish to remain in my employ, you'll have that blasted wheel fixed before nightfall."

Pulling her fur-lined cape more firmly about her, Julia started slowly down the road. Within three steps her costly satin slippers were soaked completely through and her feet had turned to ice. Stomping through the mud and cursing the stains that now marred the hem of her gown, she angrily reached the side of the inn. But as she rounded the corner, the sight before her made her draw back. A couple stood on the front step locked deep in conversation. The wind stung her cheeks, but something about the pair made Julia hold her ground. Carefully she edged around the corner to get a better view. As the woman turned toward the carriage, the wind tore at her veil, sending it flying. The large man captured the bit of cloth within a step but not before Julia's eyes grew wide with recognition.

She flattened herself back against the wall. What ever was Samantha Cortland doing here? Cautiously she inched forward to watch again. The large, unshaven man helped the duchess into the carriage, then motioned for the driver to be off. Despite his wretched clothing, he seemed untouched by the chill of the wind as he watched the carriage disappear around the bend. When it was completely gone from sight, he mounted a dappled mare that stood waiting, then he, too, was off.

Freezing wind tore at her hair, but Julia's smile was wide with pleasure. So Alex's little bride had taken a lover, she thought. Suddenly the trials of her day seemed insignificant. What would Alex say when he found that his precious darling was little more than a country whore? And . . . Her smile deepened. What would Edward pay for this new piece of information? With a spring to her step, Julia followed the path. And when she reached the spot where the couple had embraced, her laughter filled the air.

Alex closed the cabin door against the stiff March wind and moved to the fireplace. What was she thinking of? He struck his flint, and within moments the small flames began to grow. He was going to cheerfully strangle her for pulling such a stunt. He tossed more logs into the fire and straightened. Reaching into his pocket, he withdrew Samantha's note. Why had she not entrusted Judd with the information, he wondered, instead of insisting they meet? True, it was taking longer than he had first thought. But the safety of his country was at stake. And he was so close to having the proof they so desperately needed. Why could her patience not have lasted just a little longer? He pictured her sitting at the table, her hands wrapped around a cup of tea, and his scowl softened. She wasn't even here yet and already her presence filled the cabin.

Alex closed his eyes as the warmth of the flames took the chill from his body. In his mind he touched the silken softness of her hair as it slipped through his fingers. He tasted the sweetness of her lips, more potent than a heady wine, and her scent. He opened his eyes . . . Her scent was always in his thoughts. A smile touched his lips as memories of their last hours in the cabin surged forth. Mayhaps he would make love to her first, and then strangle her.

He moved to the table and frowned at the dust that covered its surface. Using the sleeve of his coat, he wiped it clean. Then he began to pace. Three months since he had last seen her, held her. His body throbbed with anticipation. He calculated the hours time would allow them to spend together and found them wanting. Three long months . . . His pacing stopped abruptly and his eyes darkened. By now her body would be well rounded with his child. The thought thrilled him, but would he be able to make love to her after all? Sobered by the realization his frustration returned twicefold. Mayhaps he'd strangle her after all. But as he took the bucket and left the cabin to get water for her tea, Alex knew he would be more than content just to hold her close and feast his eyes on her again.

Returning from the stream that supplied the cabin with fresh water, Alex smiled as he viewed the small, open carriage already tethered. His step quickened. He set the water bucket down and closed the door behind him. The room was empty, but a strong floral scent filled the air. He knew it well, and it did not belong to his wife.

"Darling, I thought you'd deserted me," Julia's voice purred from the entrance to the bedchamber.

Alex felt the beat of his heart change from surprise to anger. "What are you doing here?" He strained to keep the emotions from his voice until he knew full well what she was about.

"I missed you." Julia pouted, moving into the room. She'd shed her cloak and her pale-yellow gown floated about her. "Besides . . ." She paused before the fire, letting Alex see that she wore nothing beneath the thin robe. "I am tired of the arrangements."

Alex fought hard to suppress his disgust for her. "And what arrangements are those?"

"You know very well of which I speak." Her voice grew hard with agitation. "You were with me and then you married that little twit. Now you leave her pregnant in your home and come back to me. Well, I won't have it."

Alex leaned back on the table. "'Twas you who sent the note." Suddenly he was very relieved that Samantha wouldn't be coming. The least he could do was spare her this.

"Of course I sent the note," Julia hissed. "And I'm not at all pleased by the way you scramble when little wifey crooks a finger. I've had enough, Alex, and I mean it. You take me to the theater and out to parties, but I want more." Bent on her tirade, Julia never noticed his eyes darken with anger. "She has your name, your child, and your bed." Julia paused for breath. "I care little about the child, ruin *her* figure, not mine for all I care. But I'm tired of playing games with you. I was meant to be the Duchess of Coverick and we both know it. How can she possibly wear the Cortland jewels and do them justice?"

"And what jewels are those," Alex questioned softly.

Julia threw up her hands. "Don't be obtuse with me, Alex. You know I've never seen them. But you know as well as I do that they would look wonderful on me." Julia moved closer and ran her finger down his chest. "But it's not just the jewels, darling," she cooed.

Alex raised a brow. "No?"

"I want you back in my bed."

Outside the sun faded from view as dark clouds rolled in from the sea. The wind strengthened and lightning streaked the sky. Moments later, thunder rumbled low and ominously. Inside the cabin, neither heard the approaching carriage.

Samantha gritted her teeth against the pain in her lower back as the carriage drew to a halt. Using her glove, she wiped the sweat that dotted her brow. The journey had been pure hell. But looking down at the note from Alex, her heart soared. She was here, and after three long months she would finally be able to touch him again. The carriage door swung open and she leaned heavily against Blacky's arm as he assisted her down.

Blacky supported her until she found her balance as the wind whipped about them. "Are you sure you don't want me to wait for you?" He looked down the path to the cottage where another carriage stood waiting, but Samantha shook her head.

"Nay, I shall be fine. Besides, if you wait, you risk missing your transport to Falmouth." She reached up and laid a hand against the prickly new beard on his cheek. "I shall miss you."

Blacky took her hand and placed a courtly kiss against her knuckles. "You could come with me, I would marry you, you know."

Samantha's laughter danced on the rolling thunder. "I am already married, you fool, and well with child." Blacky glanced down to her stomach. Even though her cape was cut full, it barely covered her treasure. "And you, dear friend, already have two wives. What story would you concoct for them if you brought home another?"

Blacky had the good grace to look sheepishly guilty for almost a minute. "Now that you mention it, I am having a bit of a problem in that direction." He scratched at the itchy new growth on his chin and Samantha laughed again.

"Ah ha, so you are growing that thing to hide your face."

"Madam, you wound me to the quick."

Samantha shook her head. "Just don't let it get as wild as your hair," she teased, giving one of his long ebony locks a healthy tug. "Or all people will see is that huge black beard." For a moment the two stood silent. Then Samantha reached up and placed a fleeting kiss on his cheek. "Go now, Dancer won't wait forever and he'd thank me not for making you late." Blacky gave her shoulders a squeeze, then climbed back onto the carriage.

Samantha turned and slowly walked toward the cabin. The pain was back again. She bit hard on her lower lip, but she didn't stop. If Blacky thought anything was amiss, he would insist on seeing her to the door. And after all the months of loneliness, she wanted her first sight of Alex to be perfect.

Pausing at the threshold, Samantha caught her breath and tried to straighten her back. Would he be pleased at the sight of her? Or would he be put off by her misshapen body. Of late it seemed she waddled more than walked. Her fingers shook with nervous anticipation as she tried to smooth her hair back into place. Taking a deep breath, she turned the latch.

The wind caught the door, pushing it wide open, and Samantha watched her world crumble before her. He was there, not four feet away, with Julia plastered to his side.

"Well, don't just stand there, Samantha, darling," Julia purred, pressing closer to Alex. "You do know how to close a door, don't you?"

Samantha took a step forward on legs that trembled. Her eyes never left Alex's face. "I don't understand . . ." She tried to keep her voice steady but pain seeped through.

"What's to understand?" Julia moved to stand before the fire. "Your husband and I have been keeping company in London for the past two months. I thought it only fair that you know."

Samantha felt the words pierce her heart. She

watched a cold expression touch Alex's features and her being filled with dread. "Is this true?"

"Of course it is true," Julia snapped. "Do you think I'd go to all this trouble and come to this godforsaken place if it weren't?"

Samantha looked about the cabin. Memories of their last meeting blurred with her tears. The magic was gone leaving only dust and old furniture. Her eyes turned back to Alex, begging him to say it was not so. But only his silence filled the room.

"Do you hear him denying it?" Julia paced before the fire, confident of her plan. "He won't say it, because he knows that I can give you the dates and places of each time we met, for always were there people about." She turned to Alex. "I'm sorry, darling, to put you in such an awkward position, but you really can't continue to have us both." Julia watched Samantha pale further and gloried in her victory.

Surrounded by Alex's silence, Samantha felt the last of her defenses crumble. But she would not disgrace herself further by shedding tears for Julia's amusement. Turning, she fled the cabin and into the growing storm. With the wind at her back, she navigated the paths faster than she would ever have thought possible, until exhaustion halted her motion on the cliffs. Collapsing on a boulder near the earth's edge, she tried to gather her wits and her emotions.

Tears mingled with the rain to streak down her cheeks. Rejection. When was she ever going to learn to stop setting herself up for rejection? She caught her breath as the pain in her back bloomed again.

How many years had she tried in vain to secure her father's love? And now Alex. Her body trembled with spasms of pain. His silence had hurt more than the blows given by Edward. Her arms locked around her stomach as she held her child. Why did she always need love from those who were incapable of giving it to her?

"What's wrong with me?" she cried into the storm. "Why is it so impossible for someone to love me?"

The rain stopped as quickly as it had come, letting the sun streak out from behind its clouds. The gulls climbed high to soar overhead, then dove neatly down to gather their supper. On the edge of the cliff, Samantha sat like one made of stone as she watched the hypnotic pull of the sea. Waves crashed on the rocks below, sending their salty spray to sparkle in the sunlight.

Samantha shivered from the chill. Somewhere in her flight she had lost her cape, and now the ocean breeze struck her wet clothing. She knew she should leave, find some safe port for herself and her child, but she had no strength to move.

"Samantha?" At the sound of his voice, she shuddered. She thought she could not possibly hurt more, but she was wrong, "Come away from the edge, love."

Slowly she turned. Alex stood several feet away, but he made no move to reach her. Wearily she stared at the ground at his feet. "I have no plans to jump, if that is your worry."

Alex winced. He had hurt her, and the pain of it cut deep. Silently he wondered if she would ever allow him the chance to make it right. "Look at me," he said quietly. He waited until eyes filled with pain locked with his. "I sent Julia away. I know there's much I need to explain to you, but you must move away from the edge."

Samantha felt her heart twist in spasm. She wanted so much to be gathered into his arms. But would his words of comfort be truth? A low, moaning sound mingled with the cry of the gulls and she frowned. Could one hear a heart breaking?

Alex stepped as close as he dared, but still he could not reach her. "Samantha . . ." His voice was soft but urgent. "Stand up slowly, love, and step toward me now. You're in danger."

Samantha watched him like one stricken of mind. How much did he think she could take? Did he truly want both of them as Julia had said? The images conjured by just the thought of it made her stomach protest. The strange moaning sounded again as pain ripped through her and fetal water soaked her gown.

"Look at me," Alex commanded sharply. "I love you." He watched a glimmer of hope spark in her eyes and struggled to find the words to fan it brighter. "I love you. It seems I have loved you forever. But you have to trust me. Love that has no trust has no hope for survival. Now stand up and come to me. Show me that you care enough to fight for this."

As his words burned through the fog of pain that encased her, Samantha felt the strength of his power seep in. He loved her. He'd never said the words before. Could she believe them? *He is the sun*, reason argued. *How can you not?* On legs that she never thought would hold her, she stood. Hesitantly, she took one small step toward him, then another.

Frantically, Alex reached forward, scooped her

into his arms, and quickly moved back from the cliff's edge. The earth moaned again. Then in horror they watched the boulder on which she had been sitting disappear from sight. Crashing down the rocks, it plunged into the churning sea below.

Samantha shuddered and buried her head against Alex's neck. Her tears started anew and, try as she might, she could not bid them cease. Well away from the cliff's edge, Alex chose a flat-based rock to sit on. Heedless of her wet gown, he cradled her on his lap. His arms shook as he pressed her tighter to him.

"My God," he whispered against her forehead. "I almost lost you." For several moments they both were content to stay silent, savoring the touch and feel of the other. But when the contraction hit again, Samantha doubled over with pain.

"What is it? What's wrong?" Alex tried with little success to keep the panic from his voice, praying his suspicions were not true.

Samantha struggled to regain her breath as the gripping pain began to ease. "The babe," she gasped. "I think your son is tired of waiting."

Alex tipped her chin up to better see her face. Her eyes were ringed with fatigue and filled with fear. "Is it not too early?"

Samantha's eyes filled with tears. "I don't want to lose the baby," she wept softly. "Not both of you in the same day."

Alex took his handkerchief and dried her eyes. "You'll lose neither of us, love, on that you have my word. Please trust me just a little longer."

Catching her breath, Samantha struggled to regain her composure. She was so weary of it all, and it felt so good to be held against him again. The warmth of his body soothed her, and within the circle of his arms she felt safe. His hands rubbed absently up and down her back easing the ache, instinctively bringing her comfort. Looking up into green eyes, she found no answers but saw truth. And in that truth, the weight of the world slipped from her tired shoulders.

Reaching up, she traced his lip with her finger. "I trust you." Her voice was the softest whisper. "And your child and I love you."

Alex felt his chest swell with joy. She grew more precious with each passing day and he feared it would take him more than a lifetime just to show her how much she meant to him. He kissed her fingertips. "Thoughts of you and the babe have been the only things that have kept me sane these past weeks." His breath was warm against her cheek. Their eyes locked, each filled with love, hope, and the most fragile of all; trust. Then their lips met, starved for the magic that only the other could grant.

Another spasm tore through her, and Samantha doubled with pain.

"We don't have time to get back to the manor, do we?" Alex asked quietly as he carried her back to the cabin.

"I don't know." Her head rested limply against his shoulder. "I've never had a baby before. But . . ." Her words never came as another pain twisted within her stealing her breath and her confidence.

"Relax," Alex crooned gently. "As in all things, we're in this together."

*　　　*　　　*

Hours later, Alex finally sat back in his chair to watch her. Her face was pale. Lines of pain still etched her gentle features and her eyes were dark with fatigue. Never had she looked more beautiful. He looked down in wonder at the tiny bundle now sleeping peacefully in his arms.

"So perfect." He let his finger touch the softness of her cheek. "She's absolutely perfect." He marveled at the tiny hands and delicate brow . . . the patch of dark hair that capped her head. His daughter. His eyes filled with love and admiration as he turned to his wife. Indeed he had been twice blessed. He watched her cuddle the small bundle she held. Wrinkled and red like a wizened old man and bald as a doorknob. His son. Alex felt his chest grow tight. He had witnessed her cost in giving such a gift. Never would he be able to repay her.

"A daughter and a son," he said quietly, his voice thick with emotion. "Leave it to you, madam, not to be able to make up your mind."

Samantha shifted the babe closer to her side and reveled in the love that radiated from her husband.

"Then you are pleased, m'lord?"

Reluctantly, Alex placed his bundle back with her mother on the bed, then, leaning over, kissed each baby on the forehead.

"Madam . . ." His lips brushed against hers. "You are my life. Know that from this moment on, the only thing in life that I shall cherish more than my children is you."

Chapter XXIII

The lusty cries of a hungry baby snatched Alex from his dreams, jerking him upright in the chair on which he slept. His mind was awash with confusion, then reality set in. He was a father! Gingerly he scooped up the crying bundle and began to pace in the cabin's main room. Samantha had been exhausted when sleep had finally claimed her, and he wanted her to rest as long as possible. But how did one get a baby to be quiet? He tried holding him and patting his back, but the child wailed all the louder. Alex felt his anxiety grow. It was obvious the babe was hungry, but the cabin held nothing that would satisfy an infant. With his screaming son on his shoulder, Alex searched through cabinets he already knew were empty. In desperation he took the babe back into the bedchamber, relieved to see that Samantha was now awake.

"What are we going to do?" Frantically he paced before the bed. "He's hungry and there's no food."

Samantha could only smile at the rumpled sight he

presented. Just hours before, he had lovingly and competently eased the babies from her body and into the waiting world. It was Alex who had washed them clean with warm water, then wrapped them in blankets. Alex, who had been her pillar of strength throughout all, now stood befuddled by the cry of his day-old son.

Samantha winced as she raised herself in the bed. "Give him to me," she chided gently. Taking another strip from her discarded petticoat, she remedied the babe's first problem. Then, blushing, she pushed the sheet lower and settled her son against her breast. Her eyes grew wide as the hungry mouth found her nipple and began to suckle with undisguised lust.

Entranced, Alex stared at the picture they presented. Mother and son . . . wife and child . . . His family. His chest swelled with pride and his heart beat knowing that as the years passed, he would never grow tired of watching her. A stirring from the other bundle drew a smile to his lips.

Samantha watched with pleasure as Alex followed her example. Gently, he cleaned his daughter, then wrapped her in fresh linens torn from her mother's petticoat. But unlike her brother, who demanded immediate attention, she was content to stare at her father in fascination.

Alex held her close and cooed gently. "Do you think she knows who I am yet?"

Samantha felt her heart overflow with joy for her daughter. "I'm sure she does, m'lord," she replied softly. "I'll even wager she knows how deeply you care for her."

Alex looked up and found himself lost in eyes of azure blue and wondered how he would ever be able to leave her again . . . knowing full well that in a few short days, leave he must.

Later that evening, snug in her own bed, Samantha rested wearily against the pillows. Getting their new family home from the cabin had become quite an event. Enchanted with the new additions to the Cortland estate, servants and tenants alike had lost no opportunity to view both their mistress and her new charges. Good wishes and congratulations were offered. Small gifts appeared, and even a talisman to ward off evil spirits and guarantee long life had been presented. Samantha accepted their outpouring of love and knew the memories of the day would stay with her forever. Yet now, as the hour grew late, she found no peace. The babies were settled for the night in their nursery with Hanna. And as she shifted in her bed, Samantha knew it was not thoughts of the children that plagued her mind. They had been home for hours, yet Alex had said nothing about the improvements she had made. She had watched his eyes travel from place to place, but except when he preened about the babies, he remained silent. She curled onto her side. Had she gone too far with the restorations? Her breath caught in her throat. All she had wanted to do was please him. If he found something at fault, why did he not just say so? There was nothing that could not be changed back to the way it was.

The clock chimed eleven times and the door to her

chambers opened. Silently she watched Alex enter to take the chair beside her bed.

"You should be asleep," he chided gently, watching the firelight dance over her pale features.

"Is that why you waited so long to come to me?" Surprised as much as he by the pain in her voice, Samantha turned her face to the wall. She heard him rise, felt the bed sink with his weight, then he was turning her to face him.

"Did you miss me?"

Exhausted from the day, she had no energy left to spar with him. "Don't toy with me, Alex." Her words were sharp and full of frustration. "I'm sorry if I've done something that has angered you. I thought you'd be pleased with the changes I've made. She glanced about the room and felt her eyes well with tears. "I realize that I might have been wrong to press on without your consent. I only wanted you to be happy when you returned. And now you're not and I don't even know why." Her last words rushed forth as a single tear gathered, then dripped down her cheek.

Alex's frown deepened as he pulled her to sit against his chest. "What madness do you prattle about, woman?" His hand brushed the silken strands of hair from her face. "Why are you crying?"

Samantha collapsed against him. "I don't know."

"Shh." He rocked her gently and kissed the top of her head. "Why ever would you think that I'm displeased with our home?" he questioned softly. "You are a miracle worker. When I left, the walls and floor were barely cleaned of their dirt, yet I return to find a home as grand as any in London." His hand traced down her back, then he shifted her away so he could see her face. "Why would you think me not pleased?"

Samantha sniffed and, feeling foolish, wiped the tears from her face. "You said nothing, and for hours now you've scowled like a captain with a torn sail."

Alex released his breath and again gathered her close. "I apologize, love, for not sharing my thoughts sooner. I but wished to be alone when I expressed my appreciation for all you've done." His lips traced down her cheek in lazy anticipation. But Samantha was done with waiting, and taking his chin in her hands, she placed his lips exactly where she needed them to be. Alex felt his blood begin to pound as the headiness of her kiss destroyed his sanity. Intoxicated, he raised his head to look down at her.

Samantha lazily traced a line from his forehead down his nose. "Are you finally going to tell me what plagues you, m'lord?"

Alex smiled and nipped at her finger. "I thought of much last night . . ." he started slowly. "I watched you slumber with our children at your side. And I was distressed." In the firelight, she watched his face grow solemn. "I have told you we are partners in all things and in my heart I know that to be true. Yet I find myself in a situation not of my choosing and I am not at liberty to share it with you."

Samantha felt her chest tighten. "You have to go away again, don't you."

Alex nodded reluctantly. "The matter is not yet resolved, and I have given my word."

Julia's name was on the tip of her tongue, but Samantha fought back the question. "Will you tell me all when it is over?'' she challenged.

"Aye love.'' Alex rested his head against hers on the pillow. "And if I have my way, we shall never be separated again.''

Spring bloomed quickly in Cornwall. The snowdrops had faded to give way to sweet violets and wild daffodils. And as sprays of glorious yellow and purple covered the land, Samantha discovered the joys of motherhood. They had named their son Francis after her father, for of the two, he was definitely the most demanding. Catherine Elizabeth carried the names of both her grandmothers and a temperament that was sweet and loving. She seemed to accept her brother's needs and waited patiently for her mother's attention.

With her days full and happy, Samantha passed the hours and waited impatiently for Alex's return. But her nights were another matter. She struggled not to think about the rumors that had surfaced on the heels of his departure. Alone in their bed, she longed for his arms and the feel of his hard body against hers. And she fantasized on the pleasures they would share when next they were together.

The babies were just two weeks old when Samantha put them down for their afternoon naps and Mrs. Brown appeared at the nursery door. Samantha placed her hand to her lips and, leaving Hanna to watch her sleeping children, she joined the housekeeper in the hallway.

"Beg pardon, Your Grace.'' Mrs. Brown's eyes were full of worry and her slender hands worried her lace handkerchief. "Lady Harwick has arrived."

Samantha's eyes grew wide. "Julia is here?"

Mrs. Brown nodded anxiously. "I didn't know what to do so I put her in the salon."

Instinctively, Samantha reached up and touched her necklace. Strange there had been no warning. Turning, she touched Mrs. Brown's hand in reassurance. "That will be fine. Have tea brought and then tell James that Lady Harwick is here."

Wondering what mischief Julia had planned this time, Samantha slowly made her way to the salon. But the sight that greeted her brought her up short. Julia paced before the fire in complete disarray. Strands of hair had slipped from the intricate style she wore to tangle about her face, and her gown was wrinkled and the hem well stained from travel.

"Julia?" Concerned, Samantha entered the salon, closing the door behind her. "Are you well?"

Julia caught her breath, then, turning with tear-filled eyes, she faced her hostess. "I came to apologize." A huge tear traced a silvery path down her cheek. "My jealousy almost destroyed everything and I have come to try to make amends."

Samantha moved closer, touched by the woman's distress, and urged her to sit.

Julia let her tears continue for several moments before she spoke. "I have behaved like a spoiled child because Alex wed you and not me." She sniffed loudly and tried to smooth the wrinkles from her skirt. "I am here to beg your forgiveness and to try and start over." At Samantha's silence, Julia continued. "I am resigned that Alex no longer loves me. And since I have recently come into an inheritance, I have decided to move to Cornwall."

Samantha steeled her nerves and wondered how she would ever manage if Julia were to become a neighbor. Memories of her pressed against Alex wearing little more than a smile still stung sharply.

"And to show you I mean well," Julia continued, rummaging through the large sack she had placed on the floor, "I have brought you a present for the baby."

Reluctantly, Samantha accepted the brightly wrapped silver package. "This was very . . . thoughtful."

Julia smiled gayly, all traces of tears gone from her face. "Alex's son deserves the very best, so I went to the most costly silversmith in London." She plucked the package from Samantha and began to unwrap the shiny paper. Carefully she opened the velvet case to reveal a set of intricate silver spoons. "They cost a small fortune," Julia continued, rubbing a gloved finger over an imaginary smudge. "But what is money between friends?"

"Indeed?" Both ladies jumped at the sound of James's voice in the doorway. "What games do you play at this time, Julia?"

"Don't be cruel, darling," Julia cooed. "Come and see the beautiful gift I brought for Alex's son."

James sauntered into the room and gave Samantha a knowing wink before looking at the box Julia held out for his inspection. His brow raised in appreciation and he whistled between his teeth. "They are indeed expensive." He glanced down at her mud-stained gown. "You must have traveled straight from London to deliver them. But tell me, Julia, are the children to split the set, or did you bring something else for little Catherine Elizabeth?" James suppressed a chuckle at Julia's blank stare. "Oh, no." He feigned surprise. "Had you not heard that Samantha gave birth to twins? Not only is she beautiful, but she presented Alex with a daughter as well as a son. Don't you think that's spectacular?"

Samantha watched Julia's eyes widen with surprise; then for a fleeting second they seemed to harden in anger.

"Darling . . ." Julia turned toward Samantha and slowly closed the velvet box. "What a simpleton I am. I shall return these and get something more suitable for both."

"Nonsense." Samantha reached for the box and placed it on the low table before them. "They are a lovely thought. You are very kind to be so generous." James started choking on his cheroot and Samantha sent a threatening look in his direction.

"Oh I did so hope you would like them." Julia beamed. "And now that we have mended all our little differences, I do hope I can persuade you to come for a carriage ride with me."

"A carriage ride?"

Julia rose and picked up her reticule. "Ladies only, darling." She patted James on the cheek. "The Langston estate has come onto the market and I am thinking of purchasing it."

James passed behind Samantha's chair. "Julia for a neighbor?" he whispered. "Tell her the mansion's haunted or something."

Samantha struggled not to laugh. "I have no knowledge of the estate, Julia, so I would be of no help. Why don't you take James with you if you're looking for company."

"Oh no." Julia gasped, then she smiled slowly. "I need you. You've done so much to this old place, I must know if I shall be able to do the same. You must come with me."

Samantha gave her a skeptical look. Somehow she couldn't see Julia having much care with the restoration of fine plaster. Still, her curiosity was beginning to take hold, and mayhap if they were alone, she could find what Julia was really about.

"Well . . ."

"You must come," Julia insisted. "I simply won't take no for an answer."

Samantha rose from the settee and handed the spoon box to James. "'Tis still early, and the twins won't wake for another hour or two. I think a short ride might be quite . . . educational."

James took the spoons and tucked them under his arm. "Are you sure?"

Samantha smiled and followed Julia into the hallway. "I shall be home shortly." She patted James's arm. "Do not fret so, or you'll sound just like your brother."

James watched with misgivings as the two entered the small carriage and Julia took the reins. She waved happily back at him, then, giving the horse a quick flick of the whip, they were off.

Whistling as he strode down the stairs, James stopped short at the sight before him. Alex stood just inside the door handing his hat and gloves to Brown.

370

"Well, well, two unexpected visitors in the same day." He hastened down the steps and embraced his brother warmly. "Samantha will be beside herself."

Alex returned James's greeting, but his eyes searched the wooden staircase. "And where is my wife?"

James laughed. "First tell me how your scheme went. Are you home for good or does this spy business still call to you?"

Alex shrugged out of his coat. Damn, but it felt good to be home. "We were a success. Richard is armed with the arrest notices, and even as we speak, he is on his way to round up the lot."

"And you didn't stay to watch the final scene? I would have thought after all the time spent away from your new bride, seeing the arrests would indeed have been a moment to savor."

The smile left Alex's eyes and his face grew stern. "I have done my part. There was no need to stay further. Now where is my wife?"

James couldn't help but grin at his brother's impatience. Alex, who had always been so untouched and aloof where the ladies were concerned, now paced anxiously before him. "Well, dear brother," he chuckled. "Fate, it seems, has crossed your path again. Samantha is not here." He watched Alex's scowl deepen and knew he could push no further. "Never fear, Alex, she's just gone for a carriage ride."

Alex tried to stem his disappointment. "When did she leave?" Then, changing his mind, he called to Brown. "Have a fresh horse saddled and brought round immediately." He rubbed his hands briskly together. "'Tis a wonderful day for an afternoon ride." He turned back to James. "And a shame you can't join me. Which direction did you say Samantha went?"

James's laughter filled the foyer. "You won't believe this, but she went with Julia to look at the Langston estate. It seems your old flame is thinking of becoming a neighbor."

"She *what?*" All joy fled Alex's face, and his hand clamped onto James's arm like a steel band.

"She is considering moving to the Langston estate."

"Nay." Alex's voice was sharp. "You said that Samantha was with Julia?"

"Yes, they left not more than a quarter of an hour ago."

Alex felt his anger rise until the room all but blurred before him. "James, do you know the Wayward Traveler?"

James nodded, then at his brother's surprise, hastened to explain. "There is a barmaid that . . ."

"Never mind," Alex snapped as he pulled his brother out the door. "Get Judd to saddle your horse and ride with haste. Richard has gone there with his men. Tell him that she must have been warned. She's flown the nest and I would bet she's gone to the cabin."

James frowned with confusion. "Alex, what is wrong? Why is Cavandish at the Wayward Traveler and why are you so upset?"

Alex swung easily onto his horse and prayed he would not be too late. "Julia is the one that Richard went to arrest. It's been Julia all along." Without waiting for his brother's reply, Alex turned his horse and was off down the drive.

Samantha's brows drew together as Julia turned off the main road and headed toward the sea. "Julia, this is not the way to the Langston estate."

Julia turned to her companion with a pleading look. "I know. But, well . . . when I was at the cabin with Alex, I departed so quickly that I left some of my things behind. I didn't want to just go there on my own to get them lest someone see me and accuse me of trying to cause mischief again. And . . ." She lowered her eyes sheepishly. "I was afraid that if I asked you outright, you'd say no. Do you really mind if we just stop quickly? The bracelet I left is precious to me, and I would be most distressed if it became lost." Julia gauged Samantha's reaction with a side glance. "I could have asked Alex, but I thought as a gesture of good faith I would come to you."

"And are you really interested in the Langston estate?"

"Oh, yes," Julia replied brightly. "It will only take me a moment to get the bracelet and then we can continue on our way."

Samantha groaned inwardly. For an instant she had hoped that Julia's plan to move to Cornwall was just a ruse. She tried to hold her patience as the carriage rocked along the familiar path, but in her heart she knew she would never be able to accept Julia as a friend. Surely Alex would not ask that of her. She shuddered as a chill ran up her spine, leaving gooseflesh in its wake. The path before her was suddenly misty and gray. "Julia . . ." Samantha tried to call out, but her breath locked in her throat.

"Here we are." Julia's voice was shrill.

"Wait . . ." Samantha's hand clamped on Julia's arm. She blinked and her vision cleared, but the scene of danger that surrounded her was almost stifling. "Something's wrong, there is danger." Samantha's eyes darted about the familiar scene but nothing looked amiss.

"Don't be silly." Julia climbed from the carriage. "I see nothing to be afraid of. Come on, get down and help me find my bracelet."

Reluctantly, Samatha climbed from the carriage, her nerves tense, waiting.

Julia turned the latch and swung open the cabin door. "Well, well," she cooed. "It seems that we are not alone after all. Samantha, come and see who is here."

Samantha felt her blood turn to ice as the immense form of Edward Chesterfield filled the doorway. "Julia, move away quickly." Amazed that her voice was so steady, Samantha started to back away from the nightmare before her.

"What ever for, darling? 'Tis only your uncle. You look as if you have seen a ghost. Don't you recognize him?"

"Elizabeth? Is that you?" Edward Chesterfield stepped into the sunlight. His size had increased, bloating his features until his eyes were no more than slits under thick folds of skin. His cheeks hung in jowls and his waistcoat buttoned only at the top. Even from a distance, the stench of his unkempt body gave offense.

"Get away, Julia." Her voice was more urgent now. "He's dangerous."

Julia's laughter filled the clearing. "But, darling," she cackled. "That's why we've come."

Samantha took three seconds to curse herself for a fool, then catching her skirts high, she turned and fled. Branches snagged at her clothing, and the stones that covered the path cut through her thin satin slippers. She could hear Edward crashing down behind her, and using the last of her strength, she increased her speed. Her heart pounded in her ears and a stitch caught her side. Still she ran. But as the path narrowed and the end came into view, her mind screamed in silent panic. She had taken the wrong turn and now only the cliffs were before her. Spinning around, she watched in horror as Edward slowed, then began to stalk her.

"You shouldn't have left me, Elizabeth," he huffed, heaving his massive body slowly forward.

Samantha glanced frantically from side to side. There was nowhere to run. The sea was at her back and Edward swayed before her. Her hands rubbed anxiously down her skirts. Desperately, she hiked her skirt to her waist and fumbled with the deep pockets of her underskirt.

"I want you, Elizabeth." His words slurred as he struggled for breath. "You have the money and it should be mine."

Samantha shuddered as she watched spittle dribble from his mouth. "You're right, Edward," she struggled to keep her voice soft and calming. "I have the money and it's right here." Edward started forward.

"Stop," she commanded. Startled by the sharpness of her voice, Edward halted. Samantha stole a fleeting glance behind her. The edge was now less than a step away. Taking a steadying breath, she faced her uncle.

"If you come any closer, Edward, I'll jump."

"Then jump, dammit," Julia spat, staggering to Edward's side where exhaustion from the run dropped her to her knees."

"Fine." Samantha's words were soft and low. "But if I go, then this goes with me." Her hand tightened around the Midnight Star as she pulled it from its pouch. Then she forced her fingers to relax and her arm stretched forward to show her treasure.

Edward gasped. Never had he seen a jewel of such size. The brilliance of it brought tears to his eyes.

Julia staggered to her feet. "Where did you get that?" she demanded, watching the sunlight dance from the stone.

"You can have this, Edward," Samantha offered softly. "But you have to set me free."

"But I want you, Elizabeth," he whined, his eyes never leaving the sparkling stone.

Julia gave his shoulder a swat. "That's Samantha, you fool. And the jewel is mine. 'Tis one of the Cortland stones and as soon as she's dead, they'll all be mine."

Samantha felt her stomach turn and gritted her teeth to keep her wits about her. If she could get a head start, she could find the path down the cliffs and, once on the beach, mayhap she could locate one of Blacky's caves. Edward took a flumbling step closer, and she knew there really was no choice.

Slowly, she knelt and placed the diamond on the ground beside her.

"'Tis called the Midnight Star," she said softly. "And worth a king's ransom. Just think, Edward..." Carefully she took a small step sideways. "Think of all the food and drink you could enjoy. Why, as the owner of the Midnight Star, people would pay your way just to have a glimpse of the treasure."

Blinded by the brilliance of the stone, Edward knew only that he wanted it. "'Tis mine and I'll have it now."

"But you have to let me leave, Edward," she threatened. "Or I'll kick it into the sea."

Edward growled and straightened to his full height. "I'll have the diamond and I'll have you, too."

"Nay!" Julia's scream echoed about them. "'Tis mine, and you'll not have it. You wanted her." She pointed toward Samantha, who was steadily edging away from the stone. "And I brought her for you. You want to kill her, remember?" Julia grabbed the front of Edward's coat and slapped his cheek with a stinging blow. "You want Samantha."

Edward's meaty palm swatted Julia from his path like a worrisome fly. "I need the diamond." His words were slurred, "Then I'll get Elizabeth. She'll not leave me again."

"Don't move, Edward."

Samantha spun around at the sound of Alex's harsh command. Giddy with relief, her hand raced to her heart to stem its frantic beating.

Edward gave Alex a backward glance, but his steps

377

continued toward the cliff's edge.

"Nay, you can't have that," Julia screamed. Heedless of the danger, she struggled to her knees and clumsily stumbled after Edward. The hulking giant reached the cliff first, but it was Julia's quick hand that closed around the stone. Edward's roar of anger sent the gulls soaring with fright as he lunged after his small prey. His hand stretched out and caught her skirt, sending Julia crashing to the ground as he fell to his knees behind her. With the diamond in her grasp, Julia turned in fury. Her foot lashed out but landed only a glancing blow against Edward's huge girth.

Edward struggled to his feet, but as he reached to grab the diamond, sunlight struck the stone. Piercing his eyes, the dazzling light blinded him. He staggered as his eyes burned, then filled with tears. Julia scrambled backward, then, with the diamond firmly in her fist, lunged her small body into Edward's frame. He stumbled, frantically trying to gain his balance, but his feet encountered only emptiness.

Samantha watched in horror as Edward careened over the cliffs. His death cry echoed in her mind, then she was moving; half running, half stumbling until she was clasped within Alex's arms.

Julia's hysterical laughter filled the air. "'Tis mine," she cackled, hugging the diamond to her midsection as she rocked back and forth on her knees. "It's all mine. I've won."

Alex tightened his arm about Samantha's shoulder and kept his gun at the ready. "You've won nothing, Julia." His voice stopped her laughter.

"Oh, but I have, darling." Julia flopped back on her heels. "I have the diamond." Holding the stone to the light, she was mesmerized by the colors that streaked forth. It was worth more than a king's fortune, and it was hers.

"Julia, Cavandish knows all. Even now he's on his way with a warrant for your arrest."

"What?" Samantha gasped, and her eyes grew wide.

Alex tightened his grip about her shoulders. "Julia has been doing more in France than just shopping. Isn't that right, Julia?"

"I don't know what you're talking about, darling." She flicked her hair from her face and gave Alex a smug look.

Alex only shrugged. "It matters not. Richard has all the evidence he needs to see the deed completed."

"Alex, you can't send her to Newgate." Samantha's voice trembled as she imagined the horrors. "Whatever she's done, you can't let that happen."

A wicked grin tightened Julia's smile. "I'll not be the one going to Newgate," she taunted. "I come from an important family. No one is going to believe you. Besides . . ." Her eyes sparkled with dangerous lights. "You'll never believe the stories Edward told me." Samantha felt her heart leap to her throat. "Wouldn't dear Richard Cavandish just love to hear the one of how you met your wife?"

"It won't work, Julia," Alex replied evenly. "Edward Chesterfield was a madman."

"Alex?" Samantha's voice trembled.

"Never fear, love." He brushed a kiss against her hair.

379

"Oh, but do fear, love," Julia taunted sarcastically. "If I go to Newgate, then you can rest assured that you shall join me there." A low moaning rumbled about them.

"Julia!" Alex and Samantha spoke in unison. "Come away from the edge. Quickly."

"Julia, you're in danger. The edge is going to crumble," Samantha cried. She could hear the trampling of horses and knew Cavandish had arrived with his men.

Julia's laughter rang out, and she held the diamond high before her. "I'll not fall for that old trick. And you . . ." Her eyes slashed hatred at her former love. "You should have married me, Alex. But you've made your choice. And now you can think of all the happy hours you'll have while your darling little wife spends her days in Newgate."

Richard Cavandish reached Alex's side as the earth again sounded its protest. "I see you've found her." He motioned for his men to remain mounted.

"Look, Richard." Julia held the diamond high, letting the sun fill it with fire and beauty. "'Tis mine, now, all mine. And since you're here, why not ask Alex . . ." Julia's threat turned to a shrill, piercing scream as the earth about her began to crumble. Alex lunged forward, but Richard caught him back. In horror they watched the earth give way and Julia disappear from sight.

Alex struggled, but Richard stood his ground. "Don't be a fool, man, 'tis nothing to be done for her now."

"Alex?" Turning to Samantha, Alex felt intense relief soar through his veins. Gathering her close, he

380

felt her shudder as she struggled against tears.

"Could you tell what she held in her hands?" Richard questioned. "For a moment, I thought it was a diamond." He stepped closer to the raw edge. "But thinking back, 'twas much too big to be a jewel." Small stones scattered, tumbling to the waves below and hastily he moved back again. "'Tis a tragic ending to be sure, but certainly more merciful than months in Newgate and then a hanging."

Samantha felt the blood drain from her limbs, and her head grew light as Julia's death scream echoed over and over in her mind. "What will happen now?"

Richard smiled and executed a courtly bow. "Our mission is complete, m'lady. He took her chilled hand and kissed it gallantly. "I have kept the anxious bridegroom long enough from his marriage bed. And after seeing you, I can more than understand his reluctance to leave his home. So with my thanks and the king's blessings, you may take him home to stay."

Chapter XXIV

Samantha leaned against the rail and turned her face into the stiff wind and raced across the decks. Looking up, she watched the gentle sway of the masts in the clear azure sky. The deck of the schooner rocked gently beneath her feet like a mother welcoming back her wayward child.

Alex stood on the deck and watched his wife. It had been a hard decision, but in his heart, he knew he was right. For the moment, all was well and France would no longer gain English secrets. But there would come a time, of that he was certain, when the king would again prevail upon his service. But worse, as long as they stayed in England, Samantha's past would always hang in threat like a dark cloud above them.

The wind tugged her hair from its moorings, and Alex smiled in appreciation as it molded her cape to her slender form. Her eyes sparkled with anticipation and his satisfaction grew.

"Are you warm enough, love?" He stepped close and settled her cape more securely about her.

Samantha looked deep into the green eyes that she loved so dear. "I am fine, but I keep thinking you've made a terrible mistake."

Alex pulled her into his arms. "My only mistake was not recognizing a bedraggled stowaway for the bewitching sea nymph that she was."

"So many years ago . . ." Samantha shook her head. "But are you sure you'll be content?"

Alex smiled. Never in his life had he been so certain. "James will do well as the new master of Coverick," he said easily. "And the responsibility will do him good. Besides, if we feel the need, we can always take the children and go back for a visit." Keeping her in his embrace, Alex turned her so they could both watch the last glimpses of Land's End.

Safe within the comfort of his arms, Samantha watched England fade from sight. He had given up much for her, leaving behind all that was cherished and familiar. But together, she vowed, they would create a new home in the land called the Colonies.

Alex pressed her more firmly against him. "A new family." He kissed her brow. "A new land." His lips touched hers. "A rich life."

Deep within the churning waters of the Atlantic, the Midnight Star drifted with the currents. For years it would stay hidden, silent within the murky depths. Then, as with all things, it would surface. Like a star plucked from heaven itself, it would wash ashore on a new, untamed land. Half covered by sand it would wait patiently for the slender young hands that would find it and again fulfill destiny's promise.